DEDICATION

To Craig and Anya

History Lessons

Jennifer Mueller

ISBN-13: 978-0692589533

The Sinclairs of Wrathe are descended from William, a younger son of Comte de Saint Clair in Normandy who came to England with William the Conqueror. Through early fortunate marriages, this branch of the Sinclair family acquired the Lordship of Wrathe very nearly Kings in their own right and since the twelfth century have made their home in the Castle Am Binnean built upon the foundations of a ninth century watchtower. Fortunate marriages haven't ended over the family's history, the Princess of Navarre most notably.

Despite their far-flung seat, the Sinclairs have long been prominent in Scottish affairs. They supported Robert the Bruce in the struggle for Scottish independence and fought at the battle of Bannockburn. After independence they were given the title of Duke of Cairnmuir. Sinclairs of this line have fought at the Battle of Bauge in 1421, the battle of Flodden in 1513, the battle of Killicrankie in 1689 only to name a few. So many men of the clan were lost in several previous battles that they escaped involving themselves in the 1715 and 1745 Jacobite attempts to retake the crown and thereby saved themselves having their lands forfeited. More recently, they have fought in the Crimean and Nile River campaign as well as both World Wars.

Male members of the family generally pursue military careers. The Black Watch has always boasted a large presence of Sinclair men in their ranks. The family has produced military heroes who have no less than fourteen Distinguished Service Orders and three Victoria Crosses. The current generation has all followed the family tradition, Hunter in the RAF, Broderick in the Royal Navy, and Lorne is a highly decorated Captain in the Royal Marines with the 45 Commandos. Not just fighters the family has a long history of attending St. Andrews since it's founding in the 1400's. Phillip Sinclair helped found the Royal Society during the Restoration, a prodigy who had started university at 12. In 1886 Arran Sinclair was made Fellow of the Royal Society for his medical endeavors.

Titles in the family include Lord of Wrathe extinct since 1328, Duke of Cairnmuir, Marquess Braydallin held by the heir, Earl of Ravensgard, Viscount Stronchergarry, Baron Sinclair of the Marches and finally Laird of Creag. The 35th Duke, David Sinclair, and his wife, Lady Janet, of the clan MacLeod, live in London.

CHAPTER 1

In the Year 2004

Ayda Rogers stopped the car as it came to the top of a hill, the entire North Sea standing before her. Half hidden in the misty dusk stood the castle Am Binnean with only a nineteenth century bridge linking it to the world. Hovering ghost like the castle sat on an island where an ancient tower protected the bridge from being crossed in addition to the castle battlements. Perhaps in far off times it had been a proverbial drawbridge. Beyond lay the orange grey sky and the matching sea. Not one tree broke the monotony of short grass in every direction except a single line of lindens that ran along the road. A pair of golden eyes stared back at her as she checked her hair in the rearview mirror before she descended the hill into the small village. All of one street facing the water surrounded by a small cluster of white washed houses. She wasn't expected until tomorrow, though, so she pulled her rented car into the inn where she had a reservation just short of her destination. The village of Wrathe clawed almost to the bridge well under the eye of the cannon that once protected the battlements.

An entire summer in a Scottish castle. No one in her doctoral program could believe it. Even more so, when they read the list of paintings that hung on the walls. She had written the letter to the castle in a moment of craziness. It was a self-esteem thing, seeing as she had worked at preeminent auction houses, studied in far-flung museums around the world, and worked with leaders in the art restoration field. Granted it was all as grunt labor and assistants. A little part of her always worried that Brad would somehow steal every new job away from her too. Still she never thought they would answer her at all, the family held titles, a castle and the list got too long for reasons they shouldn't have. She about died when a letter inviting her had actually arrived.

The village was tiny when she stepped out of the inn. A dock with fishing boats all around, a post office, a few shops pretty much summed it up. Some old warehouse took up one whole area near the pier with the very unScottish name of Trowbridge Shipping. After a brief look in the fourteenth century chapel that stood in the center of town, the only other place to go was the pub, surprisingly ancient 1500's the sign said and filled with wood worn dark over centuries, and not to mention droll. Its name, The Cock in Hand. Despite the size of the village, the place was full. One lone table waited for her, and then another couple came in behind her. The woman waiting tables looked around and her shoulders fell. Somehow Ayda had a feeling they weren't full often.

"Why don't you join me? I'm alone."

Ayda turned to find a man already at a table, grinning at her. His dark red hair stood out in the room of blond and brown. "Thanks, so what's the best to try?" she asked, sliding in as the couple behind her took the last open table.

"Anything with fish, I catch it meself. If ye'll trust me."

"Sure."

With his accent, she couldn't catch half of what he called to the waitress, even though she was certain he spoke English.

"What brings ye to town? Ye don't look like ye came on the tour."

So that's why it was so busy. "No, I'm here for the summer, I'm going to be working on the art collection at the castle. I'm doing my doctoral thesis on the collection."

His eyes widened, and Ayda felt a little uncomfortable, as he looked her up and down. "Well, that is news, not many good-looking women come to stay. Ciaran Maceachran. You'll have to let me take you to the festival at the end of summer, the social event this far north." The waitress called something and his glare finally left her. She let out a little sigh.

Before he turned back to her, the door opened and a man came in. Ayda had to try hard not to let her jaw drop. The newcomer was gorgeous to a fault, maybe thirty two, with dark blue eyes and thick brown hair streaked with blond. Just a sweater couldn't hide his solid lean build, but it showed off the reddish brown tan of a man who spent a good deal of time outdoors.

The man she shared a table with leaned over near her ear. "If it's the castle ye be staying at, ye best be watching out for the Sinclair boys or ye'll be their next whore." It wasn't whispered, though. The entire room heard it. The man at the door turned his head from the counter. Only a few steps to reach the table, and he hit the red haired man solid in the jaw. Damn hard at that. Her companion slumped in his chair. One punch and he was out.

"When he wakes up, remind him his sister didn't do anything she didn't want to do. The woman was old enough to leave." That was whispered to her alone before he walked out of the door. Looking over at the man across from her, Ayda grabbed her purse and took her food to go.

~

The road ended at the castle itself, well a car park across the bridge. Am Binnean seemed fairy tale-like with its plaques set in the walls, each a tiny piece of artwork with a family crest. Sinclair in the middle and largest, surrounded by those who must have married into the family. It was a veritable "who's who" of Scotland and, judging by some of the plaques, from further afield. The interview that had brought her to the castle in the first place ran though her head.

As part of the anniversary of the end of World War II, I'm interviewing Elise Dutton who served as a spy during the War. I'll get right into the questions. Now, Elise, I see here you live in Scotland, were you part of the British effort in the war, then?

Elise: (a bit of laughter) No, I was one of those odd Americans that were caught in Paris as it fell. My college roommate's boyfriend was quickly part of the resistance, and he recruited me for a special purpose. There was a German general in Paris that needed a secretary, and with my degree in languages and having been a model, he figured I would be a shoe in for the position.

What is he up to now? This boyfriend that snagged you into the job?

Elise: Unfortunately, he was killed in the same betrayal at SOE that sent me into hiding. If not for that, I never would have ended up on the shores of Am Binnean castle. Marie, the roommate, was killed as well and who knows what happened to his family. I put the marker for his grave up myself when I realized there was no one to do it.

So you were part of the SOE then?

Elise: No, the Resistance group I belonged to just reported to them. François didn't want there to be any leaks with the group, so he was the only one I was in contact with. The SOE had my name, it was supposed to be safer that way. I was at the doctor's sick the day the Germans started killing everyone on the SOE's ranks. Someone had given up the names.

HOW DID IT FEEL WALKING AMONG THE ENEMY AS THOUGH YOU WERE ONE OF THEM WHEN IN ACTUALITY YOU WERE A SPY FOR THE OTHER SIDE?

Elise: (A vague smile) I had worked as a model, so I made fairly decent money in addition to being a translator. When I took the job with the general I was pretending to be a different person, so I had to give up the more lucrative jobs, even as a sideline. I think the part I missed the most was a bathtub, I couldn't afford a flat with one of its own after that. From the fall of Paris in 1939 until June 1943, I was Lili Muller with the same background. Sitting in an office working, it wasn't too hard to keep the secret, as odd as that may sound. Everyone took me at face value. When I washed up on the rocks at Am Binnean, I was just going to stay long enough to get out and then run to deliver what information I had gathered before I was forced into hiding. Now staying there, I think I had the hardest time of all with pretending. Four years of being someone else and suddenly I'm having to be Elise again, trying to hide where I had been for four years. There was a leak, and so not only were the British wondering where I had landed, if at all, but the Germans were wise to my attempt at leaving from Norway. It didn't help things that I walked down to dinner one night to find a German spy as a guest.

MY RESEARCH SAYS THAT YOU WERE ALSO STATIONED IN DENMARK. HOW DID THAT HAPPEN? IT'S QUITE A WAY FROM PARIS AND IN THE MIDDLE OF A WAR.

Elise: after the whole to do at Am Binnean, I was taken back to London to fill in the blanks in the information I had secreted out. General Turnbull had a need for a snooper, as he called it, who could speak Dutch. I was put in by parachute to do almost the same thing. I worked for a major for the last few years of the war, but in the evening, since I was attached to a group by more than one strand like in Paris, we worked at helping POW's escape, sabotage since I was the one that filed all the orders the major received. I had to walk a fine line, though. If we hit anything that was too classified, it would have jeopardized my position with the Major. In Paris I was never the one that was doing the work. Copenhagen was another thing all together. I killed my first man there. It took me quite a while to get over that.

I SUPPOSE THIS WOULD BE A GOOD TIME TO ASK HOW YOU ADJUSTED AFTER THE WAR WAS OVER?

Elise: Not very well at all. It was quite a while before the dreams of Germans catching and shooting me subsided. During those first four years, I couldn't send messages or anything without gathering attention. My parents had died, no one in town knew anything of my activities. To them, I had shirked my duty by not helping the war effort. The first time someone said anything about it, I could only stare, I just couldn't get the words to form to spill all those secrets I had held for so long. I mean, how do you just come out and say I was a spy to an almost stranger. I sold my parents' house and bookstore and headed back to Paris. I knew enough people to have a job lined up easily.

I suppose the readers would like to know if you ever fell in love with the enemy. If so, how did the relationship end?

Elise: (real laughter) No, I was able to keep my skirt down when it came to Germans. Pretending I was one, working in an office with them, not sleeping with them was about the only way I could keep some bit of me reminded I wasn't German. I guess I knew that getting involved with any of the resistance members, even just civilians, would put me in a position I didn't want to have to explain to my German bosses.

"Welcome to my home," an elderly woman said as she opened the door. There was no diminishing the blue eyes staring out despite the woman's age. "I'm Mrs. Sinclair." The woman sold herself short she was a Dowager Duchess after all.

Ayda realized she was coming face to face with the woman she had read about so many times. A boy with a great mop of red hair, little more than three, popped his head around the corner. "Oh, and this is my great grandson Duncan." She looked down at the boy. "I thought you were supposed to be getting your bath. You go find Mary or you won't get dessert tonight, young man."

Ayda couldn't help but smile as the boy ran off with a groan. "I can't tell you how great it is you opened your collection to me. I was beginning to think my thesis was going to have to be about one of the museum collections like everyone else," Ayda sputtered quickly.

Her hostess laughed faintly. "My mother was an artist. I know I spent days unable to believe what hung here. Unfortunately, she died before I married, so she was never able to come see them all for herself. I have always regretted that. I think it might be why I agreed to your request. It's been years since anyone catalogued them all. Should be done before I die and leave the task to my grandchildren."

"Duchess, you don't look a day over ninety." Ayda grinned. Despite her age, the woman dressed impeccably in the height of Paris fashion.

"Then I'm in trouble, seeing as I'm only eighty-seven." Ayda felt her cheeks turning red. "Call me Elise, my daughter-in-law claims the title now, and I don't feel old enough to be called the Dowager Duchess however grand it sounds. Supper is at seven and I uphold the old tradition of before dinner drinks if you care to arrive in the drawing room half an hour before."

Ayda tried not to laugh at the custom from sixty years before. "If you say I have to dress, I'm afraid I didn't bring formal wear."

"Dressing for dinner has gone, so you're in luck. Come, I'll show you to your room."

Ayda could only gaze in amazement as she was lead down the tapestry-filled hall. A bowling lane peeked out of one door, another showed pure gothic architecture. Then her eyes lit on the art on the walls and all else was ignored. They passed by a Hogarth, a Cole, a Hans Holbein, a Van Dyck. Oh Lord, a Gainsborough and a Rembrandt. When Mrs. Sinclair opened the door, Ayda froze. Papered in green brocade with an elaborate plaster ceiling and accented with gold, the room was magnificent.

"I can't stay here. Maybe a servant's room." Ayda argued. She was, after all, just an American graduate student with a master's degree in art history trying to get her doctorate in art restoration. When the letter had said a room would be provided, she was practically expecting the dungeon or the keep. Not a room worthy of any history of decoration textbook.

"Nonsense." Mrs. Sinclair plunged into the room and opened a connecting door. "I figured you could use an office for your work. The desk has phone, internet connection, whatever you might need. The boys insisted we upgrade into the twenty-first century. Now you get settled and I'll see you for supper."

Dear lord a Canaletto hung on the wall. One of his series painted in England.

~

Ransacking her bag for anything that wouldn't look ridiculous standing across from the Dowager Duchess of Cairnmuir, Ayda couldn't help but curse herself for only packing work clothes. Now she just looked frumpy in t-shirt and jeans while surrounded by splendor. With no bathroom that she could find attached, she just pulled her auburn hair into a tail and peered out the door. Mrs. Sinclair hadn't told her where the drawing room was, either. The Modigliani nude on the wall jarred with the ancient surroundings as she searched down the hall. She smiled faintly as she remembered she wasn't in a museum. No, not with a bowling lane behind one door. But then more modern paintings appeared as well Gauguin, Chagall, Degas, Rivera, Matisse.

"Ah, taking yourself on a tour already. Let me get you a whisky and I'll show you proper," Elise said as Ayda stuck her head in a room, at least she had found the drawing room.

"Where did those modern paintings come from? Was there someone in Paris in the 1920's? Those were all living there then?" Paintings swirled in Ayda's head, halls mixed, doors seemed endless until she was certain she wouldn't be able to find her way again.

"Ah yes you know your art don't you? Phillippa the 32nd Duchess. That's a fancy way of saying my husband's step mother. We have friends that own an island off Greece, and between the wars, they would spend time in Paris on the way there. She picked some up for a song, she wasn't even the Duchess when she started. I wonder if she realized they would become the pride of the collection when she spent a few francs on them. There was a contact we had too that we bought some during the war when Hitler was calling them all degenerates."

"An island? Really?"

"Kapheira was decimated during WW2, they've been working on rebuilding it from the maybe 30 families that survived, and some refugees from other places that have arrived since. It used to be a country, now it's more of a ruin. Maybe a holiday after you finish your doctorate. Just tell me if you want to and we have a house there sitting empty. There's a lovely church with old frescos and Greek and Roman ruins, Victorian shopping lanes. I'm sure an art historian like you would find interest besides beaches."

Ayda could hardly believe her ears. Here and there, as they walked, were tiny alcoves put into the eight-foot thick walls with leaded glass windows that looked into the courtyard. There had even been tiny gun slots, long since glassed in, that gave light to the curving walls of the towers. One hundred twenty rooms in all and she had been shown only a handful before a small ancient and weathered door was opened.

"This is the heart of the castle. A watchtower built to keep the Vikings at bay. Didn't work, of course." Elise grinned as she sat on a bench. "The Sinclairs decided if they couldn't beat them out, they might as well just marry them."

There were no amenities, just stone walls and cannons, very old cannons. Proof that the castle hadn't always been so peaceful. The early summer sun still shone through the small arrow slit windows now filled in with glass. The fog of the evening before had burned away leaving views of the North Sea that rivaled any postcard.

"So?" Elise said quietly. "Your letter told me all of your academic record, why you would be the perfect one to come and catalog and clean the art in the house, how it would help you get your degree."

"You're asking for a resume while I have jetlag, no fair."

Those blue eyes bore into her. "No, I've heard every reason except why you wanted to come here. We have a castle on the edge of the world and while we have art, there are collections that are far more impressive. Why did you write that letter?"

Ayda lowered her eyes. "What if I said I saw an interview with you? I came across it researching a history paper on the war and something about it caught my imagination. A castle on an island in the ocean, a spy that washed up on the shore. When the time for my paper came, it was stuck in my head. An actual art collection and how it evolved over centuries. It was just because you are on the edge of the world that the restoration aspects would be so difficult. No one ever mentioned the modern pieces were here."

Elise smiled vaguely. "Then I suppose you've learned all the history in preparation. You knew all about this watchtower, for instance."

Ayda laughed, she couldn't help it. "I found pages, doesn't mean they say much of anything. There are pictures of the castle in the books on Scottish Castles, but actual history is hard to find. If your branch was larger perhaps, but there are mentions of happenings in the clan books, never anything definite. No one seems to have taken the time to write it down. Even you. That interview at the anniversary for end of the war was the only mention I ever found of you being a spy."

The old woman's smile turned rather devilish. "My granddaughter Isobel did that interview for a class project 20 years ago, she said. Next thing I knew, I was reading about it in a magazine."

"Then you actually know the history of the castle and the family? I'd be able to get it for my thesis. There hasn't been a detailed history I could find really."

Elise took just a sip of her drink. Just because she held with the tradition of drinks before dinner, it didn't seem like she really drank while upholding the tradition. "Of course I do. You're sitting in a building that has been inhabited continuously since 1328. The foundations were actually started many years before that in 1183, but it was uninhabited during the Scottish fight for independence forfeit by Balliol, rather the reason we sided with the Bruce so we can't claim the years in between. The television reception is terrible here, it gives one time to hear all of the old tales. But right now I believe supper should be ready."

"You live here alone?" Ayda couldn't help asking as they wandered the halls seeing no one at all.

"Oh on and off. My grandsons' all make their home here. Hunter is in Edinburgh for the moment, seeing to some business. He's here full time, the others are off doing other things right now, Broderick is at university after he left the Navy and Lorne is in the Royal Marines. The Duke though lives in London, he's only here now and then. Isobel lives in Edinburgh with her husband, but comes to visit often, she's the one whose interview you read. There always seems to be some relation around. With 120 rooms if you include the service spaces it really can feel empty even with more people here."

Ayda tried to hide her grin, but it was hard as they passed yet another antique that her professor would love to see. Not to mention the dining room painted blood red with white trim and handsomely carved walnut furniture, complete with side chairs that sported gothic arched backs. It was not some great hall, but the private dining room for everyday use. Even still, the service that stood around the room sported the names of the finest makers there had been. Meissen figurines decorated prime spots for all to see, someone had a bit of an eye for the ladies. All looked to be of nude women, mythological or real life.

~

Sleeping late due to jet lag even though she had landed several days before by then, Ayda walked out of her room to absolute quiet. It was a good ten minutes before she caught sight of anyone at all.

"I'm Mary, the cook." Mary was a thin, older black woman with a glorious English accent.

"Where are Elise and Duncan?" Ayda asked as a cup of coffee was put in her hand.

"She has a doctor's appointment in Inverness tomorrow. She had to leave today to get there in time to do some shopping as well. Duncan is at preschool. Not many children for him to play with here."

"Where are you from?"

"Manchester. The Duke's car had trouble outside the café I had there, and fell in love with my cooking while he waited. Before he left he'd offered me a job and who really turns down a job in a castle. Charlie gave up being an engineer to come, he calls himself a handyman but don't listen to him. His family had a connection to the castle. It's a full time job keeping a 900 year old lady from falling down. We married after we got here. Some 20 years now."

"It must seem so odd to have two or three people for such a large place."

"Not that few. Hunter set up income-making schemes like so many big houses have. They rent out the new wing for meetings, weddings, shooting parties, fishing stays. That section that sticks out like a thumb from this part, it runs down along the wall after it wasn't a protective castle anymore. You never see them in this part of the castle, but I see to them and people from the village are employed for cleaning, guides, and servers."

After a long drink of her coffee, Ayda noticed a painting on the wall in the dining room. "So I suppose I should get started now that I've settled in. I only have three months and I swear someone's been sneaking more paintings on the walls. Every time I walk around, they've multiplied."

Mary smiled politely. "You're set up in the old kitchen. Just let Charlie know which painting you want to start with and he'll get it down for you."

"An old kitchen? Isn't there anywhere else with some more room to spread out?"

Grabbing a hot plate and pot of coffee, Mary just smiled wider and walked out, leaving Ayda to follow, past more paintings until a door was opened. She could only gape. The room had to be twenty feet by forty feet with a low barrel ceiling and a fireplace taking up one end, the stone dark from years of fires. Four large plank tables were set up, magnifying lens, moveable lights, and an array of tools were spread out all over giving her more than enough room to work and spread out.

Mary was plugging in the hot plate to empty her hands. "Large enough for you? The equipment's just borrowed, so no throwing it at a wall in frustration."

"She did all this for me?"

"Well, Elise asked Hunter if it was a good idea when she got your letter, and he asked at the University, he has an old friend that works there. They loaned him all the equipment they thought you would need. So, where do you want to start?"

"Hell if I know!" Ayda looked around the ancient room. It was definitely older than the parts being used or at least not updated. "My idea is to track the collection through history. I don't suppose there's been any sort of cataloging done, no matter how old. That way I can find the oldest ones and start there."

"Insurance list is over on the desk. The family papers would probably have notes on when pieces were actually purchased. Those are up in the drawing room."

Ayda picked up the list and searched through it. "Then let's find Charlie and he can bring me, let's see, this says it's in the ball room, west wall picture twelve. If he knows which one that is."

~

Ayda stopped dead in the hall when she saw the library several days later. A two-story room of mahogany paneling surrounded her, shelves from floor to ceiling, while a railed walkway gave access to the second floor books. The shelves were filled with rare and old classics of Scottish history and law, many in ancient leather bindings. A huge carved Renaissance mantle surrounded the fireplace.

"Oh, my god." Ayda murmured. The room belonged in some university or men's club of old. Not all the pictures were from famous artists though, one drawing caught her eye, the signature at the bottom was Cora Sinclair 1761, obviously a relation. Unlike all the professional portraits, this Cora had caught the highland lord to perfection, not posed in the house, but in his surroundings not the land through a window. Looking around, Ayda couldn't help but pull the ladder over on the second level and climb to look at one ancient volume she spied on the highest shelf. Ayda reached high to pull the book from its place when the ladder suddenly started to slip from beneath her. An eerily glowing figure, dressed in a kilt with long black hair, had his arms out but she fell right through. With nothing to grab hold of, she found herself falling over the side of the railing to the floor some twenty feet below. Ayda watched the ceiling recede as if in slow motion, knowing she was going to break her neck. Suddenly she stopped falling, and more importantly, no overwhelming pain filled her body. Turning her head, she found herself nose to nose with a man who wasn't Charlie. No, it was the man that had punched someone out several days before.

"Did you see ..." Ayda started to say but was unable to continue. She'd sound like a crackpot if she mentioned a ghost. It was her imagination run wild.

"Are you all right?" he asked. "I'm surprised no one told you the stop mechanism is broken, the book appraiser we had in here a month ago is still in a cast." Gingerly he sat her down on the sofa. "You're sure nothing's hurt?"

"If you hadn't been here, I'd hate to think of what would have happened."

Mrs. Sinclair rushed in as fast as her legs could carry her. "Don't tell me it happened again, Hunter. Are you alright, Ayda?"

Still trying to take stock of the fact she was indeed not hurt, it took a moment for her to answer. "Fine, but if he hadn't been here, I don't think I would be." She was certain he recognized her from the pub, there was a hint of uncertainty in his eyes. He took her all in but there wasn't the lecherous look she got from the red haired man.

"Hunter, I remember ordering you to fix that ladder," Mrs. Sinclair announced with her hands on her hips.

He only went and kissed her forehead. Not the actions of the man on a rampage a few days before. "Yes, Grandmother, you did. Parts for a two hundred-year-old system take time to get. The company said they still wouldn't be here for a few weeks yet. I had it roped off. What happened to that?"

"Oh ... Charlie had to take it down to get the last painting that Ayda wanted to work on. I guess it didn't get put back up while she had it."

"No harm done, why don't you go back to your bridge party?" Hunter suggested. Straightening her dress, Mrs. Sinclair left the room, nodding, before he sank on the sofa. "You took five years off my life, you know."

"Then I think fifteen came off my life. I was the one that actually fell."

He turned with a grin. "I'm Hunter Sinclair, since we weren't introduced earlier. Are you angry at me for hitting your friend?"

"Ayda Rogers."

"Yes, my grandmother has been telling me all about you whenever we're on the phone. If she had mentioned you were the young side of fifty, I would have come back sooner. She didn't do you justice at all."

Her heart beating fast from a near miss at serious injury turned very quickly to beating hard from that grin. "I was just sharing a table with him since the place was full. Since I don't have him to champion me, I'll have to say myself I don't think your grandmother would approve of you making such statements to a stranger."

His smile grew wide as he leaned near her ear. "It's an old Sinclair family tradition to flirt with beautiful women, and we take tradition very seriously. It makes up for the fact there's no television."

"I have to get back to work." Hunter was still grinning when she looked back before leaving the room. It was a little boring in the evenings. She was halfway down the hall before she remembered the warning about ending up a Sinclair whore. Had she just received proof it was true?

CHAPTER 2

Working on a painting from 1412, Ayda checked it carefully for any damage and washed away the centuries of dirt. The list of paintings she looked at was longer than she imagined. If each one took her several days to clean and a few days were the easy ones, she would only finish a small portion of the total. Even if there were no paintings from thc very earliest date of the castle, there was still some furniture around from that period. The place needed a full time conservator, or more like five.

"Supper time."

Her head was still bowed when Mary entered. "Supper? You mean I've been working all afternoon? I didn't even notice."

"Must mean you love your job."

"I'm not going to finish it, either. I think I was told about half of what there is on the walls." Ayda muttered, hating the fact she wouldn't ever see all of the collection. That list told of many more in storage.

Mary's eyebrows rose. "You're not?"

"There are so many paintings and then the history is vague enough to make it hard for me to get a good grasp of it. I'm going to have to spend more time than I thought just getting that all straightened out. 1328 is when I'm told the castle has been inhabited since, but no books seem to even mention the name of the man."

"Eaduin de Sancler, rode with Robert the Bruce, as did his brother and father. His family was originally from

France, coming with the Normans. He was the first Duke of Cairnmuir, but not the first of the line, they were the Lords of Wrathe for generations. Still makes those new titles seem like toddlers to hear David is the 35th. They don't know so much about the Lords though, 9 I think." Mary rattled off as if it was she that had gone to school to become an expert.

Ayda just about dropped her brush, could she actually hear some real history. *Finally.* "Tell me," Ayda asked quickly before they could get off the topic.

"Unexpected relatives, don't you always love those. Well, as I heard it, it all started at one of the last battles for Scottish independence. Eaduin and his brother Iohne had been with Robert the Bruce for over a decade, their father had died in the fighting at Bannockburn when they were just children."

As Mary's words flowed, Ayda could see it happening before her very eyes.

In the Year 1327

"Sancler, take your men and move around the left flank. Leave the horses behind, sneak in as close as possible before you are seen," Robert the Bruce ordered.

"Where's Iohne?"

"I sent him with a message. You'll be short him today."

With a growl, Eaduin de Sancler took his men out of the camp as soon as they had set foot in it. "Henri, stay by my side. We have to get you back to see that wife of yours. How long has it been?"

Henri grinned wide. "Five years."

There was something wrong in that statement though. He knew the man's home they had been within reach of it many times and yet he's never gone back. Even less how could someone stay away from a woman he claimed was the most beautiful in the land and fucked like a whore to boot. No something was wrong, but in 5 years he'd never figured out what. The battlefield lay out before them, but at the edge, they bore left and stuck to the trees that grew on one side. The sound of the main fighting reached them even at that distance. Looking closely they could see the Bruce leading the charge, his armor glinting in the sun. Chaos erupted as English horsemen came barreling into the trees. Standing to fight, they were no match for the mounted soldiers. The sword came out of nowhere, taking Henri's head in a single blow, and Eaduin felt the sting in his arm as the same sword bit into his arm. He fell in place. Before he could even move, Tomas had landed on top of him. A giant of a man, there was no moving him. As Eaduin closed his eyes, all he could see were Henri's eyes staring at him, lifeless.

~

"He's coming around." Eaduin heard his brother saying. "I was worried there for a while."

"Who won?" Eaduin croaked with a parched throat.

"We did, with God's grace. The English horsemen were in retreat when they found you."

As he slowly pieced together the memories from before he passed out, he remembered the blow to his arm. "I don't feel my arm. It was taken clean off?"

"No, brother. Your arm is whole. It might not work properly, but it's there."

Iohne scrambled from the bedside when Robert the Bruce entered the room. "Eaduin, I'm glad to see you woke."

"Thank you, sir."

"I think I might have something that will make your recovery quicker. Full independence from the English. When you're well enough, you'll return home as the Duke of Cairnmuir. Your family's service is worth an elevation." Elevation? They were Lords of Wrathe, they fought as equals, but when Eaduin's father wouldn't claim allegiance to Balliol as a vassal since he wasn't a vassal the lands were taken. They'd joined the Bruce's claim to get it back.

Eaduin could only stare. No, he was still asleep and dreaming. They'd been held hostage for all intents, help fight and well give it back even after Balliol was out of the picture. "It's been over two decades."

"That's why I made sure yours was one of the first that was in line when it came time. Your brother can stay here with me in your place and you can go restore your home. You've close ties with the Norse. We'll need all the diplomacy we can get."

How diplomatic he put it. "Then you can double the lands if we're so important to you."

~

Eaduin closed his eyes, and he swore it had only been a moment, but when he opened them once more, the room was empty.

"I dreamed it all, did I not?" he asked the woman that brought food in for him.

"Dreamed what, sir?"

"I have my lands back. Duke. Independence. Was that the fever?"

She smiled prettily. "Not the fever, my lord. You have your home back. Your brother has been crowing about it to everyone in sight."

"Of course he's crowing, he has both arms. He wasn't even on the battle field," Eaduin snapped, annoyed. He could only watch in bewilderment as the woman closed the door slowly and pushed the lock home.

"Tell my husband of this and I'll take your arm from you."

Eaduin would have thought it impossible in his condition but there was no doubt of the effect her words had on him. Pulling the blankets aside, she slid on him easily.

"Lord, I'll have the surgeon come check on you. I knew you had a fever but not this bad." Slowly she moved, knowing he could hardly lift his head. As he felt his end come quickly, she buried her mouth in his neck, muffling a cry. Her breath teased his ear with each gulp she took to calm herself once more. "No woman needs two arms as long as your third arm is sound. That was for you. You have nothing to worry about, I expected nothing for me." She rose just as quickly. The door unlocked and food at his side, she forced him to eat. People came in and out as she did, without a look or glance to give away her actions.

She looked back one last time before she walked out with a twinkle in her eyes that she had kept from showing earlier. "No feeling sorry for yourself. Any woman would be glad to have you, one arm or not. I'll send the surgeon to have a look. We need to get that fever down."

~

Eaduin rode his horse over the rise. The storm clouds were building quickly as he gazed upon the castle, at least what was left of it. *So much for a glorious homecoming.* When they took the lands from his father, the roof was in need of repair ... it was completely gone now. The harsh winter storms had taken their toll. Another ten years and the entire building would be beyond repairing. Eaduin looked back to find the wagons had fallen behind.

"Asmundr, we have to get moving if we're going to have any shelter tonight," Eaduin called pulling the plaid tighter around his body. It was spring, but by the weather, it was hard to tell. The castle had to be livable by winter. Am Binnean, the name meant pinnacle, was the highest point around. An island connected to the mainland by only a narrow ramshackle bridge, the castle that rose from its crags visible in all directions for miles.

Crossing the bridge, Eaduin scared some birds from their roost while the horses' hoofs echoed off the bare walls. The oldest part was an old watchtower built against the Vikings some five hundred years before, but Asmundr inn Katneski was proof it had done little good. Vikings had overrun the area long ago as residents not conquerors, he was only one of many. The Norse still ruled the Orkney Isles not so many miles away, and Eaduin's ancestors had married well among them. The first Lord of Wrathe gained the watchtower in the deal and built another tower connected by a large great hall. That had been nearly 150 years before. Never large, little more than ten rooms all total. Nor was it lavish. It was, never the less, the seat of the Sanclers of Wrathe, and now home to the Duke of Cairnmuir. With the wind whistling through the broken walls and the rain starting to fall, he was home.

~

The next morning the wagons were unloaded in a flurry of activity that the castle had not seen in some time. Asmundr ordered the men about while Eaduin took out his horse to see to all the tenants. They had until winter to get it livable, and Eaduin had only a few weeks to get food delivered for the workers. Each day as the roof scaffolding slowly took shape over the weathered remnants, Eaduin rode out to let all that were bound to his property know he had returned. They would have protection once more, in return for food. A mill that had been around longer than even his family would be his first stop. The younger boys would come to the castle and train to fight. Older men were arranged into groups to be called on if needed. The furniture they had hauled back after two decades of exile sat unused stored in one room that still had a roof. A chair would nice. Food was the biggest problem. A dovecote would be needed soon enough, fishing boats vital. Eaduin headed down to the shore to look for shellfish.

~

Standing on the scaffolding, Eaduin let out a sigh. The woman he had married as a young man had died in childbirth with their first child. There was little else to redeem her as a wife. Perhaps there might have been, but her passing within the first year never gave him much of a chance to get to know her. He had married a stranger. Even then, he had been gone often, trying to save his home she never saw. Now there were new neighbors to have to find a balance with, the Sutherlands to the east, the MacKays to the southwest, half a dozen more tucked in between. Eaduin growled as he tried to lift his arm to pick up the tools on the ground. It didn't move at all. The damn English might as well have cut it off with as much as he could do with it now.

"Asmundr!" Eaduin called down to the work below. Asmundr had fiery eyes and a shock of windswept white hair. He had been the Sancler's factor since he was a young man, some forty years now. Even though the castle was taken from them, it hadn't changed Asmundr's belief that they were the masters of the castle. "Make sure the village is gone over and secured. I don't know how many remain from the original settlement. There might be houses that are inhabitable with some work. We'll need protection."

"Protection from Vikings, you mean." Ulfr called with a grin. Asmundr's son was as pretty as a man could be. Not handsome, pretty, and he knew it, and so did every woman in walking distance. They at least ate well every night from the women loitering around.

"Hate to tell you this, but they've already raped half the female population on my land." Eaduin called to the very Viking doing the only pillaging.

"Rape never, they all gladly invited me in." Ulfr yelled back up to the tower.

A cheer went up as the news of being allowed to build their own shelter made the rounds from the men hauling stone. That at least brought a smile to Eaduin's face. Three weeks and the tents weren't adequate even in early summer from the winds the North Sea had to throw at them.

From his vantage point, a slow plodding coach came over the rise with ten men accompanying it and the smile left his face. *Now what?* "We have company coming!"

~

Eaduin could only stare even though he was being spoken to. His brother could not be that much of an idiot could he? He could not be. But no, the women standing there were real enough.

"I am Lady Aeschine of Creag, your brother's wife, I need rooms," one said, regal but a little ugly. The gold that covered her was obviously the most important thing to Iohne.

"Your husband deserves to be beaten, then. You have no roof to sleep under. He knew that when I saw him last. He obviously holds you in little regard if he sent you here without benefit of a house even. Keep in mind he's the younger brother. I would not start ordering me around."

Aeschine gaped at him, her slightly buck teeth showing fully. "I am the only daughter of the Laird of Creag. He has received permission for the estate to pass to my husband upon his death. I would speak better to me."

Eaduin grit his teeth. "And I am the Duke of Cairnmuir. I am the one that owns all the land you can see for days. I would keep that in mind." It was no wonder his brother had sent her home as he looked at her again. Spoiled was the word that came to mind more than her looks. Of course the name rang a bell, she was the child of one of the new neighbors. A man with no sons had married his daughter to the land that butted up against his. Iohne would gain a good deal when her father died, no castle but land enough to improve his income considerably. His brother was an idiot but not stupid. "I was just discussing that the village should be reestablished for the men that have come with me, and now those with you. Ulfr can show you where. You can put your tent up there until a more permanent house can be built for you. If you are very lucky, there will be a roof over the castle by winter and you can take a room there. I speak truthfully that my brother holds you in very little esteem. There is no place for a woman here. Not yet anyway."

~

From the top of the tower, Eaduin watched as the men erected a tent down near the bay. Aeschine had glared at him and hissed air through her nose, but he watched her eyes dart around the island. Her shoulders fell just enough to show that she knew he was not being a stubborn ass and that he was speaking the truth. A scrape behind him was quiet, not the sound of Asmundr or Ulfr. He turned to find the other woman standing there. Her back straight, head held high, she looked as though she expected him to start yelling.

"Yes, what do you need now?"

"After the show with Aeschine, I thought I would wait until we were alone to talk of me."

Eaduin just looked at her, and deep in the pit of his stomach, he knew why she was there. "He sent you for me, I take it. There is no church here. My mistress, then." She was pretty, very pretty indeed and her cheeks colored at his words. Black hair hung to her waist in a thick braid while her simple dress dyed dark green from the very heather growing about clung to very inviting curves. There were no jewels, though, no gold.

She would not raise her eyes, unable to look at him. "The vows were performed by proxy. The Bruce was there as witness."

Eaduin closed his eyes, trying not to yell. "What did you tempt him with, or I suppose it was your father that did the tempting? Land, money, you are much prettier than Aeschine. I am surprised my brother did not take you instead. My father chose my first wife and now my brother chooses my second, my younger brother at that." The wind was all that broke the silence.

"My husband died at your side. Do you think I wish to be here anymore than you? You survived in his place. Your brother chose me for no other reason than I was pretty and I survived giving birth to my first child. He pushed it with the Bruce. With my husband dead, I have nothing. I bring no land, no money. I guess your brother figured you'd suffered enough for the sake of the family with your first wife. Sees me a fitting brood mare."

Eaduin opened his eyes slowly, hers were the color of the sky around him. Gray, ready to storm, and he was the one to be struck by the lightning.

"Who was your husband?"

"Henri."

The visions of his death made the bile in his stomach turn. Why couldn't it have been Tomas? At least he hadn't had to stare at his severed head for hours. "Ysenda, I think he said your name was."

She only nodded without a word. "I have a son named Fergus."

Eaduin would never tell he knew far more about her. Henri liked to talk, and his favorite subject was his wife. He could guess why Iohne had chosen her if he thought he had suffered so much marrying Godit. If Henri's stories were any indication, Ysenda loved a man in bed anyway she could get him there. The look in her eyes, though, spoke of there being far more to her than man crazy. There was strength in those eyes. Iohne just became an idiot again. Henri was too, he'd never mentioned a son. "How old is he?"

"5 years."

"Henri didn't know of him?"

"If he did he didn't give a damn about us."

Eaduin turned away with a sigh. So much for believing stories told around a camp. "I hardly knew Godit, with being gone so much. I never considered her a burden, if that is the way that Iohne portrayed her. Your husband did not die in my stead, either." Despite the spray that blew off the water, one-handed Eaduin pulled his tunic off, leaving only his trews in place. The scars stood out bright red on a well-built chest, but none more than on his arm. "Our attacker only had worse aim. Even still, I cannot lift a sword from the wound hell I can't even lift a knife, and I am a poor soldier with my left arm. That is why I am here. I can no longer fight, but I can finally make my home again on the land taken from us." Ysenda stared for a long moment and then walked closer. "There is a single room that is whole, there is no furniture, and I can't use one arm. It is all I can offer you, since it seems we are together for good."

Her fingers touched the scar, and Eaduin's words died in his throat. When she lifted her eyes, the storm in them had lessened. "So you did not lose my husband to save yourself. I might not hate you anymore. I am no spoiled woman though. I have worked all my life. What task do you need done here?"

"You are a Duchess now, you don't need to do that."

A smile played at her lips. "Until we have consummated the marriage, I am no wife or Duchess. I would hate to get used to such fineness and then have to give it up when you renounce me."

Even the words just being spoken made him rise. "You wish me to take you now so you know your place is secure?"

"As much as I would like Aeschine to hear me scream, it's a little cold here to see me to it. You might find a peasant not to your liking, and I would like to have the option to leave. I heard enough stories about your first wife to know I wish to be no burden on anyone, despite your claims otherwise." Her eyes lowered to the bulge in the kilt. "I know why Iohne chose to marry me to you, but I am no church approved whore to get an heir on." With that, she walked back down the tower stairs.

~

When Eaduin followed later, he just caught sight of a boy hugging Ysenda. The boy was no doubt Henri's, he looked just like his father.

The men came running over when they caught sight of him. "I do not know how to say this, Eaduin. She is your wife. I was given the papers just a few moments ago. Some dealing with your brother."

"Aye, she told me herself. Her husband was a man that died next to me."

Aeschine loomed in front of him suddenly. "I have heard there is a room in the castle that is livable. It will be mine."

Her voice screeched and Eaduin had to fight a chill running down his back. "It is Ysenda's to use."

"She's a peasant. You said yourself this is no place for a lady. She's not a lady. She can deal with lesser accommodations."

Eaduin looked over to his wife. "No, she is not a lady, she is the Duchess Cairnmuir. She will have her due instead of others trying to claim it as their own. She is the lady of the castle."

Aeschine's eyes narrowed as she glared at him. "I will bring this up with my husband."

"Then go to him. Bring it up with him there." Eaduin snarled. His brother was a fool. Unmitigated foolish.

"There is no castle at Creag and Iohne has a meager room in Edinburgh." Aeschine whined even more gratingly.

Eaduin growled. "There is no castle here, either. There is what could be a castle with a lot of work. I don't see you trying to help. I instead seem to spend a lot of time arguing with you instead of getting things done so that there might be a room for you in the future. Go home or work." Eaduin pointed to the south and there was no denying that she caught sight of the fact that one arm hung there unmoving.

Her mouth opened several times as if her mind couldn't function without it. "Get the roof on and I will put the house in order. Iohne said the furniture that was removed is in storage at relatives. I can run a house. I have no skill at building."

Eaduin didn't want to hear it, she said the words out of pity that he couldn't handle the work he had. "Don't dare look at me like that, my one arm is still enough to put you over my knee and teach you who is in charge here. I expect to hear no more demands. Those you save for Iohne. The cottars will start bringing food soon to pay their rents. Put it in order. We have to have that last us for a while. Is that something you can do and keep out of my way?"

They all watched her gulp hard. "Yes, my lord."

~

Ysenda took one look at the one room that was livable and called for buckets of water. Cleaning was low on the priorities, since Eaduin slept in tents along with the rest, even if there was a bed, or at least the pieces to put one back together. She pulled birds' nests from the rafters, mice nests from chunks of debris that littered the floor before she scrubbed decades of dirt from every crack.

Ysenda half fell into the tent as dark came, only to find Aeschine sitting there prettily while she worked at a piece of needlepoint. There were just enough tents if the women shared one, another nail in her coffin with the woman. Aeschine walked around, ordering people about if there was a delivery of food, but for that, she did nothing. Since no house was there for her to run, there was nothing for her to do, in her mind at least.

"Still you do not share his bed? Four days now and you sleep alone. You've been saying enough how beautiful you are. I have to wonder if your lame husband is all man to stay away from your bed," Aeschine sneered as she entered.

Ysenda snorted. "I have never mentioned how I look to anyone. Now, if you bring up how I've mentioned that you're spoiled, I'll admit that readily."

Aeschine glared at her as her cheeks turned pink. "Perhaps I misspoke, but that doesn't take away from the fact that you still do not share his bed. Are you stuck with a man that was injured in more than just his arm? Or is it that he lusts after that good-looking man of his? Now there is one I would like to get in bed with me."

With her back to the woman as she washed her face, Ysenda remembered the very large bulge in her husband's trews. There were no men in sight, and he certainly had no injury, that was much was obvious. "There are more important things to get settled right now. Perhaps he is gentleman enough not to wish to take me with only a tent and fifty men only feet from us."

"Gentleman, hah, perhaps you'd like to hear about his brother on our wedding night."

"No, Aeschine, I do not." Ysenda walked out of the tent and pulled the cloak closer to her body.

Asmundr had a fire away from all the others in the keep of the castle. Perhaps as factor, they did not see him as one of the common folk. When she saw Aeschine following her out of the tent, he was as far away as Ysenda could get.

"Do you mind if I join you?"

Asmundr's fiery eyes softened. "A beautiful woman by my fire, never, my lady."

"I am not your lady, I am a peasant."

A large gulp of his ale kept him from answering immediately. "You are Eaduin's wife. You are the Duchess Cairnmuir, Ysenda de Sancler of Wrathe. You control every man you see before you, all who took the Sancler name in loyalty before the King. A man that should have the loyalty as a king from all here."

"And widow of Henri. You were there. Do you know how he died?"

"Yes, my lady. He died at my master's side. In their retreat, the English overran them unprepared."

She had been getting that same answer for months now. Even Robert the Bruce, when he ordered her to marry Eaduin, hadn't told her how her husband had died. "I asked how he died."

Asmundr only shook his head. "If you want to ask anyone ask Eaduin, but he never speaks of it. He was there when it happened. The rest of us were late arriving and missed the battle. Iohne was delivering a message. Eaduin was almost the only one that survived, and only because another man fell on him after he was wounded, hiding that he had not been killed outright. The rest were not so lucky."

Ysenda tried not to do it, but her eyes sought him out easily. Her husband was a good-looking man. Ulfr might have been beautiful but Eaduin was rugged, his only flaw that one arm hung limp at his side. Then he caught her gaze, and the smile played at his lips. No, he would take her to bed easy enough and probably put an heir in her belly faster than Iohne would the harpy's.

"You need not share your tent with that harpy, my lady. I can move my things and you two can have one alone," Asmundr said in her ear.

"I married Henri and now everyone expects me to just take to Eaduin's bed because he was bound to me against either of our consent. I am a peasant. I have no great family to push things if he does not like me one day."

The sound in the man's throat might have been a growl. "An unconsummated marriage can be dissolved, but not if you have his heir in your belly. I always knew Aeschine was wrong when she claimed you hadn't a thought in your head."

Ysenda turned her head back to stare at the man. "She says such things about me?"

"Let's just say it's a good thing there are other women around so she can't say that Ulfr is encouraging her. She likes to talk even more when she thinks it will turn you from the men's favor."

Talk or not, she had to know. "She said things about Iohne and their wedding night. That he was no gentleman. They are of the same blood."

Asmundr's laugh was loud and echoed off the stone walls. "She's never been married and with a face like hers, do you think the boy spent much time wooing her? Besides, the boy has a mistress even prettier than you that he keeps at his side in Edinburgh. She was married for future land and a dowry. Whose money do you think is paying to rebuild the castle? Eaduin's first wife secured us more land while Wrathe was held hostage. One king took it another refused to give it back. It was the younger sons turn to do his part."

"And Eaduin?" She felt her breath hitch.

The smile fell from Asmundr's face. "Eaduin I would trust with my life. If it had been a fair fight, your husband would not have died. The loss of his arm bothers him a great deal, not pain but that he must depend on others to do what he no longer can. I think it's worse that he can feel with his hand. He just can't move it. You need not fear he will replace you with a mistress. He has gone without for some time, I can always tell. He gets testy and his new sister-in-law better learn that or else you need to see to your husband before he kills her."

Ysenda couldn't help but start laughing. "Maybe I'll hold off until then. I wouldn't mind if her voice was gone from the air around here."

For an old man, his smile was beautiful. "Just don't wait too long, my lady. Every man here will start trying to fill your husband's place."

"Even you, Asmundr?" Ysenda asked.

"I trust him with my life, my lady. He can trust me with his wife."

She couldn't help but look at him and know that she could.

~

"The Duke needs a place to hold business." Ysenda announced three days later when she unveiled the finished room. The men had made plaster to smooth the old walls and painted it white at least, there was no color to improve it. Despite the bed on one side, there was indeed a table and probably every chair in miles waiting to be used. A few hangings and such warmed it faintly.

Eaduin looked down at her as they stood in the doorway. "How much of this is to get back at Aeschine?"

She didn't look at him, but the smile was obvious. "If it's yours to see to business, she can't complain. If it's mine alone, well, I had to travel all the way here with her. I can't stand to hear her speak."

"I don't blame you." Eaduin let out a sigh. "Ysenda, yes, you are a beautiful woman. I will never deny that I would gladly bed you, but can't you even talk to me? You've ignored me for a week now. I am not my brother. I had less say in this than you did."

The smile didn't go anywhere. "You are a handsome man even if you can't use your sword arm."

"Well, it is a start, from a stranger."

A high-pitched call from across the courtyard broke the moment. Eaduin was ready to send Aeschine back to his brother.

"Then how about this start, kiss me?" Ysenda whispered.

"Here with your son watching?"

"Aeschine contemplates whether you like women. She thinks that us not having taken to bed to seal the vow is because you do not wish it. She was raised with only the goal of letting a man bed her for heirs. That I have any say over the matter does not occur to her." Finally, Ysenda turned her beautiful face to him. Her eyes were stormy, but that day he couldn't see anger in them. "Kiss me."

Eaduin's hand slid around and cupped her bottom, pulling her close until she rested against his erect length. Fingers buried in her hair, he bared her neck. When she moaned at his first soft kiss, he couldn't help but sink his teeth into the silky flesh to leave his mark.

"You taste good. You must have cleaned yourself after these days of work. For me, perhaps?" Eaduin pulled back to take her look. Knowing Aeschine was coming, he ran his thumb over his wife's full lips.

Ysenda pulled it into her mouth, running her teeth over the calluses until she made him groan. "I know you want me. I said kiss me."

His mouth covered hers quickly, but it wasn't an attack. He was learning her inch by inch. Every curve of her mouth was measured with a gentle tongue until she opened her lips for him. Eaduin pulled her closer, and the growl was lost in her own mouth.

"You don't take?" she whispered in his ear.

"When you make it such, I will take what is mine." Eaduin watched her mouth open.

"Eaduin, come quick. There are some men here. They have swords drawn." Aeschine screeched instead.

Eaduin ran. Asmundr and Ulfr close behind.

~

Swords drawn! The woman was deluded. They were several men of the clan that Eaduin had been trying to get a hold of since he had arrived home. A dock would be useful in rebuilding the trading in the area. They were the builders. They carried woodworking tools, not swords. Opening the door to his new room, he stopped, a grin teasing his lips. Ysenda sat next to the fire, her dress pulled high while her fingers found her swollen mound. Her eyes were closed, she didn't know she was being watched. He closed the door quickly and silently eased the bar in place. Ulfr had been only a few feet back, and Eaduin wasn't in the mood to share. Each step across the room felt like an eternity, then Ysenda let out a moan and he felt his cock pulse in response. He knew he hadn't made a sound, but her eyes opened.

In her mortification at being caught, she didn't move her hand. The color traveled across her cheeks quickly. "Forgive me, my lord."

"Forgive you for what? Did I get you excited earlier and then not finish the job? I'm obviously neglecting my duties as husband."

Ysenda opened her mouth to speak but it died there, replaced with a gasp as Eaduin's fingers mingled with her own.

"Let me see you. All of you," Eaduin whispered, sliding a finger inside.

Her breathing became ragged quickly. When her hand fell aside, Eaduin moved between her legs. Face to face, he watched her relax as a second finger dipped inside.

Ysenda's eyes opened slowly. "Yes, I ache for a man, but you know what I fear. We didn't know each other when you entered this room. Will we when you leave it? Or will you trap me here when you've decided you hate me?"

She wanted a match as she'd had with Henri. It would be for more than just heirs that she went to his bed. A peasant was never raised with the idea of marrying for land or power, they had the choice to marry who they wished. That had been taken from her when Iohne made the match and pushed it with Robert the Bruce. Ysenda leaned forward. It drove his fingers in her deeper, and as her mouth opened to groan, he drove his tongue in with another kiss, this one far needier than the one earlier.

"How long as it been?" she asked in return when he pulled his head back from the kiss. "Truthfully."

"There was once some months ago, before that my wife and she's been gone a decade."

Ysenda raised an eyebrow. "A man as handsome as you?" Unlike his first wife, she was no shrinking virgin. He knew that the minute her hand found its way to his front. Her hand stroked the length of him.

"And where exactly are the women supposed to have come from? I had to make do listening to Henri remember nights with you."

Ysenda's hand stopped her caressing and her mouth gaped a bit. "He spoke of me like I was some common whore?"

Damn, he had never meant to say that. Gently, Eaduin closed her mouth. "He had no lands to win or lose, he fought for you. He had to remind himself what he was fighting for since he couldn't see you. He never spoke of you as some whore. I always envied him on your account, a wife who enjoyed bedding her husband."

"Godit never enjoyed it?"

"I'm rather surprised she died in childbirth, we joined rare enough. I was well prepared for battle, it took enough of one to get her to bed."

Ysenda started laughing. "Now I see why Iohne said you had suffered. Aren't we just a pair? Both of us so horny we can't think straight." Her laugh faded but the smile remained. "Will I have a match or will you tire of me and grow to hate me? There is a lot of work to do here, I know it's no life of leisure. I will not be treated as a slave or as any man's whore. If you can tell me that you will try to know me in more than just bed, I will say no more on the matter."

Pulling her hand to his mouth, he nipped at a fingertip. "The castle needs a new kitchen. Would you help me lay it out so the builders can get started once the roof is on?"

Her eyebrow rose slowly as he licked her fingers while speaking of something so mundane. When Eaduin reached for her dress to pull it over her head, she did nothing to stop him. "The village should be laid out with actual plots to save squabbles later, it was rather a hodgepodge before there should be some uniformity before the cottages left are moved into," he announced before he gently took a nipple between his teeth, smiling as it crinkled immediately. He had to hold her upright since she literally melted when he pulled it in his mouth. Her hands held him in place and she moaned when he finally pulled his mouth away from its task. "We need a dock. I have relatives that I intend to pick up trading with."

"What do you think you're doing?" Ysenda whispered as he ran his tongue down her stomach.

"I'm telling you all the work that needs to be done around here. You wish to be more than a mother to my heirs, then you will wish to know all of my business, I take it." His tongue slipped between her curls.

"Not that." She let out a little gasp.

"Showing you I'm not a selfish man." There was no answer, her moan filled the room instead. Eaduin grinned up at her. "Open your legs, wife. You'll enjoy it more."

Her eyes fluttered as they closed when he slipped a finger back in and then his tongue found her center, swollen with want. Her half-open legs opened fully, and the sigh was more than enough answer to tell him he found the right spot. He would have sworn she was too occupied to do anything but lay there until she took his bad hand and pulled it to her breast. Eaduin watched her place her hand over his, holding it to her.

"It looked lonely. Trust me, you didn't need to stop."

He pulled her into his mouth and attacked gently with his teeth. She started bucking almost immediately. The cries that fell from her lips were loud, loud enough to let the entire compound know there was nothing wrong with anything other than Eaduin's arm.

She just lay there. "Tell me how Henri died? No one would tell me." Silence reigned even though there was a faint shrill whine now and again. "I would like to know." Slowly her finger traced the scars again.

"Don't make me speak of it, please."

Ysenda lifted her head up, the storm back in her eyes. "You have enough restraint to not enter me but you can't answer a simple question. Are you all lying to me that Henri died at your side? Do you even know?"

Eaduin stood up abruptly. "Dammit, woman. It's not for your ears."

"I can't hear how one husband was taken from me and another might well follow?"

"I will never go fight again. You know that as well as anyone."

Ysenda pushed him to the bed. When he fell to it heavily, it put them eye to eye and she took his head in her hands. Ysenda just stared in his eyes as she pulled free the trews and lowered herself onto his waiting cock. "We will create life while we speak of death. If it takes me removing the possibility I can get out of the marriage, so be it. I will hear the truth."

Eaduin's hand was insistent, she couldn't just sit there. Slowly he started to move her, this was for him, and he pumped faster and faster until he poured into her. Still sitting, his forehead rested against hers as his breathing slowed once more. "You are truly worried that I might grow to hate you?" Eaduin asked.

She buried her head in his shoulder. "I have a son with no father, and if you send me away, I have nothing. A great family perhaps, but no living of my own..."

Eaduin felt his heart pounding in his ears as he lay down, pulling her with him. For a moment, she just lay there with her head on his chest. "Who are your people? You haven't acted like a peasant since you arrived even if you worked like one. Henri was..."

"You finally ask that? I expected it on the tower when I told you of the marriage. Henri was a match my father did not approve of. He left me carrying Fergus to earn a title, land. I hadn't seen him since three months after we married. My father has disowned me, I barely heard of the death when suddenly I'm told I'm being married to a stranger. You knew him better than I. I can hardly say if I loved him it's been so long. There are times I wonder if he left to fight because he did not want the woman he seduced after he got what he wanted. I was a child I wouldn't give it up without marriage. Talking about me like a whore, I'm not sure he ever did love me. I married him, I thought I was in love, perhaps it was just lust. But I do not know you and I worry that a match we had no say over will turn worse than the one I ruined my life over."

"Who are your people Ysenda?"

"It won't matter what alliances your brother thought might come of it. I ruined that long ago being an impetuous child and you stood there angry even at just hearing we were trapped. I worry when the honeymoon wears off and all that is left are family lines that you can't even claim you'll... but you need an heir, and with Iohne far from his wife's bed, there is little chance of it coming from that line. I knew I couldn't deny you, but..."

"Lying sated here from you, please don't give me such images to think of as her in bed. Even imagining her crying out with that high pitched squeal is more than my head can handle." Eaduin shuddered at the thought and Ysenda started to giggle.

"I just meant that your lands have no heir other than your brother." She lifted herself up to look him in the eye.

"Who are your people? You keep avoiding that question."

She lowered her head against his chest. "The Byset's."

"The Irish family that hid the Bruce after the defeats here over 20 years ago."

She nodded slowly.

"How close of a relation?"

"My father is the Lord of the Glens."

"Did the Bruce know of your lineage?"

Her head started shaking even before she spoke. "Henri never mentioned who I was?" It came out barely a whisper.

"We fought alongside each other, but he was usually in the camp when there was time to sit around and talk. I wasn't. Iohne probably knew of it. He's an idiot, but I'll never call him stupid. Here I thought all this time you loved him so much that you didn't dare think of another."

"I wouldn't have risked everything I had if I didn't love him, but now--I was used and I don't want to be again. It was the only bargaining power I have."

"Why say you were a peasant all this time? You don't have to listen to that woman talk to you like she does. I wouldn't have said things..."

Ysenda sat up and her back faced him, she just sat there in silence. A faint breath now and then broke the silence. Eaduin pulled her hair aside unable to resist touching her. She tensed and only then did he know why she sat. Thin lines of scars crisscrossed her back. Eaduin sat up quickly and pulled her glorious hair fully out of the way. "Henri didn't do this to you did he?"

Slowly she shook her head. "Henri was already with you, he came ahead to find a place and my father found me waiting for the ship I was to take. That was when my father disowned me, did this. Henri put me in a room in Edinburgh and said he would come back. I never saw him again. Henri wanted nothing to do with me. No matter what Henri gained in the fight, it would never bring back that he was married to a woman that no longer had the position he lusted after. I thought he... Why shouldn't he talk about me like a whore. It doesn't take high rank to desire more and more. I lost everything. I am a peasant, my father had me removed from the family records, my name is not spoken. My own mother would not look at me if we pass by. All because my eye wandered to the wrong rank. I can't stand that again, even more in the house I am forced to live when it wasn't even my action that caused it this time. You cannot go to him looking to..."

Eaduin kissed her bare shoulder and the words faded even if he could still hear the tears. "I am not looking to expand my power, I need to keep Aeschine from getting in control."

Ysenda's jaw gaped a little. "She could do that?"

Eaduin kissed her softly. "If the Sancler's are gone, there will be backstabbing and she's had more practice than you. She's tried enough of it in the last week. If you wish to be more than mother to heirs, then it would be best you learned the business of the family. Let Aeschine run the household if it makes her happy. There is no power in that. When you can conduct business when I have duties elsewhere, there will be nothing she can do then. I know I do not wish to let Aeschine have Wrathe in her hands. My brother is an idiot for marrying her. He saw it as expanding his lands when her father dies, but she'll have to be watched to keep her from running us into debt since he thrust her on me. I've seen how much she tries to spend with her plans for running the household."

"I can't be that woman. I can't be Lady Ysenda Byset."

"No, you can be Duchess Ysenda de Sancler. That's all I ask." Something still bothered him even as he smiled with thoughts he shouldn't still have. "Why do you keep asking about how Henri died?"

"You'll allow me nothing to hide?"

"Why do you ask?" He asked.

Ysenda closed her eyes. "No one will tell me how he died. I'd heard he was dead several years ago. Then they tell me again. And again. Until someone tells me they saw him personally die, I can't say for certain I am a widow. I've spent 6 years living in a hell hole that Henri left me in, I couldn't go home, and I couldn't say I was even free of the man that left me there. I couldn't marry, I wouldn't make myself a whore, I've spent the last years scrubbing floors for scraps that I used to throw to the dogs because he tossed me aside as worthless and I wouldn't have been if it wasn't for him in the first place. I want to know I'm free of him."

Eaduin pushed her back on the bed and held her in a cage even if one arm wouldn't stop anyone. "His head was taken from his body in a single blow, the same sword half cleaved my arm from me. I went down, another fell on top of me. Unable to move, I stared at Henri's severed face for hours until they came sorting the bodies and found me little more than dead myself. I can guarantee the man died last year. If you think this is a trap, I'll have a cottage built for you and you can live there with Fergus, think of this as an afternoon romp."

That was not what he should have said, her eyes were a storm ready to destroy him. "I will not be put aside, no better than Aeschine."

"Then what do you want?"

Gently she lifted his bad arm, moving it so that his fingers were in reach to pull one after the other in her mouth. That was the worst torture, unable to move them to touch her. "You were wrong earlier, I know backstabbing with the best of them. I can deal with the woman, but not being some church approved whore to get heirs on. I want a husband. I want to know I won't be put aside. I want to know I'm wanted. Show me there can be a match apart from this. You're damn good at this and god help me I've wanted you to touch me since we got here. That thing you did with your tongue, if that is in the nightly entertainment, I can promise there will be no battles. But I cannot live with nothing more than coupling as often as possible for the sake of an heir." Finally she rest his hand over her heart. "Will you know me when we leave this room? Will I sit having dinner with a stranger not a word to say like I haven't had a person to talk to in years? A prison without any walls. We had no say in this..."

"Until there is an heir of my blood, Fergus will be there after Iohne. My wife's son. I admit it's not much right now without a roof, and kitchen, and a dock, and food stores and people scattered with the wind, but whatever I have is yours. There is nothing more I can promise. But I will talk to you at dinner, trying for an heir, lounging in bed avoiding a shrill voice on the air. I can't guarantee stimulating conversation with all the work to be done, but I'll talk until you shut me up."

Ysenda lifted her head up and kissed him. "Fill me Eaduin, make me cry out so loud there's never any doubt you're all man taking his wife. Then I'll go out and deal with my sister in law, the men will mutiny if you spend all day lounging in here with me."

"They'll understand with the loveliest woman in the highlands for temptation." He didn't have to be asked twice, the sound she made lightened his heart. Maybe Henri was right about his wife loving a man anyway she could get him, but he was still a fool if he tossed that aside, hell if he left her unsatisfied all those years. Anyone would be bitter towards him.

"Yes, husband, but if I'm laying here I'm not sending word."

Eaduin lifted up to find her stormy eyes smiling. "Sending word about what?"

"Just because I can't be Lady Byset it doesn't mean I can't help with trade from my people, just not my father. I can't promise allies. A herd of cattle like you've never seen, and then of course there's wool, and leather, and grain. There are several fishermen I think could be persuaded to come fish these waters."

"I don't have the funds to purchase everything immediately. Getting the castle rebuilt is taking most of it."

"Plow my fields Eaduin, I made them yours like you said you would wait for. Plow them well and we'll harvest a fortune. I might have been disowned, but my grandfather left me his cattle, without my father's say, and the living from his mother's farm. Henri wanted more, Henri wanted to be the heir because I have no brothers. He thought when we left and there would be a child he could come back and rule. My father denied him that, remarried and got several whelps on her, and Henri didn't want anything else. I couldn't go home, but my living is there. The Duke of Cairnmuir, Lord of Wrathe can claim it."

"Why didn't you ever say that before?"

Ysenda grinned as she started moving her hips driving him mad. "Because I wanted to know you wanted me and not some cattle. You said yourself Aeschine was married for the funds to rebuild. Sow your seed Eaduin you've met my terms, it might not be love yet, but the flicker is there that it will be and a little secret, I like a good cock, and it's been years. That little show earlier just isn't enough."

~

Ayda looked around her at the very room she worked in. Finally she could see the history framework she needed to put the art around. Even if it was only a bawdy cooks story. "Are there still cattle here? I haven't seen any." She said to hide the fact she was a little hot under the collar.

"Yeah, they're over on the western side of the estate, a cross between highland cows and the old Irish stock. We don't make enough for large scale export, but they make a decent line of cheese and butter enough for us and the village. We can do most things in small scale around here. Just nothing large so the village is fading away. Hunter has started an aquaculture facility, but that's just stayed the executioner."

CHAPTER 3

Walking down the hall after closing up the workroom several nights later, Ayda said goodnight to Mrs. Sinclair, although her hostess didn't seem to hear her. Mary and Charlie had claimed a night off. Duncan was in bed. Looking around, she might as well have been alone in the castle. It was as if being locked in a museum alone overnight, but the idea of the ghost being there somewhere worried her more than the quiet. From the overwhelming silence, faintly she heard a voice draw closer to her. Just as she turned a corner, a door flew open and she screamed.

Hunter took the phone from his ear. "Sorry I startled you."

Ayda waved him back to his call as she forced her heart to calm down. He said only a few words and hung up. "You look like you've seen a ghost. Come in and sit, I was just coming to find you."

Ayda opened her mouth to answer when he opened the door behind him. She hadn't seen the Asian wonderland within during her tour. Walls covered in gold leaf set off simply framed Chinese masterpieces of landscape painting. Shelves held porcelain of museum quality, not to mention the furniture. "My god, that's a Tai Chin, oh, and a Tung Yuan, Shen Chou. How on earth did you get them?"

"I see your fright's gone."

Ayda could only grin. "I spent a semester in Taipei studying at the National Palace Museum. I did a paper on

Tung Yuan," she answered, pointing to a magnificent mountainous landscape. "How did you get them?"

Hunter looked around for a moment. "An ancestor purchased them all in the early 1820's on a trip around the world. We've been friends a long time with the Dunhams, one branch is the Earls of Moerhab, another Baronets but both richer than sin, and all sailors and owners of Trowbridge shipping. A third family the Marquess of Lisstone, the Endicott's went too. He had gone to school with the Duke. Spent almost 4 years sailing around the world. The Duchess at the time died on the trip. We still go on vacations with them since we all have a house on Kapheira. We've collected quite a few souvenirs. Have you seen the Armory? Toledo steel and just about every other fine weapon known to man from trips around the world."

Oh, yes the armory, who could forget, hundreds of guns, knives, pikes, and swords hung in precise geometric designs. "Gave me the shivers."

Hunter was grinning as he handed her a glass of wine.

Ayda knew she couldn't keep going around all summer scared of her own shadow. "Can I ask you how the castle got its ghost?"

Hunter straightened, it was obviously not the question he expected. Ayda had to wonder if he was dreading when she would ask about what had happened in the pub. "Who told you of him?"

"I've seen him."

"When you fell from the ladder." Hunter nodded as if he knew instantly. "That's why you spooked so much just now."

"Yeah."

"You have nothing to worry about. I, on the other hand, might. Back in the sixteenth century, there was a woman that lived here named Seonaid. It is a family home, I think you've seen. She was a cousin. While her father was away, a fellow named Eoin McLeod came to the castle looking for work. The days turned to weeks, and then months had passed. Over time Eoin and Seonaid fell in love, and soon they were wed in the chapel, and not long after she was with child. Seven months along when her father Lachlan returned, Seonaid and her mother were out for a walk when the men overtook them. No one imagined what would happen next.

"He sent the rest ahead with his wife and he dealt with his daughter. She was beaten to death and the child with her. Her father dragged her body back to the castle like a sack of feed behind his horse. Eoin heard all the commotion and found his wife's body. When he was kneeling next to her body, her father came up behind him and stabbed him for stealing his chance at greatness. Eoin was too devastated at Seonaid's death to fight him off.

"It's said her mother locked herself in the room with the Duchess, scared he would kill her, too. Some months later, Seonaid's father woke in the middle of the night and, we assume, couldn't get back to sleep. He was walking on the sea wall. One of the guards from the tower saw a faint glow before the screams started. He swore it looked like Eoin McLeod. No one would go up to the wall, scared of what demons they might find there to cause such screams from a man like Seonaid's father. When morning came, the men went to the wall. He hadn't been here when the whole deaths had happened. The men would only venture forth well-armed in case of trouble. He lay dead with not a scratch on him, his face frozen with horror.

"Since then, the ghosts of Eoin and Seonaid with a little black haired girl have been seen walking by the sea. Mostly he's just seen alone when a woman is in trouble, trying to save her the way he wasn't able to his own wife. A Sinclair bard wrote a haunting song about it. Not all in our history is so nice, I'm sure it will make a good story for your thesis, though. Paranormal sells."

"You don't have to get sarcastic."

Hunter sat down next to her. "Isn't that what you want to hear all this for? So you can get a good grade."

"My paper is about art, for that I only need to know names and dates so I can correlate the years it all happened. Have you thought I want to know the rest just because I like history for its own sake? You think I'm going to put the love life of a man in the thirteen hundreds in an art history thesis?"

Hunter groaned. "Don't tell me you've been talking to Mary. Next thing you know, we'll have another romance novel about the family."

Ayda started laughing. "What romance novel?"

"Mary didn't tell you?"

Ayda could only shake her head, trying not to laugh at the look on his face. Red as a beet with embarrassment.

"A writer came asking questions after an interview was published. We all assumed it would be a suspense title, next we hear it's coming out as a romance novel. Very tasteful, god, I could never handle having to read about my grandmother's love life, but still it's a romance novel. I'm surprised Mary hasn't given you a copy yet."

Finally, Ayda let the smile tease the corner of her mouth. "Old family tradition, is it?" His eyes snapped to her and Ayda put a hand to her heart. "On my honor, I promise I will never write a romance novel about what I hear inside these castle walls."

"Very funny."

"Erotic novel, maybe." He rolled his head to look at her. He would make a perfect romance novel hero. Of course, she didn't actually read them, so she wasn't exactly sure about that, but he could have been in one she read any day.

"You find that funny, do you? They started tours down in the village to visit all the places mentioned. I can hardly walk around outside the walls of Am Binnean without having some town members telling someone I'm the grandson of that woman in the romance novel. Thank God, my grandfather was dead before it came out, he would have had a fit. There isn't much to make money on this far north, I know they're just trying to survive, but damn it's frustrating to have to live with."

"I didn't know. I'm sorry." She wiped the smile from her face and tried to look business like. "So you said you were just coming to find me."

He laughed a bit at her effort. "Aye, we have a nine hundred year old castle that's in need of restoring in some parts. I've been talking about this for some time but figured with an expert here, it would be a good time to get it decided."

Ayda took a drink of wine, trying to figure out what he was talking about. "You sound so serious, like you have to decide which hand to chop off."

Hunter's eyes closed. "Close, I would like help with selling off some paintings. You've seen the inventory. I'd like an honest opinion about which ones are worth keeping and which ones wouldn't hurt the collection any to lose. Most of the ones on the walls are favorites and family. But the store rooms have paintings that have been there for decades, at least."

Just the thought made her excited. If they were anything close to what was on the walls, nothing less than Christie's or Sotheby's would be fitting. The names of artists that ran through her head filled an art textbook. "I don't suppose we could look now?"

"And here I thought I'd have to get you drunk to agree."

"That's to get me in bed. For art I'm a slut." Ayda winked, and with a laugh, Hunter led the way.

She couldn't help but watch his ass as he walked down the hall. What a sight to behold. For being warned of ending up a man's whore, he wasn't trying very hard.

Flirting yes, but he made her feel less self-conscious than the man in the pub had.

~

A cursory look the night before was enough to take Ayda back to the storeroom early the next morning. Still hoping to get as much as possible finished, going through the storeroom was given only a few days, tops. At ten, she had already been there three hours. Moreover, that was after going through the halls and checking each picture. She'd pulled some twenty down.

"You look like something the cat dragged in. I'm sure we've dusted in here since 1728." Hunter said behind her. Of course, she hadn't heard him coming and knocked her head on a shelf when his voice echoed in the cavernous stone room.

"Owww." Hunter was at her side in an instant, she'd actually drawn blood. "I'm never going to finish this. Every time I turn around, someone's showing me more pictures and now my head hurts." Ayda groaned as he put a clean rag to the cut.

"I didn't mean to add to your work. You don't have to do this for me."

Trying to keep the tears from the pain away, Ayda leaned forward, not even caring she was putting her head in his lap. "Getting all of the info that I need for my thesis isn't the problem, it's that I promised your grandmother in exchange for room and board I would clean a majority of the paintings. Only she told me there were two hundred, and getting here I find it's more like eight hundred, one hundred twenty rooms and each room has on average ten. That doesn't even count the halls."

"I think you'll find there are actually eleven hundred, give or take, but space for only about nine hundred."

Ayda could only groan. "I've done ten."

"My grandmother is just excited that it's being seen. Just do what you need to for your paper, no one will say a word about how many or how few you get to clean."

He still held the rag to her head when she sat up. "So if I helped you go through them all for a sale, catalogued them so there is actually a complete list, and cleaned the worst, it would be good enough."

Hunter pulled a loose curl from her forehead to check on the bleeding. "I am positive that it would be more than enough. Although..."

Ayda felt a knot in the pit of her stomach at what was he going to ask now.

"I'm sure grandmother would appreciate a copy of that paper of yours for the library when you've finished it. Her mother was an artist. She has an affinity for that sort of thing."

Finally she let out a breath. She could actually get through this summer without losing her mind. "Absolutely. Leather bound with gold letters if she wants it. It might be a year, though."

Hunter's eyes lowered. "Grandmother tries to hide it, but she's not well. Tell her there will be one, but she might not see it."

Somehow, even though she didn't know the woman very closely, it hit her hard. She'd been reading that interview for so long that Elise seemed frozen in time. The World War II resistance spy that had survived two countries at war hadn't seemed the eight-seven years old she was. "There was a doctor's appointment in Inverness she went to when I first got here."

"She's there quite often. Don't tell her, but my brother Broderick is planning to propose to his girlfriend Eila soon to have the wedding before anything happens. They'll be here in a few weeks to have an announcement celebration once my parents get back from their anniversary cruise in the South Pacific. You'll have more than just history to put in your paper."

Looking down at her dusty clothes, she knew she had no better. "Can I hide then? I didn't bring anything to wear for a party, not in a castle with a Duke."

"Well, the heir apparently doesn't see anything wrong with what you're wearing."

Ayda closed her eyes again. "You're the eldest son?" She shook her head, that he was a future duke wasn't what bothered her. "You're the one that said I looked like something the cat dragged in." Ayda rolled her eyes. "Clothes, I brought nothing but work clothes. Let me hide."

Hunter chuckled in her ear. "I'm afraid everyone wants to meet you after grandmother's build up, hiding just won't do. How about I help you with all the rearranging you want to do. If there's a party coming up, we can't have bare walls. Then we'll see about getting you something to wear."

Opening her eyes once more Ayda found him watching her. "Do future Dukes have jobs?"

"I am in charge of the castle and its finances. I'd already spent eight years in the Royal Air Force, a Squadron Leader. When my grandfather died, he had always done everything, and without warning he skipped my father. He's the Duke, but I hold all the purse strings. Father wanted his life in London, so Grandfather gave it to him. Still pissed my father off to no end. Doesn't leave much time for a regular job. To tell the truth, I rather miss the Air Force. What about you?"

"My parents died when I was nine, a car accident. Mom was killed outright, dad spent months in a coma before he died. My aunt raised me in Washington. I have a trust fund to supplement making nothing, that's why I can afford to take these jobs that pay nothing but look great on a resume. If I can travel for it, I have." Sitting up slowly, she found the pain had subsided and she wasn't dizzy. But more she wanted to move away from his side. Was a woman supposed to be sitting there, trying hard not to look at a future Duke's pants? "Okay, if there's a party, let's get things ready. I took down the ones I saw that aren't very impressive, and frankly, there are some in here that need to be shown. I wasn't going to go opening doors except to the rooms that I had seen with your grandmother, so I know I haven't covered much."

Hunter put a hand down to help her up. "Come on then. Let's get Charlie and the three of us can get to work."

~

There were gaps on the walls, and pictures sat around the floors of many rooms for Ayda to pour over before announcing they were in no need of repair. Each night she wrote up more notes than she ever would have if she had just kept to slowly cleaning.

"Hi, Ayda." Duncan called running in to the workroom. She had hardly seen the boy, so it was a bit of a surprise. He was in preschool during the days, and he seemed to be attached to Charlie's hip when he was in the castle.

"Hi, yourself."

"Can I help?" he asked, peering up at her with big green eyes.

Her blood ran cold, she was working on a painting worth a hundred thousand pounds. "Umm. Can you hold the swabs right there until I need them?" she blurted out, trying to think of the most harmless thing around.

"Sure." His eyes sparkled as he picked up the pile, she could see he was trying his hardest not to drop them.

"Am I going to get to meet your mom soon?" Ayda asked as she took one from him.

"She left on a long trip and we won't see her anymore."

Suddenly Ayda knew exactly what the incident at the pub was about. "When he wakes up, remind him his sister didn't do anything she didn't want to do. The woman was old enough to leave," Hunter had whispered. Looking at the boy, she should have recognized the red hair before. So, the red head was Duncan's uncle and warned her about ending up a Sinclair whore. Not an amicable split by the sound of it.

"Duncan!" Hunter could be heard yelling from the hall. The boy jumped at being caught. "Now why are you hiding? Mary made a cake and she needs help cleaning the icing bowl."

Duncan thrust the swabs back at her and vanished out of the room. Ayda was laughing until Hunter appeared, wet and shirtless, with the squirming Duncan under his arm. "Thought you got away, didn't you? This is what you get when you push me in, you little stinker." He started tickling the boy, and laughter echoed through the stone halls until Charlie took him away.

Hunter was behind her, seeing what she was doing. She had a clear view of his chest in the reflection on the magnifying lens. A tattoo graced one shoulder but she was too distracted to see of what. "Oh, god."

"What was that?"

Hell, she had said it out loud. "Keep back, this one can't afford to get wet from you drying off like a dog," she snapped as he shook his head. Ayda almost groaned when he moved out of view of the reflection. "How long ago did Duncan's mother leave you?" she muttered, finally trying to change the subject.

"Duncan's not mine." Surprised, she spun around on the stool and regretted it. He stood closer than she thought. Images of him next to her in bed ran through her head. "Lorne, the youngest, and the sister of that bastard I hit had been together since early secondary school. The summer after he graduated military academy, they had a little accident. They hadn't gotten married yet, but he took her with him to his first posting engaged." Hunter's jaw tightened. "Duncan was nine months old when she just walked out the door. Left him there alone. No one's sure how many hours Duncan sat there crying, wondering why she never came, until Lorne got home. It was probably a couple days. She's never been seen since, probably because there's an outstanding warrant against her for endangering a child. He's in the Royal Marines his unit is being sent to Afghanistan here shortly. Instead of Duncan being raised by a stranger, he brought him here. He's with him every leave he can get. Two years now. Every time her brother sees one of us, he acts as if Lorne destroyed her life. She was twenty-one when she got pregnant, not what you'd call an innocent virgin. Lorne didn't just get her pregnant, he worshipped the ground she walked on. They were to be married in three months and she would have been a lady, had an apartment in the castle, wanted for nothing, but for her it wasn't enough."

Ayda hadn't been able to keep her jaw from dropping. "Wasn't enough? Was the woman mad?"

Then he ran a finger along her cheek and she just about lost it. Take me now please. "Not all women are art sluts. Alice was a fisherman's daughter. The only explanation we can come up with was it was too much for her. Lorne's learned to live with her choice, but he'll never forgive her for leaving Duncan like she did. She could have left without endangering him."

"If your brother looks anything like you, she'd have to be mad." Oh, god, had she just said that out loud?

The corner of Hunter's mouth turned up. "With that look in your eyes, I guess I should go get another shirt on before you have me for dinner."

"Leave it off. I'll just hang you up on the wall for inspiration while I work."

Biting his lip, Hunter never the less was laughing. "Surest way to get lucky with you, it sounds like. However, while I would love to become the decoration for you, Duncan's getting a bath as we have guests coming in an hour. The fifteen-year-old girl would be rather amused to see me up on the wall, I imagine. You'll probably want to keep in here. It will be dull to no end, you at least can escape the torment."

~

"So."

The one word filled the workroom where Ayda sat hunched over a painting. Spinning around it was Hunter looking as certifiably gorgeous as always. "Yes."

One corner of his mouth turned up in a grin. "Grandmother's under the impression you spend too much time stuck down here. Worried you'll end up a pasty skeleton, but with Mary feeding you it may just be pasty."

"I probably do spend too much time here at that. What does that mean though? Or are you just here to taunt me about my rapidly fading tan."

His chuckle echoed in the stone room. Shivers. "I have to head to Fort William she thought you might want to come along see some of the country. Maybe give your paper some history and color to go along with all the art."

For a moment, Ayda looked back at the painting she was working on. How many days had she spent locked away in a lab studying the past while the present slipped through her fingers.

"It will wait a few days. If you're one picture short at the end of the summer you can blame me." Hunter said as if reading her mind.

Was she seriously considering going back in the fall and not having a single story to tell. No pictures of the highlands even, other than the little bit right around Am Binnean. "I most certainly will blame you."

"Then grab your purse."

"I'd rather grab a jacket it's raw out there for June."

"I'll make sure we find a store then you can buy plaid fleece like all the tourists who don't think it will be cold in the middle of summer."

Ayda stopped herself from perusing exactly what he was wearing. "Oh and what do you wear?"

"I have a generous collection of wool sweaters, I buy them from an old woman in the village. She'd always appreciate the income if you would like to stop on our way by instead."

"Great."

~

Five sweaters later Hunter drove out of the village laughing. "I hate to think of what your house looks like, if you buy this many souvenirs wherever you go."

"Yeah it looks like your house, stuff everywhere. I even have a Rembrandt in my bathroom."

"Pure extravagance."

Ayda smiled out the window, would he even believe her if she said she did actually have one. Granted it was only a drawing he did, some sketch for a painting, but how many could say they had a Rembrandt at all. She was finally in the middle of the highlands. With school ending only days before she was expected at Am Binnean, she had seen very little of the country. Surrounded by treeless moors and windswept valleys she felt very alone. "Why would they put a castle so far from anything? It's so empty."

He kept his eyes on the road but he smiled. "Because this is the best defensive position on the property, always has been. And once they started marrying and adding to the property and coffers, there was something to protect. The more there was to protect, the bigger the castle got. The Vikings weren't the only threat. Before the Sinclair's started building, anyone could have just landed unopposed and used it as a base for attacking other areas."

Ayda couldn't help but tease. "All that married money and they only gave you two cannon to do it?"

"I think there are 15 actually. They blew a German u-boat out of the water in World War 1. Protected the village when it was used as an allied boat refueling stop. Blew up some pirates that tried to attack in the 1620's. There are lots of stories to add to your paper."

"If I was writing a paper on military history."

"Aye, worked for me in military academy."

Ayda couldn't help but start laughing. "How did the village make money if the Laird can't even do it without marrying wealth though?" Ayda asked trying to take her mind off the fact she was thinking such thoughts about the very man's descendant. Damn he was making it hard not to imagine his clothes littering the floor, oh on the library floor would be lovely.

Hunter was silent for some time. "There is a flagstone quarry that was worked for some time. Fishing of course, there are several other old salting houses dotted around the village. For about 100 years in the 1700's-1800's there was kelping."

"What on earth is kelping?" Ayda interrupted.

"They harvest kelp and burn it to ash to make alkali for processing linen. It was mainly during the Napoleon era when the main source in France was cut off." Hunter was again silent for a moment. "Sheep of course, there was a small fabric industry, we still make plaid and sweaters. Cattle to some degree. Whatever they can find to make money really. Hiring out during harvest time to have extra money to make it through the winter. Joining the army came in that, we uhh well became mercenaries if the price was high enough always off Scottish shores. You really think we only marry for money?" Hunter asked after a long silence.

Ayda blushed again. "Well I...that is what the titled did, even into the 1900's."

"Grandmother didn't." Hunter answered simply. "There are others too."

Ayda couldn't help but grin. She knew the answer before she even asked the question. "You have a story then?"

"Aye just one or two small ones. We even have a restoration era actress gracing the family tree, one who shared the stage with Nell Gwenn."

He didn't say anything, he was being mean and making her ask. He knew she wanted to hear, knew she'd go crazy if she didn't ask. "Fine spill it then."

Hunter chuckled. "I thought you would have held out a little longer."

"When?"

"How about the Duke returning to the castle after fighting Napoleon today. Grandmother loves this one, she calls it Rose among the Heather."

In the Year 1815

It all looked the same as the Duke of Cairnmuir came in to breakfast. To see it all he might have thought nothing had changed. The walls held just as many portraits and landscapes of all eras and artists of note that they always had. Maybe there were one or two more slipped in here and there. He could add more clutter himself now with captured French and Spanish loot as he made his way across the continent.

A Duke never had to sleep in the filth like the men did, but he'd seen enough of the fighting all the same. Sinclair men always did regardless of position. How many of their names filled the rolls of soldiers that were kept in the armory, of those never to return? Dukes, the same as peasants, filled the lists of the dead. He could still rarely bring himself to look back far enough to that dark day when two hundred men were wiped off the earth and no war was even being fought. It had kept them out of the whole Jacobite fight for more than thirty years, having so few men of fighting age left to muster.

"Edward, when did you return? My God, you should have told us even if it was the middle of the night."

Edward spun round to find his mother rushing toward him, arms wide open. "Just now. I thought you would be at breakfast and came here first." She hugged him for what seemed forever. She hadn't changed either, same black hair, same green eyes, same pleasant face. Was he the only one to change since he left?

"With the ball tonight, we all ate early so we could get to the preparations."

Edward pulled back surprised. Am Binnean was days from Edinburgh. There were only a handful of houses she'd call worthy of invitation even. "We live in the middle of nowhere."

"None the less, we are having one."

"I've just spent years fighting a war in Spain and France. I don't really feel like a ball the day I get back."

"Nonsense, we were holding one without you and it's high time you find a wife anyway. We have twice the reason to hold one now that you are back. It will take you most the day to get presentable with all that filth on you. Might as well go start getting ready now. I'll find Erskine and have a bath sent to your room." She rushed off, but Edward sat down at the table regardless of her orders. A woman appeared at his elbow silently.

"Una, may I have some breakfast? I know I smell something terrible, but please."

The pretty redhead smiled. "Of course, sir. I'll bring in more of the dried heather to help you stand yourself indoors."

"Oh, and you've lost your sense of smell, have you?"

Una vanished with a chuckle.

~

The bath was waiting for him when he finished, a kettle still in his fireplace to add when he was ready. Erskine at least understood he wouldn't go without breakfast, Una's breakfast at that, not after years from home. Never even had a chance to return the first time Napoleon was sent to exile still in Paris when he raised an army again. Papered in green brocade with an elaborate plaster ceiling and accented with gold, the room was magnificent, but it wasn't the room he'd left. Mother had redecorated. Finally sinking into the tub, he closed his eyes and tried not to fall asleep. He failed utterly, and it had to have been an hour later he heard the door opening.

"Would have thought you'd try and stay away with a ball tonight. Well I suppose you can't help that can you." Erskine said as he entered. A thin man in his thirties with dark skin and thinning black hair, he could have been a pirate. That's what most thought when they saw him. Edward and he had grown up together though, Erskine's father the steward before him.

"Lord, man, when Una said ye stank, I thought a bath would have helped, not made it worse." He carried another bucket and promptly dumped it on Edward's head before opening the windows.

"Why a ball? There's only one family within a good distance and they tried to steal the castle for generations." Edward sputtered, wiping the water from his face.

"Ye didn't see them all when you came in? The castle is full, even some of the empty servants' quarters are filled with people come in for it."

"Why?"

Erskine started laughing. "Because unlike ye, your brother Bran never leaves the castle, and the Duchess wishes to find him a wife."

Edward started scrubbing and used it to try to hide his smile. "She know about him and Una yet?"

"No sir, not even the fact that the two boys running around are his." No, some things never changed much, except for his room.

"Erskine, did mother change any other rooms, or just mine?"

"The ball room has a new carved ceiling with pendants and such hanging down. It is quite impressive."

"Ahh–now I see why we're having a ball. Has nothing to do with Bran finding a wife." The beard covering his chin started itching, it was a lovely beard by the regiment's standards, but while it had been easier in the field, the itching continued to get worse. "A shave, please. I wonder if I brought back more than just me."

"Yes, sir."

Heaven help him, the woman was right. It took most of the day to be properly shaved, trimmed, and scented, but when it came to putting on a suit of clothes, Edward had to balk. "I've been in a kilt for years, Erskine. I really don't want to wear breeches."

"I burnt the one ye were wearing, and there's not much of anywhere to find one with the ball starting in an hour. Have to send away to get the plaids."

Edward started smiling. "Go see to the ball. I've been getting dressed for thirty years without help."

"I burned the others in your bags, too." Erskine gave that announcement as a parting shot.

Edward waited until he was sure the man was out of sight before he opened the door and peered out into the hall. A few more rugs lined the hall than before, but it was empty, leaving no one to see him in a dressing robe. Pushing open a door, he discovered that the storeroom was not a storeroom anymore.

"Oh, do forgive me," Edward snapped out quickly. All he had were flashes of muslin and creamy white skin as he closed the door once more, and swiftly. That's all he would claim to, at any rate. He would keep it to himself that the woman's thighs were some of the shapeliest he had ever beheld, and the bosom matched. God, he had missed a lot in France. It took a moment to find a servant, any servant, and this one looking wholly uncomfortable in full livery. "Where's everything that was in the store room? The one being used as a bedroom now?"

"With the paintings, I believe. The room off the hall tucked behind the old tower, your Grace." The original tower definitely showed its age, having been built in 856. It still had arrow slits, rough stone, and in its center stood several cannons that while not a thousand years old, were definite proof that the castle could still repeal an attack easily.

Edward found the chest quickly enough, even though the room was packed to the rafters now. He had to wonder if the woman in the room knew it would be a store room again soon enough. The chest was ancient, from the 1100's at least, but it held the oldest relics of the family. Papers from the first inhabitants of the castle, letters patent for the titles, marriage pacts and tartans, old ones from before they were banned. Even an old gold cup, no one seemed to know how exactly it got there though. Two of the footmen came down the hall and Edward waylaid them to carry it back to his room. No one probably knew that was where he stored all of the papers before he left, as the tartans covered others beneath. The plaid lengths had been found stoned up in an old niche under the stairs with a number of swords and other weapons, the same weapons that would have been outlawed. Old Johne Sinclair hadn't been willing to give up an entire armory worth of weapons when the laws came down. They might not have been involved in the fighting, but they weren't immune from the laws meant to punish. The armory had been restored to its rightful place only a decade ago.

Pulling out an old length of Black Watch and an old regimental coat, Edward finally got dressed, even if the coat he had left behind was now a little big. With dinner about to start when he emerged from his room, the hall was filled with people. No one he recognized, no one that recognized him as he made his way through the maze. His brother Bran just stared at him as they came face to face.

"Dear Lord, Edward, no one told me you were back." They were a study in opposites–brothers, yet one red-haired, one black, one with green eyes, one with blue, one thin, one stocky. Bran was the red-haired, green-eyed, stocky one. Edward was an immense man standing near six and a half feet, a dark one of the family with hair as black as night.

"How grand he looks." Some woman that Edward had never seen cooed. "Look at all his medals. What's this odd looking creature on this one?"

Edward sighed regretting ever wearing his uniform. "It's a sphinx, the regiment was awarded it for gallantry at the battle of Alexandria." He swore several of the women squealed.

"Oh were you there?"

"I was still at school." He hissed ready to bolt when dinner was announced.

"Lud Edward, I have no idea where to put you." Bran said suddenly.

Then the voice of an angel spoke. "He may sit next to me, Lord Sinclair. I believe I am on the end. I shan't mind being a little crowded. If you would introduce us."

Edward turned slowly and wasn't disappointed. No cooing child impressed with a shiny medal. The face of an angel matched the voice, the face he had seen only a flash of before her attributes gained his attention as he'd shut the door to her room once more.

"Of course." Bran stammered for a moment as his mind switched gears. "Miss Rose Beaufort, may I present my brother, the Duke of Cairnmuir."

Her dress was white but a red crisscrossed bodice held her breasts–as any man would wish he could. And her mouth formed an O. "I didn't realize. Do forgive me, your Grace."

"Nonsense. I can't think of a more delightful dinner companion, especially one offering to endure a little discomfort to accommodate me."

"I should have invited Miss Leighton if I knew you were to be here. Oh and the Marquess of Lisstone surely your old friend..."

"Is not the Marquess until his father dies, and the Earl of Altham sailed for Venice I heard before you make a fool of yourself trying to invite him now. The man is blind saving my life. I won't subject him to you." Edward held out his arm for Miss Beaufort, but it was timidly that she took it.

The great hall was a huge room, with soaring stone walls and giant beams that ran across the ceiling, each holding a huge wrought iron chandelier. The table was of an old style with the ends far across the room from one another. Several smaller tables had been moved in along the sides to accommodate even more settings. "I don't bite, Miss Beaufort," he murmured quietly, as the others jostled him. "Unless you're my mother."

"I should have never presumed to make your acquaintance. After you opened the door on me, I figured you were as much a stranger to these walls as I."

"They seem to have emptied out store rooms to make more beds available. I'm surprised they hadn't doled out my own bed. It is I who should be apologizing. Six years ago, it was a storeroom. I never dreamed I should have to knock."

"I'll only forgive you if you haven't a complaint about the view. I shall become quite missish if you are going to start ill gossip about what you saw."

It had been far too long since he had anyone flirt with him. Edward gaped for a second and then couldn't help the grin curling his lips. "Nothing ill about you, Miss Beaufort."

"Good, I should hate to imagine you thinking ill of me."

Just as Edward decided that he could indeed stand a ball in the castle on his first day back, Erskine appeared at his side. "Sir, your place is at the head of the table. I'll show you there."

Surrounded by Van Dyck, Gainsborough, and Hogarth paintings, Edward looked over at the woman on his arm–he couldn't do it. Far too long since there had been a pair of green eyes staring at him, except in war. "Miss Beaufort was kind enough to share her space at the table with an unexpected body. If you can find room for her next to me, I'll take the head, otherwise I can share the foot as easily."

Erskine wrinkled his brow at his making things difficult. "Eudard? Precedence?"

"This is to find a wife for Bran. He should be in the center of it all, not me. I'm hungry and I wish to eat."

Of course the man's eyes narrowed, in light of his knowledge of Una and the boys. They wandered quickly enough over to Miss Beaufort. "Yes, sir. I'll have a chair fit in at the foot, then."

A servant brought them glasses of wine as they waited. Hardly a guest said a word to him, had he changed so much in the last years he was unrecognizable? When all was sorted out, Edward found Erskine showing him to a table. Not the large table that everyone sat at, but a table from who knew where in the house, set for two.

"There was no room, try as we could to make it work. We'd fit too many in already," Erskine announced. However, Edward caught the wink just before he left them.

"I hope you are a fine conversationalist, Miss Beaufort."

She laughed delightfully. "I'm sure I will more than make up for your lack of companions, with no one to hear if I say something I shouldn't. Why did your steward call you Eudard, though?"

"We grew up together as boys. I'm not so strict on formality."

"No, your Grace, you misunderstand me. Ehdard it sounded like from his mouth. It is Edward, is it not? I heard your brother telling of you earlier."

"Ah, then you're not Scottish. It's the Gaelic form of the name."

"No, I was just visiting a family friend in Edinburgh. It was she that was invited. You know Lady Bissett don't you?"

"Yes, she's an old family relation actually. If you count 500 years ago, the cousin of one of the Duchesses long ago." Edward held his tongue from asking the question he wanted to until the servants had finished putting small dishes from the main table about for them to eat. "Do you always talk to strange men so, even if no one is there to say you shouldn't say such things?"

Miss Beaufort's eyes lowered. "No, I should say I do not. But there is something I can't explain that makes me want to see you smile. You seem far too forlorn for such a party in the house."

Edward's smile faded a bit, knowing she could see through him so much. She knew nothing about him, and yet she could see what no one in his family could. "Do I seem so much so, then? I shall try harder not to let my years of war darken your dinner table."

"Did you lose many friends? It was horrid of your mother to bring up a man she knew was injured."

Edward raised his head slowly. He had expected her to just move on to more frivolous topics. "A good many, Miss Beaufort. The one she spoke of would make you swoon he is so handsome a man, and if you shan't tell my mother the only reason I don't fuck like a farm boy. Introduced me to all the delights a woman can offer beyond rutting. He can't even be swayed by such a beautiful face as yours these days." Edward shook his head clearing the memory of it. A good friend that fought in the Hussars was now unable to even ride a horse. "Now I have the sad duty of riding to several of the tenants' homes and informing them their sons are dead as well."

"And you arrived home to find everyone in the midst of a party. I should look a little melancholy, too, in that case."

"Well, you could always say such things as you shouldn't, and take my mind off of it. From you, I would accept it gratefully." And there she blushed.

Still. "What sorts of delights did he show you?"

Edward couldn't stop the grin. "Maybe one day I'll introduce you to the pleasures of an orgy."

The room was suddenly quiet, hopefully no one heard that last comment. "I believe they are toasting your return," Miss Beaufort murmured quietly.

Edward stood and took the adulation, hardly hearing it. Maybe it was at higher rank, but he served no different from most others. His great distinction being that he survived where others had not. Why weren't they being toasted for their sacrifice?

Sitting down, their light mood of earlier was gone. Eyes lowered, he watched Miss Beaufort eating her meal.

"Excuse me, Miss Beaufort, I can't do this." The second course was being brought in. There was enough confusion, no one even noticed him leaving the room.

~

The fire burned brightly in the fireplace when he found his room. A mist outside made it a dreary night. A perfect night for feeling sorry for oneself. Why couldn't he just endure the night and make his family happy?

A voice came out of nowhere. "Not very gentlemanly to leave a lady at table alone in a sea of gossipers."

"I am sorry, Miss Beaufort. I assure you it is no slight to you."

A hand touched his neck softly where there should be none. A gentle thumb traced his cheek. "My name is Rose."

Edward pulled his eyes from the fire as she bent down, eye to eye with him. She glowed, there was no other word to describe it. Golden skin, copper hair, emerald eyes. "You blushed earlier, and yet now act as if we are long engaged."

"Have you thought that is perhaps why I am here? No one has made me blush before and many have tried. My heart pounds, my knees are weak, and thoughts are in my head no one has put there before, not even my dead husband."

His knuckle traced the edge of her low-cut neckline and she gasped. "Miss Beaufort, is it?" He asked it as her eyes closed, when his hand dipped beneath the dark red muslin. Full breasts, with nipples that turned hard the moment he touched one.

"Lady Bissett brought me as companion when she received the invitation. I believe she imagines that your brother would find a Miss more desirable a wife than a widow, even with the stigma of marrying so soon after my husband died. Biggest matchmaker in Edinburgh, so I hear. My husband fought in the peninsula. He came back different, not the man I knew. He wouldn't even let me comfort him. And then Waterloo took him for good."

Nothing stopped him as he pulled one breast from its confines. "Rose, you should stop me."

"I came to comfort you, I suppose, the way I was never allowed with Graham. Please don't send me away. I think it's gotten turned around now."

Edward pulled on her gently and she fell in his lap. "Send you away?" Her face was hidden in his neck, but it left the breast he had bared only a hair width from his mouth. The sigh that escaped when his tongue touched her was pure music. Rose turned, giving him access. "God, it's been too long. Did you at least lock the door?"

Her smile was radiant when she pulled back. "Of course."

Edward reached behind and undid the few buttons holding her dress tight. She seemed even more eager than he was as she pulled it over her head. The corset and chemise followed quickly. The brief glimpse he was given earlier was nothing compared to the full view.

"No indeed, Mrs. Beaufort, nothing ill about you at all."

She sat there on his lap nude and smiling as she offered up her breasts once more. Suckling made her moan with pure abandon. "More," she sighed breathlessly, and almost screamed when Edward broke off, moving her from his lap until she was straddling him.

"Please, Edward."

Such wide green eyes pleaded for release. "How long had Graham not let you comfort him?"

The words never came, though, as he ran a finger through her folds stretched open across his lap. Wet for him like no one before, she cried out as he slipped three full fingers deep within her. As he slowly thrust them in and out her eyes opened, lids heavy.

"How are you when you have room to maneuver?"

His thumb swiped through her folds once more, this time laying claim to her mound, and she shattered. Even with the noise of the dancing in the other wing, she bit her lip to keep from crying out at full volume. Edward stood as her head rested on his shoulder, and carried her to the bed. She looked like Aphrodite lying there on the bed, sated.

"It was 1812 the last time, and you know well when Waterloo was," she murmured. There was no way any sane man could have ever denied her, looking at him with those eyes. Away in battle yes, but lying next to her and denying her had just been cruel.

"I want you, Edward, all of you." Her hand ran up his thigh. With nothing under his kilt, there was nothing to stop her finding out how much he wished the same.

He let out a curse in Gaelic when her thumb ran over the top of his cock. She wasn't making it easy to get his clothes off as she stroked him throughout his attempts. Rose licked her lips when the kilt finally fell to the floor. "Please," she whispered, her breath coming short. But as much as she pleaded it didn't hurry her fingers tracing the scars that covered him. A knock on the door made them both freeze.

"Are you in there, Eudard? Your mother is worried." Erskine called out.

"Never better." He grinned wider as he climbed on the bed, hovering just at her opening. "I've been on the road a long time, I just need some rest. I'll play the good Duke tomorrow."

Rose ran her fingernails up his back. He knew she was trying to pull him inside, but he resisted for just a moment longer.

"And what are you tonight then, the naughty Duke?" she whispered in his ear, as Erskine said goodnight.

"The luckiest Duke in the world. Never a finer welcome home a man could have."

Her lips curled up in a cat-like grin. Only then did he slowly push his way in, watching the grin fade as her mouth opened in a silent gasp. He lay there unmoving, inhaling deep the scent of her, gratitude–a woman to comfort him, when war was always in his mind. Lucky didn't start to describe it.

Rose picked his head up from her shoulder. "Come with me this time." Her kiss was soft, and with it, she set the pace as he started moving. When she moved faster so did he, harder so did he, and just as he felt the start of going over the edge, she rolled. She sat there on him unmoving, holding him captive, her breasts barely rubbing on his chest.

"Rose?"

"Say it again. I like hearing you saying my name with that burr of yours."

"Rose, don't tease."

With that, she sat up. "I never tease. A proper welcome isn't over in five minutes." She held his hands, kissing each fingertip before pulling one into her mouth. Edward swore he felt matching pulls on his cock.

"A proper welcome can happen over and over and over," he corrected. With that, Edward started thrusting, while she rode him like a horse. He'd never look at a woman on horseback the same again. It didn't take long before she was on all fours again, matching his strokes, forcing them harder and harder. This time he took her cries away as he kissed her. It was his last thought before he found his end.

~

In the morning, Rose's eyes were closed as he licked the nipple that was temping him so much. As he made sure the other wasn't neglected, her eyes opened. "I'll be woken here soon. You should get back to your room unless you are prepared to marry a stranger."

Rose stretched like a cat. "For a moment there I thought I was dreaming and I would wake in an empty bed as usual. I'm sick of empty beds."

"As long as I'm around, you won't have an empty anything." Edward kissed all the bare skin he could find, he wasn't pushing her out quickly.

~

Around them, there were others of the party that wanted some exercise after the long night dancing and waking late. Rose and Edward walked in silence for much of the way until they reached an aged stone bridge half looking ready to fall down. The castle actually stood on a spit of land out into the sea. That bridge was its only connection to the mainland. Beyond, the castle with its clan seals set in the walls stood the blue grey sky.

"You're quiet this morning," Rose finally announced.

"Could you make excuses for me? I need to go talk to some families. I'm afraid that it will be on my mind until it's done."

"Of course." Watching him walk off, Rose wished there had been someone real to tell her Graham was gone. The letter she had received took weeks to truly hit her. For weeks she kept expecting him to walk in the door any minute, just as she had every other time he was gone. At least until she watched the others that had left with him returning to their homes. Returning to the wives she knew so well. It had been two months before she finally cried that he was gone. Lady Bissett had finally invited her for a visit determined to rid the grief, Rose had taken the offer, but being forced on every eligible bachelor on Edinburgh had not been the answer. Nothing had helped, not until she saw a man that looked just as out of sorts as she was, one that stirred more than just her compassion, too.

~

Edward and Bran played billiards in a room filled with hunting trophies, not all as local as the Highland stag, as well as dozens of reminders of the Sinclair penchant for the military. Women were never allowed entrance to that male enclave, probably the reason Bran had suggested it. The ball may have been to show off the ballroom, but at the ball mother had let slip that Bran was ready to marry and of course, now that Edward had returned, he would be looking as well.

"Do I just tell mother the truth?" Bran asked quietly as he aimed, speaking low enough that the men smoking cigars on the other side of the room couldn't hear.

"Will Una even take you if you asked?" Edward inquired in turn, and Bran completely missed the shot.

"Damn it, Edward."

"I'm the Duke. There's not much mother could do about it if you just took her over to the church in the village and married her, claiming Ainsley and Gavin as yours. Mother's going to start noticing who the father is soon anyway. They look more like you than ever."

"So mother can just stop talking to me and make my life hell?" Bran hissed.

"Are you sure her not talking to you is hell?"

Bran started laughing. "Well, perhaps not."

"Go marry the woman. I'll miss her cooking, but we'll have the best run kitchen in the country." Bran just stood there. "Well, what?"

"I'm not really sure she would accept me."

Edward snorted. "You think the woman dreams of cooking for us the rest of her days? I don't want to see you again until you're married." Edward had said his piece, it was up to Bran now. Still, he couldn't help but laugh at Bran gaping like a trout as he left him there.

~

Chaos filled the dining hall when Edward entered for supper. Lots of women's heads huddled together whispering. So Una had accepted him, then.

"Ah, Miss Beaufort. I hope you had a pleasant afternoon after I took leave of you."

"You'll never guess. Bran just announced he's married the cook, and that her children were his." Edward tried not to smile and look stern, but the woman saw though him easily enough. She moved her head imperceptibly closer. "You knew."

"Since they were sleeping together when he was fifteen. I told him I didn't want to see him again until he was married. It was that or have him hiding in the billiards room for the remainder of the party. Man loves her. It would have made many people miserable if mother had succeeded."

Rose lowered her head, trying to hide a grin. "But all these women that came at your mother's invitation? Oh, you like difficult circumstances."

"I could tell them where we were last night and take their minds off of it." Edward whispered softly. "Or maybe that the idea of an orgy intrigues you?"

"I'll force you to marry me if I hear one word out of your mouth."

"You say that as if it would be a punishment."

Her eyes went wide. "I'm all but a stranger."

Edward started smiling. "You know where I sleep. We can rectify that situation." Walking off, he heard her gasp. He'd heard the same gasp the night before. He'd bet ten guineas she'd be back.

"Mother." Edward kissed her cheek when he saw her standing there in front of him, hoping she hadn't been close enough to hear his conversation with Miss Beaufort.

"Hiding it under my very nose, Edward."

"Only to those not looking. He's loved her since they were bairns. Now I think we shall have a wedding party."

His mother looked positively ashen that he had known all those years. "He made me look a fool. I invited all these people to see him married."

"Precisely, and he is married. If they read into it to send their daughters to snare a husband, then that is their fault. You were misunderstood, nothing more. I wasn't going to see my nephews deprived of a father because you forced him to marry someone he cared nothing for. Bran never has stood up to you. I'm going to propose a toast. You should either leave or go find a glass."

It took a moment for Erskine to get the room quiet, but finally Edward stood at the head of the table, as was his place. He could hardly see Rose, buried as she was at the other end. "Ladies and gentlemen, a marriage was mentioned in the invitation for coming, and a wedding we have had. While the ceremony was kept intimate, since the local church isn't large enough for us all, the celebration will not be small. Raise your glasses, everyone, to the Lord Sinclair and Lady Sinclair. May they long be happy. I invite you to enjoy their wedding feast before they leave for their honeymoon."

"What honeymoon?" Una asked out of the side of her mouth, as everyone sat.

"Edinburgh, London perhaps. I'd suggest Paris, but I'd wait a few years more."

"I'm the cook," Una countered.

"You're Lady Sinclair, and you have been, to my mind, for years, so don't forget that."

Una lowered her eyes to her plate, unable to look at him. "Thank you, Eudard."

All through dinner, Edward could see the whisperers, but he kept talking to Una as if it was the most natural thing to do. Fortunately, she was so happy at finally being married after years of being the mistress that she just teased and taunted him, as she always did. They were laughing through most of the meal, definitely not looking like a scandalous wedding had just taken place. As they stood around before brandy and cigars, Edward watched Rose walk over. The black dress she wore with a white bodice drew his eyes to every curve. The little van dykes of black that webbed down from the neckline over her breasts were like arrows pointing the way to her treasures. Lifting his eyes to meet hers, he knew it was a challenge to his earlier comment. She was trying to make him come to her instead of the other way around.

"Congratulations," Rose announced, with a wide smile. He was sure it was more at his reaction than over the couple's marriage.

"Thank you for saying that. I feel as if everyone in the room is staring, and not in a good way," said the new bride.

"They're all jealous. You have what they want."

Una's eyes widened. "Oh, is that what it is? That I can deal with. I thought it was just that I was the cook." A sly look filled her face. "Then why are you talking to me?" It was an impertinent question, but she was, after all, the cook, and partook of the legendary cook's temperament.

"I've my eye on another, Lady Sinclair."

How on earth she knew, neither of them could figure out, but Una leaned close to Rose's ear. "Well, if he's anything like his brother, I don't blame you."

"Una!" Bran hissed.

"You'll forgive me for leaving early but I need to pack for my honeymoon. If you'll excuse me, Bran, Eudard, Miss Beaufort." Una walked off as serenely as anyone could.

"Edward, I'm sorry." Bran apologized, but as he looked between them, the look on his face changed. "You aren't protesting much for something over which you should be outraged. You ken she was right."

At that, Edward felt Rose leaving his side, as it had been suggested there be music. The group was retiring to the music room. "She was right?" Bran asked again.

"Yes." Edward left him at that. The look on his face just as astonished as it had been when he'd ordered him to go marry Una.

Rose wasn't heading in with the crowd, though, and Edward followed her as she made her way down the hall. Losing sight of her as she turned a corner, he heard voices before she was back in sight. For a moment, he could only fume as he found Rose against a wall with a man very close to kissing her. Edward felt a fool. After all, she'd come to his room, who's to say she didn't go to others?

Just about to turn around, he stopped cold. Only feet away from her was an eerily glowing figure, dressed in a kilt, with long black hair. He was truly from another age. His huge broadsword lifted and came down in a wide arc, as if in slow motion. Rose screamed, but it was drowned out, the music from the other room had started.

The castle ghost had been a story well known since he was a bairn, though he'd never seen it himself. Supposedly it was known for protecting women when they were in danger, and having a ghost trying to cut off a man's head was surely that. Edward's fist connected with the man's jaw as well. No sense trusting entirely to the supernatural.

Erskine heard the screaming, and came careening around the corner. "Sir."

"Throw this man out now. He tried to attack Miss Beaufort."

Without comment, Erskine grabbed him by the collar and dragged him away. The rough treatment bringing him to, he tried to struggle, but there was no breaking Erskine's grasp.

"Let me go!" He yelled before he was out of sight.

"He said he knew, and as we are not engaged, I must be..." her words faded as Edward slid the small sleeves of her gown down, baring pale white shoulders. "We are in the hall," she whispered quietly. Edward couldn't help it, his fingers ran along the red mark where the man had held her too tightly.

"Did he truly hold you so tight to cause such marks?" Only looking down did Rose see what Edward did. The handprints were clearly visible upon her. Edward took her hand and led her to his room, only a few doors away. Her own room was clear on the other side of the house. He didn't have to guess where she had been headed.

Edward poured a glass of wine, hating that he had thought the worst of her. How much would she have had to endure if he had turned and walked away?

"This is what got us in trouble in the first place," Rose announced, as she took the wine he handed her.

Edward sank onto the settee and leaned his head back. "Is this when we are forced to marry because you've been ruined when he tells why he was kicked out? Una will keep her tongue still, other than to tease me."

Rose started chuckling. "With me the one that came to your room, I don't think ruined is the right word."

"Compromised, then?"

Rose smiled as she straddled him and drank her wine with a twinkle in her eyes. Such eyes staring into his soul with such thoughts so easy to see in them. She was a vixen. "Edward, I would gladly marry because thoughts of last night still make me ache for more, and I could endure that usage for the rest of my life. But I will not be forced into it, or into having a man resent me for committing him where he did not wish. I'm a widow no one can condemn on that fact. That is not how I wish to live the rest of my life. Duke or not."

"Ache, is it?" Edward pulled her down and gently kissed each mark on her pale skin. "Try not to be seen when you go to your room this time," he whispered.

~

Saddling two horses, Edward took Rose for a ride about the estate. The village was tiny. It was hardly more than some hundred buildings clustered around a bay where numerous fishing boats anchored. After a brief look at the fifteenth century chapel that stood in the center of town, it was the mausoleum next to it that was impressive though as she walked around seeing the graves of all his ancestors. Large carved stone monuments and effigies of the important, not in a closed in tomb but opened to the sky. The breeze blew her riding habit about her legs as she read the stones. Only since the 1440's though, those before were in graves only known by local legend and not a stone marker. All around were wide-open grasslands where sheep grazed.

"You cleared the estate for sheep?" Rose murmured.

Edward let out a sigh. "No, we did not follow that practice. The land isn't fit for farming in the first place. The same families still live here that did a hundred years ago, three hundred years ago, six hundred years ago. That's why so many serve in the army. There is little to feed them besides fishing and sheep."

"The castle is so grand. How do you ever afford it with so little to bring in income?" Rose put her hand over her mouth, shocked she had said such a thing.

Edward couldn't help but grin. "We married well. Or we turned mercenary for the right price."

Rose's hand fell from her mouth. "Then I truly am only a mistress. To save my pride, I should like to think you were at least considering it, if only faintly."

Edward rode close enough so he could reach over to her cheek. "There is none I have ever considered more.

The party leaves in two weeks. You might decide that you are too far from London in that time." Her mouth hung open, and Edward closed it gently. "You did not expect me to consider you? The one who's best by far at keeping the horrors of the last years at bay? I have not slept well in some time, and with you, I have. I do consider it greatly."

"A minor officer's widow? What about marrying well?"

"Aye, I'm a Duke, but I live on the edge of the world. You think I'd look at a woman that would hardly talk to me and I would take no pleasure in? That castle full hardly speaks to me other than yes your grace, no your grace. Would you care if I dally with your title? I have a sickly daughter who will make your life hell because she hates Scotland and will surely never give you any comfort, but she has thirty thousand pounds so you'll get along well."

Rose started laughing and Edward pulled her over, his mouth covering hers. Stunned or not, there was no denying her mouth opened for him as readily as she had offered everything else to him. He truly did think on the matter a great deal.

When at last their lips parted, he looked deep into those green eyes. "Don't sell yourself short again, Rose. People died around me and my own family doesn't seem to care. When I get quiet, you know where my mind has gone. Maybe an officer's widow is exactly what I need." Edward mounted and spurred his horse on, Rose just sat there stunned. As he had with Bran, he had said his piece, the rest was up to her.

~

Rose wasn't in his room when he retired from the billiards room. Not that he expected her to be catering to him, but she was sleeping in the old storeroom. He should have let it rest, he knew that in his head, but

Edward couldn't help slipping into the hall and making his way to the other side of the castle. There was no answer to his knock, and even putting his head in, he could see that she was not there. Hell, the castle had over a hundred rooms and that didn't even include the storerooms. She could be anywhere. Heading back to get some sleep, he happened to glance out the window, and saw her on the sea wall. A storm was coming in, the waves crashed into the rocks, spraying into the air around her. The wind battered him as he pushed open the door.

"Rose, what are you doing out here?"

She lifted her finger and pointed. Down on the rocky beach walked a trio, two adults and a bairn. They were glowing green, the same way the ghost had been when it had tried to protect her. Edward had heard of the ghost being around but never seen it, and now twice in a week.

"They must have died horribly to haunt the castle still," Rose whispered.

"His father-in-law killed him, when he returned from war and found he had married his daughter without permission. He killed his daughter too, and the bairn she carried."

Rose turned slowly, tears running down her face. "And now you give your brother permission to marry whom he wishes."

Edward still stared down at the little family, oblivious to the storm that blew in around them. "Not exactly. I told him to marry Una because I'd returned home and found my nephews were looking more like their father than ever. Either he married her or else endure the gossip, and then live in torment if mother found him a wife. Because it wouldn't be long before even a dull witted woman knew where his heart lay."

"Couldn't let me have my little fantasy."

Edward wiped the tears from her face gently. "It's going to start pouring soon. Let's get you warmed up before we have to call the doctor."

"I'm feeling a little lonely all of a sudden."

Edward led her to the library, a two-story room with a fire already burning brightly. Shelves from floor to ceiling surrounded them, while a railed walkway gave access to the second floor books. The shelves were filled with classics of Scottish history and law, many in ancient leather bindings. Where the shelves didn't cover, there was mahogany paneling, while a huge carved renaissance mantle surrounded the fireplace. Meissen porcelain figurines lined the shelf, all of nude women.

"Not your room?" Rose asked.

"If I'm going to get caught, it will be something worth getting caught for. Getting you warm, we can use a public room." Still he locked the door as she sank on the chaise. No sense adding fuel to the fire. Alone even in the library would cause enough talk.

"I can think of one thing that will warm me quite well."

She stretched out looking for all intents like a painting of a courtesan, if only her clothes were off. "You're a little vixen, you know that."

"There's room for two, Eudard, come hold me till the loneliness has passed."

Rose curled into a ball in his arms when he sat next to her. How could he ever forget she knew his sadness as well as he knew hers?

~

Every night Rose slept in his room, every morning she slipped back to her room before the servants came to wake him. Every morning they ate breakfast on opposite ends of the table as if they hardly knew each other until Edward's mother took his hand and led him to the sitting room as the party neared an end.

"Now your brother getting a fine match out of this is lost, but you still can. Mrs. MacKay has been expressing quite a bit of interest in a match between you and Lenore."

"Christ, mother, the MacKays have been trying to get the castle for more than two hundred years, or did you forget that? Might have been by sword then, but it's no less a scheme to do it now with a sum of sterling."

"Well then, what about Miss Leighton?"

"Who? Has she said one word to me since I arrived?"

"Oh no she wasn't here, but her father sent a letter asking about an arrangement."

Edward raised an eyebrow and his mother shifted in her seat. "That's it? I'm supposed to marry the woman on that?"

"And her excellent five hundred thousand pounds. A bankers daughter, she surely doesn't have the breeding, but by god Edward the fortune."

A slight noise drew Edward's eyes to the door. Rose stood there, eyes as wide as saucers, with several others that were coming for tea, just there long enough to have heard the mention of fifty thousand pounds. Rose fled. Not that he was wavering much about asking her, but the sight of her running off, shattered, was the last straw.

"Yes, Mother, I have decided on one, if I can persuade her. I don't intend to marry Miss Leighton's five hundred thousand pounds." Edward pushed his way through the crowd at the door, and made a stop at his room before he found the converted storeroom, door open. Rose was packing quickly.

"Rose, stop." It only made her work even faster.

"I told you I'd only like to know you were considering me even a little, but I don't have to stand there while you wed another," she snapped.

"The only one I'll consider marrying is you, if you'll have me."

She stopped everything, only the sound of her breath coming short broke the silence of the little room. Edward kissed the expanse of neck that was bare before him, but there was no sound until he held out the ruby ring surrounded with diamonds. Then there was a distinct sob.

"I've told you what my mother is like and that she would be pushing others at me."

"I have nothing to give you. No five hundred thousand pounds."

"I don't intend to go back to war and fight a wife every day for the sake of money."

Rose's head fell back on his shoulder as Edward slipped his hands to the slopes of her breasts.

"Easily worth a million each." His hands cupped her without hurry before caressing her hips. "Ten million each."

"That's all? You seemed to appreciate them far more last night."

"I'm not done yet," he rumbled in her ear. Her skirt slowly lifted, baring her before his hand cupped one last place, and a finger slipped inside easily. "Fifty million alone, Rose. You'd bring the best dowry I've seen in all the offers I've been presented."

Rose turned her head, a grin clearly lighting her face. Edward started pulling his finger out, and then watched her melt as it slowly returned inside, with a grin of his own. He added his thumb to her mound and whispered over her moan. "There's a chapel down the hall if you doubt me."

Her hand clapped over his as he went to remove it. "After you've finished what you've started."

Even after prolonging her pleasure, it wasn't long before they were down the hall and his Rose among the Heather was staying for good.

~

"And they lived happily ever after isn't that how the stories end." Ayda murmured.

Hunter let out a noise she didn't expect. "She was dead about 10 years after. Having the heir just about killed her within two years, she was told to never get pregnant again. Her second pregnancy killed her. Twins actually, cut out of her moments before she died in South America. Doctors here couldn't have done anything so they kept plans for their around-the-world trip, let her live life to the fullest knowing she'd probably be dead the moment she started labor. Money and title were no cure to childbirth in the 1820's. Edward went on to marry Tessa Endicott, the widow of a good friend, there were three friends that all fought. They rather had orgies among them and the wives. Edward had fallen for her, her husband Rhys knew about it even, she slept with both of them from what we know when they were together. She was married to Rhys though for almost 20 years. There's a book we found that kept track of them. We assume so they could tell if a pregnancy might, well to make sure certain children didn't marry among the three families. Find it all romantic now?"

"Orgies?" Ayda whispered.

"Are you asking to have one?" Hunter just laughed as she turned red and stared out the window to hide it. "It must be wars that bring it out of people, brothers in arms to survive the horror. The 1920's seem to have been the same way. The three families all fought and all fucked. They were commoner wives then too."

"Is that your way of saying you're just a normal sort of family that just happens to have a title?"

"No just my way of saying it's not all romance and fantasy. We've been poor, we've been almost wiped out, we've had murders and bastards in the sense of nasty men as well as some on the wrong side of the sheets. Dukes that die in a prisoner of war camp trying to save a friend from being emasculated, it didn't save the friend either.

He was one of the Dunham's, spend any time here you'll hear them mentioned. They're talking of being here for Broderick's engagement party. My father tries to pretend there isn't anything bad, it's all being the DUKE and prestige, they're off on their anniversary trip when we know full well he's gone up to women saying I'm the duke service me it's your duty. Well probably not that crudely put, but that's his meaning. 900 years of nothing but grand deeds and he'll mention kings and queens that have stayed. I'd take what he says with a grain of salt, he even tries to sweep his mother under the rug because she isn't born to the blood. She's just married into it. My grandfather was nothing like that, we can't guess how he turned out that way. If this was 400 years ago and he could get away with it he'd probably be a tyrant. Grandfather not dying until a few years ago kept him in check, there's a reason grandfather left the finances in my care. I might have told you a little lie that he wouldn't take care of things and I picked up the pieces. Well it was more like grandfather's will cut him out knowing it would all be blown on private planes and whatever else, he got the title I got the castle and the money as long as my father gets his allowance. He can get nasty when he comes around, he'll usually keep it in check when there are outsiders around so I have hope when he comes he'll be pleasant. That's why I was a little standoffish about you wanting to dig up the past. My sister is a tabloid staple, if any of this gets out..."

Ayda looked over slowly. No some of the shine fell away with that. "I just..."

"I know. You want old dirt, not new dirt. I guess that's my apology for being like I was when you first arrived. I actually thought he sent you to spy."

"You're kidding?"

Hunter just shook his head. "Until it was clear you were an art slut and that we had to drag out of your workroom. Besides if he was going to send a beautiful woman to tempt me it would be one with a title."

Ayda closed her mouth and turned back to the window.

CHAPTER 4

After hours of rolling hills and a nap, Ayda opened her eyes to a majestic mountain before her, overlooking a loch as still as a mirror. The sky had turned dark though, a storm threatening.

"Ben Nevis and Loch Linnhe." Hunter said at seeing her wake up. "I have to visit the distillery you're welcome to come with me or I can drop you in town and let you do some sightseeing. I have rooms for us at a bed and breakfast tonight."

His rather dark mood earlier was gone. That or he was a good actor. "Oh I'm sure I could do some damage at the distillery gift shop."

"Should have known. More souvenirs."

Ayda bit her lip trying not to smile. "Bottle of whisky to soften up my professor." Raindrops started to pelt the car and the surface of the loch grew pitted. Hunter soon pulled off the road and under a carport. A man came out of the back as soon as Hunter was getting out.

"You brought the bottle? I have high hopes for it."

"In the back." Hunter pulled the back up as she got out.

"And you brought us another treasure. Welcome fair lady." The man kissed the back of Ayda's hand gallantly.

"Ayda Rogers this is Jamison Forbes. He left Wrathe to find work and became one of the finest whisky makers in the country. Ayda is working on getting the paintings in Am Binnean in order again. She's with us all this summer. Grandmother thought she should get out and see something before she thought we had her imprisoned."

Jamison grinned over at Hunter as he put his arm in Ayda's. "Now you're just trying to butter me up to move back. Come my dear Ayda I'll give you a tour of your very own."

"I thought you were eager to get this bottle." Hunter argued.

Jamison beamed over at Ayda. "That's before there was a woman to woo. You're here for the night there's plenty of time."

"You can finish your business with Hunter first, I can just go look at the gift shop. I wanted to get a bottle for a professor of mine."

Jamison waved his hand in dismissal. "Nonsense. Hunter has all the time in the world. What else does a future Duke do in life after all?"

"Jamie ..." Hunter growled. The man was a retired fighter pilot, not the thing to say at all.

"Now my dear that tour of yours." Jamison pulled her off without much chance for Hunter to say more or Ayda to get a word in edgewise.

Jamison was definitely different from Hunter. Red haired for one, a thin and wiry 40 if he was a day, but certainly cute. His accent also seemed to thicken as he explained the entire workings of the distillery. If Ayda had to guess she'd say he liked playing the highland rogue to all the passing female tourists. Hunter didn't have to play, a highland duke, even future, everyone and their sister must have been after him. Good thing Ayda didn't have a sister. She wasn't in the mood to share.

~

Somehow, Ayda ended up leaving the distillery with an entire case of whisky, not paying for a single bottle. Jamison sure did woo hard.

"Could we get some business done here?" Hunter asked, he'd not gone in with them. "I'd actually like to get Ayda to her room before dinner."

"Jealous?" Jamison asked.

Hunter only glared.

"All right, all right." Jamison disappeared back inside and returned with a glass. "Pour some on me cousin. I still can't believe that I wouldn't have known there was a distillery just down the street. I lived there for 20 years."

Hunter poured dark amber liquid in the glass. "Grandmother said she remembered the man when she was there starting in '47. It was never a commercial distillery. He ran batches and sold it locally in plain glass jars. They only found the stills when his son died in Edinburgh and the house was to be sold."

Jamison laughed. "Some man making illegal whisky out of his basement. It can't be any good." The laugh died as the nose of the whisky filled the air, even Ayda could smell it, pure ambrosia. "Shite Hunter! Heather ... honey ... is that ginger? Autumn mist?"

"Taste it. When was the last time you got a free bottle of 50-year-old whisky?"

"50 you say."

Finally, Hunter started smiling. "You can taste the sea air Jamie and the heather. You don't think I would tempt you back home with anything less."

Ayda still wasn't sure what she was hearing. "What are you trying to do?"

"There's most everything sitting there for a distillery. It only needs a manager someone that knows what he's doing and a building to set it all back up, make it a commercial operation size instead of a basement operation. Jamie's right it was in someone's basement. Where no excise man would find it with as far out from anywhere that we are."

If Hunter was going to say anything else, it died at the sounds that started emanating from Jamison as he sipped the nectar in his glass. He wouldn't have need for a woman for some time. "What was this man's name? He deserves to be a god, there are 40-year-old bottles going for 1300 pounds apiece. This has to be a 5000 bottle at least. How many casks are there again?"

Hunter winked over at Ayda. He knew Jamison was hooked. "I bought the lot, equipment, filled casks, and each one has a year on it. The newest is 1989 and they go back to 1947. Must be about 200 in an old salting house on the edge of town. There's a wash still and spirit still and probably another 50 casks at least that are empty."

"I can do whatever I want with it. I can do whatever I want with a 70 year old cask of this liquid gold. 70 bloody years, those could go for 15,000 a bottle."

Hunter was shaking his head. "You can do whatever you want to set up a distillery, you would have full control over the production and bottling. I'd see a business manager was hired who would deal with that side. Everyone else hired would be local if at all possible. I've set aside land near the salting house to build the new distillery."

"You'd try to lure me back with that? A distiller."

"Oh and you want to sit around designing bottles, labels, marketing plans, payroll ... or would you rather be perfecting the recipe and the cask selection. You'd be the master distiller."

"True." Jamison took another sip, inhaling the aroma for some time.

Hunter grinned, full of promise, all Ayda could think of was how many woman had he used that grin on. They all surely melted at the sight while he hid the family secrets that took him from what he wanted. "I promise to hire you an attractive assistant you can flirt with endlessly."

Jamison waggled his eyebrows. "Ayda's looking for work is she?"

How'd she get thrown in the conversation? "Hey I've got an art restoration dissertation to get done. Don't go putting words in my mouth."

Jamison started laughing. "Well it will be hard to reconcile myself to loosing you Ayda, but you might just have yourself a deal Hunter."

"Go get changed and we can discuss the details over dinner then. Unless you plan on quitting now when they find out you're plotting to leave."

"What I can't come now? I was practicing my resignation speech in my head already."

"There's nothing for a master distiller to do with no distillery. Let me know everything you need and we'll get it built to specification. I figured you could stay put until the premises were built."

"I've got to get a few things done before I'm done here. I'll see you at eight then. Pick me up and I'll show you the best place in town." Jamison ran off without time to argue.

"You really convinced him to pack up and leave in 10 minutes?"

Hunter looked over with a smile. "Sorry about him and no I've been on the phone with him for weeks. He likes to hear how great he is so I have to go through it all every time we talk."

~

The bed and breakfast was nothing like Ayda expected, not the castle on the edge of town for one thing. It was a run of the mill Scottish stone house, 200 years old if a day. Her room not more than a postage stamp was cozy, the opposite of everything at the castle. Was this the real Hunter, taking on the responsibility he was born to, but just wanting a simpler life? Still in the

RAF even? Rain continued to fall when there was a knock on the door.

"Ready to be fawned over?" Hunter asked from the other side of the door.

"Isn't every woman?" Ayda opened the door and just about dropped her purse. Why did Hunter affect her so much? It's not as if she never dated any, Brad definitely fell in the category of very good looking. But this drooling over a man was unprecedented. He just wore a sweater and jeans and she was weak in the knees. Then again good looking never meant they weren't rotten inside after all. Brad definitely fell in that category.

"It was cute when he was married flirting with his wife like that, with her gone its every woman now. She died about 3 years ago."

Men. Couldn't he see himself in that. "And you aren't flirting with every woman? Making your evenings less boring with no TV?" One corner of Hunter's mouth curled up in an impish grin. Get your mind on matters Ayda. You've got a doctorate to finish. Your paper won't get done watching him smile. "Dinner time then?" Ayda added trying to change the subject.

He didn't take the bait. No, his hand touched her cheek. Her breath caught in her throat when it moved to her lips. Tracing them gently was enough to drive her mad. Then he leaned his mouth near her ear. Ayda felt his lips brushing against her ear as he spoke. Certainly not keeping her mind on art. "Every woman? I can't think of any others around but you." Slowly he pulled his head back so she could see into his dark blue eyes. "As far as making my evenings less boring I can't deny that, but then I'm not art, I can't affect you at all so I'm told."

Ayda felt her cheeks heat up at such words. "I never said affect me at all. Just it wouldn't be as easy as if you were art. You'll have to work at it."

"Then my evenings will certainly be less boring. I've always hated flirting when I knew it was a lost cause." His lips brushed against her cheek as he spoke. Ayda couldn't stop herself turning her head and his lips were covering hers. Oh lord.

"No, my dear lady I know he's staying here. He told me so himself." Jamison's voice carried up from the floor below.

"I pride myself on discretion and if the Queen herself was staying here I wouldn't tell the likes of you." The woman at the door countered.

Ayda felt an ache of longing as Hunter stepped away.

"Suppose we should go down before they resort to blows." He headed down the stairs, Ayda couldn't hear a word he was saying. The blood was pounding in her ears. She hadn't just kissed him had she? Six months she'd told herself she wouldn't get involved with anyone, get her paper done then she'd worry about that sort of thing. He hadn't just kissed back had he?

~

Jamison didn't let them get a word in as they ordered dinner. He'd shown them the most expensive place in town of course since Hunter was paying. Debating in her head this whole wrinkle in her plans she hardly heard a word he said, she just ordered the whisky menu filled with recipes made with of course the local whisky. Jamison beamed at what he took as a complement to him.

"Has Hunter showed you the Sinclair golden chalice yet?" That she heard and it pulled her out of her thoughts of getting Hunter in bed and what complications that would bring up.

"What chalice?"

Hunter shrugged his shoulders. "You asked about paintings I didn't know you were doing decorative arts too."

"I'm not but it would be cool to see. What era is it?"

Hunter took a drink of his whisky, smiling all the while. He hadn't made anything of the kiss. He didn't expect her to take him to bed over it. Hunter had just kissed her knees weak. She was smarter than to let a little lust ruin her plans. Wasn't she? "If the stories are true it's Viking. Legends always start somewhere, but this one that's all it seems to be. It's the only true link anywhere that the family has been able to find. No ones found anything more yet, so it's a legend and the books speak of the history that can be proved. There's just a cup with no names that we can't say how we got it other than a probable marriage. If you heard Mary's story about Eaduin that's about as far back as we know things reliably. Prior to that it just an incomplete list of wives."

"You have to show me."

"Your wish is my command." Hunter replied with a smile and her thoughts drowned out Jamison starting up again.

Not of Hunter in bed, of finding out the truth behind the legend. That would definitely be an interesting way to tie all the ends of her paper up.

Jamison grinned wide enough to beat the Cheshire cat in a contest. He opened his mouth yet again and without warning stood up. "Nadine! I didn't know you were back."

Just like that, they were alone at the table.

"How about you tell me more about you? We talk about my family enough." Hunter asked out of the blue.

Had she kissed the same man earlier? He acted so proper almost as a stranger might. "I've told you. My aunt raised me after my parents died. Traveled whenever I could."

"Why art restoration?"

Brad still put himself in the way no matter how much she put him behind her. "Why did you join the Air Force? Same sort of thing it's where I had an interest."

Hunter smiled with a bit more of his old flirting showing again. "But the military is a long tradition in the family. Not many job opportunities for a Duke either. Were your parents' artists, your aunt and uncle, some trip to an art museum? Why art?"

The scene filled her head almost immediately. "My mother took me to the Louvre when I was eight while my dad was on a business trip. I still have the postcard of the painting I fell in love with. Made them send me to art classes when we got back. It was all that was left for a while after they died. Dad didn't die outright, months he lingered in the hospital in a coma before...I sat there every day, school didn't matter as long as he knew I was there. I could copy that postcard identically even if I was hardly old enough to think I would be a forger. The room was filled with pictures by the time he was gone, buried with him."

He didn't actually smile, but Ayda would have sworn he was. A sad one that said he understood. Jamison returned as quickly as he had left and all talk of old Sinclair stories and chalices were forgotten. Nadine dominated the conversation and she wasn't even at the table.

~

When they left after lunch the next day Hunter took with him pages of notes that Jamison provided as being vital to creating a proper distillery. Ayda drifted off to sleep as he was talking on his cell phone about designs, building costs, staffing, even sherry casks from Spain and wine casks for some new revolutionary taste to whisky. If the half she heard was any indication while he might have put a local at the helm he wasn't just taking one man's advice. Half a dozen distilleries were mentioned by name.

"Where's this salting house you mentioned?" Ayda asked as they arrived in the village.

Hunter pointed down by the beach. "It's that big stone warehouse we're coming up on. Salted fish was a big export to Russia and Scandinavia at one time." Only a moment later he pulled off the road to give her an up-close view. The wind blew brisk even in the middle of summer as they got out. There couldn't have been a more picturesque place to live. A small highland village on the sea, dotted with fishing boats.

"No one really knew it was full of whisky?" Ayda asked contemplating the building, it was right on the edge of town not as if it got lost for being in the middle of nowhere.

"It had been boarded up for 25 years. I got the feeling that the son saw it all in there untaxed and didn't want to deal with it. So he just boarded it up. It was assumed empty until I went in to see if it was worth buying. I had been thinking it might make a good sports facility. Give everyone a chance to have some fun without driving hours. We don't own the village, just everything around it."

Ayda pulled her eyes from the nondescript stone building. It was old, nothing special, sturdy was all that came to mind. Still boarded up in fact. "This is the business you were gone on when I first got here?"

"Aye. I didn't want to get anyone's hopes up about jobs in case it came to nothing. I didn't even tell grandmother I was buying it. Just picked her brains about the old owner then took some of it to Edinburgh to have it tasted. Find out what kind of taxes had to be paid to make it legal."

Ayda tossed an idea about, it would take away some time she needed to get her paper done, but they'd put her up for free, fed her, in addition to letting her research everything in the house. "Hunter, you don't usually end up in restoration unless you're an artist to begin with. Would you want some help designing the label? I'm no businessperson but that I can do. Pay you back for some of everything you've done for me this summer."

"It's not something we'll need to be done until the building is finished so we can actually bottle it to modern standards. But if you have any time and want to try your hand at a design, I'm starting from scratch so I'll take any help I can get."

"Now what did I tell ye? All of ye end up the Sinclair whore if ye spend any time in the castle."

Ayda spun at the voice breaking the calm of the windy day. Not quiet but it was calm at least until the red hair chap came strolling up.

"Fuck off Ciaran." Hunter ground out between clinched teeth.

"I can go anywhere I like. Call the constable on me for trespass if you like, we can get ye taken care of for that assault too."

"I don't need the constable to tell me you're a pain in the ass. I seriously doubt that Ayda likes you calling her names when you don't know her from Adam."

Ciaran made a noise that wasn't flattering in the least. "The whole village knows the lot of ye." As if that was enough to condemn an entire family.

Hunter straightened up to his full height. "Aye the whole village knows the lot of us, but they know you too. You're making a fool of yourself every time you open your mouth. Your sister isn't a whore, my brother didn't turn her into one, she's a fool is all, the same as you. Your nephew could have died if Lorne hadn't come back from maneuvers a week early."

"Ye dare ..." Ciaran rushed at Hunter in a blind rage. Face red with anger, it almost matched his hair.

"What do you think you're doing there Ciaran?" A new voice and Ciaran turned to it, his momentum carried him forward though. He rammed into Hunter, but the interruption lessened its impact.

"Nothing to concern yourself with Roddy." Hunter answered hardly straining at keeping the attack at bay. Ciaran hit like running into a brick wall, he stopped dead. "Ciaran here was just protecting his sisters' honor again by blaming it all on Lorne. The same as always."

Ayda turned to find the very constable they had threatened to call standing there.

The constable's wide face broke into a grin. "Christ Ciaran I watched her making doe eyes at the boy as soon as she was old enough to notice boys." With a single hand, he grabbed hold of Ciaran's collar and pulled him away from Hunter. "You seen your sister?"

"I'm not saying." Ciaran growled.

"Leave the man alone and stop calling strangers names. I got calls from Effie you were disturbing the tourist when you called this fair woman names, and her just arrived in town. One last chance and then I'm putting you in jail to cool off next time." Roddy still had Ciaran by the collar as he dragged him off. "Good day to you Hunter and you Miss Rogers."

"How'd he know my name?"

"Very small town. Sorry about that."

"You don't spend much time in the village do you? It's easy to hate what you don't know well."

Hunter started to climb back in the vehicle. He sat there waiting in silence as Ayda went around and got in. "He was my best friend. Maceachran's came to town with a step great grandmother in the 20's, they were her brothers. He might as well have been family."

Ayda stared over at him, but he just drove back to the castle in silence.

~

Not until Hunter sat back after dinner did Ayda remember her request.

"Grandmother has the chest been moved since the last time the chalice was needed? Ayda would like to see it."

"No it's in the store room as always."

"You're up for an adventure then I hope?"

Ayda couldn't help but smile. Everything seemed to be an adventure when it came to finding things in the castle. "Of course." Ayda followed as Hunter led her near the old tower to a tiny room off the hall tucked behind the old tower and the stairs. It was a place that she'd never really been in the castle, but that wasn't saying much.

Hunter found the chest quickly enough, even though the room was packed to the rafters. No as Ayda looked around she was in the old tower, she'd gotten turned around. But the sight of the chest made her forget anything about the tower. The chest was ancient, from the 1100's at least, was it even the one that Robert had pulled things from in Hunter's story. When Hunter opened the lid, it was obvious it held the oldest relics of the family. Tartans, old ones from before they were banned. An ivory chess set that looked even older than the chest and then he pulled out the gold chalice. Glowing dully in the faint light it was magnificent.

It was the oddest place to keep such a treasure. "Why keep it here?"

"No one would come here to find it, keep it out on the mantle for anyone to see and it might get stolen. Here it remains part of the legend. We only pull it out for christenings."

"I suppose there isn't really a proper bank in the village to have it in a safe deposit box, is there?" He held it out for her and she felt her knees go weak as she held it, heavy enough she had to struggle not to let her arm fall under the weight. Not huge, it wasn't much taller than a modern wine glass with a very wide stem, but the base was almost half an inch thick. A large knob in the stem held two crests one the Sinclairs that was over the door of the castle and the other was unknown to her. A glint caught her eye over the top of the chalice and she lifted her head to find Hunter held another cup. "Another?"

"This one we know about, Spanish silver 1400's."

He said it like it was nothing. Like he wasn't holding two cups worth she couldn't even fathom how much. The silver one was much more elaborate with semi-precious stones and enamel panels, the whole cup was decorated with filigree design.

"Another dowry I suppose?"

Hunter smiled. "Aye part of the dowry of the Princess of Navarre."

Ayda moved closer looking over his shoulder. "What all is in that chest?" Those were the only precious items, the rest old but everyday things. Rare in their condition, but not materials. Sentimental in other words. Ayda stood up and looked out the door to the hall, lined with paintings. "They bought most of this just because someone liked it didn't they? Its only age that made the men masters, the prices exorbitant."

Hunter sat back despite the room being covered in dust. "Probably, despite being Kings of Wrathe for all intents, the family was never fabulously rich, or the most landed. There's always been talk though that the Bruce handed us the title of Duke, because when we were Lords of Wrathe we were rivals, others with the titles were vying to control the country, as Duke we were vassals. We just had titles and what we could make of ourselves, marriages to help things along. Things sold off to build or rebuild, pay men's ransoms. I mentioned the shipping heiress married into the family, we've been flush since 1840's is all."

Ayda bit her lip. Dare she ask? "Would you mind if I maybe tried to see if the legend could be proved?"

"I thought you had a paper to get done?"

"I do." She said sheepishly. A mystery would sidetrack her as much as an affair would.

"If you have the time you're more than welcome." He grinned up at her and there was her reminder they had kissed. God this was getting complicated.

~

Hunter was nowhere to be seen for several days as Ayda got back into the rhythm of work again. The buzz from town was answer enough though, a surveyor had arrived. Staying at the inn, his evenings were filled with telling everyone the reason he was there. The idea of new jobs from a distillery had everyone excited. While her days were filled with paintings and paper research, Ayda couldn't keep her mind from turning to the chalice once supper was over. Digital photos of every angle sent to Rowanne, a historian she knew specializing in medieval art not to mention her old roommate through 6 years of college. Pictures of the crests sent to heraldry offices, names punched in the internet. Everywhere she turned there were more distractions. Hunter, a chalice, a bottle design that had nothing to do with her paper at all, but a morning fog over the sea when she woke up wouldn't wait until after she had more time. The whole design scheme was based off a swirl of mist. The lower grades were etched with swirls making it look like a cloud of mist and fog. The 50 year old bottles were encased in swirled metal with the same design only the bottles were blown into the form. Each decade older vintage had a different metal and yet she was bored. No wonder it was a Sinclair family tradition to flirt. Only she had hardly seen Hunter in days to even practice that. Elise was to her room much of the time. Duncan was off to his uncles for a few days. She couldn't even seem to find Mary and Charlie's room. Finally, she knocked at Hunter's door, she had to talk to someone or else go crazy.

"Come in."

"What do you do around here? I need something to do in the evenings." Ayda opened the door and found him sprawled in a chair surrounded in his Asian splendor. Papers were everywhere. It was a far cry from the clean Chinese wonderland she had caught a glimpse of before. Obviously the maid wasn't on duty now.

"You've lasted longer than I thought you would." With a grin, he walked over to the armoire and opened it up. He was hiding a damn TV.

"You said ..."

"I still haven't seen shows in two years. Reception is nonexistent, but I can get you a movie. You can go to the pub in town if you want TV, they have a dish."

"And run into what's his name I like not being called a whore thank you very much."

"Sorry about that." Hunter muttered as he looked through the stash of DVD's. "I thought you were hot on the trail of your paper or I would have offered sooner... Pull up a chair."

It seemed odd to be pulling up an antique Chinese chair to watch a hidden TV in an equally antique armoire, but she didn't care. "The paper is to the stage I have to wait and get more done before I can write about it. I even have a bottle idea almost finished but, I'm going crazy. I just need some time not working for once. There's nothing to do but work so I work. Where is everyone?"

"And what was Fort William? That was only a week ago."

"I consider fighting off Jamison very hard work."

"Good point." Hunter finally decided on a movie and put it in the machine.

His sitting next to her changed it from a friendly visit to her mind drifting where she didn't want it. Like what that tattoo was she had glimpsed but not seen close enough? Like they'd kissed once and never even mentioned it again. Slipping his shirt off to find out, running her fingers over every inch.

"All right it's killing me, what's the tattoo of, I didn't see it clearly when you came after Duncan. A circle was all I could see."

Casablanca was just starting. "The Sinclair crest."

"I would have thought RAF for my first guess."

"That's the other arm." He just got it out when the room plunged into darkness.

"What happened?" There was only silence for a moment before a flicker of light shone forth as he lit a match from the fireplace.

"We sit on a rock there's nowhere to dig the lines in and if they put them on poles the wind hits them too much so they're attached to the underside of the bridge to get them here to the castle. They get knocked loose now and again especially when there's a storm, the weather said one was moving in. I'll have to get the generator running until they can fix it."

"Should we go check on your grandmother?"

Hunter looked over quickly as he was lighting several candles. "Yes." He all but sprinted out the door grabbing a flashlight from a side table, out of sight by the time Ayda made it over. Candles on the mantle gave the only break to the little light that the clouds leaked through. Despite the thick walls all around, the wind of the storm whistled quietly with no sound to mask them. The hairs on Ayda's neck stood on end as she realized the ghost could show up any moment. A flash of lightening shot out of the air and Ayda jumped. Get a grip Ayda! He keeps the women from harm, a blackout is not deadly. It was stubbed toe worthy but not deadly. Unless maybe you were an old women wobbly on her feet and the lights went out without warning.

It seemed an eternity before the flashlight's glow pierced the darkness. "You want to stay here or do you want to come with me until I have the generator going?" Hunter asked.

"How's your grandmother?"

"She was already in bed so no harm done."

Asleep? It was barely eight at night, only dark at all because of the storm. That far north the sun set late, after 11 now that it was mid-summer. "I'll come with you if that's okay." She refused to mention her paranoia that the ghost would show up. That hadn't surfaced once she heard the story explaining his history. Hunter led the way down to the ground floor and then they had to sprint in the rain to an out building. She'd thought it was a garage all this time, but opening the door, the room was almost filled with an immense generator. Not to mention it looked like it had been there for 50 years.

"This used to be the only source of electricity. Talked us into switching saying it would be more reliable. Fourth time this year it's gone down already, I think the generator broke 4 times the entire time I was growing up." Hunter said, but he wasn't really making conversation he was distracted getting the contraption going. Two minutes though and it whirred loudly to life like the day it was made. He looked out the door and the lights in the castle were already coming back on. Few that there were though with everyone gone. Finally, he was smiling as he turned around. "You want to know what we do? I'll show you the best view on the estate."

Ayda followed him back into the castle ducking her head now that it had started to rain. Without a word he lead her not to any room she had ever seen, it seemed to be the servant's quarters. A room tucked up in the eaves of the roof near the old tower. It was dark even when he turned the light on, the window blocked from getting any real light. Hunter looked over his shoulder with a dare you to smile before he opened the window and crawled out. With that hook, there was no other option but to follow. She didn't have to go far once she scrambled through, there was a 5 foot ledge where the roof of another level kept the rain off. With Hunter already out there, room was tight as she sat, but the view went forever. Even with the storm clouds darkening the sky, a light show more spectacular than any technology could produce flashed in the distance. Only the rain itself disturbed the surface of the ocean. It was surprisingly calm after the wind that must have pulled down the electric wars.

"Oh my..." Her words were lost as the thunder caught up to them.

Hunter leaned near her ear, with the thunder it was the only option for her to hear. "I would come out here when I was in trouble. Found it when I was six. Never was found out."

"Well now what are you going to do, I'll be able to tell on you when you get in trouble the next time."

Hunter sat back laughing silently. "A reason to keep to the straight and narrow for certain."

Another flash of lightening lit up the sky with a double bolt. It seemed close enough she could hear the sizzle. "Okay maybe I could see why they would put a castle here."

"You say that with a slate roof over your head, they were huddling in tents until they could get houses built."

The thunder kept her from answering, but she started laughing anyway.

"What?" Hunter mouthed, this thunder too loud to even whisper.

She waited though until only the rain pelting the roof was disturbing the silence. "Well if Mary's story is true, they were too busy getting it on to notice a little rain outside."

"Come here." Hunter said suddenly.

"I can't get much closer."

Still he pulled her over, actually in his lap. Arms around her but he was pointing out to the sea. "Look there."

Ayda started to ask what, but then she saw it. The roof angle where she sat had kept hidden a whale, a humpback whale was surfacing in the water. Then another and another, three at least.

"20 years ago you never saw them, with the fishing changing they've started coming in closer, the ferry ride to the Orkney's has all sorts of sightings now."

His breath caressed her neck as he spoke and the fact she was sitting in his lap had new meaning. "Hunter, why did you kiss me?"

"Would you rather I have just stood there, a quarter inch from you?"

Ayda turned in his arms, "I ..." Ah hell. She was kissing him again entirely her fault. His hand slipped up and cupped the back of her head, not letting her pull away and even worse she didn't even feel herself trying in the least. What woman in her right mind would pull away from a modern day highland warrior? Inside she was laughing, how much that sounded like the romance novel she swore she would never write. Reluctantly she finally pulled back, her forehead still rested against his though as she tried to calm her breathing. This was getting very complicated.

"I'm months away from finishing my Doctorate." Ayda whispered. "I have to get through this summer and get my thesis done. I've spent 9 years getting here."

"I'll try my hardest not to kiss back next time you kiss me then."

Ayda could hear the smile in his voice. She slid off his lap, not that there was far to move away. The whole ledge wasn't more than 4 feet by 5 feet. "Don't joke. I know I'm making a fool of myself."

"Ayda it's a kiss. It's not ruining your entire career plan."

She couldn't look at him, her look turned back out to the sea, the wind was picking up again, the sea choppy now.

"Let's get back inside, with the wind changing we'll get soaked."

Sitting back inside watching Casablanca, Ayda held her tongue that if Hunter knew how much she thought on him, he'd know why she worried so much about her career.

CHAPTER 5

Ayda stretched her legs from her crouch on the floor and went back to digging in the family records. No one had said they would be in low cabinets, but they were all there. The drawing room was bathed in dark red as the sun set outside a large stained glass window showing the family crest. Sure it was research for her paper getting dates all correct, but she hoped something was overlooked too in regards to that cup. With gloved hands, she leafed through old marriage contracts, land deeds, old inventories of the castle, some even six hundred years old. While there weren't any paintings from as far back as Eaduin, his marriage contract along with the patents for the title with the very signature of Robert the Bruce had to be worth a fortune. Definitely nothing mentioning a mysterious cup though. Much in the house, and even the estate itself, came as part of marriage contracts and was listed in the agreements. Price lists for remodeling a single room at a time hundreds of years before were there, the 1660's and 70's were especially busy with such papers. It really wasn't so much the history of the family as the history of the castle, of Wrathe itself.

"So, digging up all the family skeletons I see."

Ayda spun around to find a man in his mid-sixties, perhaps. He looked a lot like John Forsyth in his Dynasty days. Dressed as nice, too, as he stood there in a very expensive suit. Ayda sneaked a peek down at her dusty jeans. "I, uh..."

"David Sinclair. Mother told me you were about somewhere."

Ayda jumped up and reached out to take his hand, then realized she still had the gloves on.

"God, you are a historian. If you're going through all that mess, you probably know the family better than I do."

Despite the book in the library, there was too much she didn't know. "Dates maybe, family history very little."

"That makes it sound like you have a question."

Ayda could still see the page staring at her. It was still a sore subject, dare she bring it up? "I found an order removing all the tenants from the estate. It was well before the majority of the clearances happened. I just wondered."

David poured himself a drink and settled in the old leather wingback chair. "You mean that's still around? I thought it was long gone. But no, we never emptied the land for sheep."

"Then why is it here?"

He laughed slightly. "It was all part of the Jacobite rebellion, actually. The woman that wrote that was put to death for treason and murder. Her niece kept it from ever being enforced."

Hunter walked in the room, making her stomach churn. Despite this, she couldn't help but ask. "Tell me?"

"She seemed to enjoy Mary's telling of Eaduin, and she's heard about Rose, you might as well not leave out any of the details, Father," Hunter added.

Ayda narrowed her eyes as Hunter grinned at her.

"I believe my great grandfather was interested in history, and through family stories and records of the time, he pieced it all together. The politicks of marriage, he called it. Those steamy details, well, most those hot and bothered parts came from the old cooks. I rather think they like embellishing." David started and Ayda closed her eyes, envisioning the stormy wind tossed coast as Alexander made his way.

In the Year 1714

"Bluidy Sinclairs. Canna they live on dry land?" Alexander Lindsay cursed to himself. The rain blew in horizontal sheets around a tall, dark haired figure. It didn't disguise the large claymore on his back. As the wind whipped by, making it impossible to keep the plaid covering him, the ocean rose out of the seabed and came ashore as if to swallow him whole. It didn't really matter, he was already soaked to the bone. Three hours he had been walking without sight of a single hovel, even. He knew roughly where he was before he had been attacked for accidentally interrupting a little cattle stealing. It was still another hour before he sighted the castle in the gloom. Thank God, it was day. Staring at the chasm of sea that separated him from the island where the castle stood, he knew he would have drowned before finding a way across at night. Now, even during the day he was left with only one option, cross the ancient stone bridge that was the only connection to the rest of Scotland. Not to mention he could feel the blood sticky on his leg as he walked.

~

The door swung open at his endless banging to reveal an ancient woman hunched and frail. "Shelter, lady."

"Come in, come in," she croaked as she stepped away from the portal through the massive drawbridge. Was that the usual way across the chasm? It seemed far sturdier than the crumbling bridge. "Ragged though ye look, the ladies of the house will be eager to know there is a man about again."

"Again?"

The frail head bobbed as she shook it back and forth. "Havena ye heard of the terrible battle? Two-thirds of the Sinclair men are gone and only a few have returned from the fray even now, none of them castle men. The heir is too wounded to bring back."

Looking back outside as she closed the door, it was obvious why they kept the gate up. The same remoteness that he had complained of to reach them was the only thing protecting them with no men around.

~

Alexander woke in a large bed with little memory of anything past entering the front door. Lifting the covers, he found the old woman had obviously gotten more than just his plaid off him. It was easy to take stock of his six foot four inch frame. The gash in his leg had been bandaged, as had one on his side. A little unsteady on his feet, he made it over to the fire to find his clothes hanging up. They were bone dry. How long had he been asleep? Slipping the shirt over his head, it was obvious they had been washed of the grime of the last few months. Wrapping himself in his plaid, he opened the door to find himself staring into the face of a remarkable looking woman. She was older, but her red hair was as brilliant as that of a twenty year old. Even more remarkable was the costume she wore. There on a rock in the middle of nowhere, she was dressed in the latest of court fashion for the lowlands. London even. Rich brocades and lace, the only thing missing was powdered hair.

"Ah, you're up. I'm the Duchess of Cairnmuir and welcome to Am Binnean. Call me Elspeth. There's no one here to mind formality."

"Alexander Lindsay. I'm sorry to hear of your men." Not one to mind formality, and yet dressed like she was. He had to hide the snort threatening to offend the woman if she heard it.

The duchess crooked a red eyebrow. "A Lindsay, you're a long way from home to be on our shores. You're not one of those idiots that go running off to fight for glory and leave us to mourn, are you?"

Alexander lied. "My boat capsized in the storm." She seemed to know nothing of his wounds. That he had been working his way toward passage to sign up for the French army didn't seem to be the best way to make a good impression. She didn't need to hear that after everything she had to live with.

"Then I'll show you to the great hall. In this weather, we keep the fires high." She smiled faintly as she turned from him to lead the way down a maze of halls. There were several rugs and paintings here and there to warm up the bare stone walls. More than he would have expected to see. Elspeth suddenly threw the door open, and he was confronted with the great hall. Huge fireplaces bracketed the room on each end while large chandeliers filled with candles gave light. The clan crest hung over the fires, Several family coat of arms broke up the long expanse of bare walls. Plaid of several different setts warmed up the vast space. "Here we are. My niece, Geneva. Do be a dear and keep her occupied. She gets restless when the weather keeps her inside." Elspeth left them and walked out without another word.

That she was the niece of a grandly dressed duchess showed in no way, dressed as she was in just a blue plaid bodice, a blue skirt, and a braid in her hair. Peasant clothes. But good God, the woman had skin as pale as winter snow. Her hair was like the darkest red embers dying in a fire and her eyes were pools of deep blue. The women deserved to have him bow before her. "My lady. Is it that she wants to put me in a good disposition before asking a favor of me that she introduced us?"

"Knowing her, probably." Not even a smile crossed her lips to say it was a joke as she walked past him and left him in the empty cavern of a room.

~

In the morning, Alexander prepared to leave, not that he had any money to continue his way to France now. As he headed to the main gate, the ancient woman stopped him. Caitriona, he had heard her called.

"The Duchess wishes to have a word with you," she rasped before she vanished down the hall, expecting him to follow.

Elspeth stared out the window, looking out over the wind tossed sea. "You have pressing business that draws you now that you leave my hospitality so quickly?"

"No, I lost all I owned when the ship went down and haven't the money to continue on to my destination now."

The Duchess laughed faintly. "Too many would have seen that as a reason to stay indefinitely and live off my estate." She turned finally. "If I have to ask, so be it. Perhaps you might stay on here for a time. I have need of men and have money to pay them. You could earn back what you have lost, if not more, and have a roof over your head until then."

The offer didn't take much consideration. "I would be glad to help ye out, but your niece seems to be offended at my presence."

Elspeth snarled, seeming to know exactly what the problem was. "I don't have the leisure to turn away those that might help me to spare my niece's feelings."

Alexander nodded, even though he had no clue what was going on. "What's the first task ye need done, then?"

Alexander felt eyes on him as he walked through the courtyard. One was clearly Caitriona, the other was a red head barely noticeable through a window, and there were more than one of them in the house. Elspeth had all but given him run of the estate, so he couldn't see her watching him, so that left Geneva. A woman that showed no sign of liking him, but he wouldn't mind her staring around a corner at him. He sobered knowing why she probably was watching him. She waited for him to do something wrong to get him kicked out. Of course, there was a glint in her eye. He wouldn't count out her having a knife hidden in her bodice, ready to take care of him herself if he dared try anything.

~

It felt good to work again. Actual work. Most tasks he was given before coming to the castle involved fighting for money or stealing cattle. He'd been drifting for too long, ever since his wife had died two years before along with his child. He pushed that from his mind and nudged the horse to a canter, wanting to make the next cottar by lunch. The men of the castle had been gone some two months, and the few that survived had been trickling back only in the last few days. Elspeth needed agreements signed, and a roll taken of who was under her care. After several days of hard riding, he was almost done with the list the duchess had given him. She had lost husband and brother in the fighting. It was about the only reason most of the families didn't feel any animosity towards her husband taking the men from them. Flying out of the bushes, a streak of red caught his eye. What on earth was Geneva doing out like that?

"Sir, please help me. He is after me!" Her hair was loose to her waist and her clothes were torn. As she pulled the hair from her face, it was obviously not Geneva, older for one and then there was the wild look in the woman's eyes.

Alexander slid off the horse quickly at the terror in her voice. Try as he might, though, he couldn't hear any sound other than the birds and the wind. He was far enough away from the ocean that the sea couldn't cover any sound. There was no one. "Perhaps if ye rode the horse, I could get ye back home. Where is it ye live?"

"Am Binnean, but it's him that's after me," she cried in a small voice.

Alexander narrowed his eyes. No man graced the halls of the castle, not even a servant. Hamish was a boy of twelve, the only other a boy named Iain was fourteen. There was no way he would have been entrusted with the tasks he was if there had been men about. Neither of those boys was strong enough to put that much fear in the woman. "Would ye care to ride with me while I finish my errands? I'll keep ye safe from him."

"Oh, thank you." She fell on his legs as if she was truly in danger and he was her salvation.

Alexander helped her up and led her on to the next house. Only after the business was taken care of did he dare ask, "Do ye know who she is?"

A small sad smile came to the woman's face. "Tis Isabella. Geneva's mother. Mad as can be now."

Alexander led her away to the next house. The last few were in a cluster, so he didn't have to take her far. She sat on the horse, content now, not saying a word. She nodded and smiled as if in some private conversation.

~

The gate flung open as soon as they neared. "Weel, don't just stand there looking proud. Geneva's out looking for her and there's a bad storm coming. I can feel it in my bones," Caitriona ordered as she took the silent Isabella.

"Thank ye, too," Alexander muttered after the door was shut in his face. He turned the horse around and rode back off the island. The sky was cloudy but it didn't look like rain. Almost as soon as the words were out of his mouth, lightning filled the sky. "Of course," he muttered pulling the plaid over his head.

The rain started shortly after, driving across the sky in horizontal bands. Drips started to fall over his eyes from the material and the smell of wet wool filled his nose. He had gone close to a mile when there was no mistaking her red hair in the haze. At least he assumed it was her unless more than one ran around he hadn't met. Kicking the horse into a gallop, she took off running as soon as she saw him coming.

"Geneva, I found your mother," he called after her, but a flash of lightening zinged through the air and the clap of thunder rumbled in the sky, drowning out his words. The lightning made her run more. He could only watch as she fell in a ravine, crashing into a bush. She scrambled up the other side and kept going.

"Hell." He sped the horse up and was able to get in front of her. Her face was so wet, he wasn't even sure she could see him. She was just blindly stumbling about, looking for her mother. Sliding off the horse, he grabbed hold of her before she fell. The feel of hands spurned her into action and her shoe collided with his shin. He could guess what was coming next. Putting his hand down, her knee collided into it instead of softer parts. Alexander grabbed hold and pulled her off balance. Geneva fell in his arms and he held her tight. She squirmed to break free to little avail.

"Don't hurt her." She pleaded, her breathing ragged from fighting.

He pushed the hair from her face and wiped away the water from her eyes. "I found your mother. She's safe at the castle. No one will hurt her. Let me get ye back." The squirming stopped, but there wasn't very much trust to see.

She stared with haunted blue eyes for a long moment before she nodded faintly. When Alexander picked her up and put her on the horse, she said nothing. When he swung up behind her, she said nothing. It had been a long time since he'd had a woman so close. She was by far the most beautiful woman he had ever seen, and that included his wife, God rest her soul. Leaning forward, his long dark hair fell over her shoulders, making a cocoon as solid as his arms around her. "Who wants to hurt her?" he whispered in her ear.

"If I have no son and Johne dies, it goes to the nearest male, and right now, that's a MacKay. They want to cover all options and arrange a marriage to me, with Johne on his death bed."

"Is that why ye snarled the first time we spoke?" She was shivering as the rain pelted them. Alexander pulled her closer, covering her with the free end of the plaid as much as he was able. He had to force his thoughts onto something else with her so close between his legs.

"Wouldn't you be annoyed? Every man in the area has come offering himself to me. My daft mother is threatened with kidnap for the sake of pressuring me to marry. There are no men about to stop it from happening. Who knows if they'll try to take me next? After all, marriage by rape is more certain than wooing."

Another flash of lightning filled the sky, and she jumped in his arms. "How did your mother get out? We'll need to make sure it doesn't happen again."

Her head bowed forward, giving answer before she did. "I took her out. She loves to walk on the beach."

"If they're so intent on ye, it might be best if ye didn't go out. I would hate to make your aunt forbid it."

"Couldn't we go out with you? She'll go mad stuck in these walls." Her hands went to her mouth. "Oh God, what did I say."

Alexander started laughing at her reaction. He coughed as he swallowed and it went down the wrong pipe, but he couldn't keep the laughter from falling out. He could feel her laughing in his arms, too. Alexander felt the stirrings telling him it was more than protection he felt for her, or at least from her sitting so near.

"Maybe we can figure something out."

Alexander pushed the horse fast to get out of the rain, not to mention she had him worried now about men bent on rape and kidnap. The door opened at their approach. Someone had been watching. Elspeth bustled Geneva away and again he was left alone. He couldn't help notice Geneva looking back over her shoulder. "Ye're welcome," he muttered to no one.

~

In the warm kitchen, that if the date carved in the fireplace was right was already near to four hundred years old, the cook slid a bowl of thick soup in front of him. She was a large, heavily padded woman, but to call her fat wouldn't be right. She was solid, but a ready smile had greeted him as he entered, and around that house, it was a friendly sight. Alexander had been on a horse all day seeing to the outlying cotters. All he wanted to do was sit and eat some supper.

"That will warm your blood after a day out in this weather."

Alexander hadn't even gotten the first bite in his mouth when Caitriona came storming in. "The Duchess needs your help." She smiled like a proper young flirt as her hand tried to slip under his kilt. "Have a nice sword for me today? Fill out a kilt better than any of the boys I sent off to die. Strong thighs, wide chest, tall, handsome face, long black hair, deep green eyes. Ye shouldn't sleep so soundly. Never know what old women might do while they have ye at their mercy."

With a growl, Alexander slapped her hand. "Christ, woman, ye sound like a camp whore with talk like that." Caitriona opened her mouth. "I'll cut out the tongue in your head if I don't finish my supper first."

Caitriona's mouth gaped like a fish out of water. When it looked like she might speak, he reached for the sword. Her mouth shut quickly enough. The cook turned back to the fire, hiding the smile. Bryde was expressionless when she brought over some fresh bread and a large mug of ale. His supper was going to last a while.

Only after two bowls, three mugs and most of a loaf of bread did he sit back and acknowledge the old woman's presence. "Now talk."

"Ye always eat like a pig?" Caitriona snapped, looking down her nose at him. A little odd to see since her head bobbed, so it didn't have the same effect she probably thought it did.

Alexander's chuckle was low. "When I haven't eaten all day, aye. Now what does her highness need?"

"The MacKays are here. Elspeth won't talk to them unless ye're in the room. She's worried they may do something."

"Then waiting was good for them." He pushed away from the table. "Thank ye, Bryde. Good as always." He liked leaving Caitriona to watch him walk off for once.

The potential bride was nowhere in sight. At least Geneva had taken the warning to heart. Alexander entered the drawing room which was bathed in dark red as the sun set outside a large stained glass window showing the family crest.

"Where have you been?" Elspeth snapped. "I've been sitting here worrying they might sneak off and find Geneva."

"Then why let them in the castle at all?"

Elspeth's breath came quick. "I don't think I'm happy with the tone you're taking."

Alexander took Elspeth's stare. "Caitriona, bring them in. The Duchess has business to attend to," he called out, never looking away. She was still trying to get him to back down when the MacKays entered.

"Duchess Cairnmuir, so good of you to find time to speak with us," one called as they entered.

They were quite the opposite of Elspeth's sort. No clothes of court, they were highlanders through and through. They wore kilts, all of them, though of a finer sort than the cotters he'd dealt with. Alexander couldn't help but let the grin tempt the corner of his mouth. No wonder she wanted him there. A highlander to keep the highlanders in line. Especially when he was certain the one standing to the side gave him the wound on his leg. Cattle thieves, too, as well as out for kidnapping. The eldest, for a sixty year old, was a magnificent looking man. A thick head of white hair flowed to his shoulders, setting off his blue green plaid. There was no rhyme or reason to the rest of the men. They might have shared the same name but not the same weaver.

"What do you wish to discuss this evening, gentlemen?" Elspeth asked, pulling her stare away first.

"We've heard word that Johne has worsened from his wounds," a MacKay announced, stroking his bearded chin as Bryde brought in tea. There was noticeably enough for only one.

Elspeth's breath caught in her chest, but she kept it quiet. "That's what the messenger said, yes, but there is still hope my son will survive."

"While you sit here unguarded."

"It's only from you that we need protection. Isabella wasn't just being taken for a leisurely stroll two weeks ago," Elspeth snapped, trying to sound calm.

"Andrew will inherit the castle when Johne dies. If Geneva is wed to him, it will save your home for you."

Elspeth straightened as much as her five-foot frame would allow. "It's a Sinclair castle. It will stay such."

"With no man to pass on the name, it will change no matter who she marries. At least with Andrew, there is a connection and it won't go far out of the line," the MacKay elder hissed. He started to walk closer to the small woman, but at the last moment he caught sight of Alexander and pulled up short.

Elspeth took confidence in seeing the man halt at the mere sight of her protector. "IF my son dies. He's not dead yet. Alexander, see them out. My decision is final. There will be no marriage arranged."

Walking down the hall, Alexander caught a door open only slightly and a deep blue eye peered out. The MacKays were in front, but as he passed, it was him that Geneva watched go past. Just before he lost sight of her, she dipped her head briefly in thanks. It was more than he got from the woman that asked the task of him.

~

Dear Uncle,

I have found myself at the Sinclair castle in Wrathe. I seem to have missed the news while traveling that the men all died. The duchess has offered me a position as her factor. I can be found here until such time I have earned enough to continue my journey or she grows tired of me, which might be closer to the truth.

your nephew,

Alexander

A fire in 1608 had caused one whole side of the castle to be rebuilt. Centuries younger than the rest, that wing now held the family's quarters. While much of the rest was still medieval, that wing ranged had a sameness of the 1660's style. Alexander was rarely required to intrude on the upper floors, there was little need for him to visit the apartments. Geneva bid him inside when he knocked on the door.

"Caitriona swears in her bones that the weather will be nice and I have to go to the village to buy supplies. I thought ye and your mother would like to get out."

As a cat might, Geneva lay in a sunbeam, her hair on fire in the light. "Mother's not doing well today. She's sleeping."

"How about you, then? Would ye trust me within arm's length alone? Ye look like ye could use some fresh air," he asked quietly, seeing the woman on the bed nearby.

Geneva nodded silently and grabbed a length of faded hunting plaid. She wrapped it about herself until she truly looked no different from any cotters wife in their arasaids outside those walls, but as she pulled the fabric over her hair, her reason became obvious. Her hair was a dead giveaway. Then she walked out, leaving him there as he had been left so many times in the last few days.

"Could people stop doing that?"

Her face peered around the corner. "Doing what?"

"Slamming doors in my face, walking off like I'm not even here. I don't have to stay, ye know. I can leave anytime I feel like it. I keep my tongue with your aunt only until I have enough to get somewhere and even that I am finding difficult." She turned red and Alexander couldn't help but notice it extended down her chest to disappear below her bodice.

The corner of her mouth curled up in a grin. "I'm used to doing it with my aunt when she's trying to push marriage on me. There isn't anyone else around that I have to practice niceties with. I'll try harder to remember. Could ye please accompany me on a walk, sir," she finished to make up for it.

Alexander started laughing. "Aye. If ye're past taking my head off now?"

It got her to smile at any rate. "Only two days before you arrived, the cottar William came upon men leading my mother far from the castle. They hadn't had to force anything. They just had to tell her they were going to show her something and in her state, she followed blindly. If it wasn't for William insisting on seeing her home, I hate to think of what might have happened. Then you showed up claiming shipwreck."

"That's what your aunt referred to the other night, and ye assumed I was abusing the hospitality given to me."

"My aunt thinks only of the lack of men."

"Ye do need to get men in this place again. Too much clishmaclaver going on."

A grin tugged at the corner of her mouth. "Us gossip, never."

"Then how do ye explain the old woman?"

Away from the room where her mother slept, Geneva laughed, a full out laugh, no tittering for her. "Caitriona? She's been like that since I was a girl. You should be lucky she's out of practice. You'll get a hand up your kilt yet if you don't watch yourself."

Alexander let out a groan. "Oh, she's already done that. Hate to think of what she did while I was asleep, since it seems she was the one that undressed me."

Geneva's grin grew and she bit her lip trying to stop it. "No, Bryde and I did that. Caitriona's a dirty old woman, but that doesn't mean she can lift a full-grown man to see what wounds he has. Young Hamish was keeping watch, and when he saw the blood staining your shirt, he came and got me." Geneva started laughing. "Even the bairns know not to leave a man alone with Caitriona when he can't defend himself."

Alexander crossed his arms, suddenly enjoying playing with her. There was nothing of the woman he expected in her when she wasn't protecting herself from all that was going on. "If ye're going to start laughing, get undressed so we're even. Then I'll listen to it."

Geneva leaned near his ear. "Never seen a grown man get flustered at a woman seeing him naked."

"Not flustered. Disappointed."

"Oh." Her pale white skin turned brilliant red, none more so than the skin at her cleavage.

"For a flirt, I wouldn't have expected that color."

She was still rather red when she looked over at him with those deep blue eyes. The blush did not go with her hair at all. "More men than I care to count have shown up lately wanting marriage, caring nothing for me, or else they're pigs, asking me if I want a cock in me the moment someone turns a corner. You aren't being coarse. I guess it threw me off guard."

"Should I stop then?"

Her smile grew but the red was fading. "In this castle, it might be the only entertainment I get. You don't want me bored, do you?"

It wasn't until they were clear of the towers and off the island that Geneva's shoulders loosened and she took a deep breath.

"Can ye explain what is going on a little clearer? I got quite clearly that the Mackays want to make a marriage and the house needs an heir."

Shrugging her shoulders, she tugged at a piece of grass. She indeed looked far more the peasant than a lady of the castle. "If you tell me the truth as well. The wounds I bound came from no shipwreck. I would guess a broadsword if I had to put a name to them."

Alexander couldn't keep from smiling. "No, there was no ship. Your aunt had mentioned the men dying already. She didn't seem in the mood to want to hear I was anything like them, so I told a little lie. It kept a roof over my head, if nothing else."

Geneva looked out of the corner of her eye at him. "The English gave you the wounds?"

"Lord, woman, ye must think the worst of me. No wonder ye snapped as if I was dirt when I arrived. I'm a brigand on the run then, is that what ye believe? No, I seem to have run across some of your very MacKays with some stolen cattle. They weren't in the talking mood. What if I said I think I recognized some of the men standing in your Aunt's drawing room when they came to discuss marriage?"

Geneva's laugh was glorious to hear. "Now that I would definitely believe."

"Your turn to spill a few secrets."

"My uncle formed a group of men to go in aid of a kinsman. Now most of them are dead, my father and uncle included. My cousin lies at death's door. If he survives, it will be a miracle. That leaves Elspeth, my mad mother and me. A handful of women stayed to work. With no one to serve, the rest went home to take the place of the men that died in their own families."

"I got most of that part. What about this marriage thing?"

Her head nodded. "The title Duke of Cairnmuir was granted as such that it can be inherited by the closest male relative, it doesn't have to be in the direct eldest sons' line like some. The lands and castle are part of that. My aunt, God bless her mercenary little heart, is too old to bear any children, and refuses to part with it to a MacKay. If the now dead Duke's niece has a son, however, that knocks the MacKays out of the situation. They're only fourth cousins. My mother and aunt are only related by marriage. I'm the closest with blood ties and until I'm gone, any son I bear will inherit even if it's in 20 years and they take control now. My child can always knock them out."

"And now they're willing to try tricks to get in there."

Geneva gave a laugh. "What a dirty little mind you have."

Alexander scratched his neck to hide the grin. "That's not what I meant."

Still she chuckled. "Aye, they're trying tricks now. But then so is my aunt. Her views and my uncle's didn't match politically. They married for money, after all, not love or even affection. Now that he's gone, she's trying to push me to marry someone allied with her ideas and get an heir out of the match as well. If it's a relative of hers, she'll be able to stay master in her home."

"Some poor but well blooded man that won't mind being lorded over by his female relations for the sake of a castle."

Her eyebrows rose high. "Played these games before, have you?"

"I knew the steward of a castle a few years ago. I got to hear all the sordid stories." Alexander wasn't in a hurry, and when Geneva veered down to the beach, he just followed. Granted with the sight of her pulling up her skirts to keep them clean, he would have followed even if he weren't walking with her. Grabbing a stick, she started digging in the muck, pulling up clams.

"What happened to your mother?"

Slowly she raised her head. "Want to hear my sordid little story, too, I see."

"Didn't ask that."

"Maybe it will explain why I fight it so much. My aunt politicks for a marriage when the goods aren't as pure as she's claiming. Maybe I prefer to stop the matches before they denounce me for being a whore."

Alexander raised a dark eyebrow. "She's lying or she doesn't know?"

"Doesn't know," she admitted pulling another clam. "I think my father was getting suspicious that I had feelings for the boy. He went and married him off a hundred miles away. That was three years ago. He has twins now and I remain unmarried at twenty. Not just anyone was good enough for him. He was worried he was losing control of me. I was his ticket to power, marrying me off could get him what he wanted. As a second son, there was no castle, no land, and no power. Marrying my mother gave him money, marrying off his children was supposed to give him the rest, and there was only me."

"What happened to your mother?" he asked again.

Geneva nodded faintly the way Isabella did so often. It was a shock to realize the mad woman had to have been quite a beauty in her younger years. "When I was eight, my mother gave birth to the son my father always wanted. About two months later, he died in his sleep. First and only time my father laid hands on her, screaming that she wasn't a fit mother. She was distraught with grief already when he accused her of the boy's death ... she wanted more children, always had. The thought of not being a good mother was more than she could handle. Now she's mad for it. Spends her days being the perfect mother to children that aren't there while I raised her along with myself. My father couldn't get rid of her, so he ignored her. The day I have children, they'll never have to wear the same clothes twice from all the clothes she's made for the ones that don't exist." She stopped for a moment as she pulled a clam, then raised her head again. That look of hers bore right into him. "No matter how worked up she gets, give her a chore, especially cooking, and she'll turn and go do it as if the fit never happened. At least the food we can eat."

Alexander squatted down near where she worked. "What is it ye want?"

"Clams for lunch."

"I've heard what your aunt wants. What is it you want?" he repeated quietly.

"I don't know, Alexander. My mother wouldn't do well being taken somewhere else. She does well most times as long as my father's name isn't mentioned. Of him, she remembers only that one time he beat her. I think he might have killed her for it if the castle ghost hadn't intervened. At least that is what my mother claims happened. Daft as can be, but fine. Elspeth can't handle her alone. So I'm stuck with some wimp of a man that will do his aunt's bidding like a servant. No one cares what I want. Never have."

"Like having clams for lunch."

Geneva started smiling as she put her head back down to her task. Alexander wasn't quite sure, but he swore he saw a faint blush at her cheeks. He wasn't sure it had anything to do with getting bored.

~

"I'll bet she's a damn good roll in the hay," the cottar William cracked as Alexander sat to lunch at The Cock in Hand, the only tavern in fifty miles, the only village in fifty miles for that matter. Half the men he had met were sitting there with food or drink.

"And just who would that be ye're wondering about?" Alexander asked.

William's smirk slid through the room. "Geneva, of course. Half the MacKay men would marry her if they could get their hands on her. The other half are already married or they would, too."

"They want a castle. They'd marry her regardless of what she looked like," Alexander argued.

William slammed his hand on the table as the laughter poured out. "True."

"She turn ye down, William? Is that why ye wonder so much?" Alexander asked, and the rest of the room took up the laughter, answering the question as if the red at his collar didn't.

"Oh, and you've gotten so far in your weeks in the castle. Do tell, what's she's like in the hay, master?"

Alexander took a long drink of ale to force down the smile. "Wouldn't know. Never been near any hay."

"Bed, then?"

"Not even close."

William slammed the table again. "See, ye're no better than the rest of us."

"Never said I got anywhere with her. Just hate to think of what tongue lashing ye'd get if Caitriona heard ye talking about her Geneva like that, is all." The laughter picked up again. "That woman might be a horny old biddy but she'll kill anyone who's say the same about Geneva."

"Maybe you're looking to marry yourself a castle like all the rest of us." It was a new voice and everyone turned to the door.

"Don't remember inviting you, MacKay," William growled.

Alexander couldn't help but take a glimpse of the man all the Sinclair didn't want to marry in to the family. He was a rather good-looking man, so their decision wasn't based on disgust. Well-built and trim, fair complexion, dark blond hair, a man with Viking blood, perhaps. The Sinclair castle itself had a Viking era watchtower, not that it had kept them out of the area all those years ago. Alexander knew more about him than he probably wanted him to. That blond hair was a dead giveaway. Alexander had wounded several of the men that had attacked him, but a blond haired one had taken the brunt of his resistance. So that was why the man hadn't come to press his own suit for marrying Geneva.

The blond man grabbed a mug and purposefully sat next to Alexander. "Andrew MacKay, since I'm sure you don't know me. No need to introduce yourself, Alexander. My father told me all about you." Andrew took a long drink of his ale. "Must be hard to live with being ordered around by a woman," he added as offhanded as he could make it.

Alexander couldn't help but laugh at the words though. "I don't know that Geneva doting on me as the only man around could ever be called torture. If ye want a good word about finding a wife, though, I think Caitriona would like a husband. Should I inquire for you?" He dipped his head in thanks as the man brought over his trencher of food.

"Who the hell is that?" Andrew asked, confused as the room tried not to laugh.

"Must be what, men? Seventy. I think she's simmered down enough even a man like ye could satisfy her. Then again perhaps its best you stopped in the tavern, you can take things in your own hand like the name says. Be the closest you'll get to Geneva." The laughter spilled out the building as poor MacKay pushed away from the table and stalked out. Alexander was just about knocked off the bench as William pounded him on the back, laughing loudest of all.

"Only an outsider would have said that." Someone announced, but it was said without malice. "But lord that was funny."

"Said what?" Alexander had to ask. As an outsider, it was gibberish to him.

"The taverns name." William started laughing anew. "When the village was but just started, there was no public house. The original owner got kicked out for annoying his wife some 200 years ago and he was hungry something awful. Old Nellie's cock was running around and he caught it said right here by god he was going to build a place where the men could get away from the cackling hens even if it meant him cooking to make it happen. He and Nellie's family been fighting ever since cause to this day his family has never paid for that stupid cock."

"I like my story better. Sure did get rid of Mackay in a hurry."

William made a rude gesture in reference to the name, almost falling off the bench in doing so. "Good riddance."

~

The door opened quickly, waking Alexander from a sound sleep. His hand found the handle of his claymore, but he stopped it short only inches from Elspeth's throat. Her breathing was ragged and she looked as if she was ready to wet herself as she stared down the blade.

"Ye tell me men are trying to kidnap people in this household and then ye do this when I'm sleeping. Hell, woman, what do ye need?" He dropped the sword and rubbed the sleep from his face.

"I understand you were implying that you were having relations with my niece!" Elspeth cried, easily shedding the fear in her eyes only moments before.

Alexander groaned loudly. "No, as I recall I was saying I hadna."

"What could induce you to speak of a lady in a public tavern at all? It is bad form, I tell you."

"If it's such bad manners, next time ye see Andrew MacKay, ask him this question. I responded, I wasn't bringing the subject up."

"Andrew was there?" she asked as Alexander lay back down and closed his eyes.

"Aye, Duchess, he was. I'm surprised your gossiper didn't tell you that part. Next time I hear of your niece being spoken of in a tavern, I can ignore the questions put to me. I'm sure that will cause more gossip than dealing with it. I know how to handle men's talk, while your gossip here in the house will kill me yet. Can I get back to sleep? I have a long day tomorrow with a shrew for a task master."

Elspeth stared at him for a long moment before the laughter started to spill from her. An annoying little titter that grated on his ears even as she walked down the hall.

~

"No." Geneva hissed. "I refuse to let you do it."

Alexander stopped in the hall when he heard that. There was more going on in the castle than a little marrying off. What was the question?

Elspeth took a sip of her wine. "But it's my castle now. I see no reason why I shouldn't be able to see to it as I want. The cottars hardly keep body and soul together with farming and fishing."

"You know your husband and son would never approve of kicking them off their own land, for a damned hunting preserve even less. Last I heard, Johne wasn't even dead. It's not yours to rape yet."

"The messages all say soon enough, and everyone complains that there is no entertainment here. If I am to entertain properly, we need hunting." Elspeth was suddenly not the woman that she had shown Alexander since he arrived. She was a bitch. There was no other word to describe her.

Out of the corner of his eye, Alexander could see Geneva leaning over the older woman. She smiled, but it was a predatory smile as the older woman sank in her chair. "Then get a man to keep you entertained. Your husband is dead, we know that for sure. If I am to keep you your damn castle to entertain in, you will do as I wish, and I wish to follow the legacy your husband and son started. If you raise one finger to remove even a single tenant off this estate, I will walk out the door and marry the first MacKay I see. I can have you kicked out on your ass in a day if I want to. Keep that in mind, Aunt."

"I will see you married to whom I choose. I am your guardian."

"I may not like the MacKays anymore than you do, but I will carry out my threat if it will keep my mother in the home she knows and stop you from destroying everything this family has worked for. On this I am firm. Grandmother would beat you senseless if she heard this rot. Pity she died for I'm in the mood to see you whipped for your own good." Geneva pushed away from the woman. Elspeth looked truly scared as Geneva stormed from the room.

At the sight of Alexander sitting in the hall, she pulled up short. "I don't want to hear it. I don't want to hear you ask if this is what I want."

"She would put all of them out?"

That stopped her for a moment and then she nodded. "She showed me the order before you obviously started eavesdropping."

Alexander rested his head back against the wall as it all rushed back. Maybe if there was someone with as much backbone as Geneva had, his wife and child might have been spared their horror.

"Alex, what's wrong?"

He thought she had walked off, but when he opened his eyes, she was in the chair next to him, looking very worried. "I was married, lass. She was carrying our first child when the house was burnt to the ground with her inside."

"Over land?"

He closed his eyes again as the sight of the ruins of the house they had shared came to mind. "Aye. I wasn't there. I returned a month later when the child should have been born to find a grave instead. I was just wishing someone had stood up to the one in the castle that gave the order. It's a nasty way to die." A faint kiss gently between his eyes came as an answer, no words. Forcing the thoughts away again, he opened his eyes to find Elspeth staring down at him. Geneva was nowhere in sight.

"I don't pay you to sit around."

~

Elspeth may have paid him and given him orders, but it was Geneva he worked for now. He could protect her the way he hadn't been able to for his wife.

"Bryde was saying crab was your favorite but with the men gone, few have been putting lobster pots out. Bryde says she'll cook them if we can catch them,"

Alexander offered. It was the opposite of everyone else, crab were usually thrown back when they got in the lobster pots.

"Lobster... oh, Geneva, your brother loves lobster. We'll have to make sure to get some," Isabella cried with glee.

Geneva sighed. Obviously twelve years of children that didn't exist being better treated could get old. "Put on a scarf, then, Mother, and we'll go find some lobster for little James."

Isabella picked up a scarf and ran out of the room.

"I didn't know she would do that, sorry." Alexander apologized.

"I've been scolded for eating food she's saving for James. Oh, and she still thinks I'm eight," Geneva answered before rushing out after the rapidly vanishing woman.

~

Outside the castle walls, Isabella slowed to a walk and started picking heather, the rush for crabs seemingly forgotten.

"She never wakes up, I guess ye could call it?" Alexander asked quietly.

Geneva shook her head slowly. "Once about two years ago, she looked at me for a long time and asked when had I gotten so big, wanted to see James' grave. That was the only way I knew she was herself those moments. When she saw the grave, she started screaming, asking why I would play such a cruel joke on her." The gull's cries filled the air when she spoke no more. They walked in silence for a while before Geneva stopped, eyes sadly watching her mother. "Do ye suppose that is my future, to never see my children grown, to never know anyone dies, hearing people that don't exist?"

"I can't see ye ever going mad. Ye're too stubborn to let someone else tell ye want to do."

Her sullen face turned to laughter. "It's been a long time since I laughed. I might decide I like you just on that."

"Like me? And ruin the idea that ye carry a knife ye're just waiting to use on me?" Alexander could only watch as her fingers disappeared between her breasts, and when they emerged, they brought a rather lethal looking dirk with them.

"You mean this one?"

He tried not to smirk but he couldn't help it. "Aye, that one."

Geneva laughed louder. "How could you guess when even Elspeth hasn't a clue? I haven't always been the last hope of bearing an heir. Johne was one of six children. Over the years, the others have gone through sickness and fighting. It was only a year ago we were the last ones left. Her mother in law died about then too. How can you see that and not the part I play now to appease my guardian?"

"Then your aunt never looks at those eyes of yours. They are not those of a bidding, innocent woman."

Looking around, Geneva jumped slightly. Isabella was nowhere in sight. "Mother, we need to go to the village for lobster pots, remember."

Isabella's head popped up from a bush not far away.

There was no denying the sigh of relief Geneva let out. "She's going to be the death of me yet," she muttered. "What, no jokes at hearing that?" came out as an afterthought.

"I see nothing funny in what your mother has to live like. I just can't see ye going mad yourself. Driving me to madness, maybe."

"You, how?"

Alexander glanced over out of the corner of his eye. "Ignoring me so completely when I flirt with ye. I can think of one entertainment the castle has to offer, and ye've not been offering at all."

"And a man like you waits for an offer. I lock my door nightly to keep from being ravaged."

Now there was the woman that fit the look in those eyes of hers. "Your mother screaming at the merest visit is all the guard ye need. I've heard her when the maid comes to wake ye. Man would have to be certain of the reward to risk that. Ye forget I guessed about the knife, too."

Geneva grinned. "And so you wait for an offer?"

"Only proper thing to do, seeing as I could get thrown out on my arse without any money if I launched an unwanted assault."

"Then I'll stop locking the door and sleep soundly." A wink accompanied the grin as she left him behind to catch up to her mother.

~

Mucking out the stable, Alexander could only stop and stare when Geneva came running in. She was not dressed for riding or even as a peasant, for that matter. She could have stepped into court without changing a thing.

"Hide me," she hissed.

"What now?"

Geneva looked over with a grin. "Suitor come to call. I'm being difficult."

"Come on, then." He threw down the shovel and led her up the stairs to the hayloft. "With the pile of horse shite in the way, no one should come looking too close."

Disregarding her dress, she flopped on a pile and let out a sigh. "What if I told you it was a Lindsay in the drawing room?"

He caught the look out of the corner of her eye. "What, ye think that I wouldn't want to meet a clansman?"

Geneva started laughing. "Thought crossed my mind."

Alexander threw a handful of hay at her. "Does nothing satisfy ye that I'm not a brigand out to rape ye?"

Geneva sputtered, trying to get hay out of her mouth. "Then why are you running?"

"Nothing left for me there."

Her laughter faded. "I know your wife died, but you've nothing at all at home? That's very sad."

"Geneva, are ye oot here, girl? We have a guest here to see ye," Caitriona could be heard yelling outside.

Alexander flopped down next to her so he could whisper. "So if ye hate the idea of marriage so much, what are ye doing coming to a man to hide ye?"

"You like flirting, don't you?"

"Me, flirt, never." He answered, mimicking her words about gossip. "Ye plan on staying here until he leaves in disgust?"

Geneva shook her head. "No, I'll go soon. I just won't make it too easy on my aunt."

"Since there's no mirror, I suppose I should help ye out." Alexander pulled a stick of hay from her hair gently before he started laughing. "Oh, no."

"What?"

"No, I couldn't tell ye."

She leaned back against the mound where she sat. "Tell me or I shan't leave." Geneva's grin belied the well-dressed woman that sat there. She was a little vixen.

"William was asking what ye were like in the hay and here ye are in the hay with me."

"You often discuss me in public with every man around?"

"Don't ye start. I already had your aunt busting in on my sleep. I was trying to get them to stop and William decided I must have had the pleasure to be standing up for ye. Not to mention Andrew Mackay was there accusing me of trying to marry a castle."

"You would never marry me for the sake of a castle." Geneva argued.

"Glad ye know that."

"No, you would marry me to get me in bed."

"Ye say that like it's a bad thing."

Biting her lip was all she could do to keep a straight face. "Help me get the hay out of my hair. Time to go face the suitor."

As Alexander pulled the last piece from her hair, he had to stop himself from leaning over and kissing her. "Lindsay, ye say. Maybe I'll have to make an appearance," he said to stop the urge.

"Go, then. Let me have a few moments alone. I get few enough as it is. I'll be up in a while."

The drawing room was a blue-papered room with an elaborate plaster ceiling and quiet when he walked in, even though Elspeth held court with a man. Looking over, his eyes felt like they were deceiving him. It couldn't actually be someone he knew, even more that it would be a relation. One he knew Geneva would hate to end up married to, Ingram Lindsay was well known, and not in the least for being faithful.

Elspeth jumped up at the sight of him. "Alexander, I hope you've seen Geneva."

"She said she would be here shortly. Caitriona just found her to tell her ye had a guest."

She just looked between them for a moment. It was obvious they were related, same dark hair, same tanned skin, and similar build. "I suppose you're here to see your clansman, then."

He hated having to ask, the words stuck in his throat. "If it is all right with ye that I speak with my own cousin, my lady." The woman froze. Alexander knew he was being raised a notch. Ingram Lindsay had money, land, and an ear at court. Alexander Lindsay wasn't the poor destitute man she thought. Alexander didn't feel like correcting her that he was on the wrong line to get anything.

"We weren't expecting company. Could you keep him company while I go tell cook to prepare something special for supper tonight?"

"Gladly."

Elspeth rushed from the room. Alexander poured himself a drink before he turned back to the man. "When I heard it was a Lindsay here, I didn't expect it was ye, Ingram."

Ingram walked over and joined him at the table with the whisky. "I expected you in France by now."

"The lady offered me a position to fill my purse, what with all the men gone."

Ingram leaned near Alexander's ear. "I suppose you came to talk me out of marrying the lady."

"Only heard there was a Lindsay here. Didna know it was you." Alexander started to laugh. "Why would I do that? The woman is beautiful, clever, and funny. Any man would want her in his bed."

"And?"

Alexander's laugh settled into a smirk. "And she's the ward of the woman ye just met. I'm sick of her and I'm just here to earn some money. I wouldn't want to be under her thumb for any amount of money if I had the choice, no matter the size of the castle that came with her."

"Speaking quite forthright about us, Alexander. Are you going to introduce me to your clansman?" Geneva said from the door.

"This is no clansman of mine. Ingram is my cousin and no greater wretch will ye meet."

"Pour me a drink then before she comes back."

Alexander handed her a glass while she remained as straight faced as could be. She downed the contents before the smile started to tease the corners of her mouth. "Well, save me being petulant all day, Alex. Do I only flirt or do I consider marriage with the wretch? We both know I have to let her think I'm at least considering some of them."

"You are a sneaky woman." Ingram raised his glass to her as she turned to him.

"That I take as the greatest compliment," Geneva said sweetly.

Ingram's laughter filled the room until Elspeth's return made it die quickly.

~

Alexander made a round of the outer wall of the castle. It made him feel better more than anything, since he was sitting on an island on the edge of the North Sea. The castle filled the island, so there was hardly any gap for someone to get a hold to storm anything. An ancient tower in the center was filled with several cannons that aimed in all directions. Two more towers stood on either side of the bridge over to the mainland, so that approach, too, was covered. Fifteen cannon in all protected the walls. There was nothing to fear as long as there were people there to operate it. There was nothing to fear, unless a rather mad woman got loose and they had to go find her. They needed men. There was nothing else to it.

"Man could make a fine place for himself here with all the men gone," Ingram said from the door of the guardroom as Alexander was staring out the window.

"What are ye doing here, Ingram? Give me the truth."

"Truth. I read your letter to my father and had to come try my hand at the finest castle in the north. The woman to take to bed doesn't hurt things."

"Geneva isn't showing any sign of agreeing to a marriage anytime soon. Don't get your hopes up."

"Maybe you would like to marry her yourself?"

"Don't joke about something like that," Alexander growled.

"Mairaid's father would be most impressed that you hold his daughter's memory so dear, but I saw the way you looked at Geneva. It's been two years. No one would fault you if you were getting feelings for her."

Alexander looked over his shoulder. "For her, maybe, but I spoke the truth about her aunt."

"And what did she do to receive your disgust?"

"Was ready to kick out every cotter she has for the sake of a hunting preserve. Geneva's threatening to go marry the man next in line was all that stopped her."

Ingram settled against the wall with a smile. "Now I know why you looked at her the way you did. You'd look at a hag with doe eyes if she saved Mairaid for you."

Alexander smiled as he turned back to the window. "Elspeth's your problem. Just remember, cousin, I'll keep Geneva from any of your trouble."

Ingram nodded slowly. "There's spirit there. I'll let you know how she is." The grin spread across his face.

~

A luxurious brocade settee held Geneva as she read a book of poetry, at least until Ingram sank next to her.

"A word, Geneva."

"Of course. Any cousin of the man who's kept our house together is welcome at my side."

"Good to hear."

Geneva put her book down as Ingram's hand slid over and rested on her thigh. "So, did Alex ever get back to you about if I was worth marriage or only flirting?"

Laughter filled the room. "You put so much stock in your poor cousin's opinion of you?"

"Only that I would hate for him to be telling untruths about me." His fingers moved higher, bringing the skirt with them. Geneva's pale thigh was very visible.

"Why, Ingram, I do believe you are a scoundrel with words like those, not to mention my skirt is going up."

"Well, if you've never had the pleasure of a man, I'll be more than happy to take a kiss, then." Ingram started to lean over when Alexander's cough stopped him cold.

"Keep going if you want to be thrown out on your ear. I have a woman's reputation to uphold. I'd take pleasure in that duty. Not to mention the duchess is coming."

Ingram's hand stopped with only inches to spare. Geneva was almost bare to view.

"My aunt will choose my husband. Seducing me might get you a feel or two, but no castle," Geneva whispered as she stood.

Ingram stared into those deep blue eyes, suddenly knowing his job would be much harder.

~

From the tower guarding the gate, Alexander could see a carriage moving closer. Not feeling like more orders from Elspeth, he just sat there out of sight, watching. Soon a woman was alighting from the steps of the coach.

"Cristeane." Elspeth hugged her tightly with a squeal. They were obviously a pair. Alexander had never seen a woman so grandly dressed before and he had spent time in a castle often enough. She wore a smoky blue silk gown with mauve bows that ran down the bodice, not to mention the lace erupting from the sleeves. A dark haired woman who carried herself as proudly as the Duchess Elspeth with her hidden rotten core.

"Now what is she doing here?" Alexander muttered.

"Paying her respects over the death of her uncle." Geneva said behind him. Geneva with her French name in the midst of Scotland, but the plaques set into the wall of the castle told a story that there was more than one French family represented in her blood.

"Great, another woman to deal with," he muttered, but when he turned, he found Geneva was as dressed up as the woman in the coach was. They were a study in opposites. While the newcomer was covered with decorations, Geneva shone in an ivory gown of heavy brocade. The golden design of the fabric was about the only ornamentation she allowed herself other than a few tasteful bows at her bodice. She glowed, the woman outside flashed.

"Does she have children?" Alexander asked.

"She's related on Elspeth's side, not the Sinclair's, and unmarried. She's not a threat that way. I'll wager you a guinea she's here to help my aunt decide on the husband I should have among her relations." Geneva laughed faintly. "She's always an easy touch for a good looking man. If you're tempted, remember she always burns you in the end." With that, she walked past. "Cristeane!" she called brightly, hiding all the feelings she had just shared.

"Geneva, my dear. You look positively radiant. I'll have to talk your aunt into letting me take you to Edinburgh and away from all these rustics. I've been talking with the most delightful man. He's eager to meet you."

"Meet me for what, Cristeane?" Geneva asked sweetly.

"Ah, there you are, Ingram. You must come meet my niece on my side of the family. This is Cristeane Stuart," Elspeth called.

"Shite!" Alexander hissed under his breath. They weren't just poor tenant farmers. Just how close were they related to the exiled King James? What had he gotten himself into if they were Stuarts? A relation to the pretender, life just got a lot more complicated.

Alexander came out of his spot watching Ingram and caught the clenching fist hidden behind Geneva's back. Ingram had the king's ear. Johne and Braden Sinclair from what he'd heard supported the king, but he wasn't so sure about Elspeth. Ingram was there for marriage, sure enough, but it was to secure a castle for the king. Still no one cared what Geneva thought.

~

He'd never eaten dinner with the family, but that night he was told he was requested. At the grin from Cristeane's face, it didn't take any guesses as to who requested him.

"So my aunt tells me you're keeping house and home together for her now that her men have abandoned her and many dead," Cristeane announced.

"As long as she needs me, yes. I'm sure when Johne comes back, I'll no longer be needed."

Cristeane's grin was filled with deviltry. "By then I'm sure I will find a reason to keep you around, or shall I make do with your cousin?"

"How did I suddenly get to be second best? I'm the one with the castle here," Ingram complained.

Cristeane's giggle floated through the room. "Dear Ingram, we all know you're enamored with Geneva. I have to make do with the help."

Alexander's jaw clenched at her words. Sneaking a look at Geneva, she caught his glance and raised her eyebrows as she reached for her wine. She knew the woman well, didn't she? "Me, Lady Stuart? I doubt that. You're far too accomplished to find anything to want to hold onto in me."

Cristeane's laugh was honey filled. "It's been my experience that the more accomplishments a woman has, the more she finds a man with strong legs and long black hair attractive. Did I ever say anything about holding on to? I only said keep you around, didn't I?"

Elspeth's arriving ended Cristeane's taunts. She just grinned across the table at him every time his eyes passed by her.

~

"Ahh, Alexander, just the man I was hoping to find," Cristeane's coquettish voice called out.

The words made Alexander freeze in the hall as he passed by the game room. He was finding it difficult to get away from Cristeane at all. "Yes?"

"Well, come here, man. I have a task for you." Cristeane commanded.

"What now?" he asked as he stepped in the room. Elspeth sat there with her needlepoint, and Isabella was looking rather coherent for once. That left Geneva and Cristeane playing a game of chess.

"Not sure I'm happy with that tone, either." Elspeth started. "But I find that Cristeane is right on this point. We can't send Geneva into marriage without having ever had a proper kiss. So kiss her, and like you mean it."

"You make it sound like we should be children and you're daring him to do it," Geneva argued.

"Geneva is resisting all attempts at the discussion of marriage. We need to awaken her passions so she will relish the idea of her marriage bed. You're the only man around, so kiss her," Cristeane prompted.

"Again, I find that highly objectionable. I am a man, am I not?" Ingram huffed, crossing his arms.

"Yes, but we need an impartial teacher here, one to break her in without attachment. I've seen you drooling over her daily. Nothing impartial there."

Geneva pushed herself away from the chess table and stood in front of him. "Well, then, I'm hungry, and they won't let me leave for our meal until I've been properly shown. Let's get this over with."

"Don't need an audience," Alexander growled before he pulled her into the hall. Geneva pulled free of his grip and backed away as he walked slowly toward her. Only when she hit the wall did she stop. He didn't touch her as he placed his hands on the wall beside her. Alexander took a deep breath, taking in the smell of her, committing it to memory. He wanted to do a lot more than kiss her as she stood there looking a little smug. The crook of her neck was too inviting and he couldn't stop himself from nipping at it gently. Geneva yelped, not expecting it. Even that light of a touch left her skin discolored.

"What did I say, Aunt. She would positively not be able to allow a man next to her in her marriage bed. Try harder, Alexander," Cristeane announced loud enough for them to hear.

"Ye have something to do with this situation?" Alexander finally asked in a whisper.

"Aye."

"Then ye've wanted to kiss me?"

"Aye."

Slowly he moved his head until he was looking in her eyes. Cristeane was dangerous, giving the woman what she wanted. There was no denying Geneva wanted him.

"If ye've wanted it, take it," Alexander whispered.

The quiver in her breathing might have been fear, but there was no hesitation before she licked his bottom lip slowly, then pulled it in her mouth and sucked gently. The quiver came again, and this time he knew it was anticipation. Geneva's head only had to move an inch for her to claim the rest of his mouth. Tentative at first as she explored his lips, tasting him, the moment he opened his mouth, she plunged in. Her tongue seemed to be everywhere, dueling with him. Every spot she touched him he could feel the heat radiating off her. She bit her lip to trap the moan that rose from her when he pulled away.

"Ye didn't have to arrange this charade," he whispered in her ear before he pulled the lobe in his mouth and heard her breathing come short. "Wanted ye in bed since the day we met, since our ride on the horse, I've wanted to protect ye. Since the day ye stood up to your aunt, I'm pretty sure I'm falling in love." The stubble on his face rasped gently along her neck as he ran his tongue down to the top of her chest displayed perfectly in the bodice. With a quick hand, he dipped beneath and pulled out a snowy white breast.

"If you've wanted it, take it," Geneva whispered.

Alexander grinned as he bent his head to the task. Geneva could only watch him as he slowly pulled her nipple in his mouth and swirled his tongue around it. It had been too long since she'd had any pleasure. Her breathing grew ragged. Her hand clutched his hair, but it wasn't enough to keep the moan from escaping. With equally quick motions, her breast was back in its place and his mouth claimed hers as he heard the swish of satin and silk behind them.

"See, Cristeane, I knew she wasn't the cold fish you thought, and here Alexander is all but a stranger. Just think what a husband will be able to do. Time for lunch, Geneva. You said you were hungry."

Her voice was husky with want as she murmured, "Aye," only loud enough for Alexander to hear.

~

Alexander flopped on the ground with a groan. Two days of being ordered around like a slave was getting to him. If Elspeth wasn't sending him on a chore, Cristeane was, but he hardly had enough saved to make it across the channel, let alone live until he could find work.

"You really feel something more than lust or greed?"

He didn't lift the arm covering his face at Geneva's whisper. "What does it matter?

Through a gap between arm and face, he watched her head lower. "I would like to know. It would matter to me."

Alexander pulled the arm away. God, she was going to be the death of him. He knew he shouldn't say it, but kissing her was more than he could stand to fight against, not after what she had said. "Aye, Geneva Sinclair, I'm finding a lot more that I like beside the idea of your castle."

Geneva sank down next to him. "My bed, I suppose."

There were no bashful glances from those eyes as she stared down at him. Alexander ran a hand up her thigh and slipped under the bodice. With a good hold, he pulled her over on top of him. "Given the chance, I won't say I'd ever turn down taking ye to bed," he murmured just before his lips found hers. There was no chance of anyone seeing them, and she opened to his onslaught. She didn't lie when she said she was hungry, that much was certain. Her breathing was ragged when she pulled away. She only turned her head to the side as she gasped for breath, leaving her neck ripe for pillaging.

"I don't have to remind ye to breathe through your nose, do I?" he teased. "Has it been so long?" Her breathing wasn't showing any signs of calming with the kisses to her neck. "Can I ask ye a question?"

His tongue running up the length of her neck kept her from answering, though, and then he found her ear lobe. "Ummm."

"If that was meant to be a yes, did ye ever have fencing lessons? I swear I felt a parry in there."

It was enough that Geneva lifted up to look him in the face, laughing. "Did you know my grandmother was a breeches actress on the London stage? She could duel with the best teacher they could bring in and she never thought a female was anything less than a male, she taught me well. A spy for Charles II before his return to the throne. My aunt doesn't like to remind people of that dip into the common sorts. Does it scare you off?"

"Your aunt wants to marry ye off and my cousin is in the running. If that didn't scare me, what's a little steel going to frighten me?"

The quiver to her breathing gave away her thoughts long before her words did. Alexander rolled suddenly, pinning her to the ground. "Breath through your nose this time," he whispered as he dipped his head.

"Geneva, your sister needs her shawl. Can you go back and get it?" Isabella yelled.

"How did she get out?" Geneva hissed.

"Aye, I'm daft for it, but I want ye. Neither of ye should be out alone. It's time ye get back." Alexander lowered his head the last inch, but the kiss was gentle and short.

~

Cristeane and Geneva were out in the courtyard taking some air, as Cristeane had called it. It looked more like a reason for her to show off a fur cape to Alexander. Unloading the wagon of supplies that had been delivered from the village, it was not as if he was included in the exercise, but every time he looked up, he found eyes on him. Cristeane's.

"Perhaps, cousin, I should order Alexander to kiss me as well. I would hate to think that I went to marriage untutored. If he got you to moan, perhaps I will learn a thing or two."

"If ye order me to do so, I will try." Alexander answered. He couldn't look over at Geneva, else Cristeane might realize her cousin wasn't quite the inexperience virgin she thought. He swore he could feel her eyes burning into him, though.

"Here, now." Cristeane pointed to the ground in front of her.

"I see being demanding runs in the family," he muttered under his breath only loud enough for the cart driver to hear. Standing in front of Cristeane, he leaned over and kissed her.

Not a few moments later, she pulled away. "Mary, mother of God. Geneva, you are inexperienced if you found that exciting enough to moan about. Where is Caitriona? I have to go wash now that the man slobbered all over me."

She had vanished through the door before Alexander started laughing. Looking over his shoulder, he found Geneva watching him. Her expression was statue like. He'd probably just ripped her heart out, was all he could think.

The cart driver watched him for a minute before he realized what he had done. "Ye are a devil, aren't ye?"

"I guess I just need the proper inspiration to perform to my best and 'here now' doesn't do it," Alexander replied, looking quite innocent.

"That witch is a beautiful woman. What kind of inspiration do you need?" the cart driver asked as he pulled another sack off.

Bless the man, he gave him a perfect opening. "To hear a little quiver in her breath like she can't wait to taste me. To see a woman's eyes grow heavy with want when she looks at me. Then there's always the smell of her arousal, best perfume I've ever known."

"You're a handsome lad. I'm sure you have beautiful woman wanting you all the time to throw that one over so easily," the cart driver countered.

"Lusts after me, maybe. All the inspiration I need is a woman that truly hungers for me. Doesna matter what she looks like if that is there."

The cart driver rested his arms on the cart. "And just how many have you met that hunger for you more than food?"

"Only two, and my wife is dead. Only one alive that fills me with want, and it's not that witch that just ordered me around." The cart separated the two men, so the driver couldn't see Geneva's hand slide around his chest from behind. Behind him, Alexander could hear that quiver again as her hand rested over his heart. Well, he'd been forgiven at any rate. Alexander took the hand from his chest and traced her lifeline, hardly hearing the words the driver was saying. It was all they touched. He couldn't even feel her against his back. Alexander pulled her around so she was against the cart, watching him.

"That's a pretty perfume ye're wearing, Geneva. Is it French?"

Her lips twitched, trying not to smile. "Scottish, if you must know. I made it just for you."

Everyone would have seen if he kissed her, so he had to be content with putting the mound of her hand to his mouth, but even that was enough to make her breathing hitch. Then the cough made Geneva freeze. Elspeth's, if he guessed right.

"There ye are. Ye should be more careful around this old wood on the cart. That splinter was deep. I think I got it all," Alexander announced rubbing his thumb over the spot. "I never thought ye one to be scared at the sight of a little blood."

"Get that cart unloaded, Alexander. There's another task I need you for as soon as you're done."

~

A heavily wigged man that looked as if he could have been a woman from all the decoration his clothing had, stood in the drawing room when everyone entered.

"I'm so glad you dressed well tonight. I would have hated Charles to think you had gone rustic," Cristeane offered as she held out her hand as if Geneva was on a platter being offered up for dinner. "Charles was ambassador to France until recently."

Ingram froze as the sight of the man. Had he still thought he had a chance? He must have missed Elspeth looking like she'd sucked on a lemon every time he was near Geneva. He was fed and plied with whisky, but there were never negotiations, never time alone with her, not after that first time.

"Geneva, my little juniper tree, Cristeane has told me so much about you. Come sit by me and we can get to know one another," Charles offered.

"Did ye know he was coming?" Alexander murmured as she passed him.

"This one they brought for me, the others came on their own. I would have sworn I had more time." She shivered faintly in horror. The man's wig almost reached to the elbow he had crooked. His jaw and bottom lip thrust out and up, while his long nose hung down almost to meet his lip. Maybe if he had dressed somberly, it could be excused, but he wore the most fantastic bright green coat with gold breeches.

"Bring us some wine, Alexander. Charles brought some fine French stock back with him. I told him the cellar here wouldn't be up to his taste," Cristeane ordered.

"I brought some Chinese silk, too, as a gift. It's all the rage in Paris," Charles called. "Could you unload that?"

"Aunt Elspeth, I think you have something to tell Alexander," Geneva announced as Alexander started to turn. "He's here, and you've been telling me for days you mean to talk to him."

He just froze and looked at her. What did she have going through her mind now?

Elspeth fanned herself even though the room was cool. "Oh yes, of course. You've done very well with the tasks that needed tending here. I think I've given it enough time to see the sort of man you are. I'm asking if you would like to stay on for good, run things for us in our men's absence."

Somehow, as much as he wanted to get away from the Duchess he couldn't bring himself to leaving Geneva alone with all the scheming, even if he might never kiss her again. "I would be honored, Duchess. Perhaps then you can tell me about the actress in the family? It must have been so exciting to hear her stories. Did she know the King then?"

Elspeth glared at him. "Good, that will clear my mind up and I can concentrate on finding a husband for Geneva."

Alexander caught Geneva's hand clenching into a fist again as he turned to leave.

~

Coming in from checking the fish catch, Alexander found the courtyard filled with horses. "More MacKays?" he asked Hamish.

"No, sir. The Sinclair men have returned. Johne is dead, but they haven't told anyone to give them time to put their affairs in order. There's no time left. Geneva will wed."

"Aye. Anyone that belongs here in the castle?"

"Three only. When things have settled down, they have orders to find ye."

The boy was small and disheveled, seemed to be even after his bath. Alexander knew he was more observant than most thought. "Any of them likely to resent the place I have now?"

Hamish smiled. "Might have if any of them could stand Elspeth."

"Alexander, go to William the cottar's house and tell Geneva the news. She's there with his sisters while he's away." Elspeth ordered.

Alexander walked off, chuckling even though the ride would take him hours.

~

William's house was an old style crofters house, thick stone walls, thatched roof tied down with hanging rocks and the roof seeming like it was smoking from the fire within. Elspeth was right in one thing, they were barely keeping body and soul together. The two sisters in question were twin girls, perhaps sixteen. They would soon marry and William would replace sisters with a wife of his own.

Geneva's head flew up from the embroidery in her lap. By the looks of the work, there was the suggestion that marriage was sooner for the girls than later. Geneva only stared at him for a moment. "Johne is dead?"

Alexander could only nod, and her gaze fell to the window.

"You promised," Maire protested, "you would help us finish, and it's far too late to head back."

"She is right," Alexander agreed as the last of the light faded from sight. It would be Geneva's last night of freedom. Sitting there by the fire, she reminded him of his wife Mairaid. Only she had no one pulling strings, her heart was her own to give.

"Is there enough food for supper for an extra mouth?" Geneva finally asked, still not looking at him.

"Jamie brought by several fish from his haul today. If Alexander would like to get them ready while we keep working, there will be plenty."

"So Jamie would be?" Alexander asked and watched one of the girls blush. Geneva only laughed, giving all the answer he needed.

~

Alexander lay by the fire after the women retired to the only other room. He was sound asleep quickly, at least until he felt a very female form cup herself in the curve of his body. The fire still burned high. The twins would be able to see very clearly if they looked out, even more, the door stood open.

"There are two girls ten feet away."

"They'll turn a blind eye."

The quiver of anticipation in her breathing was strong enough it made him rise just at the sound of it. "Then ye aren't here for a kiss or two."

"I'll lay with the man I want while I have the chance."

He couldn't keep his hand from running up her thigh, pulling the shift up and leaving her open to view. She shivered as fingers grazed her stomach lightly, barely brushing the hairs there. "Is that truly what ye want?"

"Knew it the day you asked what I wanted when no one else had."

"I was hoping ye'd say that." Without warning, he put a hand on her stomach while he slid in from behind. Geneva's mouth opened in surprise but she covered it before any sound could escape.

"You might have warned me," she said, trying not to laugh.

"That quiver in your breathing would have given ye away if I had."

He explored every inch of her with fleeting touch. Barely there, teasing at the back of her knees, the juncture of her hips, the underside of her breasts, the long slope of her neck. His fingers left a trail of heat at every touch. There was no hurry, even though he was already inside her. Alexander gently slid his hand down her stomach. Her face slackened at his first touch. With a grin, Alexander kissed her ear.

"I've wanted to feel love, that's all, and I've wanted it from you," she finally whispered.

A touch like the wings of a butterfly as he kissed her cheek, Geneva opened her eyes staring straight into the fire. "I could get used to this," Geneva murmured just when Alexander didn't think she had a solid bone left in her body.

"My wife used to think herself lucky. Long winter nights with no money to spend, ye take your pleasure where ye can get it. She was a very enjoyable pleasure."

"Is that why you left? Why you weren't there when they died?"

"Aye. A child on the way and no money. I took a job as a soldier to keep them fed. I was no farmer, it seemed."

"Is this when you tell me I'm a very enjoyable pleasure?"

"That ye are. One I could get used to, given the chance." The only noise in the room was her stifled moans as he assaulted her from both directions.

Slowly with no hurry, he began moving in unison with his hand. Enough she was constantly on the edge but never enough to send her over. Time stood still except that the fire burned lower. Those twins would be well asleep, and it was only when he could hear snoring from the other room that he thrust faster.

When the first waves of her climax started to ripple through her, Alexander rolled her to her stomach and thrust quickly. The end hit her hard, wave after wave even after Alexander had released his seed. When he felt the last one flash through her body, he lay down next to her pulling her back into his arms.

"Sleep well," he whispered, seeing her eyes half-asleep already.

~

When the door flew open, Alexander lay by the fire alone. Geneva was smart enough to have left him at some point in the night and gone back to bed.

"Where the hell were ye?" Ingram yelled.

"Don't suppose ye noticed what time it was when Elspeth sent me. It was pitch black when I got here as it was."

"Don't think very much of me as a possible wife do you, Ingram?" Geneva snapped as she emerged from the other room. "You think he should have tried to kill me to get me back? Now that it's light, I have a cousin to mourn. Are you gentlemen going to see me back?"

Geneva climbed on the back of Alexander's horse even though Ingram offered his hands to mount his.

"I'm sorry, Alex," Geneva whispered when Ingram fell behind them.

"For what? Saying ye want me? I promise I didn't mind."

She leaned back against him with a sigh. "For having to deal with Charles. He's said as much you'll be gone."

"Even more if ye end up carrying my child."

Geneva entwined her fingers in his and rested both of their hands over her stomach. "I had time before, but with Johne gone, the wedding will be soon very soon. Perhaps only days."

"I know how to deal with Charles. Not being able to touch ye again, that's what ye should be telling me sorry for."

"But I would have to admit I never want ye to again if I said that."

When Alexander started laughing, Ingram and the men who had led him there rode closer, not wanting to be left out.

~

Isabella's scream ripped through the castle walls. Most of the house was out in the courtyard, taking in a warm but windy day.

"What now?" Elspeth snapped.

"Johne is in my room. I have to make him tea." Isabella chatted quickly to no one in particular.

Cristeane growled. "Then why scream?"

"He'll be hungry, I imagine," Alexander offered without waiting for her to answer the question. "Isabella, why not make him some rabbit stew. I have some animals from William."

Geneva's mother started beaming. "Best idea I've heard in a long time. It's his favorite, you know."

"No, I don't know that. If it's his favorite, ye best get started."

Isabella wandered off, nodding to someone that wasn't there again.

"Why do you encourage the woman?" Cristeane snapped.

"Would ye prefer her down here screaming or busy with a task that will take her half the day? Ye seem to be annoyed if she's around." Alexander looked over at the door. Isabella hadn't disappeared yet. "Perhaps he would like a bottle of that wine Charles brought. That should go good with rabbit."

"Now that is just too much," Charles protested.

Alexander went back to the books that he was going over. "She seems to have been quite the hostess. Ye wouldn't want her thinking she hadn't served a guest the best she had."

"He doesn't exist," Cristeane sneered.

Alexander put a finger over his mouth. "She doesn't know that."

Cristeane stared at him for a moment, then took Charles' arm. "Come, let's go find something amusing. Everyone here seems to have become quite droll." Elspeth rushed along with them as they made a pretty exit.

~

The stable needed work, and even with three more men in the castle, that left Alexander to do it. Young Hamish helped, but young was the major word there. It wasn't as much help as Hamish claimed it would be for him to take care of the highland ponies.

"Tis a poor stable you have here. That will change once I'm in charge."

Alexander's back straightened as he recognized Charles' voice. "Then ye haven't figured out Geneva yet, have ye?" he muttered under his breath before he turned around. "I'm told it was a rather good stable until the men took all the better horses with them. Fighting has a way of changing things, or did ye forget that they all just died?"

Charles picked at his teeth as he looked at his reflection in the water trough. "Marriage has a way of changing things, too. Your services won't be needed when I take over." He smiled slimily. It had the oddest effect of making him look like he was sucking on the end of his nose. He had Elspeth's word, which was all he cared about.

"Ye only referring to the stable?"

It stopped Charles mid pick and he lowered his hand from his mouth. "You are exceedingly rude, sir, to talk about a lady such."

"To treat her like a piece of property for the sake of a house isn't rude. She deserves a hell of a lot better than ye."

Charles' chuckle rumbled through the air. "You've fallen in love with her, is that it? Noble of you to protect her from a husband so you can keep her for yourself."

Alexander held his arms out. "Now what would she even want with me?"

"Glad you see your place."

Alexander's smile was enough to make Charles squirm. There was nothing happy or joyful in that smile. "Which is why as factor here I can say it would be a mistake for this estate to ever let ye anywhere near it."

"It is the Duchess's decision."

"We can see about that. Perhaps I'll go tell Geneva about your assumptions. She was rather forceful the last time her aunt tried a stunt. Or I could just take your head off and dump ye in the sea. Ye wouldn't think any less of me, I'm just an ignorant after all."

Charles ran.

~

The guardroom of the tower seemed to be the only refuge Alexander could get after they buried the old Duke in the mausoleum in the village. Sinclairs valued family that was obvious. Fighting men all by the look of their monuments. Staring out the window, Alexander let the brisk winter gale blow the distaste for Cristeane, Charles and even the fact that Geneva was nothing more than an affair from his mind.

"Could you use a drink? You've looked like you could use one."

Alexander turned to find Geneva there, holding out a pewter cup. She was back in her peasant clothes, looking far more comfortable than she had since Cristeane arrived. "Thanks."

The whisky burned down his throat. "What can I do for ye? Ye're dressed for going out. A walk again?"

She slowly pulled his hand to her cheek. Dark from the sun and pale as the snow contrasted greatly. While his callused fingers barely brushed her skin, her hand still held his. A smile grew at her lips. "Before you ask any stupid questions, I'm letting you seduce me, what does it look like? A man that's nothing I wouldn't want anything to do with."

Alexander's chuckle rumbled in her ear. "Charles didn't tell ye of that."

"Hamish. You sold yourself short, too. I can think of quite a few reasons I'd want to keep you." Geneva closed his fingers around the knot of her laces and pulled it back. The knot came free and she slipped his finger beneath the first rung. Using his guided fingers, each rung came loose.

His tongue traced her lips until she opened for him and he plunged in. Her fingers still wrapped around his hand as he found the edge of her skirt. Alexander pulled his head back to watch her as their hands traveled up her thigh. His fingers parted the hair and slipped in. When her mouth fell open to moan, he forced his tongue back in. Alexander kissed her jaw before running a line down her chest and finding a nipple beneath the linen she still wore. With hasty fingers, Geneva pulled the tie of her shift loose and ripped it open, giving him free access. With the merest touch of his tongue, her moan filled the room.

"Please," she whispered.

Alexander slid his finger deep inside her and sucked her nipple deep in his mouth. Geneva buried her hands in his long hair and held him close, unwilling to let him pull away. The faster his fingers caressed, the harder she ground down, trying to bring him further in until she was the one to throw up his kilt and slipped him inside her. Alexander grinned as he cupped her ass and started moving her up and down. She was close, damn close, as her breathing grew shallow.

He pulled her even closer, bringing her sensitive flesh in contact with his abdomen each time she slid along him. One last deep thrust and he felt her tightening. He claimed her mouth to keep her cry from echoing through the bare stone walls of the guardroom. It was the last thought he had as he felt his own end rushing forth.

Geneva slumped against him, her head on his shoulder when he opened his eyes. "Well, that's one thing I can give ye."

She pulled back to grab her bodice discarded on the floor. She still hadn't moved from his lap as she dressed once more. Then her kiss was slow, with none of the rush of just a moment ago. The hand that ran along his chest started to shake.

"What?" he asked as his hand closed around hers to stop the quaking.

Geneva stared straight into his heart. "It seems forever ago since you asked what it is I wanted. I know. I want to marry a man that makes me feel safe. I want to marry a man that makes my stomach tighten every time I see him, makes me wet with want with only a glance. I want to marry a man that makes me feel beautiful without ever saying false words. I want you. I'm asking if you'll wed me, put an end to all this politicking going on."

Alexander only stared for a moment. "And what of Charles?"

"Will you be the one person that lets me have what I want and wed me? After all these games being played around me, I will take no man that doesn't want me. Would it be giving you what you want as well?"

Alexander narrowed his eyes, she had ignored his words completely. Something was going on still. "Aye lass, but ye didn't have to seduce me first to get me to say yes."

Geneva kissed him softly between the eyes. "Meet me in the chapel tonight after dinner. I'll be there with Pastor Declan." With that, she rose and walked out the door, but not without flipping his kilt back down, returning him to respectability. Alexander took a deep breath before the smile took hold.

~

There in the midst of the dark, blocky castle built to withstand attack, weather, and sea, soared an airy gothic chapel filled with stained glass windows. When Alexander walked in, the pastor quickly shuffled him off to the former confessional. Presbyterian now, the room was not destroyed, but sealed off during the reformation and uncovered when it was over.

"Only sin I've committed was sex out of wedlock and I'm marrying the woman," Alexander protested.

Pastor Declan looked around, even though no one was there. "Cristeane is coming with Geneva for evening mass. Not that the woman has ever been faithful in her life. I'll find a reason to keep Geneva after. Just stay in here and keep quiet."

There he was again getting a door slammed in his face.

~

"Geneva, let's get this done before anyone comes back looking for you," the pastor finally hissed, looking worried after a service that seemed to want to never end. She looked stunning in a dress that made her eyes shine like emeralds. Alexander had to get married looking like had just woken up.

~

"Tell me what Alexander was like as a child." Geneva asked Ingram when Alexander brought in papers to sign.

Ingram's eyes sparkled, perhaps not thinking he was discounted again.

"If ye're asking about me, can I tell tales, too?" Alexander countered.

"About what?" Geneva asked brightly.

"Don't you dare!" Ingram hissed.

Geneva's laugh grew devious. "Now you absolutely must."

"Are ye saying, Ingram, that ye don't want me to tell how ye asked my wife to be your mistress?"

"A bachelor and a peasant. It often happens." Elspeth replied taking the tea Bryde had brought.

Ingram was looking a little green. Geneva smiled as if she knew there was more to come. "On the day of our wedding, at the wedding feast, as a matter of fact. Offered to make me a cuckold."

Elspeth's tea ended up sprayed across the desk. "Get out of this house immediately," She cried. "Show him out, Alexander. This instant. Boys may play, but not married to my niece."

~

Ingram just glared at Alexander as he packed his things. "You had no right."

"I only told the truth. Did ye think I would let ye play ye're games only to cuckold her on your wedding day when ye saw the next woman at your wedding feast?"

Ingram shook his head. "Should have left the day I saw you here."

"Ye got fine food and drink out of it for a month. I wouldn't complain too much. Ye never had a chance, not while the Duchess is in charge."

Ingram lifted his head from his trunk. "You knew why I was here all along?

"It annoyed Elspeth to no end that a well-known king's man was in the house courting her niece. I held my tongue, but Geneva knows herself she'll marry Charles in days to keep her mother in the only house she knows. Johne is dead. When it becomes known, the MacKay's inherit and everyone gets kicked out."

"Then I'll tell the king, the MacKay's are loyal."

Alexander couldn't shake his head fast enough. "There's something going on and Geneva follows her uncle's leanings. Keep ye're tongue. If they wed, I lose my job, so I've got an interest in stopping it."

He started shaking his head again. "Suppose I should be lucky you didn't hand me my head over it. Mairaid probably told you the day you wed, didn't she?"

"Aye, she did. Ye should thank her for distracting me from the insult or I would have had your head."

Ingram started laughing as he ordered his servant to grab the trunk. "See me out." His laugh died the instant he walked out and found Elspeth glaring at him.

~

A picture stopped Alexander cold as they walked down a hall where he had never been before. The woman wore a dress of ivory embroidered in red and black, the sleeves and much of the bodice were solid black fur lined with red. Her hair covered in an elaborate headdress lavished in pearls. The only jewelry was a single ruby pendant at her neck. It was the size of a quails' egg.

"Isabella Gunn before she married. My father married her on the promise of that portrait," Geneva whispered as she followed his gaze.

"I'd swear it was ye, but she doesn't have the look in her eyes like she's ready to stab a man through the heart." His hand slipped inside her bodice and he could feel her nipple pucker at his touch. There was no knife there now. "Ye must feel safe if ye stopped carrying that little knife of yours."

"You have the only sword I need." Geneva led him in a door only feet away.

"No please, no sword references. Sounds too much like Caitriona."

Geneva turned in his arms and kissed the base of his neck. "What about plucking my womanly rose and savoring all its beauty?"

"Where did ye hear that shite?"

"Elspeth was describing the process before you came along and showed me how to kiss."

"Ye kept your tongue after hearing that?" Alexander leaned down and slipped his hand beneath her skirt. She tried not to giggle as his hand trailed up her thigh. They were face to face again when he started smiling. "Someone's rose is covered in dew."

"That sounds even worse out of your mouth than it did hers."

Alexander looked around quickly, they weren't in a bedroom. "Go hop up on the table and I'll lick the dew away until the rose unfurls. My first wife always begged for a little gardening. I'm sure ye'll enjoy it, too."

Geneva put her hands over her ears. "No more flower comments, please."

"My tongue will be too busy, but when I'm done, I promise." With only a finger and a grin, he pushed her over to the table and lifted her onto it.

Geneva leaned back on her elbows as Alexander pushed her skirts above her waist. His thumb slid over her mound as he stood between her legs. "Ye don't look like ye've regretted wedding me."

Geneva had to drag her eyes open. "Suppose I'll have to repay the favor, else you'll regret saying yes."

"Have practice at that, do ye?"

"Was trying not to get with child the last time. It comes in handy."

"And your boy wasn't willing to show his appreciation. No wonder ye got rid of him." Alexander pulled over a stool and, before she could correct his words, he licked the first of the wetness from her thigh, each time moving closer to her center. She was watching him as he moved towards her center. But with a grin, he moved to her other thigh and started the process over. Only when he saw her eyes had closed did he start at the very bottom of her slit and slowly run his tongue up. As if he was taking the dew off the petals of a rose, he moved slowly closer to the center each time.

"Alexander, I think I'm going to owe you after this."

"This is nothing." He parted her thighs wide, rubbing his thumb over the very spot he had been missing before he parted her wide. She just lay there, watching him as he thrust his tongue slowly in, her hips rose to bring him deeper.

"Geneva!" came Cristeane's call from the hall outside. "Charles wishes to hear you sing."

"I don't sing, never have," Geneva growled.

"Shhh," Alexander murmured before he moved further up and took her in his mouth. She shoved her sleeve in her mouth to bit off the cry that came. It didn't take long once he started and Geneva bucked. Once the first wave passed, she tried to sit up, but Alexander refused to let her. Another wave came quickly, and another.

Finally, he stopped with a smile. "Ye can repay me some other time. Ye shouldn't feel like taking their heads off anytime soon after that."

~

Elspeth's smile when Geneva walked in the room was enough to make her stop. The end had come.

"Get a good night's sleep. You marry in the morning."

"I have no dress yet. Maire and Iona have just a few more days left to embroider. Let me have the dress. I refuse to let them work so hard on it and then not use it."

"Oh, Aunt Elspeth, I thought it was finished," Cristeane argued. "It is the most beautiful thing even if peasants did the work. She has to have her dress."

Elspeth stared for a moment before she nodded. "If it's not done in two days, you marry with nothing on. Charles doesn't look as if he would mind."

Geneva's hand clenched behind her back once more.

~

The flash of red hair caught Alexander's eye as he looked out into the courtyard. A moment later, Charles went running after Isabella. Isabella's scream filled the air as Alexander ran around the corner. Charles was standing frozen into place while a green ghostly figure held a sword at his throat.

"Alexander, help me," Charles hissed.

Frankly, the sight made the hair on his own arms stand on end. Alexander walked slowly by, but the apparition paid him no mind. He just caught the last of Isabella disappear into the chapel. Peeking inside, he found her sitting in a pew looking like a disheveled child waiting to get caught.

She spun around guiltily. "Geneva will hate to marry that man. Charles is an evil one." She looked down at her dress and picked at a frayed spot. "I had hoped she would marry you."

"Why would ye say that?"

Isabella leaned near his ear. "I saw you in the library. I was getting a book for Johne."

"The library?"

Isabella turned as red as Geneva had gotten that first time they went for a walk. How alike they must have been at one time. "The flower unfurling," she whispered.

Alexander tried not to laugh. He wasn't even sure he would have recognized the room if he had seen it again without her giving name to it. He'd been more than a little distracted.

"She looked so happy, happier than I've ever seen her."

Opening his eyes, Alexander couldn't help but look closely at the woman. She didn't sound quite as out of it as she usually did. Was she actually in one of her rare moments of waking to the present?

"Don't worry. I think Geneva will find a way to get out of it. I don't think she wants to marry Charles, either."

A great smile broke Isabella's face, as he had never seen from her before. "Ahh, Johne will help her, then. They were always great friends."

Alexander took a deep breath in preparation. "Johne is dead Isabella." There was no scream, though.

"I know, but I see him in my room still. I see him and Geneva talking often. He keeps James awake to all hours telling him stories. They are going to make Fergus mad and he'll hit me again."

"I need to go. Ye'll be all right?"

"Tomorrow as she weds, I cry that my daughter will not be happy. But the ghost will keep me safe when I tell Charles what I think. So yes, I will be all right." Isabella patted him on the leg before she turned and nodded as if there was someone else next to her she had to listen to.

Alexander looked back from the door, wishing Geneva had heard those words, for once knowing that her mother did care for her at least as much as she did for her children that didn't exist. Charles still stood in the hall, even though there was no sign of the ghost. It distinctly looked like Charles had wet himself as Alexander passed.

~

It was the wedding day and still nothing had been said about a prior marriage. When he saw her as the dress was delivered, she bowed her head briefly as if it would be all right but nothing more. The banging on the gate brought Alexander from the kitchen. Opening the through door, he found himself face to face with a very well-armed group of men. Looking past them, he could count some fifty that surrounded a coach.

"Yes?"

"The Lady Ravensgard is here. Open up."

"And why should I do that?"

"Hospitality for a relation."

Alexander didn't want to come out and say that he was the only man over twenty in sight or let fifty men in to find the truth. "The house is in mourning. We aren't prepared for hospitality right now."

One man ran to the coach and after a few words, a woman emerged, walking purposefully to the door. She wore a dress of fine silk plaid, a bright red set that complemented her dark hair.

"What was that banging, Alexander?" Elspeth asked, emerging from Geneva's room where they were hard at work preparing her for her vows.

"The Lady Ravensgard is here asking for hospitality."

"Mary Forbes. What on earth is she doing here?" Elspeth hissed, rushing to the door.

Mary smiled sweetly. "Not so in mourning as he made out, I see." There was nothing sweet about the words out of her mouth. There was no denying the bright sage green gown Elspeth wore with no hint of black in sight. "It's Mary Sinclair, though, I'm afraid you're the dowager duchess now. I'm here to see Johne."

"We had word he was dead." Elspeth whispered.

"I see you're mourning him well, but he left my bed a month ago quite alive with me carrying his child. Now I'll see him."

Elspeth was as green as her dress. "Alive?" she stammered as Charles and Cristeane emerged.

"Aye, Mother." A voice rang out from behind them. " Quite alive and listening to all your scheming. I needed proof for you putting my own father to death along with most of my kin."

Slowly Elspeth turned to the man standing across the courtyard. Isabella stood at his side and everyone knew the rants were truth. He had been there for her to cook for, hiding in the one place no one would believe if a word was said.

"Why aren't you dead?" Elspeth whispered as Johne walked closer. He was an immense man standing near six and a half feet, the dark one of the family with hair as black as night.

"We stopped so I might marry first and then father continued on. One man wouldn't change the fight any. A week of marriage and I'm roused out of bed with news that all but thirty of more than two hundred men that left me only days before were dead. More disturbing was the news they hadn't even made it to your family. All this because you couldn't stand me marrying anyone that wouldn't forward the Stewart return to the throne."

"What proof do you have I killed Braden? It's an outrage," Elspeth screamed.

Geneva appeared at Johne's side, holding up a piece of paper.

The green of Elspeth's face was replaced with a sickly white as all the blood drained from it. "You were working against me?"

"No one comes to visit you but family. Whom did you have to impress with a hunting preserve for entertainment? But I would imagine a relative that was king who was grateful for you securing him a chunk of land in the midst of a king's stronghold, well, you would want to impress him. Of course, there was an even more devious plan I've considered. After I was out of the way with several heirs, there would be all this land to give away and even women desperate for men. Would they care the name of them if you gave your word? I suspected something was going on even before Johne came back telling me all. Doesn't really matter which guess is correct. We know you prepared the massacre of the Sinclair's."

The men outside were suddenly surrounding Elspeth. "Don't forget her niece. She isn't just here for the hospitality," Geneva added.

"You're just in time, then. You can give away the bride. It is your cousin's wedding day," Charles offered with a big smile as if he was blameless in all of the mess.

"I gave her permission to wed who she wished two weeks ago. I might have been out of sight, but I witnessed them myself. Shall I have you taken into custody for bigamy while they are here if you continue?"

Charles slid out of sight as Elspeth spun around even with the men holding onto her. "What!!!" Alexander felt Elspeth's eyes bore into him as if she could carry out with them what she couldn't with her hands even before he felt Geneva's hand slide around from behind.

"Good Lord, Geneva, you can't have married him. The man can't even kiss," Cristeane cried.

"No, I was smart enough to marry a man that knows how to run off women he's not interested in," Geneva answered. "He was married for several years. Do you think his wife would let him drool all over her without correcting the matter, not that she had to. Have you ever thought he just wasn't interested in you?"

Cristeane's jaw dropped as the men took her away.

"Can you forgive me for keeping secrets from you?" Geneva whispered, her forehead resting against his back.

"Ye found out he was here the day we wed?"

"Aye."

"Then ye got what ye wanted?"

"Aye, but I want to know that my lies haven't changed that you want me, too."

He pulled her around to face him and heard that quiver to her breath as he backed her against a wall. "I want," he whispered putting a hand on one side of her head, "to pull that wedding dress off of ye." A hand on the other side of her head. "I want to hear ye cry out the way ye haven't been able to with us sneaking around." He nipped at her neck, but there was no yelp this time. "Ye wouldn't have threatened your mother with eviction if something hadn't changed. Might not have known the dead would come back to life, but I knew ye were up to something." When he raised his head to look her in the eyes, a smirk spoke before he did. "If ye want me to pretend some slight, though, I'm sure I can find a way or two for ye to make it up to me."

Geneva started smiling. She never took her eyes from Alexander as she called out, "Cousin, it's time I had a wedding night with my husband. You'll have to settle in yourself. Nice to meet you, Mary."

"When you're done with him, bring him to me. The four of us have a castle to get back on its feet," Johne ordered with a grin.

"Next week maybe," Alexander called as he lifted Geneva off her feet.

The courtyard was filled with laughter, Caitriona's.

~

"Is Isabella's painting still around?" Ayda asked as soon as she knew David was done.

Hunter could only laugh. "It's moved from the hall, but yes."

"You really should put all of the family paintings together in one room. The great hall or the ballroom, perhaps?" Ayda offered.

David nodded his head. "Now I'm sure your mother is wondering where I am. I just said I was looking for a hanger to put my suit on."

CHAPTER 6

With the post arriving a day later, her chalice search really took off. Not that she learned much or quickly, but slowly the pieces started to form. The original patent for the title was perhaps the most intriguing. Alasdair was a third son, of the main Sinclair family and in 1179 he was granted the title Lord of Wrathe. The original piece of land was from William II for establishing a castle to keep the Norse at bay. But the crest on the cup was Norse. It couldn't be!

What was Wrathe in the terms of anything? The original inhabitants dating back to the 1st century called the property Bad A'cheo. Place of the Mist an apt name with the mist hanging around the castle as if it was floating in space. A few early records remained, the income was nominal, its tenants numbered maybe 20 farms and a mill, Pictish descent by their names. 1182 was the date the castle started upon the foundations of the earlier Viking tower, but there were several brochs not far away that perhaps said there were other people at one time. No one seemed to know much of all but a few names until 1328 when the title Duke of Cairnmuir was granted and then things were well documented. Wives were missing, or only a first name known. After all the details for the Sinclairs, Ayda was a little put out that the name of a wife was omitted. One statement in the family history that was known stuck 'married well among them'. Married well with a gold cup to mark the occasion and a

Norwegian title. The marriage had to be a high ranking woman of...?

A few days later Rowanne confirmed the Chalice's age as 1100's, perhaps as early as 1090's. It was certainly Viking, and the crest that of the King of the Orkney's. The idea that it was from a marriage held up too, seeing as the Sinclair crest dated much later. Added to an existing cup, it wasn't created special for the occasion. What it meant was Hunter's assertion that it was a legend was about right, there wasn't much proof that the chalice meant anything certain at all. Ayda sat up from reading her letters. No, it meant that the Sinclairs avenues of searching had been covered. Had anyone looked on the other side of it? The Orkney's were just a ferry ride away if there was anything there they would have found it long ago. But the Lord of the Orkney's was a Viking, a Norsemen. Ayda started sending emails not to Scotland, but Scandinavia.

~

With a mission to restore some older parts of the castle, Hunter had researched the castle indeed just as Mrs. Sinclair had said. Ayda had already seen all those records though, Hunter had handed them over some time ago. Each room had been ranked as to its need of repair. He hadn't written down names, to Ayda's regret. It was only a record of dates and condition, not so and so Sinclair married so and so another clan and the dowry built this wing, redid the room, bought this furniture and paintings. Perhaps there was the reason for the stories Mary and the others told. It gave a face to the often dry stories of lineage and finance. It turned the list of arranged marriages into the start of a romance at least, in some cases even more. The ghost, proof that not all stories were so picturesque, no one made up stories for how Seonaid and Eoin met, how she was beaten to death with her child... Ayda focused on the job at hand again. The idea of that story was too depressing, too dark.

"A fire in 1608 took the east wing," Hunter mentioned as they wrestled a painting ten feet tall back into place. The great hall was a huge room, with soaring stone walls and giant beams that ran across the ceiling, each holding a huge wrought iron chandelier. The table was of an old style with the ends far across the room from one another. It was one of the few rooms to resist renovation. "That's when all the family apartments were moved to that side. It's primitive by today's standards, but it was built to the height of sanitary beliefs for the time. Personally, I think it was the wife's excuse for completely remodeling. There isn't much left of the décor from before that. I suppose it's a good thing she enjoyed herself, since there was a marriage arranged just after the fire, I would imagine for a dowry to rebuild."

For most of the castle, however, opening a door was like opening a tiny time capsule into the taste of some former owner. The old dungeon was little more than a hole into a cavern under one of the walls. No one had been in there since the 1820s when the castle had caught some smugglers off the coast. The chapel reflected a time six hundred years earlier. There in the midst of the dark, blocky castle built to withstand attack, weather, and sea soared an airy gothic chapel filled with stained glass windows. When the sun shone, the floor danced with brilliant colors. Billiards were in a room filled with hunting trophies, not all as local as the Highland stag and dozens of reminders of the Sinclair penchant for the military. Each room explored for paintings to be catalogued, cleaned, rearranged. All family portraits being moved to the great hall.

"All right then, come on," Hunter announced when it was in place.

"Where?"

"Edinburgh. You said you needed clothes and I have some business to take care of."

Ayda looked around at the chaos. "Take a vehicle we can haul some things in, then. I have some paintings to take down there. Charlie, these three are small enough to hang yourself, they go over on the east wall. The Scottish gentleman can go to the entryway in place of the one we took down. The rest go to the workroom. Mrs. Sinclair had mentioned guests coming later. There may be some spaces on the walls, but at least we can clean up the mess."

Charlie just grinned. "Yes, ma'am."

~

As the sea disappeared behind them, Ayda kept glancing over at Hunter. "Are you short on money? I'll know how hard to push when I take these in."

"What brought that up?"

She turned red at the thought of actually saying it out loud. "How many owners of these old castles and estate can't afford to keep them up? Rich in property, poor in cash. I know how much death duties used to be. You're selling paintings to do restoration work, aren't you? To pay for the building of this distillery you're busy with. You already rent out the castle for people to tramp around your house."

His laugh filled the Land Rover. "We invested heavily in the North Sea oil business in its infancy. We have more money than we really know what to do with. There was a shipping heiress 150 years ago that pretty much ended any money troubles the family had in the past. We've used that to kept it growing ever since. And we rather missed out on the death taxes."

"How?"

"My great grandfather it seemed had turned it over to his son, Lorne, when they made the announcement that soldiers were exempt from death duties. So when

Lorne died in the war and it went to my grandfather, his younger brother, it came free. He was in his 20's then, only died a few years ago so he missed out on the 65% it was at one time. We have paid it, but missed out on the death knell taxes that have destroyed houses."

"Then why did you explain it the way you did? You made it sound like you had to sell the paintings for the money."

"Suppose I did." He tapped his fingers for a moment on the steering wheel. "All right, I think this will explain it better. At the time my grandfather died there was no reason to worry about money. But the North Sea Oil fields have hit their peak. The barrels a year put out has been going down since 1999. The village relies heavily on those platforms for income. Town is the closest place for supplies for two or three of the rigs. On leave they come in and drink, eat, stay in the inn. The lower production has already hit here. The shipping warehouse folded a long time ago and we lost those jobs which weren't many, the building still sits empty. The only real thing left is tourism, a few day trip buses from Inverness a month is about all, the festival coming up is the only big thing in the area. Preserving Gaelic culture and arts, but it's one long weekend a year, nothing that keeps people with enough to live well. So I opened a wing of the castle up for events, weddings, fishing, shooting, etc. It pays the keep for that wing plus a bit more and gives jobs to the town. I'm overseeing the building of an aquaculture sector to try to take up some of the slack. That trip to Fort William and the whisky distillery will mean export and jobs. Managed wisely, the money we do have can be spread to support everything it needs to without us going into ruin for generations, but when I see a chance to not spend, I try. Perhaps if I don't have to take funds out of the bank to pay for the restoration work in the main castle there will be another use for it that will create more jobs like building the distillery and the aquaculture. We're in the middle of nowhere like you pointed out it's not easy to keep money coming in."

"Sounds to me like the lord of the castle still sees to his clan even if they aren't bound to him anymore."

Hunter looked out the side window but Ayda caught the smile before it was out of sight. "Not many care to hear of it. I have a title, so I must go to Ascot, have tea with the queen, and shoot things."

Ayda smiled at the back of his head. "You forgot charm women into your beds, vacation in Monte Carlo, and gamble a fortune on every game."

"Don't get me started on what I think of trust fund kids."

Ayda stuck her tongue out just as he turned back to catch her.

"Don't stick that out unless you're prepared to use it."

She narrowed her eyes. There were times she wasn't so sure the flirting was a game, there were times she had to wonder if he really meant it. He wasn't doing anything, but it must have been all the flirting, because she definitely noticed him a lot more than she had any man in some time. What worried her most was she was entirely prepared to use more than her tongue if she thought it wasn't all a joke.

~

Hunter left her at the art dealer's while he took care of his own business. After about two hours of conversation under the watchful gaze of Edinburgh castle, he returned, and Ayda handed over a check for more than fifty thousand pounds. "The others are far more valuable, we'll need to set up an auction to get you their full value."

There they stood in the middle of the Royal Mile, but she doubted any of the tourists walking past had the money on them they did now. Hunter raised his head from the check, eyes rather wide with surprise. Why did having him stare at her with those big blue eyes make her want him to lean over and kiss her? Have him show that she wasn't just making a fool of herself and kissing a man that wasn't interested. Kiss, hell, she wanted him to do a lot more than that.

"I take it I've underestimated how much is hanging on the walls at home. This was twelve paintings."

"Probably. I have counted at least several hundred that are easily a hundred thousand pounds apiece. A dozen or more that are possibly a million, but the prize are the modern paintings, that collection some 1920's duchess bought on her way to some island those 30 alone are I could hardly guess. The rest are nice but not of that quality. In sheer numbers, let's just say the rest will go for ballpark ten thousand apiece, and I'm sure many are more than that. Just selling off the extra - well, you get the idea."

He looked down at the check once more. "I'll buy what you need. Where do you want to go?"

The smile returned. "You tell me. How formal are family gatherings at home?"

"Don't let Broderick's girlfriend hear you say that. She's a fashion designer, and father will surely point out the Countess Baiyle. Only formal will do."

"Oh god I'll never fit in."

Hunter started laughing. "Just remember the designer part, she was a bar maid to put herself through school, worked downstairs of Brodie's flat while he's in school for Marine biology. I knew her for several years before I knew about her title. It's all but defunct, father cares though." Hunter stared at the display when his cell phone rang.

"Matt?" He answered. "What are you calling for, aren't you out in Pacific somewhere?" He listened for a moment. "No I'm in Edinburgh. I had some business to take care of, I'm down with an art restorationist helping cull the paintings in the castle." He started grinning. "No you can come have dinner with us, maybe we can talk her into an orgy, she blushed when she heard about the family's pastime on occasion."

Ayda narrowed her eyes at him and his grin only got wider.

"She has to find something to wear for the engagement though, no one told her she'd need formal wear, see you at...how about the usual and you can tell me this big secret. I take it this means you aren't coming to the engagement or you'd tell then."

Hunter shook his head. "Yeah at 8. I'll call and make sure they have a table."

"You always offer up a woman for orgies?" Ayda snapped.

Hunter didn't rise to the bait. "He's supposed to be on..." He wandered off looking worried.

~

While shopping for the perfect dress, it wasn't to impress Hunter oddly enough. She was worried what Mrs. Sinclair would think. She was worried what an 87-year-old woman would think instead of a hot gorgeous man she had kissed more than once. Something about the way he talked she was worried. He wasn't flirting for one thing.

"Hunter who is coming to dinner?"

"Matt Dunham. Commodore, he's supposed to be on a ship out at sea. He's been out there for months. The fact he's here at all means something is up."

"And?"

"His surprises usually mean you need to worry. I wouldn't serve you up for an orgy until I've at least grown tired of you and that means you have to grant me a first night to get the ball rolling." Well he had heard her. He just looked up a number and dialed.

"Mind if I pick out something for dinner tonight, if I suddenly have two handsome military men to take me to dinner, I'm not wearing jeans."

"Sure." He said distracted.

Ayda turned to the shop keeper with a grin.

~

They were early to the restaurant and she excused herself to the restroom to change. She had clothes that weren't dowdy and ready to slog through dust and filth, a castle on the edge of the North Sea she really hadn't thought there would be a need. The shop keeper was more than helpful. Everything needed was purchased when she walked out. She could see Hunter talking to someone when she came out, his words died in his throat when she stepped into view. It was a lace sheath that hugged everything, see through to a point. She wouldn't get arrested for indecent exposure, but there was clearly skin and nothing else underneath silvery black hematite lace. Ayda knew how to stop a room when she wanted to. The man with Hunter turned and froze. He was gorgeous.

"You said art restorationist, I expected some 60 year old woman with glasses for some reason." He murmured as he stood like few gentlemen did anymore when a woman came to the table.

"Lord Matthew Dunham, this is Ayda Rogers. She's come to finish her doctoral thesis on the family collection, would that not give you the impression of grandmother?"

Ayda shook his hand, but his eyes had trouble not wandering. "I heard Hunter say you were supposed to be on a ship, I couldn't very well show up in jeans now could I?"

Matt started laughing.

"Does that mean you'll actually tell me what this secret is then?" Hunter asked.

Matt sat back down and poured her a drink from a bottle of whiskey. He stared at his own for a moment. "I was accepted into the SBS. I report in a week, I wanted to come tell someone. I need you to keep it secret that's where I am though."

Hunter looked up slowly. "Sure you did this just so you wouldn't have to face my sister?"

"That's low. There's something you don't know about that whole deal and I'm not bringing it up now."

"What's the SBS?" Ayda whispered.

"Special Boat Service. It's special forces."

"You mean like Navy Seals."

Matt nodded. "Same idea, yes."

"Then why not tell anyone?"

Hunter took a long drink of whiskey. "Ayda maybe I should mention Matt is one of the richest families in the world; Dunhams, Trowbridge Shipping, Shipbuilders, but not the playboy one always in the news that's his brother Benedict, the Dakar Rally fanatic. He's also a damn good helicopter pilot which is how he got here. He was calling from London before."

"If you could keep that quiet Miss, I'd appreciate it. I'd hate anyone getting hurt if it got out I could fund a small country off my ransom."

Ayda put her hand over her mouth as it sank in. "Then I'm glad I chose the dress."

"Trust me so am I even if a very appreciative friend has given me one hell of a sendoff since she heard."

The waitress appeared and they ordered quickly. Matt seemed to have half the menu, lobster tagliatelle for starter, and the Sirloin for entrée, the best wine, and even a dessert.

"I..." His phone rang and he excused himself, pacing outside the room as he talked.

"Is that what you would be like if you hadn't been saddled with responsibility?" Ayda whispered.

"I don't have a billion dollars sitting there as a consolation for not being heir."

Her jaw dropped and just sort of sat there. "You're joking?"

"Him and his sister both, they've got lots of money and their father all but ignores them. He dotes on Benedict and the man is a scoundrel. The family would be far better off in the long run if Matt was heir and Benedict was out."

Matt came back and downed a drink. He was not happy.

"What's wrong?" Hunter asked.

He just shook his head. "I'm getting off topic, what will it take to get that dress off you?"

"This from the shy boy that couldn't ask a date to his senior dance." Hunter teased.

"That was a lifetime ago, in the time before that dress."

Ayda just started grinning. "Well if you hadn't said you had a very nice sendoff I might have considered taking it off and hoping I didn't spill supper, but as it is bribery might work, I have student loans to pay off." She couldn't take her eyes away from Hunter. If he asked she would pull it off then and there in the restaurant. She could easily imagine him slipping his hand beneath the tablecloth to pleasure her as they ate. That sort of dessert she could make room for.

Despite the comments about the dress, Matt wasn't obsessed with sex, before the wine had arrived he was talking about art like he was the one with the degree. Then again the family had a 500 year old country house, a massive London mansion, and they owned an island all while having more money than anyone knew what to do with. The walls were filled with art. He even offered to let her come bury her nose in the collection when she wanted a break from her slave drivers. Before she knew it Matt had begged off needing to take the helicopter back.

"Hunter?"

"Yes."

"What was that talk about him and your sister?"

He laughed faintly as they walked down the cobble stone street to work off the last of the alcohol before he drove again. "He's been in love with her since he was 10 I want to say, long time at any rate. I know they slept together, but he left for the Naval Academy when they were 18 and she married someone else before he came back. He has not been in the same room with her since she married. He always finds an excuse to beg away."

"How long has she been married?"

"Must be 6 years now. She was 21 then. Never have understood why she married Jack. She's a huge party girl, and Jack's just this stick in the mud. Never figured she'd be the first one married. Or the first with kids. She plays the perfect wife, but they fight like cats and dogs. She's the most modern woman you'll meet, and Jack wants her to be the 1960's hostess it feels like. Go flirt with that man to get my career ahead, make sure you get invited to this party I would never be able to get through the door. It's like he married the Duke's daughter rather than Isobel. If it lasts I'd be surprised, but with the kids she'll probably let it go on longer than it should." He shook his head slowly. "Her and Matt were perfect for each other and no I'm not saying that because he's filthy rich. He was shy as could be and she'd drag him out of his shell, she has a habit of getting in trouble, he always kept her in line without dragging her down to boring. They knew every fault of the other including the fact his father never gave a damn about them. Matt calls us family more than his own father. Isobel more than most, she was there for him when his mother died. Our father didn't raise us, he lives in London, when we were each about 4 he shipped us all back to the castle. Isobel spent a while here, but she begged to go back to London. She all but moved in with them after his mother died at least for a while. They came back here every break. Our grandfather raised us 3 to be who we are, Isobel was more of father's doing. I have to wonder what Matt won't say even now though. That sounded like more than just they drifted apart while he was gone, or they had a fight."

"I didn't mean to bring up, I'm sorry. I thought..."

"No, it wasn't just a one night stand and I tease him about it. You might want to keep everything you heard since Matt showed up to yourself. You'd break Isobel's heart if she knew he refuses to step in a room with her."

~

Hunter pulled up in front of a row house in the old part of town. "Well, here we are, the Sinclair family townhouse."

"If you tell me you got it as part of some woman's dowry, I'll have to decide your whole family is mercenary."

"Won it in a poker game four hundred years ago."

Ayda tried to find some hint he was joking as he opened her door for her. Tried and failed. "Really?"

"Well, maybe it was three hundred seventy-five years ago and I'd be careful what you say about mercenaries, I never did tell you how recent we hired out to fight." Finally, he looked up at her, grinning as her mouth hung open. "Actually this part of town had deteriorated and, on the condition we fix it up, we got it for free. Grandfather had a connection in the city when they were giving them away to developers trying to revitalize the area. Figured it was a good way to get some money to come in if a title would restore an old house here. It's only been ours for about fifteen years. You're looking at the last time the castle was cleaned, instead of having a rummage sale we decorated this place. And you've still seen the mess the store rooms are in."

"What am I going to do with you?" Ayda went to push him away as he helped her out of the vehicle. In that split second, Hunter's hands circled her waist, pulling her close. Only his thumbs touched her belly leaving a trail of heat through the lace as he slowly caressed.

"You're pretty good at the family tradition." Ayda whispered.

He didn't have to move his hands far and his thumbs touched the sensitive undersides of her breasts. There was a downside to not wearing a bra, horribly easy access. "Open your eyes."

He was very close when she opened them, very close as he brought his hands high enough. Her nipples gave away her secret even through the fabric. No matter what she said, she wanted him.

"I said the family tradition was flirting with beautiful women, touching them, now, that's a whole other story, and I was raised a gentleman. I would have kept my hands to myself, but I just keep getting the idea you want me to touch you. No matter how much you tell me you don't want to get distracted from your paper every time I look over you are devouring me in your head."

He was a damn mind reader. "I think we better take this inside."

He kicked the car door closed with his foot and walked her to the door without moving his hands. "The keys are in my pocket. The large silver one, or do you want me to stop?"

Those thumbs that had caressed moments before were quickly bringing her nipple to hard peaks. Ayda couldn't stop the temptation to grab hold of him as she found the keys. By the streetlight, she saw his eyes fill with want. The moment the door closed behind them, he had her against the wall, mouth covering hers. The buttons on his shirt popped off and she ripped the material from him. Her dress was off in one quick pull leaving nothing. The dress had some thicker layers of lace in strategic areas. She'd had nothing else on. It was like waving red in front of a bull. Ayda watched as a future duke hoisted her up, legs around his waist. Her head fell back with a moan when he took a nipple in his mouth. How he made it up the stairs she couldn't tell, but he lowered her onto a bed soon enough. As her legs stayed locked around him, his hands caressed her hips.

"I was watching this ass until you fell. I'd like to say I was just at the right place at the right time, but seeing it framed in the door with you stretched out on that ladder, best picture in the entire house." With her legs open, he had a view of everything. "No, I was wrong, now is."

With a grin, Ayda sat up as he took the view in. "A gentleman wouldn't leave me here while he stands there fully clothed." There was no protest as she unzipped his jeans and lowered them to the floor. Nor when she pulled his shirt off. For a moment, she could only stare at his erection. Then she put her lips to it and it bucked to life. Hunter groaned as she wrapped her lips around him. Then she felt a hand on each side of her face and he pulled her up to him.

"I've been dreaming of that ass while I was inside of you." He tilted his head slightly as if asking permission and when she nodded, he bent her forward over the bed. A heated tongue dragged across her back before he straightened up behind her. It must have been long enough for him to put on a condom, she could feel it, still cooler than the heat of the rest of him. Ayda gasped when he was suddenly inside her. Hands caressing her ass, he moved slowly as she accustomed to his size, each stroke getting a little faster. Each stroke and his breathing came ragged in her ears. Ayda couldn't move as he ran his hands down her arms, her stomach before his fingers found her ... Close already, she bit off a moan, trying not to have it over so quickly.

"Next time can be slow. Let it out," he rasped as if reading her mind. Her back arched in an instant and her cry echoed in her ears. No, it was Hunter matching her own climax. Legs a little wobbly, he picked her up and laid her down. Ayda watched him across the room, Hunter Sinclair was no spindly, pasty Brit. Well, okay, Scot. What those sedate sweaters and business suits hid was a well-muscled physique. A six-pack she still ached to run her fingers over. A stubbled chin she could all too easily imagine rasping against her thighs. And indeed two tattoos, one on each shoulder, the Sinclair crest and the RAF crest.

"How long ago did you quit the Air Force?"

"Five years ago."

Ayda walked up behind him, and before he could turn around, Ayda's hand ran along that stomach from behind. "Don't look like a soft bodied aristocrat, that's for sure."

Hunter turned and a very hard body pressed against her. Ayda ran her hands over his chest and grinned when, without much of a touch, his cock grew hard once more.

Kissing her neck, his whisper gave her goose bumps. "I like the view I had earlier, go spread your legs."

"Only if you let me reciprocate." She didn't have to say it twice. He followed as she went back to the bed. As she was lying back down on the bed, he was gone from her side. In the dark she couldn't find him until, coming from the other side of the bed, he kissed her upside down. Slowly working his way down her, each breast was paid homage before she gasped at the first flick of his tongue between her outspread legs. It took Ayda a moment to remember she had offered to reciprocate. Just as she opened her mouth to take him in he plunged his tongue in, making her gasp.

"Oh, yes!" There was only one option to make her hold out. She reached up and took his him in her mouth, the first swipe of her tongue over the tip lessened his assault. Ayda could feel his heart beat as her lips rested on the vein running his length. Using her teeth, she dragged a groan from him.

"Hunter, please" she rasped. He forgot her and slowly thrust in her mouth. Thrusting faster with each lick she gave him, he slid in and out as she urged him on. When she reached up and took him in her hands, he moaned against her. Only a few more thrusts, harder, urgent and he came in her mouth. He fought for breath as she took all he could give.

"I was dreaming of that."

Hunter crawled off her. "Well, if there's no urgency, I'll get more comfortable." He settled with his head back between her legs, his stubbled chin rough against her thigh. His tongue was gentle as he went back to work. This time Ayda knew she was going to be tortured for some time to come, what with that grin of his wide even then.

~

Hunter's arms were still around her when she woke. The only thing she could see without waking him was a painting hanging on the wall. What she had just done sank in. Her whole future hung in the balance as Brad's face stared back at her from the painting. If they fought and she got run out of the castle, she would never be able to finish her thesis. Now that she heard the townhouse was filled with the leftovers from the castle there was even more to do. She would have to find another collection to work on, wasting time to start over. Brad would have won again. Hunter stirred but didn't wake when she got out of bed. Outside she flagged a cab for the train station. She needed to ... she needed to think.

~

The storeroom was the most secluded place she could think of. And she hated to think of what hid there that she had yet to see. The insurance lists were incomplete to the point of being ridiculous. She spent five hours cataloging that one room alone. Half peeking out from behind a pile, the corner of one made her freeze. Checking the number she could see with the list in her hand, all she got for it was Venetian painting of Virgin Mary 1519, purchased for the chapel 1527. Value five thousand pounds. Ayda uncovered it carefully. No tears, no flaking, which was amazing in itself for a five hundred year old painting. Tall and narrow, it was on its side, and even then she knew it had to be a Titian. 5000 pounds my ass!! The style, the colors, the subject was very like the Assumption of the Virgin he did for the high altar of S. Maria Gloriosa dei Frari, though smaller. Ayda could see why it had been put in the storeroom, for the small chapel it was huge. Perhaps the buyer had miscalculated the size of the room, been gone for a long time and forgotten what it looked like.

"Stop it, Ayda!" she told herself. Why didn't matter. There was only one thing to do, prove it was a Titian. "Charlie!"

~

Ayda just couldn't look Hunter in the face again. That was not the way to keep good relations with the Dowager Duchess and the Duke. That was not the way to keep her mind on her doctoral thesis. Her search for the Chalice origins was enough of a distraction already. She only had to get a paper written and she was finished. No more school, and she could apply for most any job in the world she wanted. Going early to the workroom and coming out late as she threw herself into the painting she found, she managed to avoid Hunter. Cleaning the painting carefully so she could study the brush strokes, so others more expert than she could examine it properly. Not to mention pouring thorough the records, trying to find who might have been in Venice in 1527.

Coming around the corner, Ayda ran straight into Hunter, literally. His hands caught her before she could fall.

"So, do I get to find out why you're avoiding me, why you ran out the other morning?"

She hadn't realized that she had ignored him for so long. That first day, yes, to give her time to think, but had it really been days since she had found the painting? Her mouth opened to tell him all about her find, but Mrs. Sinclair's voice filled the air instead.

"Ah, here you are, Ayda. A Mrs. Lamond from the village showed up with a painting she swears is worth a fortune, and she refuses to leave until you've had a look at it. Could you please tell me what Antique Roadshow is? She keeps going on about it. She just refuses to believe we don't have a television hidden somewhere."

Hunter let go of her arm reluctantly. The look in his eyes was enough to know it wasn't over. "The BBC did it first and American public television started an American version. Experts set up in a big hall and people bring in their treasures to see if they're actually worth anything. I'll come see what she has."

~

After she had finally broken free of the Lamonds from the village, who were overjoyed to hear their painting was worth about five hundred pounds, Hunter was nowhere to be found. It was dinnertime though and despite tea in the village, her stomach was growling. Ayda headed into the dining room.

"Do I get to know the reason you're avoiding me?" Hunter asked quietly just after she had settled into a chair.

Ayda's head spun around, gold eyes narrowed, she was alone with Hunter and hadn't prepared for the meeting at all. All she could see was Brad dumping her when he got what he wanted. "So I was a little weak the other night. Should I throw away the chance to be able to finish my thesis because you decide you're sick of me after a roll in the sheets? I've worked too many years to ruin this. I found a painting, I've been busy with it. That is why I am here."

"You kissed me first. Should I be worried you'll throw me off now that you've gotten what you want." Hunter crossed his arms with a faint smile. "What if I said I was considering offering you a position here taking care of that entire collection you won't be able to finish this summer? I would have asked at dinner when we were in Edinburgh, but you kept looking at me with that gleam in your eyes. I had other things on my mind, very pleasant things. You wouldn't have to leave at the end of the summer. You would have access to all of them until you had your paper done."

"In exchange for what?"

"Oh, show a little interest in a woman and she thinks he has ulterior motives for everything. I want to make the offer for just that reason, you show more interest in the art than you do me. If we're going to bring someone in to have it done right, I want it to be someone that will appreciate it properly."

Her heart was beating in her ears, her throat, everywhere but in her chest. She couldn't let him think she was that cold hearted. "You act like this all the time, I imagine, flirting with every woman that comes to visit. I'm just an uncultured American who doesn't know the difference. I left before I started caring for more than jumping into bed with you. Before you got tired of me and sent me on my way." Her heart stopped when she felt his mouth on the curve of her neck.

"Has it occurred to you that I want to offer you the position because I would like to keep you around? Because you are an uncultured American that doesn't give a damn that I'll have a title?"

From his position behind her, he caressed her cheek, and Ayda couldn't stop herself from leaning into his touch. She was caving and she knew it. "Hunter."

He stopped, but his breath caressed her neck. "I've seen a woman that showed she belonged here more than anyone born to these walls. You sit there with my grandmother, pulling stories out of her that I never even knew existed, you act as if this is your personal museum, arranging rooms until they are perfect. I saw you up on the outer wall watching the sea and you fit. You love it here, anyone can see that. There is a but in there, Ayda. I've still wanted you since the day I first saw you. I want you to stay regardless, but I'm not going to be able to ignore that I want you to stay for reasons that are more selfish as well."

"Supper." Mary announced as she pushed open the door from the kitchen.

"I have to think about it. Any job offer has to be duly considered." She didn't want to make it sound so businesslike, not when her heart was telling her just to turn her head and his mouth would be on hers. Her head was telling her flings ended one day.

~

For once in her life, Ayda couldn't concentrate on paintings. For trying to leave the distraction behind, she was doing a poor job of it. Everywhere she looked Hunter was there. Ayda stalled leaving her room by checking emails. Three jumped out at her among the everyday ones. Three places she had asked about the Lord of the Orkney's. Opening up each one, two said nothing more than please send a research fee and we will look into it for you. Copies extra. The third though ...

Dear Miss Rogers,

Attached you will find the family history for the title Lord of the Orkney's. It was the closest I could find to answer your question.

That's all it said, nothing more. Ayda opened the file to literally find a picture of 900-year-old documents. Someone had taken the time to document and catalog it, but not for her. The quality was far too good for a person with a digital camera. A program to keep the ancient documents safe then? Photographed and then put into permanent storage for only real scholars to see. If it was all computerized it would have taken only moments for the person who answered to have put in a search, found the relevant photos and sent a reply. Hurray for technology. Even with her artists' eyes, she still had to blow the photo up to 300% before she could read the ancient lettering. Then it was only a matter of finding a date close to the right time frame. 1183 jumped out at her. The rest though she had to decipher by IM'ing Rowanne, besides medieval history, the woman could speak something like 4 or 5 languages. Or was it 6.

Ayda grabbed the laptop and ran down to Hunter's room to no answer. Only then did she remember he was out visiting a distillery in Wick. She headed to David's office instead, she had to tell someone.

"Can I interrupt?"

"Of course." He said pushing away from the massive desk. "Leaving things to Hunter, it's all busy work anyway. Requests for art restorers to come up for our summers and that sort of thing." He was grinning at his little joke the way Hunter did. It was an odd statement though considering that Elise had said he didn't even live there. Not to mention Hunter was annoyed with him it seemed.

"I've gotten a little caught up in your mystery. I think I have an answer for you."

He knit his eyebrows together, maybe Hunter hadn't told him she even knew of the Chalice. "What mystery is that?"

"How your golden Chalice came into the family." Ayda waited for some sort of acknowledgement but the excitement got to her. "Jamison mentioned it when I went to Fort William with Hunter during your trip. He showed it to me, and ..."

"It was a marriage."

That stopped her cold. "Hunter said no one knew."

David laughed. "Everything was a marriage. If we have a French gothic chapel it's a French marriage, etc."

"But I know who. I can tell you her name, I think I can even guess a lot more."

That made David Sinclair, 35th Duke of Cairnmuir raise an eyebrow. "Can you now?"

Ayda went around the desk and opened her laptop back up. "I went about it like I assume you all have, going through the Scottish records. But that didn't give me anything more than what you already know about the Sinclairs themselves, since about 1328 when the Dukedom was conferred. I sent pictures of the cup to a friend though, and the crest on the cup belonged to the Lord of the Orkney's. Viking kings. I sent some emails to Scandinavian archives. And one got back to me with this." Ayda pointed to the date that she had of 1183.

"Aye that's about the right date, but I don't read ancient Norse."

Ayda read the transcript of the IM she'd gotten, "Eyja youngest daughter of Lord of the Orkney's given in marriage to Alasdair Sanclar. From what I've seen Alasdair was given Wrathe to build a castle here to keep the Norse at bay, and a title Lord 1179. Then he's marrying essentially a Norse princess. Lord's were kings practically at that point at least for the Norse rulers. But look right here there's one more sentence. Fulfilling the agreement with William the 2nd Rex Scottorum. They married the problem out instead of fighting for it. Alasdair is made Lord, married to some 15 year old girl when he's not much older. This is centuries before the main Sinclairs are made the Earls of Caithness and it became Scottish, but next to Caithness is a firm Scottish presence at peace with the Norse. A marriage would keep that safe especially when they are fighting England about that time, William had to give up Northumbria. Her father was Lord of the Orkney's, her cousin King of Norway and another King of Denmark. I've heard it said that you were given the Dukedom because they were worried about the family getting uppity and trying to claim more power. You never had a blood claim to the throne, but you had a power claim. The old king put you here to be the link to the Norse and from what I've seen a number of the wives I can track down after her aren't all good Scottish families back then, they're all rivals to the crown. It's half and half. When Balliol forfeit the castle from you while he was in power within a few generations before the Lord of Wrathe at the time had connections to just about the whole of the northern highlands and islands. If he'd just stepped up and gathered them all together it could have been another true kingdom without a war. I think it worked better than had been hoped. There was peace with the Norse, but there was a new threat when it came to Scots. Until the Bruce said you deserve recognition and had you swear loyalty to him, you really could have taken over."

David sat back in his chair. "The books have always said we married among them well, a princess would certainly explain the ties we have even now. If you want to start telling the story though Mary won't let you off unless you embellish it."

"I'm not writing a romance novel. I promised Hunter."

The Duke laughed heartily. "Mary likes details to flesh out her stories. I think you'll find them now that you have a name to search for. Me I guess I'll have to write the people that write all the clan books and make them change things."

CHAPTER 7

Setting a picture right after hanging it, the hand on her shoulder made her jump. Expecting it was Hunter wanting an answer, she spun around, but it was Mrs. Sinclair.

"Come with me, dear."

"Not another antique appraisal, I hope."

Elise smiled faintly as she led Ayda to a sitting room with ivory silk walls and teak furniture covered with sage green brocade. She had been there several times in her rearranging, but had never just sat there. Calm and quiet came to mind, so she had filled it with impressionist paintings of nature. Slowly Elise lowered herself in a chair, her gaze making Ayda uncomfortable, but there was no leaving.

"A long time ago, I washed upon the shore of this castle, trusting no one, and on the run. I haven't been able to wear it in some time, but I think you have need of it as much as I do."

Ayda raised her head to find those piercing blue eyes staring into her soul. She'd never realized they were Hunter's eyes. In Elise's hand lay a large emerald surrounded by diamonds, held in the most gorgeous art deco setting Ayda had ever seen. "Did Hunter tell you to speak to me?"

Elise started laughing. "Oh, god no, the boy would be furious with me if he knew we had this chat."

Why was she having trouble getting her heart to calm down? "But you know?"

"It wasn't hard to notice you left for Edinburgh together and came back separately. What did you do that took the sparkle out of his eyes?"

The tears threatened to fall down her cheeks, and she closed her eyes trying to stop them. "I left him asleep without a word. Do you know how many years I've spent getting to where I am now? It's too easy to fall for him, too easy to get distracted."

Elise took Ayda's hand and placed the ring in it. "Broderick put this ring on my finger to save my life, and it brought me back. Granted I was returning it, but I never would have found out he never meant for me to take it off by the time I left. Let it bring you back here. Now might not be the right time, but let it bring you back when it is."

Finally, the tears slipped down her cheeks. "I can't take this. Your children, your grandchildren, your great-grandchildren will want this to stay in the family."

"Who said it won't stay in the family? I've not seen him like this before with any woman. And you my dear aren't tearing yourself apart over a chance night with him."

"What if it's too much?" Ayda whispered, forcing the words out.

"You mean like Duncan's mother? Oh, child." Elise closed Ayda's fingers around the ring. "No one's asking you to give up your dreams. Alice never knew what she wanted, there is no forgiving how she left, but she came to me before she vanished. Blubbering about how much she wanted to live in a castle and having people fawn over her. She had some vision from the village at what life was like here and she got a very rude awakening when she went to live with Lorne in military housing with a newborn while he was gone much of the time on maneuvers. Came back after the crying stopped to tell me she really loved Lorne and not to think badly of her."

"What about you? Going from being a spy to this?"

"I speak seven languages, well, eight now that I learned Gaelic. I was a translator before the war, I was a model, and yes, I spent quite a few years behind German lines snooping." Elise started grinning. "I've used those skills more times than I can count in carrying out being the wife of Retired Lt. Colonel Broderick Sinclair Duke of Cairnmuir, Marquess Braydallin, Earl of Ravensgard, Viscount Stronchergarry, Baron Sinclair of the Marches and Laird of Creag. One day, god willing, I would like to know that you have at least given it a chance. Hunter would hate to hear this, but yes, I went and told his grandfather that I wanted him to help me forget the war. I kept the details out of my stories to that writer, but that man ... best distraction I ever had. We started with that and had fifty years. A little distraction never hurt anyone, and you never know where it will lead. You have to take what time you have. You never know how short it will be."

"Tell me what happened, please? Not some romance novel Mary might give me."

"It's called Once upon a Spy if you ever want to find a copy, though it's hard not to find one in the village." Elise sank back in the chair, the sage green silk surrounding her like a picture frame. A faint smile formed at her lips. "I remember thunder and lightning. Hitler's speeches crackled as the radio's reception cut in and out. Rain so hard it stung. Rising and falling, the boat tumbled in the waves. Hunger pains burned my stomach like fire. Darkness everywhere, unable to breathe. Lifesaving air filled my lungs. Darkness again, dank and musty. Pain slammed into me. Eyes open for only a moment. Too hard to stay awake. Castle walls rose out of the gloom. Sleep. The smell of raw fish made me gag. Voices broke loudly into my half dream state. I opened my eyes suddenly,"

Ayda closed her eyes and listened the old woman speak, her voice like velvet even at 87.

In the Year 1943

Elise stared at a strange ceiling. A wood paneled room. The four-poster bed felt like a cage as it reached in the air.

"Did you find out who she was, Emmon?"

English voices. How long had she been asleep? How long since the water choked her?

"No, she was dead away when I found her on the rocks outside. However, I think we should stop talking about her as if she was dead. I believe her eyes are open."

She turned her head and found two men there. They looked at her as if she had risen from the dead despite their words. Where was she?

"I'm sorry we woke ye. The Master and I just arrived and wondered of your condition. Ye came ashore two days ago. Hugh here was worried ye were dead." His grin removed the menace from his appearance. He was dressed in a muted kilt, a thin man in his thirties with dark skin and thinning black hair. With the scar from his eyebrow to the middle of his cheek, he could have been a pirate in another age. "I'm Emmon."

They said she had lain there two days already. Those who expected her must think she was dead. Elise lifted the covers to get up and put them back down just as quickly. "Where are my clothes?" She croaked, her voice hoarse from all the salt water she had swallowed.

"Mrs. Buchanan, the housekeeper, took them off ye to keep ye from catching your death. They are cleaned and pressed, what is left of them, and in the closet." The other man was an elderly fellow, though perhaps not as he showed few signs that the ravages of time had taken hold. While his hair was white, his eyes were bright and his skin unwrinkled. If not for the hair, Elise would have sworn he was little older than her own twenty-six. Taking all that into account, fifties would be her best guess about his age. "I'm Hugh."

"Where am I?"

Hugh clasped his hands behind his back. Something in his demeanor said he was in charge. "If it means anything to ye, this is the castle Am Binnean. There's nothing but sea between us and the Orkney Islands."

"Damn it all to hell," Elise cursed, but the men paid it no mind.

They turned to leave when Elise tried to smooth the tangled mass of hair on her head. "We'll leave ye to get dressed. When you are finished, there's breakfast on."

As soon as the door closed, Elise threw back the covers and checked the waterproof packet attached to her torso. Was Mrs. Buchanan ready to ask questions when she saw her next even though it hadn't been removed?

Elise surveyed her appearance at the dressing table. The sand in her sable hair just had to stay there, as the room wasn't equipped with much more than a washbasin. Pulling it back to hide the sea's damage was the best she could do.

Not much of an improvement from the sea-battered woman she had stared at before. She was too pale, too thin, and her height made her seem even thinner. Always self-conscious of the fact that she stood near six feet, she now looked as if she was a battered scarecrow. She didn't like the comparison.

Hugh waited with hands behind his back as Elise emerged. All she wanted to do was slip away to complete her mission. He led her past many lavish rooms without a word. She glimpsed richly upholstered furniture everywhere.

"Is that a bowling lane?" Elise asked peering in one door. Hugh didn't say a thing.

The walls held portraits and landscapes of all eras and artists of note. Her mother, as a painter, would kill her if she couldn't have recognized a Rembrandt or a Hans Holbein. It was the Chagall, Degas, Rivera, Matisse, Cole, and Modigliani that made her stare. Looking down at her clothes, Elise felt even shabbier. Why couldn't she have washed up on the door of some fishing shack?

"And here we are. Breakfast is served," Hugh announced. They were his first words since he had left her to dress.

The dining room was painted blood red with white trim and handsomely carved walnut furniture, complete with side chairs that sported gothic arched backs. It was not some great hall, but a private dining room for everyday use. Even still, the service that stood around the room sported the names of the finest makers there had been.

A man already seated looked over papers at the table. Grudgingly, he lifted his head at their approach. He was handsome to a fault, maybe twenty-eight, with dark brown eyes and thick brown hair streaked with blond. Just a sweater couldn't hide his solid lean build, but it showed off the reddish brown tan of a man that spent a good deal of time outdoors. The paperwork seemed ill fitted to the man.

Despite looking as if he didn't want to be distracted, he stood when Elise entered and bowed deeply as if she was the Queen instead of a shipwrecked peasant. "I'm Broderick Sinclair. Welcome to Am Binnean."

"Elise Dutton." The room smelled of heather that stood dried in vases here and there. She took a deep breath to will the nervousness out of her body.

"Mrs. Buchanan, could you please get our guest some breakfast and perhaps see what we have that she might be able to wear that isn't going to fall off her at any moment?" At Broderick's command, a short plump woman shuffled out of the next room with a tray of food. The smell alone made Elise's stomach growl.

Elise watched her out of the corner of her eye. So this was the housekeeper that could blow her secret if she had felt the packets. Seventy, at least with her hairdo thirty years out of date, she didn't look much of a threat. Mrs. Buchanan didn't give her more than a passing glance as the food was set out. Had the packet truly gone unnoticed?

Elise forced herself not to shove all the food in her mouth at once. After two days without food, she had to work at it.

Broderick took a drink of his coffee. "So do you mind my asking how you came to be on this spit of land in the middle of a storm?"

Elise lifted her head quickly as memories flooded back. "The boat captain, was he found as well?"

Broderick turned to Emmon who only nodded and disappeared. "I will let you know. If he hasn't made his way to shore before now, I wouldn't hold out much hope for him. Do you know his name or the boat's name so we can notify his relatives?"

"His name was Per. I don't know his last name. He was a refugee from the war who had escaped with his boat. I'm not sure he has any family here to notify." Elise answered. She kept her answers as much to the truth as she could. If she had learned one thing at all in this charade of hers, it was that.

Broderick looked up from his plate. "What on earth were you doing on a boat in a sea known to be patrolled by enemy ships and subs? In a storm no less?"

Elise opened her mouth to speak. There was the faintest pause, as she hesitated to consider how to respond. "Neither of us had any rations left or money for that matter. Should we have starved when there are fish in the sea?"

Broderick's eyebrow raised a fraction. "You're not British. What is that accent I detect? Are you an American?"

Elise looked at the man with a critical eye. How could he guess her speech? "I didn't think that I had much of it left after university at the Sorbonne before the war." Elise hoped her answer covered her disquiet adequately and didn't bring up other questions. She had worked hard to rid herself of any trace of an accent.

Broderick smiled. "I suppose the point was more that you didn't have a British accent."

Elise smiled back. She could have easily let her guard down and shown him far more than just a smile. It would have been easy, but other thoughts were in her head besides flirting, despite the great temptation. "And where is yours?"

He laughed. "You were expecting a highland man to be a brute in a kilt with a claymore strapped to his back? Oh, and the brogue so thick an Englishwoman couldn't even understand him to know her virtue is in danger."

It was Elise's turn to laugh. "It's 1943. I'm not expecting the characters out of a novel to be played out before my eyes, but I would think sounding like a Scot wouldn't be out of line."

Mrs. Buchanan laughed bawdily. "See, we told ye that ye spent too much time in London with those English friends o' yours."

Broderick actually looked as if the old woman's comment flustered him. "Well, perhaps I have. I forget that I sometimes lose it when I've been away from home, one consequence of an Eton education I suppose, I guess St. Andrews didn't put it back well enough."

She had played the grateful guest long enough, Elise thought. "May I make a phone call to my friends and tell them I'm safe? I should have been back to Aberdeen two days ago."

"Generators can give me power, coal heat, but the storms play too much havoc on the lines to try to run phones here, but don't fear. There is one in the village." Broderick shrugged his shoulders. He had given that answer before. "We'll see that the search is started and show you the phone. I have a runner that brings any messages. Just give your friends the number. We'll have to walk to the village. You're up for that, aren't you?"

Elise nodded. "A short walk I could handle, especially if it will get me out of your hair. You look too busy to have to be seeing to me too."

The grin that grew on his face was enough to tell her that her unexpected appearance wasn't too much of a hardship for him. "I should have been here yesterday if the infernal car hadn't broken down, so now I'm behind. I'm afraid I can't be of much help getting you out of here until it's fixed."

Thank God, a car. She could get out of there. No. Wait. What had he said? "There's only one car for the entire castle?"

"With rationing, we only have enough gas and tires for one to be kept running. We wouldn't be much of an example to the others if we flaunted the rules just because we have a castle now, would we?"

Elise smiled, but inside she cursed. Those packets needed to make it to her contact and fast. Her enemies had to have realized she slipped the cordon. Escaping those who chased her was the only redeeming benefit of landing in the middle of nowhere.

~

Despite the mound of paperwork that Elise had seen in front of Broderick, he took it on himself to show her to the phone in the village. It was hardly more than some fifty buildings clustered around a bay where numerous fishing boats anchored. Accustomed to the stink of German cigars in the office where she worked, Elise welcomed the scent of the outdoors. Even the stink of fish was but a faint memory. The wind blew too hard for the smell to linger there. Broderick left her to her call but, only when the door closed did she dial the number she committed to memory. It was too open to view, but she had little choice.

"Davis, please." Elise could hear the sounds of voices on the other end. She wasn't on hold, someone had only set the phone down.

"Tell me it's you, North Star. We expected the worst when you didn't make the pick-up in Aberdeen. With that storm raging, we weren't even sure if you had left," Davis finally spoke on the other end with relief. Then he remembered the task and asked. "What happened? Where are you?"

As she sorted out the memories that flooded back the longer she was awake, Elise had worked out the last few days in her head. "We left safe enough. The storm came up out of nowhere. Considering where I think I must be, we blew well off course before the boat capsized. I only woke up a few hours ago. A search is on for the captain of the boat, but I fear the worst."

"But where are you?" Davis demanded.

"I don't know exactly. North Sea on three sides for sure, but I was told something about the castle Am Binnean. Does that mean anything to you? I haven't wanted to ask too many questions in case they get suspicious."

Davis laughed, but it was not a merry sound. "It means you're a hell of a long way from Aberdeen. Little wonder Devon couldn't figure out where you disappeared."

Looking out the window Elise watched as Broderick spoke to the villagers. The situation was getting worse by the second. She was stuck. "But I'm also without transport. Mr. Sinclair's car is in disrepair."

"You mean he's there?"

Elise could have sworn his voice cracked. How young were they recruiting agents? "Well, why not? It is his house, isn't it?"

"I saw him in London just a few days ago is all. I'll call when I can get someone there to pick you up. It may be a few days before I can arrange it though. Devon was pulled out when you were over two days late. I don't have another agent in Scotland to help you. Get on the first train to London if you can find a way out before I do. Damn it all! You might as well be in Berlin for all the good that information is doing us. Blast that storm!"

There was a pause and Elise thought the line had gone dead. "Are you still there, Davis?"

"Is the phone safe? Can you tell me the information now?"

She growled. "No one would consider it reliable if I just popped it out of my head."

"Don't you have it with you?"

Elise was getting a bit annoyed at his tone. She was the one who risked her life for four years and by the sound of his voice, he was little more than a schoolboy. She had to wonder what the man she had never met looked like. That was the problem with blind contacts. "It's safe and even if it was right here in front of me, it's coded so I can't just read it like the newspaper. I was compromised, Davis. One of them was there at the dock when I arrived. I had to sneak aboard in a damn crate of fish. Don't snap at me like I'm your secretary."

"Just get here as soon as you can. I'll work on it from this end."

"Perhaps it was a blessing. If our boat didn't make it through, no one could have stuck to us. A body in the ocean doesn't show up so easily." The line went dead before she had even finished.

Elise hung up the phone and watched as the men scattered to start the search. Inquiries told her nothing of Per before she was shown the phone. She let out a sigh. It was not one of relief. Grey clouds still filled the sky since the storm that had shipwrecked her had still not fully played out.

"So when can they send someone to get you?" Broderick asked to break her out of her reverie.

He made her look up at him when she usually had to stare eye to eye with most. Before the war, he would have occupied her fantasies. Now it was little more than a passing thought with so much else on her mind. Still, he was a fine man to look at and she'd had very little to distract her of late. "I'm afraid you're stuck with me for a few days, if not longer. It will be that long at least before they can come up with enough gas rations to come get me."

"I have some guests coming at the weekend. You're welcome to join us. The young doctor plans to propose to his lady while they are here. She would probably appreciate having a woman here to 'ooh and ah' at the ring afterwards. I'm sure if they have room in their car, they could take you to more habited lands when they depart. If they can't help, then there's always the postman that comes once a week. You can catch a ride with him."

The sea air buffeted Elise as she left the haven of the post office. A look around at the little village showed there wasn't a boat, there wasn't a car either. Other than maybe taking a horse and cart all that way, she was stuck right there and she didn't see many horses to steal for that matter. They were all busy with gas so hard to come by. "I thank you for the invitation, but I do have to use that tired old saying that I've only the clothes on my back." It would look suspicious if she turned down the offer since she had no other options.

"Mrs. Buchanan is a master at creating something out of nothing I'm sure we can find enough to keep you covered at least."

"I'll be sure to practice my oohs and ahs before then." Inside Elise grimaced at the picture of the woman she created. Four years she had pretended she was someone else. Surely, she could do better. Figure out someone interesting at least.

They walked in silence for much of the way until they reached a bridge. The castle actually stood on a spit of land out in the sea. That bridge was its only connection to the mainland. Elise made out the date 1844 carved into the stones on their lifeline to the rest of Scotland. Beyond, the castle stood against the blue grey sky. Even without sun, it seemed fairy tale like to her war battered eyes with its seals set in the walls. Tiny pieces of artwork. Sinclair in the middle and largest, surrounded by those who must have married into the family. It was a veritable "who's who" of Scotland and judging by some of the pictures from further afield. Surely, here in Scotland, Elise could pretend for a little while at least that life was normal.

"How old is your home?" Elise asked finally. It seemed the most normal thing she could think of to ask.

"The original tower was built by the Vikings. It's been added to significantly since then, of course. My grandfather was instrumental in the more recent changes. 120 rooms it was the logical place to bring all the children of our London friends. We have a school practically on the third floor."

"Definitely a haven in a storm. Thank you for taking me in."

Broderick smiled as they reached the castle. "I'm afraid I must be a terrible host and get back to the work you saw earlier. If you can excuse me for the day, I'll give you a full tour this evening after I can say I've accomplished something."

Elise had to force the thoughts from her head, a handsome man, indeed.

~

Free after lunch, Elise looked over her shoulder when she saw the library and slipped inside. A two-story room, shelves from floor to ceiling surrounded her while a railed walkway gave access to the second floor books. The shelves were filled with rare and old classics of Scottish history and law, many in ancient leather bindings. Where the shelves didn't cover, there was mahogany paneling, while a huge carved renaissance mantle surrounded the fireplace. On a table near the door sat a book on the families of Scotland. It lay open to the Sinclair family.

The Sinclairs of Wrathe are descended from William, a younger son of Comte de Saint Clair in Normandy who came to England with William the Conqueror. Through early fortunate marriages, the Sinclair family acquired the Lordship of Wrathe and later the Dukedom of Cairnmuir. Since the twelfth century have made their home in the Castle Am Binnean built upon the foundations of a Viking era watchtower. The family has strong ties to the Earldoms of Caithness and the Isles, with which they are closely related, and to the Sutherlands by marriage. Fortunate marriages haven't ended over the family's history, the Princess of Navarre most notably.

Despite their far-flung seat, the Sinclairs have long been prominent in Scottish affairs. They supported Robert the Bruce in the struggle for Scottish independence and fought at the battle of Bannockburn. Duncan Sinclair was a Knight of The Most Ancient and Most Noble Order of the Thistle. Male members of the family generally pursue military careers. Sinclairs of this line have fought at the Battle of Bauge in 1421, the battle of Flodden in 1513, the battle of Killicrankie in 1689 only to name a few. So many men of the clan were lost in several previous battles that they escaped involving themselves in the 1715 and 1745 Jacobite attempts to retake the crown and thereby saved themselves having their lands forfeited. More recently, they have fought in Crimean and the Nile River campaign. The Black Watch has always boasted a large presence of Sinclair men in their ranks. The family has produced military heroes who have no less than twelve Distinguished Service Orders and two Victoria Crosses.

Titles in the family include Lord of Wrathe extinct since 1328, Duke of Cairnmuir, Marquess Braydallin held by the heir, Earl of Ravensgard, Viscount Stronchergarry, Baron Sinclair of the Marches and finally Laird of Creag. The 32nd Duke Robert Sinclair and his second wife Phillippa of the Clan Maceachran reside in Am Binnean Castle with his two sons by his first marriage and three children of the second union.

Elise couldn't help but notice that the last line was crossed out and rewritten in a precise hand. The 29th Duke Lorne Sinclair is serving as a Captain in the Argyll and Sutherland Highlanders. The spiral stairs drew her up to the second floor. No one was there to see so she slid a book off the shelves that had to be worth a fortune. An original 1831 copy of The Scottish Gael or Celtic Manners as preserved among the highlanders. Before Elise opened it though, she caught sight of something in the corner. There from floor to ceiling were ribbons, medals, and honors of all sorts. Order of the Thistle, Order of the Garter, Order of the Golden Fleece, military medals a lot of them. The sound of someone down below didn't distract her from the objects.

"What sort of man is Mr. Sinclair? All that paperwork doesn't fit in with this." She asked as she looked at one in particular. Was that picture of him with the King of England? Wait! Was the one behind with a Russian Princess? She picked it up to have a closer look.

"I'm the second son, my brother was the one raised to do the paper work. I'm just filling in while he's fighting in Malaya." Very definitely, Broderick's voice filled the room.

Elise closed her eyes silently. She cursed that he caught her and set the picture back where she had found it. Now he thought her a snoop and a flake after the ring comment.

"You admire books, I see. Found the oldest ones in the castle quickly. If you're looking for some more popular reading, ask Mrs. Buchanan to show you."

Elise looked back at her other hand and straightened. "Do you mind? My parents own an antique bookstore. I was just admiring your collection. It makes theirs seem like a child's next to this."

Broderick only shook his head. "Life in the same house for centuries. It seems to accumulate no matter how much you try to tame the clutter. One hundred twenty rooms make it difficult to keep track of where you leave things."

Elise looked over the railing. "I saw some papers over on the side table if that's what you mislaid." Elise picked up another photo, one of Broderick in full military dress uniform, a Captain and she thought he was gorgeous in regular clothes. "I never heard you served."

"Currently serving. My father died last year and with my older brother away, it came to me to see to the estate. My step mother went back to work, she was a nurse during the first war, she's running a hospital at the moment. My half-brother and sisters aren't of age yet and away at school. I had to argue to my superiors that they didn't want to send an estate to ruin for lack of a short leave."

"I'm sorry to hear of your loss." It seemed the only decent thing to say. Nevertheless, she saw Broderick's look as he picked up the file off the side table. Broderick worried her with that look, but he walked out without a word.

The book in her hand was heavy and as Elise looked back down at it, she suddenly missed her parents. It had been years since she had seen them, since she had run her fingers over the books in their store. She couldn't risk contacting them. Surely, in Scotland, she was far enough away that she could at least send a telegram to let them know she was alive. Elise grabbed her jacket and headed for the post office.

~

The wind had picked up since their walk that morning and Elise pulled the coat around her neck tighter as the wind blew the sea in a fine spray over everything. If nothing else, the castle was well protected from land attack. An ancient tower protected the bridge from being crossed in addition to the castle battlements. Perhaps in far off times it had been the proverbial drawbridge. The village was barely off the island well in its protection and just as Elise was about to push open the post office door, Broderick's voice filled the tiny building. "Carol, how did you get this number?" Of course, Elise had gotten a little lost finding her way out of the castle and she spotted a horse nearby out of the wind.

"We haven't seen each other in months and last I heard you were with Ronald. What makes you think I wanted you to come on this trip?"

"Yes Magda came with me! The woman just found out her husband died in a German prisoner camp after being shot down last year. Did you really think in the middle of a war I was going to throw a ball and you were getting left out? I came on business and heaven forbid I brought a friend for a break from death and war." Elise stifled a smile as she heard the phone hang up. She slipped around the corner out of sight, but Broderick still wasn't coming out. Elise could see a store down the street and went for a look until the horse vanished. At the last minute before she entered, the horse wandered back around the corner.

"...then what are you doing to get Lorne out? Maybe I'll just have to do it myself." This time the hang up was angry and Elise had no time to move out of the way as Broderick came storming out of the post office. He pulled up short at the sight of her. There was no smile or polite host this time.

"I have work to do. It will have to be later." He muttered as he grabbed the horse's reins.

"And a good day to you, too." Elise said, but he was already gone from sight.

~

It felt as if Elise was warm for the first time in years, as she looked out over the sea in all its wind-tossed glory. She could only hope Per had faired so well. There was a knock at the door and the gentle Mrs. Buchanan entered the small sitting room. How a woman her age could keep a castle of that size going was anyone's guess. Then again, she had seen a number of people around that probably did the actual work.

"I was told ye needed sum clothes." As if to make up for Broderick's loss of accent, Mrs. Buchanan's seemed even thicker now.

"I do, but why don't you just tell me where the clothing store in the village is. I can go back and buy what I need there now that I know the way." Elise watched her closely. She waited for Mrs. Buchanan to say something about feeling anything in her ministrations, but it never came.

Mrs. Buchanan tittered lightly. "Dear, the highlands aren't known fur their access ta readymade clothes even before the war brought all this rationing. For those we usually have ta go ta Inverness."

Elise wrinkled her brow. "Then what did Mr. Sinclair mean about you helping with some clothes?"

The housekeeper clasped her hands over her large chest with pride. "I was the duchess' personal maid and her seamstress before her death. When old McLeod died, I was promoted."

"Well if you're going to make clothes for me, I insist you let me help." Elise offered.

Mrs. Buchanan smiled, but her eyes showed her surprise. "You know how ta sew? I thought all ye young ones were gettin' away from that."

"Can one live nowadays without being able to repair what they have? I've had to learn to use what I can find same as you." Elise didn't know how much news of the American depression made it to the Highlands of Scotland. She'd learned how to make do when rationing was only a dream. If she really thought about it, wanting more during the depression had lead her down the path she was on now.

"We'll have ta work hard ta get ye into a wardrobe by tamorra evenin'. There are outfits left here by accident over the years before the war. They shouldn't be too terribly out of date. We'll change what we can on them so they fit. Come look with me and pick a dress for us ta copy. What they left are day clothes, no one would leave an expensive evening dress. And call me Iona."

Elise looked out the window once more. She was to find new clothes while the man that had brought her was dead or freezing on the beach. Nevertheless, it was war and many things weren't fair. "Perhaps we should see what there is to work with. We won't have any bolts of cloth to use I'm sure."

"Of course I should have thought of that myself." Iona toddled off, leaving Elise to follow. The sewing room hidden in the attic of the castle was a room full of windows. Iona pulled open a large chest full of remnants. There were exquisite pieces of lace, silk, brocade, taffeta, and chiffon. Mostly small pieces. Another chest held enough clothes to have been her old wardrobe before the war. Even if some were more than a decade out of date, they would have a lot to work with.

Elise tried on the clothes left behind and as she went through the pile, each dress was pinned and taken in where needed. Slowly, Iona put together a wardrobe out of clothing that hadn't seen the light of day in years. Several other women appeared, excited about the opportunity to dress someone. With no parties, not even a family to take care of, frankly, they were bored. They all wanted to help with her clothes as if Elise had been there all along. One woman went to work on Elise's hair while Iona pulled out some fashion magazines. One magazine was even from America and was surprisingly up to date, considering how far away from everything they were on the island.

"There. I've found one we could make with what we have. There's that large panel of German lace, the nude colored slip and the ruffled dress I couldn't think of wearing cut apart." Elise said in the midst of the gossip. Those women told some very risqué stories about her host. It was a wonder he got any work done at all.

"Oh, seeing that one, I have an idea. Before I came up from London, I saw a film. There was a dress in it, the top fancy stuff, and the bottom a plain sheath a lot like the lining of one of the old duchesses' dress slimmed a bit." One woman said as she dug through the chest. She tossed aside one after the other until she pulled one out in triumph. "But the best part is the top ended here and the bottom started here." There was a gap of several inches to show a full midriff and it would allow them to use a smaller piece of something stunning.

The women all looked over at Elise's figure and nodded. It was no scarecrow they saw, instead deep blue eyes, velvety pale skin, dark brown hair and a figure that even hidden under tattered clothes that was near perfect. Soon they found several more and Elise had a wardrobe planned for the entire visit.

"So this is our little shipwrecked foundling?" A voice announced from the door. A heavily accented voice, Eastern European if she had to guess. Elise lifted her gaze to a stunner, thick dark hair, gorgeous blue eyes, she slowly pulled a cigarette from her mouth and let out a slow stream above her head. "I'm Magda Stárek."

"Elise Dutton."

"Princess do you need something?" Iona asked.

Princess! Elise tried not to get caught staring. She didn't look it standing there in pants and a heavy wool sweater. She was glamorous still, but a Princess no. Even she had to live with the dictates of fuel rationing.

"It's lunch time and nothing is out."

"Lawd, ma dear, I got caught up in this. I best get oot o' here and see supper is started too or ye'll starve. Give me half an hour and I'll have something out Princess." Iona rushed out as fast as she could.

"That one will look well on you." Magda said at the fashion photo one woman held up.

"I hadn't seen you around."

She let out another veil of smoke. "The castle is so large it's not hard to loose oneself." It was all she said before she walked off.

Elise went back to her room with an armload of clothes that had been finished. Finally, she could get out of the ragged clothes she had washed up on shore in.

~

Broderick looked up from his work and stared at the picture on his desk. It was just a simple picture of him and his brother, but he had looked at it a lot lately. There was a faint knock on the doorway. He looked up to find Hugh's young niece there with her son in her arms.

"Sir."

"Yes, Mary." She was up from London escaping the bombings. Her husband had already died.

"I saw something when I was helping Iona with our guest's clothes. Her dress has a French label."

Broderick rubbed his temples. "Mrs. Buchanan informed me of those while she was asleep still." He murmured. He had enough to do without having this thrown at him from the sea.

"And you're having us work to dress her for Sir MacGillivray's visit with all the rationing we have to live with? It's our stash. We've been using them to dress up our own miserable wardrobes. Your stepmother said we could. Did you see what she was wearing? There's enough material for two dresses in it while we've been wearing our clothes out until they're too threadbare to save for lack of material."

Women's minds seemed to go when they spent too long without something to do. A French label to him meant a spy, to her it meant she got more fabric in a dress. Woe is me. "The postman listened into her call and it's suspicious enough for me to keep her here even if I were able to help her leave. Keep her busy with a wardrobe and we'll see what we can find out this week. She's not meeting anyone to do any harm while she's here. You can have the clothes back after this week." She started to leave with a set to her jaw that was a bit defiant. Magda was the one with something to worry about. "And Mary, don't say anything that might make her run. I'd like to keep her where we can watch her." The file he had collected from the library lay open on his desk. He had to wonder just how much Elise had seen.

"Yes, sir." Mary looked like a dog with its tail between its legs as she headed for the door.

Broderick just had to know. "By the way, just what were all you telling our guest this afternoon?"

Mary's face brightened dramatically. "Oh sir, don't you worry we didn't mention anything about what sort of work you do for the government." She put a finger to her mouth but it couldn't hide the grin. "We were just talking of Isobel, Sarah, Catherine, Lucy."

Broderick tried to hide his smile. "That's all?"

"Well now that you ask. We might have brought up Francoise, Elizabeth, Alexandra ..." She wandered off, but Broderick could still hear her mentioning names as she vanished down the hall.

~

Mrs. Buchanan cleared away the dinner dishes as Broderick finished off the last of his glass of wine. It didn't fit the meal they had consumed. Far too grand.

Elise smiled satisfied as Iona took her plate. "That is the best meal I've had in months, Iona." They took rationing seriously, but Elise wasn't left hungry by any means. There was an abundance of vegetables and such that grew in the castle greenhouse, while nothing rationed was on the table in any quantity, if at all.

"It's nice ta ken sumone appreciates ma cookin'. Ye'd think the way the others around here complain, I was servin' them pig slop."

"For shame, Broderick." Elise chided and he smiled at her.

"Oh, not him!" The old woman defended Broderick with a grin. "He can't get a fresh vegetable half the time in London to save his life I'm sure."

"Would you care for that tour I promised?" Broderick offered. The wine seemed to have washed away the mood from earlier.

"Delighted."

He filled their glasses once more and led her out of the dining room. The original tower definitely showed its age. When Broderick opened the door, it was in a thousand-year-old style. It still had arrow slits, rough stone, and in its center stood several cannons that while not eleven hundred years old, were definite proof that the castle hadn't always been so peaceful. Somehow, the look of them said they were still in working order and woe to the enemy ship that came too close. Elise smiled to herself at the reaction a modern captain would have if one of those tore a hole in his ship. From the top of the tower though, it wasn't hard to notice a ship docked in the village. A naval ship, not some fishing boat at all. Before she could ask about it, Broderick turned her quickly away and plunged back into the castle proper.

"Do I ask about Magda Stárek, Princess? A woman that came to see me and yet I never knew she was here."

He stiffened at her question. "She had to escape Czechoslovakia when the Germans overran it. Her father is part of the Government in Exile, a former ambassador to China when it fell in '38, they had just gotten home when they had to flee there as well in '39. Her husband was in the air force helping to get back in his country when he was shot down. Died last month in a Stalag. A widow at 22. She's here grieving, not socializing. A friend gave Magda a house on an island he has because she's poor as can be, her son is there and last she heard the Germans had landed there and she's not heard a word if he's dead or alive."

In the depths of the castle was the old kitchen from a 1328 addition with a fireplace that took over the barrel-shaped room. The ceiling curved above them, the stone dark from years of fires. Here and there as they walked, were tiny alcoves put into the eight-foot thick walls that looked into the courtyard through leaded glass windows. There had even been tiny gun slots long since glassed in that gave light to the curving walls of the towers. Broderick swung open French doors to a fairyland of tomatoes, beans, potatoes, and peas. So here was the source of fresh vegetables in the midst of winter. Fruit trees grew on each corner faithfully clipped back so as not to disturb the glass above.

Elise sat on a seat built into the thick walls and stared at the stars that shown above like a glittering crown. "I just realized this castle isn't blacked out."

Broderick looked up. "If anyone is going to drop bombs, it's going to be some place they could get more than a handful of people. No one would even know it happened if they hit us."

Elise gazed around at life far from the war, so far from those chasing her. She'd seen the boat though. "I'll bet you brought all numbers of girls out here to seduce them. Most of those clothes I saw Iona working on weren't matronly at all." She teased, but it was more from that phone call she had overheard.

Broderick looked back down and the grin on his face spoke far more than the words. "You were obviously paying attention to the staff this afternoon. You aren't going to mention names are you?"

Elise sipped from her glass, her grin smug to say the least. "So are you going to deny the gossip?"

He laughed aloud at that comment. "I've had my fair share I'll admit. The garden house over there was a favorite haunt. Had to have a lock put inside just to keep out the riff raff."

"They all swooned at the thought I imagine." It was good to act far closer to her true self finally. That promise to get excited over an engagement ring still rankled a bit. Out of clothes that signaled another life, it started to come back easily. She was a flirt and she knew it. Most her life she had male friends more than female. They liked to play, as it were.

He sank on to the seat next to her. "Over the family fortune or a title more likely and those go to my brother. I was left with the hangers on like our half siblings."

It was Elise's turn to laugh. "I seriously doubt that." There was that grin, the one that made her heart race.

"Well, there is that pesky little fact that we have a title too even if it is only a courtesy, so it might be fiction. I think you'll find my stepmother was some years younger than my actual mother. She was the darling of society before the war started, even modeled some. I think you'll find much of those clothes are her old ones, the matronly would be my mothers. She was one of the old guard bought her husband good and proper."

Emmon appeared in the garden.

"Any news from the search?" Broderick asked as he switched topics with ease.

Emmon straightened and Elise could almost see him prepare for the reaction to whatever it was he had to deliver. "Nothing yet, sir. There is a message for you from the village. The old bull has more work for you."

"How in the bloody hell am I supposed to get my own work done? Doesn't he realize this isn't a pleasure trip?" Broderick took a breath to calm down. "If you'll excuse me, I have to go to the village and make yet another call. I'm sure Hugh would be glad to finish your tour."

"I was actually just thinking of going to bed. My swim tired me out more than I thought," she replied.

"Of course."

Elise watched them as they spoke in hushed tones to each other while she walked back into the castle proper. Somehow, it worried her. As if they suspected her.

~

Elise spent the next day helping to complete her clothes. Finally she stood at the top of the grand staircase ready to go down to supper. The guests had arrived. She had heard the commotion as they reached their rooms. There was no missing Magda at the bottom of the stairs. She glowed in a black sheath dress with a train of green coming off the waist. There was no rationing in that dress. It even looked to be silk.

"If you're worried about not fitting in, you'll make an impression on them all, a smashing one I must say." Broderick's voice her behind her made her jump.

"Where did Magda get a dress like that these days?"

Broderick laughed. "She has connections at the Hollywood studios, look close and you'll see dresses you recognize from films. She's poor as a church mouse, but knows enough people to hide that fact."

Elise had to remind herself to breathe and not give away that her heart had stopped when she saw him in person in his uniform. "Like you?"

"Yes exactly. What's a princess without a castle?" From farther down the hall, a wolf whistle broke the silence and gave her a chance to collect herself. God, she had been out of commission for too long. He shouldn't have done that to her.

Elise blew Emmon a kiss. Broderick only grinned as she took the arm he offered.

"I'll not embarrass you if you're worried. I was a model in New York and Paris an age ago it seems now. I know how to decorate an arm properly." With that, Elise descended into the mouth of hell.

At the bottom of the stairs, she was face to face with the man who was after her. The man whose face she had memorized through a pair of binoculars just before she had boarded a fishing boat. He had an oval face, thin mouth, short white hair sat on his tanned face like a crown and those eyes. Ice blue wasn't hard to forget. Such an innocent face, but the churning in Elise's stomach told her she wasn't mistaken. He was definitely the one after her. A lot could happen when a storm lifted, it seemed.

Elise could only hope he had never seen her picture. She could only hope he had never seen her. Could she pretend it was another woman they were after or was it already a lost cause? Elise glanced at the man whose arm she held. She had to wonder just how he fit into the mess she was in.

"Oh! There you are, Broderick. I was beginning to think that you weren't really here and that Hugh was just lying to us." The most elderly of the guests called as eight in all stood there to look at them expectedly. She had heard talk of only three.

Broderick grinned at Elise, but her eyes didn't share his smile even if her mouth did. "Sorry I wasn't here to greet you earlier MacGillivray, but when one has such an enchanting guest, my mind was liable to be on other things." No mention of the fact she had hardly seen him all day. Or that Magda was there. The once they had run into each other in the hall he had rather growled at her or more precisely he had been growling at the papers in his hand. He had hardly seen her.

Sir Bruce MacGillivray was an older distinguished man in a dress kilt, the only one there who wore such. He stood almost even with Elise when they reached the bottom step, but he had a decidedly stooped posture that made him look shorter. Bruce's eyes set on Elise and held fast. His grin held just as steady. There was a twinkle in his eyes that screamed he knew why she was there, only it fit Broderick's reputation not her mission. He thought she was the latest conquest.

"Everyone, this is Broderick, the son of my oldest friend who is also a distant relation and our host for the week. Broderick, may I present Dr. David MacInnes, Gladys Murray, Aubrey and Rebecca Elliot," And then of course, the man hunting her. "And finally we have Alexander and Cornelia Colquhoun." So, Alexander was his name or at least the one he was using currently.

Broderick bowed slightly, framed perfectly by the large granite columns that supported the ceiling. "Pleasure to meet all of you, and welcome to Am Binnean. This vision of loveliness is Elise Dutton and no one can forget Princess Magdalena of Růžička. Shall we all go have a drink before dinner? I'm sure you could use it after the drive."

"Wonderful idea, my boy." Bruce agreed and headed off as Hugh led them to the drawing room. "I tried calling Dunham to see if he could come up, but he's too busy by far."

Broderick held Elise back so they were the last to leave the stairs. "Is everything all right?"

Didn't it sound sarcastic that question of his, to antagonize her now that her adversary was in his house. Broderick hung her out like laundry. Then he repeated himself and she heard genuine worry. Did her mind play tricks on her? She had to watch herself around him. He seemed to be able to see through all the barriers she threw up. "Nothing a good meal won't cure."

"Then allow me." Broderick offered his arm once more, and they headed for the rest of group. It was a blue Chinese papered room with tables holding all manner of games and amusements under an elaborate plaster ceiling showing the family's heraldry in its graceful curves. "I could have told you Dunham couldn't make it, he's in the Pacific right now. Left the factory in his wife's running to join up again even at his age. His sons have as well."

"Who's that?" Aubrey asked.

"Oh, The Earls of Moerhab very old friends, we've known each other since before the days of Napoleon. He runs a shipping company, the warehouse in town is theirs, empty what with the war on. I stay in their London house, never had the need to buy one there since they always have provided. Never have to feel like I'm away from home too."

Elise listened with a stupid grin plastered on her face as Broderick played the perfect host. She could only survey the room full of enemies while Broderick laughed at some story Bruce told him and the Doctor. Dr. David MacInnes was a big boned, yet wiry man, with a square face. With blond hair, blue eyes and red cheeks, he looked more farmer than doctor. Even his clothes seemed a little more country than the rest.

Gladys, the intended fiancée, was a pretty oval faced girl with pale eyes and shiny brown hair. She wore the latest fashions, but she wore them awkwardly. Bought for this occasion, Elise gathered, and unable to feel comfortable in them yet. The both of them were in their late twenties and as they talked with Broderick, they relaxed considerably.

Broderick wasn't stuffy about the fact he had a title even if it was only courtesy, and the story he told appealed more to the common denominator than say one that involved that picture of him with a Russian Princess she had seen and a Czech Princess listened on.

The two married couples were harder to put in a category. Alexander, her hunter, was perhaps mid-forties to fifty. He had a severe hawk-like face to match his hawk-like eyes. He was indeed the hawk swooping down on its prey. Elise had felt it as she had watched him on the dock after her. However, the three with him didn't seem so menacing. Elise knew she was proof not to trust them though. If she could pretend to be someone else, so could they.

Aubrey was in his mid-thirties. He had a solid body, black hair, sunken cheeks, and a beaked nose. David wasn't what anyone would call handsome or gorgeous, but he had appeal. He was attractive in a country sort of way, Elise wouldn't have objected to dating him herself as far as first impressions went. Aubrey was none of those, he was rather ugly but was in demeanor more than looks. As Broderick made his way around getting to know the guests Elise heard Aubrey was a lawyer in a well-known firm in Inverness. Perhaps that explained his wife.

Rebecca was in her mid-twenties at best, but her appearance clearly aimed to make her appear older. She could have been considered a minor beauty but with blood red nails and her chosen hair and clothing style there was something just off. She was reaching, a social climber without the breeding to do it properly. Not that Elise considered herself well-bred but still Rebecca looked ready to take on the queen. They were all dressed for dinner but Rebecca stood out like a sore thumb.

Cornelia, Alexander's wife, had to be a decade younger than her husband and a very elegant woman. She was tall with a long horsy face. Oddly enough, her hair matched her shoes. That thought distracted her from noticing much else about Cornelia. She lit up a cigarette as Elise eyed her.

"Want one?" Cornelia offered, seeing her glance.

Elise took one from the case even though she didn't smoke.

"Don't you just hate the first night of these things where you don't know a soul?" Cornelia continued. "They seem to know each other well." Elise looked over as Cornelia tipped her head at Broderick and Bruce.

"I thought you knew Broderick?"

"Oh, no. We met Lord MacGillivray several years back. He's always invited to the most interesting parties. I suppose he finds us entertaining enough to bring us along to many of them. We've never met Broderick until tonight, though. Pity that Dunham couldn't come you know his wife is Russian nobility."

"Was she indeed?"

Cornelia narrowed her eyes as the statement. "Cornelia what was the name of that chap we met last week with Charles?" Alex called over and she was left alone again. Elise put the cigarette to her mouth, but she didn't inhale deeply. Even without the foreign smoke, she felt queasy. How exactly had she washed up on the doorstep of the one place the man who hunted her showed up?

"You all right?" Magda asked. "You look a little green."

"Oh. Here I don't really smoke, took one just to have something to say to the woman." Elise handed over the cigarette. "I'm really not used to nobility. Russian at that."

Magda gave a half laugh. "Tatiana? They haven't been married since WW1. They got divorced in 1917. Andrew married a Turkish woman the day the war ended. I can't imagine why they would mention it, occasionally she's on the island, but never as family. Her sons hardly claim her even. There's a reason the Bolsheviks revolted."

She tried to change the subject. "Broderick says you have a son."

"Augustin yes. At least I think I still do."

Elise turned to her quickly, that phone call. Princess Magda was a fabulously dressed woman. She looked like nothing she'd ever seen of recent days.

"The Germans were reaching where he was living last I knew. They care nothing for a fatherless boy who hardly knows his mother."

"No, they don't. I can only give you my hope he is safe." What else was there to say?

After drinks, they retired to the dining hall as opposed to the dining room where they had eaten breakfast. It was a huge room, with soaring stone walls and giant beams that ran across the ceiling, each holding a huge wrought iron chandelier. The table was of an old style with the ends far across the room from one another. It was one of the few rooms to resist renovation. If Hollywood wanted to make a movie about knights and ladies in distress, they couldn't do better than to use this room as a set. Did that make her the lady in distress then?

MacGillivray waylaid them as Broderick was seating Elise. She hardly paid attention to the first few words as she sneaked a quick peek at the chandeliers above, glad to see that they remained unlit. With the dust she had seen when she had hidden the packet there, she had obviously guessed right that they were there for effect alone. Elise looked back at Broderick as he sat next to her, only then did she hear what was said.

"You don't mind my asking them along, do you? It seemed a sore party with only the four of us, I didn't know you would bring such lovely ladies to join us, a Princess even. Gladys would have been without any female companions. The only down side is I don't have the rations for all of them. Four portions into ten mouths, it will be a lean week."

"You needn't worry about me." Elise interrupted. "I'm fine with vegetables alone. Iona is a master with them."

Bruce smiled at her. "No, we'll just have to figure out something to supplement what I had saved up for the occasion. I tried bringing it up, but Alexander just waved me aside. I'm afraid when I've invited them before it wasn't quite the same circumstances."

"Nothing we can't handle, but we'll figure it out after we've eaten." Broderick said as Mrs. Buchanan brought out dinner. The gossiping hens were gone, they all wore uniforms and were as proper as could be. They put on quite a show.

Talk soon started about trivial matters as they ate. Elise added what she could, even though it was hard for her to do without giving away that she had spent the last years on the war torn continent and not Britain or America.

~

Broderick sought out Bruce's guests, the Colquhoun's and Elliot's at any rate. The little Broderick had heard when he had visited on his way north was that David and Gladys hadn't much to their names. Bruce wanted them to have a memory of their engagement. That Bruce had brought it up at all was proof enough how much it bothered him the week might not be perfect for them.

They stood near the fireplace deep in conversation and as Broderick neared, he couldn't help notice that the others stopped, only Cornelia had her back to the room.

"Do you suppose she's the Lili we've heard about?" Cornelia was saying until Alexander grabbed her arm.

"Broderick, so good of you to have us," Alexander called with a smile.

Broderick didn't feel those words came in kindness as hawk-like blue eyes stared at him. What was going on in his house? First, a woman washed up on the rocks with odd words on the phone and now mysterious behavior from other guests.

Broderick smiled in direct opposition to Alexander. "So rations getting a little low and you figured you would eat off someone else's pocketbook?"

Alexander's eyes narrowed. "That's a damned lie."

Broderick shrugged. "That's what Bruce thinks after you waved him aside on the matter. He's providing the rations for David and Gladys so you're taking food out of their mouths. He's fit to be tied by your bad manners, so I suggest you make amends."

"Since he never mentioned it in Inverness, it's not like we came prepared for such a problem. Just how would you suggest we do that?" Cornelia asked quietly.

Alexander straightened. "We don't have to do anything. He invited us to a visit and we accepted. Bruce never mentioned anything about paying. I would think you of all people could afford to at least feed your guests."

"This has nothing to do with ability to pay. It's called rudeness."

Alexander started to raise his fist, but before he could throw the punch, Cornelia laid a hand on his arm and stayed him. "He's right, Alex. This was rather an imposition since Broderick didn't even know we were coming. I did hear Bruce trying to bring it up during the invitation. I think Rebecca and I have our coupons upstairs. We can head into the shops in town and buy our fair share. Vegetables seem to be in good supply but if we contributed meat, butter, sugar, I would feel better. See whatever treats they might have as well. That would make it up to Bruce wouldn't it? There's no need to get in fisticuffs over the matter, Alexander."

Alex's arm started to lower and still Cornelia continued. "You've been most generous to open your home to us. You're right that it's fair we help provide as well. No need for MacGillivray to be put out so much for our thoughtlessness."

"How about you go tell him then before he has you blacklisted by everyone he knows over the offence?" Broderick commanded and it sounded just that, a command. There was no request in his voice. Rebecca rushed off to find Bruce. Alexander still glared as he walked by.

"I would have liked to have seen you try it. This isn't some pub you're used to frequenting and I'm not a drunken lout you can take advantage of," Broderick muttered as he passed.

Alexander turned to face him his hawk-like eyes glaring. "You're just some second son to a Duke," he spat out as if it was a curse.

"Indeed, but that assumes I give a damn about being the Duke. As it is I get all the advantages and none of the responsibility. Bruce likes telling about me and my brothers' exploits, but he leaves out the more mundane accomplishments. Maybe next time you'll get Bruce to tell you of it all. I didn't get where I am resting on the laurels of my father's name. I would keep that in mind the next time you think of striking me, especially in my own home." Broderick wasn't stupid enough to turn his back on Alexander though.

He let him go first.

~

The group walked out on the highlands in the morning causing a group of birds to flush and Broderick brought down the first one of the day.

"Now you're just showing off," Elise called to him.

"You saw the trophies. I don't have to show off," Broderick called back.

Elise started to grin. Broderick narrowed his eyes at the look, at least until Elise took aim at the birds getting farther away. One fell easily.

MacGillivray laughed hysterically. "I think you just might have to show off, my boy. You've finally found a woman to match you it seems."

"But can she fence?" Broderick asked MacGillivray as if she wasn't even there.

"With words like a champion," Elise called back and while Broderick was distracted, she brought down a second bird that David had scared up and missed.

Broderick smiled broadly. "This means war, you know."

Elise held up an imaginary sword, and she bowed to her adversary.

At the end of the day, when all was said and done, they had shot bird for bird. The haul went back with Emmon to give to the cook for supper while they slowly walked back. There was one way to feed a house without enough rations.

"So do I ask how you learned to shoot so well?" Alexander asked. Blue hawks' eyes stared at her.

Elise felt her blood run cold. She had let her pride get in the way. It was a mistake, and she knew it. "The depression in America. When you are short on money, you learn to make every shot count. I don't like an empty plate."

"I suppose you're an excellent fisherman as well? Don't let rationing get in the way of a full plate either?" Broderick asked.

The whispering she had seen wasn't her imagination, after all. He suspected her story was a lie. "Maine is known for its fish. Of course I know how."

"Then you'll want to try our Scottish streams. They're known for the fishing as well," Broderick offered.

Maybe she could pull her way out of trouble with Alexander and even Broderick. Elise grinned. "Shall we have a contest again tomorrow?"

The offer put Broderick off his stride. "I don't claim to be a fisherman. Perhaps you would let me have Emmon go in my place?"

"A proxy? Not on your life! If you're going to doubt my words, you're going to have to prove me wrong yourself."

"Fishing it is tomorrow," Bruce declared with a laugh as he linked his arm in hers to walk back.

~

As they finished their meal, there was a commotion outside and Emmon came to whisper in Broderick's ear. Broderick's eyes landed on Elise long before the one sided conversation ended with only a nod on his part.

"What was that about?" Alexander asked.

Broderick smiled. "Just our ghost acting up. He went and scared a chambermaid. Havoc on keeping good help."

"Ghost! I wish I had exciting ancestors like that. I have nothing, but farmers as far back as we know," Gladys lamented, but it ended the topic and soon they were in the drawing room for brandy as a phonograph played in the little railed Minstrels Gallery. A pale peach room, the elaborate barrel, drop plaster ceiling dominated most.

As the others began to sit down, Broderick took Elise and led her to a clearing in the furniture, as much of a dance floor as he could provide. It was time to find out about the woman found on his shore. It was time to figure out just what was going on in his house. The ghost had told Emmon an interesting story.

"No one is dancing," Elise protested.

"Perhaps I'll have the ballroom dusted and we can do this properly. I have a feeling you're a wonderful dancer."

Elise shook her head. "It's been a long time."

"Nonsense." Broderick pulled her close, his arm around her waist held tight. Broderick's cheek barely touched Elise, and still he could feel the heat rising from his touch. Then again, the dress she wore left him with bare skin to hold. He couldn't blame her reaction.

"Ah, so you're not as immune to my charms as you let on," Broderick whispered in her ear.

David and Gladys joined the dancing. Despite his country ways, David looked to be a superb dancer.

"We're near the fireplace," Elise defended. It was a worthy excuse. The fireplace went from floor to ceiling and even featured caryatids supporting the upper reaches.

His smile was slow. "A likely story. Why is it you froze when we came downstairs that first day? I don't think it was anything to do with hunger." There, in his arms he felt it again. It was barely noticeable.

"Have you ever thought I just don't like being stared at?"

Her voice was calm, he had to give her that. "A model would be used to it."

Elise pulled away so she could see his face. "A man with the reputation MacGillivray hints at wouldn't need to ask how I object to being looked at. It's the way you're looking at me after all. As lustful as I've ever seen a man."

Broderick pulled her back until their cheeks touched once more, and they spun around. "I don't notice you objecting now. No freezing up at all. Rather heated if I do say so myself." He could feel the heat from her cheek getting just a bit hotter.

"Tell me, is it that I'm the only single woman in the room that has you flirting with me since Magda's in mourning? Frankly, after all those women I heard of from the household staff I'm surprised you have the time to get to me. Was Magda an old fling even?"

Broderick laughed. Interesting how her words were so cold compared to the heat from her cheek. "Magda well, she's an old friend, you should watch out for her. If she wanted me you'd be out of luck, she gets what she wants. In a room full of women, I'd still be dancing with you. The most beautiful one. If you're worried, Magda has nothing on you."

"A host just making a guest feel welcome. Shall I bring up those names you didn't want me to mention the night you arrived?"

Broderick was the one to pull away now. His grin showed perfect white teeth, but he moved back until his mouth was near her ear. His whisper gave her goose bumps. "Are you trying to say you want me to take you on a visit to the garden house? If I get you alone and use all my charms, will you tell me how an American washes up on Scotland's shore without any papers?" It was bait pure and simple, but he felt no reaction from her.

"The boat capsized after all. Everything was washed away including my pocketbook."

"Of course, how could I forget?" If only he could learn to lie that well. "I thought perhaps they were kept in the belt I was told of. Mrs. Buchanan's a little too proper to take a woman to the skin to find out. Of course, I know you aren't wearing it in this outfit." Even the slightest movement didn't give her away.

"The chastity belt my father always told me to wear. With talk like taking me to the garden house, should I go put it back on? I thought it ruined the lines of the dress."

Broderick spun her away as she grinned wide, only their hands touched. Over Elise's shoulder, ice blue eyes stared at him. A day of hunting had not changed Alexander's opinion any. The look in his eyes was enough for Broderick to know he still had an enemy.

Alexander tapped Elise's shoulder. "Do you mind if I cut in?"

At the sound of Alexander's voice, there was no mistaking the tremor in Elise's hand, but the smile remained on her face. She was some actress. "Why not ask your own wife, Colquhoun. She's looking a little bored." Broderick spun Elise back into his arms. He did it for no other reason than he disliked the man.

As Alex moved off and asked Cornelia to dance, Broderick felt Elise's head rest on his shoulder. This situation with Alexander was nothing to do with advances. It was pure fear. With all the right curves that lined up in all the right places, he did not have to fake that he enjoyed it. He did have to fake that his mind was racing to figure out what was going on in his house. Broderick was certain he had a real problem on his hands.

~

Elise watched Broderick get up from the table as she came into the dining hall at breakfast. He met her at the door and kissed her cheek. Odd after the questions the night before.

"I think it's time we were properly introduced. North Star isn't it?" he asked.

Her heart jumped to her throat. "What on earth do you mean?" She hoped she sounded normal.

"We found your fisherman alive last night. That was the commotion, the ghost was just a ruse. He was quite informative about what he was doing when he sank. I made a few phone calls as soon as I heard what that fellow had to say about you. Half of London is anxiously awaiting North Star and the report she hinted she had. Why didn't you tell me that you're a spy for our side?"

Elise couldn't match his smile. She had no reason to rejoice. "If you just had a car I could have stolen, I would have been out of here before they ever arrived. The man after me is in your home and I didn't invite him. Before that there was no reason you needed to get involved in this."

Broderick's smile faded as he looked over at the table of guests. The fear she showed took on a completely new meaning when his eyes landed on Alexander. "You really just said what I think you did?"

MacGillivray called over to break up their conference. "So, Broderick, some host you're being, ignoring us over a creature such as Elise. Then what did I expect from the likes of you? The stories I could tell would turn these ladies' ears pink and their cheeks red."

Things had changed so quickly. She was exposed. Though she wasn't completely among the enemy, she was still very much in danger. With a long look at Broderick, Elise made up her mind that he was the only chance she had to get out of there alive. "Our coldness toward each other," she muttered under her breath in an act of self-preservation.

"Lucky thing you flirted back. Make it hard if you hated me. A lovers' spat we'll soon remedy. I would say over my reputation with women would be good enough reason. Lots of ammunition to fling at me with all Bruce has whispered to you."

Elise leaned near his ear as she passed him. "I always knew you were trying to get me into bed. Some of us have willpower, though."

The smirk was clear as Broderick headed over to the table, then he saw the fishing equipment sitting by the door waiting for them to finish. "You can actually fish, can't you?" he whispered.

"Wouldn't have challenged you if I couldn't." Elise heard him let out a sigh of relief as he pulled out a chair for her.

The gracious host came back easily. "You'll forgive Elise if she wants my attention, won't you, Bruce?" He held out a chair for Magda, there was no missing his whisper in her ear. The woman's eyes turned to her widening quickly. So she wasn't just there to grieve then. Assuming she even had a husband. She wasn't going out with them during the day staying behind alone.

The old man's smile lit up the room. "Perhaps I shall have to take her aside and warn her of your sort, right in front of her you're propositioning another woman. A decent girl shouldn't be with you. If the stories are even half-true, you've lived a life of adventure. Exotic travels, wild parties, beautiful women," he teased causing Broderick to grimace.

"A boy needs to sow his oats when he's young, but I have Broderick talking of marriage now that he's a man," Elise said with a straight face. Broderick spewed out his coffee at her words, just as she hoped he would. It drew a laugh from all. "Still it can't hurt to hear of the competition now that I've just about forgiven him for the last one he brought up. You should have heard the row before you got here."

MacGillivray whispered in Elise's ear while she ate. She had washed away any doubts of her having been in his life for less than a week. Elise caught Broderick looking, and he raised his glass to her slightly. When Elise smiled back, it was the smile of a concubine. There was no denying what it meant to all who saw it, which was everyone. Elise had an ally until the Cavalry came. Until then, all it would take was one accident at the top of the stairs, one stray bullet while out shooting, and all her work would be undone. It didn't give her much confidence that she would get out of this. The thought that worried her most was if they didn't care to recover what she had found and only wished her never to deliver it.

~

When night finally came, Elise hadn't exactly proven she fished as well as she hunted, but she had at least shown up Broderick as well as the others. They feasted on trout that night at supper, her six to his one. Even Alexander only got two. After two days of outdoor activity, most of them couldn't help but yawn shortly after supper so Broderick escorted Elise openly back to his room.

Earlier, when they were out of the house, her things were moved and even put away in the dresser. Other things lay about as if she had trouble with the decision of what to wear that morning.

"Now, what is all this about spies being in my house?" Broderick asked as soon as the door closed.

Elise looked over at him and retired behind a screen to change. "Why did you never tell them of me even before Per was found? I'm surprised you mentioned nothing of my spill to your guests. An amusing anecdote to tell at dinner," Elise noted instead of answering. "Like that refueling station you're hiding in the village, in your old friend Dunham's warehouse."

"You saw that did you?" Broderick smiled. "Wouldn't you have been weary? A mysterious stranger that gives some rather flimsy excuse for what she was out doing in a boat in the middle of a storm. I had you pegged for a spy though not ally. Your clothes had French labels and no rationing in effect. However, your Captain Per seemed not to care that the doctor was talking of him remaining covered and warm, only that we keep looking for you. He wouldn't shut up until Emmon told him it was you that had sent us to look for him. He then whispered that what you had was extremely important to our efforts in the war. I knew as much last night with those questions of mine. I couldn't go to him to get any answers. Thought maybe you would give me some. Damn, but you can lie! I didn't know the details until I was able to get to a phone."

Elise shook her head. "I'm a French resistance spy that's been on the run for six months, and the man after me is eating dinner across your table. Would you have believed me even if I had told you?"

"Perhaps I wouldn't have." Broderick was silent for a moment before he continued. "That call you made, it was to London not Aberdeen, wasn't it?"

Elise nodded briefly.

"They didn't tell you I was on General Turnbull's staff?" Broderick finished.

"The old bull, is it?" Elise's words made Broderick grin. "Should everyone know of the great Broderick Sinclair simply because you have a castle to your name? Or is it that I'm a woman and should have heard of your exploits?" She didn't share in his smile.

Broderick still laughed at her words. "I don't claim such a grand reputation. The General is the man behind the scenes in the war and I'm his chief aide. The report you're protecting will be on his desk minutes after you've delivered it to whoever your contact is. You don't have to act in front of me, your life and your secrets are safe."

Elise stuck her head around the screen with a grin. "You forgot to mention my virtue in there. You make no mention if it's safe."

"So how is it you are able to resist me? Forget love. There aren't many that have the willpower." Broderick asked and then his mouth dropped, as she emerged from behind the screen naked as could be. He took in the view with pleasure there was no denying.

"Damn it, man, when you say such things it gives me the willpower to resist the King of England himself even if he wasn't married!" Elise snapped. It was only then she flicked her eyes toward the door just for a second as she searched around.

Broderick set his face and turned to find Alexander at the door, his own jaw sagging a bit. It was a view to behold after all. "Can I help you?"

"I thought this was my room," Alexander stammered.

"Four doors down on the other side, by the divan," Broderick corrected as Elise picked up a robe that was on the floor and covered herself.

"I see your argument has resolved itself," Alexander pointed out when the distraction had gone.

Elise plastered a smile on her face and sat in Broderick's lap. "Oh, we're on another now. Isn't making up always more fun after a fight? Perhaps, as a man, you can understand why he brings up old girlfriends just to bait me."

"Thank you for the directions. Sorry to have disturbed you." Alexander closed the door behind him and silence filled the room.

Broderick pushed her off his lap and went to lock the door. He turned back to her slowly. It was time for answers. He didn't even need to ask the question, she saw it on his face.

"Do you know a Lili connected to all this?" He watched her face turn pale, with her complexion, he would have thought it impossible to lose any more color. It was not the question she expected.

"Where did you hear that name?" she whispered as he walked closer.

Broderick pulled her to the bed on the far side of the room, far from where anyone could hear at the door. "Who is this Lili?" he asked sitting down underneath the dark green canopy.

"Lili Muller was the secretary to General Meierhoff. She'd been with him since he arrived in Paris after the Germans rolled in."

Broderick scratched his head. "I've heard of the man. He's in charge of military strategy if I remember correctly."

Elise nodded mechanically. "That's a polite way to put it. He's in charge of blowing things up."

"What does that have to do with you?" Broderick asked.

"I have a better question. Why is the man after me in your house? How do I know you didn't call them? All those women that have succumbed to your charms, you think I should be an easy mark. Is that your plan?"

Broderick couldn't help but let his jaw drop slightly. "You can't think I'm a German agent."

Her voice was cold there was no denying that, even if she lounged on the bed. "Even before they got here, there were whispers with Emmon as you watched me. Papers you didn't want me to see."

"I know a lot of classified information from my job. Emmon is my assistant. He went with me to London when I took the position with the General. I had to bring him back just to take care of all those messages from the general even if this is a vacation."

"Why should I trust you?"

Broderick went to the wardrobe and pulled out a gun of Great War vintage. Well-cleaned, it would kill as well as anything new. "If there are Germans in my house, you'll need this." Silence except for the sound of the chamber being checked on the pistol. Broderick took a long time as he settled back beside her before he spoke again. "Lorne is in a Japanese prisoner of war camp with the Argyll and Sutherland Highlanders. Been there for a year. Bruce's son is with him and one of the Dunham's we mentioned. Is that enough of a reason that I wouldn't be helping the enemy?" That was the main reason he had stopped in Inverness to tell Bruce of any news they had on the Highlanders. That was when Bruce had brought up the engagement party. Broderick wasn't even to have entertained them other than supper. Oh bloody hell, we mentioned to a spy Dunham was in the Pacific."

"I would have thought you'd have enlisted with your brother. Same regiment and all."

He shook his head. "We both graduated military school before the war started, but I had gotten a regular degree at St. Andrews before I had gone, a long family tradition. The General is an old friend of my father's, they served together in the Great War. He needed an aide. Lorne was commanding his own men when the General's request came. I was just a lieutenant. Lorne preferred to command and he suggested me, so, I went to London and the General."

The door handle rattled after a quick knock. Broderick forgot he had locked the door, and he pulled her over to his lap. He felt Elise's breathing stop and not from who might be at the door.

Many women had been in that position and none of them had shown such a reaction. To know one was good looking was one thing, but with that tiny lack of control by a woman that could lie through her teeth like Elise did, was something new.

"You can trust me or the man you say is hunting you. I need to know what I'm fighting. Now what does Lili have to do with you?" he asked as the handle rattled again.

It seemed like forever before she finally spoke. In reality, it was mere seconds. "I'm Lili Muller," she whispered in his ear.

Broderick let out a long breath as he realized just how much danger she was in with the words he had overheard.

"Sir?" Hugh called out from the door.

"Yes," Broderick answered.

"There's a message for you from the General. Another report from Kapheira. I thought you'd want to hear, a boat escaped they just made it to ally held land, the Princesses' son is safe. He got out with them. Safe as he can be anyway in Egypt. But the word is they were slaughtering everyone they found, the Jews that were there, the Russians, the rest they weren't so quick about, they were alive when the boat slipped away."

"What the hell am I supposed to do about it at eleven at night?" Broderick called back with a growl. He was starting to regret having ever taken the job. He should be out fighting more than a mound of paperwork. "Get word to the Consul in Cairo, Augustin and all the refugees see if you can't get them here somehow. Dunham's not able to help right now. Tell them they have my backing if anyone balks at letting them in Britain. If they still do tell Henry Dunham I need a favor." There was no answer from the door. Hugh had left.

Deep blue stared back at him as her eyes slid open. "I saw Alexander Colquhoun in an SS officer's uniform the day my boat left. If you didn't call them, then I can't figure anyway that they could have known I was here. Is there something you're working on? If there is, I'd hide it."

"Christ!" She had a harder war than he had, that wasn't hard stuck sitting in an office, not to mention she was the one to figure out his guest's purpose. He went over to a side door and knocked faintly. Magda appeared quickly. "Did you hear about your son?" It was the first smile he'd seen on her face since she arrived as she nodded. "Go, she says Alexander is SS. Get our guest out of here and the both of you leave now as soon as the house is to bed, I'll make excuses for you say you took ill in the night. Have Emmon show you the tackman's house not far from here. Get her captain out of here with you. We can't risk bringing a doctor here to see to him anymore." The door closed silently.

"What on earth do you have going on here?"

Broderick turned around slowly. "There was an escape of inmates at Treblinka concentration camp earlier this year. Magda is here with one getting information, no one is believing what he's telling about it. She's Czech resistance, she's been sneaking in and out of there since they took over. Her father is part of the government in exile, and yes she is actually a Princess. Her husband worried about her making the trips, and he's the one that died. Not knowing what kind of weapons they might have I don't want to risk the household. Can you help me keep them around and occupied until Turnbull can get someone here? I'll call first thing in the morning."

Finally, Elise smiled. "Can I be safe from the reputation MacGillivray spoke of for that long?"

Broderick laughed. "Usually the stories of Lorne and I get mingled. He is only ten months older than I. Everything you heard, cut it in half and it might be closer to the truth."

"Those would still be quite a few women."

He smiled wide. "True, and I enjoyed every minute of it." It didn't surprise him she pulled away. Still put in the position to get close to a title, many Broderick had met would have taken the opportunity. Carol for instance.

Her laugh was good to hear. However, he grabbed a blanket from the foot of the bed and headed for the couch. Elise only raised an eyebrow, having to wonder just how much of those stories were true. A flirt maybe. Elise started smiling. MacGillivray would be disappointed she had nothing to add.

~

Elise woke to find Broderick gone from the room. She could vaguely hear a voice and followed it after she dressed. She had a better wardrobe of clothes people left behind than she had as a student and only could acquire when she modeled. She found Broderick in the adjoining room speaking into a recording device. "Well, you did say you would take care of it in the morning."

When Broderick saw her, he held up his hand for silence as he finished his thoughts. He was dictating a letter by the sounds of it. Soon he shut off the device and pushed his work aside. "You slept well, I hope?"

"Fair enough. The wine and drinks last night seemed to have helped me along. It's been awhile since I've been able to partake of so much. A secretary doesn't get the chance that often."

He cocked his head. "I'm imagining that you weren't trained as a secretary. What did you do before the war?"

"I mentioned modeling I know, but my main job was working as a translator and enjoying myself royally in Paris. I speak seven languages fluently, including German and French, like a born speaker of both." Elise held up her hand and flicked off each. "Italian, Danish, German, Spanish, French, Norwegian, Polish, and of course, English. There are a few others I can make myself understood in, but I'm by no means fluent."

Elise watched Broderick's eyebrow rise significantly. "A useful accomplishment for a spy."

She shrugged her shoulders. "No kidding. I was in the office two years before the Americans joined the war." Elise looked over in an elaborate gilt mirror with a sigh. Her reflection seemed transparent as it stared back. "I haven't been called my own name for so long from those four years of pretending, I sometimes forget who the real Elise is. She's like that ghost of yours. I know I'm there, but you never see me."

Broderick sat back in his chair, letting the work fade from thought. "And who is Elise Dutton then?"

"Do you really care?"

He looked up and she saw the humor in his eyes. "You let MacGillivray and the staff, tell you too many stories. Do they have you thinking I'm that much of a cad? Tell me who she is."

Elise could only shrug. "You know most of it. My parents have that little bookstore I mentioned to supplement their income. My father is a writer and my mother a painter. My father was very big on education. I learned other languages from a toddler onward. I graduated from high school only a few weeks before everything changed. The day the stock market crashed, what money he had saved was gone. I modeled to help and when I was home, I learned to shoot well. Then an aunt died and left both my parents and me some money in '34. I used mine to go to college in Paris. I modeled there too, when I needed extra money in school."

Broderick sat there straight faced as she finished. "You're right, not quite what I should date." Then the grin grew.

"Yeah, I've heard what you will date." Elise threw a pillow at him. "I'm going to breakfast before you insult me anymore."

Broderick held up a hand to stop her. "Emmon tells me that Aubrey has been snooping already, so we'd best go down together."

"Very well, but any more cracks like that and our fake argument will become real."

Broderick laughed. "It won't be the first time. I'd make a good showing of myself."

Elise stopped with her hand on the doorknob as he moved from behind the desk. "You've seen me naked. Perhaps I should find out how long we've been together. Make it a reasonable amount of time, I don't want you to think me easy." When Broderick had her trapped against the door, Elise did nothing to stop it. No one would believe it if she couldn't even let him touch her.

"Easy never! I've seen the way you shoot. I would say a good year at least. I haven't been here in over that time so it would make sense you've never been here to learn your way around. Naturally, I've never seen you shoot or fish either."

"You thought about it, didn't you?" Elise asked quietly. She should have thought of it herself before then as she was the one used to making up lies.

"Having you parade around with nothing on is what I thought about, our history was secondary. Should I repay the view so you can lie properly?" He grinned as if he looked to see how far she would let him go.

Elise opened the door, and they tumbled out of the room. Broderick laughed until he caught the change in Elise when she saw Cornelia Colquhoun in the tapestry-lined hall.

Elise could only worry if the woman had listened at the door. She had let herself get too lax because she was on British soil. She had to watch herself more closely.

Broderick grabbed hold of Elise's arm and pulled her close. "Oh, no, you don't. You can't say that to me and not let me defend myself." He ad-libbed before he kissed her.

MacGillivray's whispers had a basis after all. Broderick was an expert with women. He was far too good at it for Elise who hadn't had a proper relationship for as long as she had played the part of Lili. She couldn't meet with too many French else the Germans would get suspicious, and she wasn't going to date the enemy.

"All right, all right. You are the best I've ever kissed. Can't you even take a joke?" Elise finally admitted, but it had been a long time before she pulled away. It had been four years after all. She needn't let it end before she had to. Broderick still kissed her neck when Cornelia finally left them.

"I think we both know your train of thought in regards to my parade last night," Elise whispered low so no one could overhear. "You should have seen Cornelia's face," she added, though she didn't want him to stop what he did at her neck.

"Sir, a tenant is here to see ye, it's young Hamish." Emmon announced, and Broderick straightened up. Elise would have sworn he was caught like that far too often to not even flinch.

Broderick just grinned at her as he arranged his clothes. "This may take a while. I'll meet you at breakfast." He walked off, and Elise sank into a nearby chair. Four years without a kiss was too long to be able to toss that off so lightly.

"Ah, there you are my dear."

Elise closed her eyes at Bruce's arrival. She knew he would be able to read everything in her eyes and would make her the next on the list of women he told everyone about at his next get-together. "Come, I'll walk you to breakfast now that you've been left without an escort and poor Magda is ill I hear I should despair without company."

"You saw?"

He took her arm lightly and helped her to her feet. Like when he told her stories of Broderick, he put his head near hers. "What I am more concerned with is what I saw when Broderick stopped by my place on his way up here. It's when we planned this little party."

"Another woman to tell me about, Bruce. I shall tire of the gossip soon."

The old man laughed, but even before he stopped, the look in his eyes told her he was in all seriousness. "I guess the better way to put it was what I didn't see. You weren't in the car with him from London, and there was no mention of a new woman to meet him here. I'm not going to say he doesn't have good taste, but even my boy Broderick doesn't move that fast to be talking of marriage in only a week." His voice was low enough no one could hear, but Alexander looked up from the dining room at their approach.

Surrounded by Van Dyck, Gainsborough, Canaletto, and Hogarth paintings among others, it took the menace away from the situation even though Elise felt her skin go clammy from the look she saw on Alexander's face.

There could be no slip-ups. "I suppose you know all about Broderick's father's exploits as well? You really must let me in on the stories. All the family ghosts as it were."

Bruce's eye narrowed, then he followed her gaze. "I see Broderick hasn't arrived yet. If that's the case, I shall show you where I found the old Duke in flagrante with one of your American film stars. No, the boys came by it naturally." He patted her hand with glee and led her down the hall.

"What do you do, Bruce?"

He chuckled. "I would have thought you'd figured it out by now. I just am. If I were young I should probably enlist and do my part, but even though I've no castle like Broderick, I have more than enough money to sponge off others."

Elise had been trying to figure out what was going on ever since Alexander had been standing at the bottom of the stairs. If Bruce didn't have any power of his own then ... "You've lots of friends in high places though, and you take along your friends, I suppose?"

"Oh, of course, my dear. Generals, Ministers of Parliament, Lords, Dukes, Union leaders. Everyone loves my stories," Bruce said as they neared a wing of the castle she hadn't been to yet. It was by far grander than the rest as if that was possible. There was the connection, though. Bruce knew people and in Inverness of all places, no one would suspect they were there to spy on anyone. All they had to do was listen to stories, and if a name came up, elicit an invitation to the next party. Ask questions about people, the Dunham's had come up a lot since dinner that night. The Dunham's that owned a giant ship builders in Bristol and ships that covered the world. Broderick was the aide to a rather important general, after all. Not to mention a refueling station that hopefully wasn't being used during the visit. She was just in the wrong castle at the wrong time.

"Loose lips sink ships Bruce you really do talk too much."

They spun at Broderick's voice. "One hundred twenty rooms. How did you even find us here? We shouldn't have had to lock the door."

"Simple. This is where Bruce always takes beautiful females he admires."

Elise turned slowly back to Bruce. "I don't suppose you were the guest with the American film star?"

Broderick shook his head, but it wasn't for being wrong. "My father was most displeased that I walked in on them at the age of ten. As I said, always lock the door, isn't that right, Bruce, old man?" The old man in question blushed like a schoolboy. "Come on, breakfast is just waiting for you two to show up."

~

MacGillivray used up some of his precious gas rations to take them out to see a bit more of the countryside. The minute Iona saw Elise walk in the door covered in mud, she was drawing a bath for her. Sightseeing hadn't been so fun for all of them it seemed. What a room to become civilized again was all Elise could think as she sank into the tub. Dark green art tiles on the floor, walls, and ceiling, even the fireplace was covered in them. Shelves, nooks, and mantles were all filled with verdant green plants. It was Broderick's mothers' bathroom, her personal addition to the castle Iona had told her. She redecorated, the step mother just made him a very happy man. Since Broderick's father had died the year before, the castle sat unused but for servants just waiting for a war to end so they could return once more. That's what she thought at any rate. There were children from many of the Duke's friends escaping the London bombings. She never saw them though, only heard mention of it. Still the servants seemed to relish having someone in the house once they knew she wasn't a German spy at least.

"Oh sorry, I didn't know anyone was in here. Just giving a tour."

Elise turned her head to find Broderick at the door he was already starting to close it as she caught sight of the three women peering in. "Just dreaming what it would be like to live as a duchess. Come wash my back would you dear I think I have mud even there."

The door stopped midway and Broderick's face peered back around with a grin. "Considering I'm only a Lord, I think I may be in trouble ladies. One more lost to my brother's title. But when a lady beckons who am I to argue."

Gladys' giggle filtered in even with the door half-closed as Broderick slipped in, trying to keep Elise from sight. Even from the door, it was obvious there weren't any bubbles to conceal her.

"I am so sorry." Rebecca called from the hall. "When I started to fall you were the closest thing to grab. I didn't know you were off balance too." She got out before Broderick closed the door.

He raised an eyebrow as he crossed the room. "I thought you didn't trust me to not try and get you in bed and now you're asking me to wash your back? Awfully forward aren't you?"

"I've had to share a tub for four years I wasn't a very well paid secretary, I couldn't afford one of my own. If I'm going to die, I'm going to die clean. Besides with all the gossip Bruce is spreading I think your tour would have been disappointed if we didn't have a little scandal for their amusement."

Broderick sat on the edge of the tub but Elise said nothing as his eyes wandered. "I think you have an admirer. Rebecca pushed me in just after you kissed me, couldn't go in without dragging her with me."

He frowned noticeably. "Sit up, let's get the mud off. You're hair looks caked with it."

Elise's groan filled the room. She didn't want to move from the warm cocoon of water. "When she tried to stand up I got used as her crutch. I was flat in the mud at the time."

"Sorry I missed the show."

"I would have pulled you in with me just as payback for all the laughing."

Broderick dumped a bucket of water over her head in answer. While Elise was still sputtering Broderick pulled her over and put in some shampoo.

"I thought you had work to get done? Seem to be busy every time I turn around." She asked at his silence.

"Talked Turnbull into another week off since I'm battling Germans this week. I'm not so pressed for time now. You in the bath, I would have found time regardless. So how is it you resist me anyway?"

Elise sounded like a cat purring when it was petted right. "Right now I have to fight it hard."

Broderick laughed at that, but even as he did, he carefully tipped her head back to rinse the soap from her hair. "Found your weakness have I?" He leaned near her ear. "In that case." With hands full of suds he ran his hands down her back and washed away the last of the mud. Elise couldn't keep the gasp from escaping when he slipped his hands around and grazed the underside of her breasts gently.

"If you didn't look like you enjoy this so much, I might stop thinking I was being forward."

Elise let out a sigh that only enforced the impression. She couldn't help it. "I'm not the one with the reputation with every person who knows you telling me stories and a litany of names. What makes this different from what you've done to all the rest? I can't blame myself for showing a reaction. It's been four years since a man has touched me."

"No wonder you got so heated at just a touch." His hand slid slowly down her stomach. Broderick didn't even hesitate a moment before a finger slid over her clitoris.

"What are you doing?" Even as she got the words out, her mouth opened to let out a moan of delight when his finger buried itself deep within her. Broderick kissed her before she let out a sound, if they were still close outside no one would know.

"Just relax. If we're making up its time you looked like you've been enjoying yourself." Slow and steady he found the right spot every time and her breath caught. "Why are you denying yourself, even a fling to remind you there's life still?"

"I refused to get someone killed because they knew me if I was ever found out, and I refused to sleep with the enemy. I'm out of practice and yes, I find you attractive, but so have a lot of others."

Broderick lowered his head, but Elise caught him biting his lip as if keeping himself from speaking, there was no denying his grin though.

"What?"

"I doubt you would believe me if I told you."

Elise settled back up to her neck in the tub, it only made Broderick push deeper inside. "Try me anyway."

He shrugged without taking his hand away. "Every story you heard from the staff is false."

Elise shook her head adamantly. "No."

"See you don't believe me."

"I didn't say that. Bruce said he'd heard you're the best kiss a number of your women had. Limited though my experience may be with your skills, I sure as hell can't find fault with that story and don't intend to have you try and change my mind." Broderick actually looked like he might have been blushing. Then again, he was sitting over a steaming tub fully clothed. "Dear lord please finish, I can't talk about nothing while..."

He shook his head. "Just relax and talk to me. Right here the war doesn't exist for a few minutes, there's no reason to rush it. I just like knowing you aren't completely immune to my charms when I can catch you in an unguarded moment."

"So what is the truth?"

He looked as smug as a cat that ate the canary. "You should try me when I don't have an audience."

"This litany of women?" Elise clarified.

"Ah yes, the truth. My staff are imaginative gossips that need something to do."

Elise closed her eyes, but it didn't keep the smile from forming. "So you're pure as an altar boy?"

"I can say without reservation that I haven't done anything more in this house than a kiss or two well until you. My father developed a heart condition. A scandal like that though... we were used to keeping such things out of his eyes and ears. Such a lovely woman, I would have hated to ruin my stepmother's life if he'd died young. We were worried about our exploits giving him a heart attack and it was his own that did him in. She came home for a visit from the hospital a year ago and he was gone before her leave was up. We saved those for the island, I'm a proper gentleman here. I'll introduce you to orgies even if you want. Just don't believe what the staff says is all I'm saying. You aren't immune to me, are you?" Elise opened her eyes to find that Broderick had leaned over her. She was staring into those deep brown eyes. It didn't take much Elise barely had to pull and Broderick fell in on top of her.

"You can tell me when we're finished." She pulled the sweater off and it hit the floor with a splash. "I've lied for so long I wouldn't trust a word out of my mouth."

Broderick started laughing. "Quite right, but you could have picked anytime when it wasn't a muddy bath."

The tap at the door barely gave warning before the door opened and Iona walked in with Elise's clothes for the evening.

"Lord Broderick, ye couldna have taken your clothes off first."

"You're right Iona." Broderick kicked off his shoes and pulled off his pants. The gasp from the older woman sent Elise into giggles.

"Grown up a bit has he?" Elise asked with a grin.

"Iona, why don't you send Hugh with some dry clothes for me?"

Elise started laughing as soon as the door closed.

"You know you might seriously ruin me for all other women. They'll seem completely uncomplicated without a single thing to talk about." Broderick whispered.

"I didn't know talking was high on your priorities."

"When someone has nothing to talk about I don't encourage it just for the sake of talking, man or woman. I rather like listening to you."

"Flatterer."

"Now where were we?"

~

Broderick remained half dressed for supper when the phone message came for him. It was a task he took seriously bedding her. Watching him disappear shirtless down the hall was a remarkable sight, but Elise caught Alexander's eyes peering from his room. She locked her door quickly and for several moments used it to keep her upright. They knew she was Lili!!! How could they not? Before it was just supposition, but they watched her too close to not know. She couldn't keep her heart from racing. Elise felt as trapped as she had when she sat in holes in the ground for days. Her nerves were all but shot. To play this part after six months on the run was driving her insane. She was certain there was a mole in the British government. The highlands of Scotland were a long way from Bergen, Norway where the Germans held sway. Even if they were there to try to find out information from Broderick, they had figured out that Lili was out of German held territory or for that matter not dead. Someone had to have let Alexander know she had reported in to the main office. Someone had... Ahhh! She was doing it again. The last of Broderick's drink still sat on the table. Elise downed it before she opened the door. How long she could keep it up was anyone's guess. The events of the last week raced around her head never giving her any rest.

Elise was still agitated when Broderick came down. True, she had spent four years playing the part, but then she knew it wasn't a fight for her life. She was Lili, end of story. Her parents owned a bookstore, she modeled, and she had been to the Sorbonne. Only places and names had changed.

"Nothing too important I hope," Elise asked of the message that had taken him away.

Broderick pulled up a chair. "Not so important that I need to ignore you. I don't need to have you start another argument with me over it."

She smiled. "As long as you've seen the error of your ways."

Broderick's voice dropped as he brought the glass to his mouth. "But the General has been held up. It will be a few days longer before he can get here. He seems to want to take care of this problem of ours personally."

Her smile froze at the thought of having to keep up the act any longer. Broderick noticed Alexander moving closer trying to hear their conversation. He took her face in his hands. The kiss that followed made Elise forget she was surrounded by spies, forget there was even a war. Broderick took his time before he finally let her go. Alexander turned away, but she was sure he didn't look embarrassed at the scene. Gladys across the room however, blushed when their eyes met. "Should have kept you in bed longer I guess." He whispered.

"Why don't you go up to bed if your headache is so bad?" Broderick announced loud enough they didn't have to strain to hear him. "You shouldn't have come down at all if you felt so under the weather."

Elise hoped the gratitude was evident in her eyes as she walked off.

At least until Cornelia ran over to her. "Here let me help you to your room. I know how bad headaches can be, I get some just awful ones myself." She took Elise's arm.

"I don't really think I need any help to find my room." Elise cursed as she left the room, for even a headache had given them an opening.

"Nonsense. What kind of woman would I be to repay your hospitality by allowing an ill woman to wander these dank halls alone? With Magda sick we have to take care of the remaining guests." Cornelia replied.

The words rubbed Elise the wrong way. She knew they suspected and it was bait to try to find out for sure. "It's just a headache and I've always found the castle anything but dank."

"How long has that been anyway?"

"This is my first visit to the castle. I met Broderick in London about a year ago." Thank the Lord they had discussed such things.

"Why not head home then?"

Was that what saved her? She sounded American and they couldn't imagine one so well placed in the Paris offices. Granted with the situation that had been in Paris when it fell, she shouldn't even be in the situation she was. Americans were told to leave, they weren't part of the war then. If she'd had to make that trip she did with Per before America joined the war, she could have gotten into serious trouble. She had gone against the whole US government's stance of being neutral. "My parents thought it was too dangerous to attempt after they heard of my dating Broderick, hoping a Lord might be added to the family." Her parents would hate her to imply such a thing. They would have been more impressed if he was an artist or writer. They valued education, not that Broderick didn't have that either. Charles and Kathleen Dutton would truly not care that Broderick was a Lord. Now, given the chance to study the art and books that the house held, they might forgive her for the lies she told.

Cornelia laughed. It sounded false to Elise's ears. Elise said little else as they walked to keep up the pretense of the headache. Truth be told, if the woman didn't shut up soon, she would have one for real.

Cornelia closed the door behind them when they reached Broderick's room. "Oh this is so much more elaborate than ours."

Elise hadn't really looked at it until Cornelia brought it up. Maybe that she was alone with Broderick in the room had something to do with ignoring her surroundings. Papered in green brocade with an elaborate plaster ceiling and accented with gold, from picture frames to curtains to gold leaf on the plaster. She had to wonder what the Duke's room looked like if this was the second son's.

"Here I keep some aspirin with me for just this reason. Take a couple and have a short nap. Perhaps you'll feel better enough to join us for cards after supper is over." Cornelia handed Elise some tablets. Before she had to think of an answer though Mary thrust open the door and jostled her way in with a tray. Cornelia started slightly.

"I was told you're feeling under the weather and to bring you your dinner and some tea. That should help your headache go away. Out all day in this wind has been known to do this," Mary chattered.

"How is Magda by the way?" Cornelia asked.

"Oh she's at the doctors' house to let him watch her close. Tricky little infection, but I hear she's getting a little better."

"Well since you're in such good hands now, I'll just go back to dinner. I do hope you can play cards later." The door closed with a resounding thud and Elise let out a sigh of relief.

"My dear." Elise put a finger to her mouth figuring Cornelia was still outside listening at the keyhole. Mary nodded and began to prattle about her favorite subject, Broderick's escapades, as she poured the tea and served her dinner. "Well when you finish, you take a nap. That's the best thing when you're under the weather."

~

After a time, Broderick came in waking Elise, as she had fallen asleep in reality.

"Is your head better? We've gotten a game of bridge together and we need a fourth."

Elise pointed to the door and he nodded. They were out there. "Much better. I guess some quiet was all I needed." He smiled relieved. Elise had to wonder what meaning it had though since no one else could see it. There was something more than play-acting in it.

~

The scream woke Broderick quickly. They were alone in the room. He quickly put a hand over Elise's mouth when he heard what was to come out of it. It was gibberish to him, but it was in German. If someone woke from the noise and heard it, there would be trouble. Her eyes flew open at his touch.

"You're all right." He said quietly smoothing the hair that stuck to her forehead with sweat. He could only think of his brother living like she had for the last months, but in Lorne's case there was little chance for escape.

"I--I--" Her breathing came ragged as if she had been trying to escape some terrible danger.

"Calm down. I'll keep you from being chased tonight." He wanted to tell her that there was no danger, that it was only a dream. He couldn't make himself, not when her terror might be right down the hall. Magda made runs home, no one ever imagined how she did it, one mention of Princess and they never looked farther. She was a damned tough woman playing a part, her sister had been the biggest slut in China, mistress to warlords, opium addict, she died while in bed with said warlord when Shanghai fell. Magdela and Magdelena, his Magda played the part of the sister perfected when in company. There was a reason that many never looked past the title Princess, she bred the impression very well. Fancy dresses, drinking, smoking, laughs all around hiding that her husband was imprisoned, the Prince that flew missions over Europe as dangerous as any posting there was. Her work was dangerous, but she never had to sit there day after day pretending she was something she wasn't. A month or two Magda went...the latest getting their guest from Treblinka out, then she'd come back and be the princess again. Any moment Elise had to dread looking up from her desk knowing they wanted her dead. No escape. His presence brought the safety that she had been denied though and she calmed quickly. "How on earth did you get caught up in this?"

Her breathing slowed as Broderick's hand rested on her neck as she lay there. "At the Sorbonne," she finally spoke. "I went to school with a member of the resistance, my roommate's boyfriend. He joined as soon as the Germans took over Paris, and through that, he found out about a job at Meierhoff's office. They wanted someone inside that could feed them information about what went on, nothing dangerous. I didn't need to seduce anyone. I didn't need to sneak into anyone's office."

She continued. "All I had to do was report on what I typed and heard in my normal duties. Lili Muller was created using most of my own background so I wouldn't slip up. We even had a contact in the Sorbonne office that changed the name on my records to give me a history they could check. That I was a model didn't hurt things either in my edging out the competition for the job. My one job was to gather information. Marie's boyfriend worked at a café. If I had anything, I would go have dinner and leave it with my bill. If I was ever caught, all I could give up was Marie's boyfriend."

Broderick leaned back against the headboard to get comfortable. "It sounds rather fool proof. How did Alexander catch on to you?"

"He didn't. I was undetected as both an American and a member of the resistance until June when traitors gave up the ranks of the Special Operations Executive. My name was supposed to be safe with them instead of the regular resistance members." Elise curled up, her voice little more than a whisper. "Obviously, foolproof means nothing in war. I've been on the run ever since. I escaped only because I was sick that morning and went to the doctor's at the time they visited my apartment and office. By then, the executions had already started and I ran."

There was one thing that Broderick wondered since he heard from Turnbull where she had left the continent. "Why risk crossing so far north at this time of year?"

"Only days before, I learned information that was a lot more important than a truck full of supplies to steal or where and when captured members were being transported. I doubt anyone would care I was out there since I was gone from the General's office except for that. I used my pass to get out of the city before the roadblocks could go up and then contacted the resistance in the countryside. For weeks I tried to make a plane pickup, but every time I was almost caught. So who would suspect anyone trying to get away from the Germans to go in the middle of their strongholds?"

Broderick had to look at her with different eyes when he heard that. He saw just how she could stand there in little more than a robe, even when he had heard her reaction to him several nights before. "Brilliant, if rather daring."

Her eyes closed as she recounted the last of her story. "I've been underground ever since, moving only when it was safe, hiding in holes under the floor for days on end, if need be. Finally, I made it to the Norwegian coast, and from there we made radio contact again after months. I told the British where I would land. Something went wrong yet again. I was waiting for the guards to pass by when I saw Alexander asking someone if they had heard of a woman named Lili looking for a boat. Luckily, he didn't notice it odd that a crate of fish was loaded onto a fishing boat instead of off it shortly after that. There wasn't a storm when we left, the sky was clear. I thought it covered any tracks I might have left, but here is that SS Major staring at me from across the dinner table." No wonder she had such dreams. She was on British soil supposedly safe and even then, she couldn't let her guard down.

It was several minutes before Broderick heard her breathing slow back to normal. There was quiet in the castle once more, but it took Broderick a long time to fall asleep. The reputation that MacGillivray had spoken of was in a good part true. It wasn't because he was an ass though, sleeping around with every woman he saw. Even with a war on, too many showed their colors, only wanting a title, a castle, money. Kissing in the garden and caught by staff there was rather a lot of that, but throwing them away after getting what he wanted. No, they never lasted long enough for that sort of caddishness to even be possible.

~

Officially, hunting was canceled due to weather, but unofficially Broderick didn't trust any of them with guns handy anymore. That and several ships were to refuel at the village, it was best they weren't roaming about now that he knew they weren't to be trusted. After the night before, Broderick was worried they were too close to her, much too close to cause such dreams. With rain falling buckets when lunch came around, they just had a day to relax. The guests were to go home the next day and the expected Turnbull was nowhere in sight. Broderick and David played billiards in a room filled with hunting trophies, not all as local as the Highland stag and dozens of reminders of the Sinclair penchant for the military. Elise was sure that not so long ago the women would have never been allowed entrance to that male enclave. Near the fireplace, the women sat talking until Broderick finished his game. Elise joined them at the table for a moment before she kissed Broderick.

"Get me out of here." She muttered.

"Alas that I were young, Elise, I would court you myself." Bruce called from his chair giving Broderick no impediment to taking her down the hall out of their sight.

Her sigh was audible. "If I had to listen to them anymore, I was going to scream. I think they're trying torture by gossip."

Broderick grinned but it faded as he opened the door to the office off the bedroom. After years in Turnbull's office, Broderick had a definite system and only a glance told him the room wasn't as he left it. The reason for the never-ending gossip became clear, Cornelia and Rebecca were the diversion while Alexander saw to business. While Elise's things lay about for looks, until then no one had disturbed anything after Alexander had walked in on them.

"What did they see?" Elise asked as he straightened up.

"Leases, buy and sell orders for stocks, household accounts."

"I thought Turnbull kept giving you work. Like that file you about blew a blood vessel over when you thought I saw it."

Broderick looked up with a smile. "I should have known I couldn't hide anything from a spy but ever since then, I've kept it all locked up in my room safe." Elise looked around trying to see if anything had been disturbed. "No, this isn't my room. The family wing hadn't been used since my father died. With guests coming, it was easier for the staff to put me here with everyone else. What about your report? We'd never know with all those clothes lying about in the other room if it was ever searched."

Elise shook her head. "I hid that the day I woke where no one could connect it to me." She jumped toward the door. Broderick ran to grab her before she could get the door open and took her face in his hands. "Calm down. If you go rushing off, they'll know something is up." He couldn't ignore that she warmed significantly at his touch. He had to try hard not to smile.

"I don't suppose anyone has searched their rooms?"

"Emmon saw to it under the guise of housekeeping after we got the truth out of you. The only thing he could verify was that Cornelia dyes her hair." Broderick let go of her face. "Now you have a free afternoon. What are you going to do with it?"

"Well if I was smart, I would probably have you take me to bed and take my mind off all this again." Her smile was almost his undoing then and there. "But I know you have work to do so I think I'll go write a few letters to people that haven't heard from me in years and probably think I'm dead."

"That is just cruel."

Her smile lost its playfulness but didn't vanish. "You are about all that's keeping me from going crazy. Please don't stop."

~

Elise's words haunted Broderick all afternoon as he finally got some work done and not for the reason MacGillivray would have claimed. She wasn't a trained spy, no one had taught her how to deal with all this. She was just a woman that couldn't stand by and let the Germans invade unopposed. A model that spoke seven languages, with a roommate's boyfriend that came to her for help. Broderick might just have to do something drastic to get her out of this. He didn't have a clue what something drastic could be though. He spent his days organizing thousands of men for battle, what to do with two when he had no equipment or men wasn't in his scope of daily problems. The collateral damage could be too high in this case.

When Hugh knocked on the door, Broderick looked at the clock to see that the afternoon passed without interruption, in itself a miracle.

"It's time to get dressed for supper. Dr. MacInnes is springing his surprise tonight."

Broderick started smiling knowing what drastic measure would clear all this up. "Pull a few bottles of champagne from the cellar. They should celebrate this properly. Oh and have Magda recover."

"Yes sir."

~

Once the meal was over and they waited for dessert, Broderick had the champagne poured. "The floor is all yours, Doctor."

David turned to Gladys with a smile. "This whole visit has been for you. I wanted you to remember this moment as something special. I wanted it to be somewhere other than my cottage in Inverness. Gladys, will you marry me?"

Tears ran down her cheeks as he pulled a ring from his pocket. "Oh God. Of course I will."

MacGillivray gave a cheer and raised his glass. "May I toast the newly engaged couple? Gladys, you deserve him, you know. After your parents died, I thought you'd never have any life of your own what with your brothers and sisters to raise. May you enjoy the greatest of happiness!"

Elise watched Cornelia and Rebecca as they admired Gladys' ring. She could understand Alexander and even Aubrey. Perhaps they had gone to school in England or Scotland before the war, lived there after school even, if they had gotten the mannerisms of the English down so well. Then war was declared and a use for their past was found. Did Alexander slip across the channel every so often to report and he had just been the one near when it was announced she was in Bergen? It would explain why her appearance was unknown. Were Cornelia and Rebecca just pawns in all this? No, Broderick had said it was Cornelia asking if Elise was Lili. Still Elise found it hard to believe there were that many German women that had studied abroad. From an Ambassador's family maybe? Were they English then and converted to their husband's ideals? Elise's train of thought vanished when Broderick put a hand on her waist.

He rapped his glass with his knife. "Excuse me." The guests slowly quieted. "I want to apologize to the two of you for this. Would you mind sharing the spotlight?"

Broderick had meant it rhetorically but Gladys took it otherwise. "Of course not. No, you intrude all you want, after giving us this."

Broderick couldn't help but smile because she was as clueless as a babe about all that went on. "I mean to take away from your moment in no way, but when I was informed of the purpose of the visit, it seemed providential. With this war going on and me busy in London, I may not get such an appropriate chance to do this again. Elise, would you marry me?"

MacGillivray's jaw dropped as Broderick brought out a ring of his own. Even if he knew they hardly knew each other, the idea of Broderick marrying was not expected. The perfect two-carat emerald surrounded by diamonds made Gladys' look like a toy. It had been Broderick's mother's ring. Elise's own mouth hung open and no answer came forth.

"Didn't you say my dear that you were talking of marriage with the boy?" MacGillivray was finally able to say after recovering from his shock.

Elise had to take a drink to think of what to say. "Of course, but I thought it would take a lot more talk on my part to get him to speak the one little sentence I just heard."

Magda laughed heartily. "Why shouldn't he be thinking of it with the most beautiful woman he's ever had the chance to bed."

"Then he hasn't been your beau?" Gladys asked.

Magda lit up a cigarette. "Heavens no. Henry Dunham, now there is a man that can teach a woman. Alas I'm invited thinking Broderick hoped for the same and he springs Elise on me. I'm off to America maybe I can find a Yank as handsome and devilish."

"Henry's a traitor, black market goods, hasn't even signed up for service while his brother is imprisoned with my son, and Broderick's brother - you dare say his name - spends his days drugged up and fucking in Tangiers." Bruce practically spit out.

"Do I get an answer?" Broderick asked finally.

Elise let the question hang for a moment. "Of course I will."

Broderick grinned and kissed her for so long that MacGillivray finally cleared his throat loudly before they stopped. No one would be able to think it was a sham. Broderick's mouth was close to her ear. "It was all I could think of to erase any doubt." He murmured as he slipped the ring on her finger to Bruce's cheer.

Gladys rushed over and congratulated her with a hug that was returned in congratulations. The champagne flowed quickly as the women admired the rings.

~

Emmon slipped into the office Broderick used after the festivities had broken up. Work again.

"Sir."

Broderick groaned. "Not another message from the general. I really am getting fed up with this constant chaos he makes for himself. He has a bluidy army at his beck and call, I can't get two weeks to do my own business."

"No sir. The postman just sent Ian with a message. It seems that Cornelia was down in the village making a phone call after dinner. Her end of the conversation sounded as if Elise was in trouble. Something along the lines of that little bitch had us all fooled. Don't worry we'll take care of her."

"Do you know who it was on the other end?"

Emmon could only shake his head.

~

Elise looked up as she came to the bottom of the stairs and felt her hair stand on end. She couldn't force herself to do anything, she froze to the spot she stood. Just feet away was an eerily glowing figure, dressed in a kilt with long black hair. He was truly from another age. His sword lifted and came down in a wide arc as if in slow motion. She felt the bite of the blade as it touched her skin. The pain made her lose her balance and as she tried to right herself, she saw the ghost's blade hadn't cut her. It was Alexander's knife from behind. His ice blue eyes blazed out of the darkened corridor, as she lay there stunned from her wound and the fall. He flipped the knife to finish the job. As Alexander bent closer to her prone figure, he too, saw the apparition. Moreover, the ghost had the sword pulled back as if ready to take off his head.

The gaping face of a suit of armor stared at her blankly as her eyes slowly closed.

~

A scream jolted Broderick from Emmon's message. He and Emmon rushed out and found Mrs. Buchanan standing there while Magda bent over Elise's sprawled body feeling for her pulse.

Mrs. Buchanan fussed with her hands. "Sir, the ghost. I saw him at her side. My scream may have brought everyone running, but I was there before he left her. Ian was there wielding his sword."

"None of that ghost talk!" Broderick snapped. "It's an interesting party story, but I'm not going to trust a sword-wielding ghost to stop the bleeding. What the hell happened?" He asked as Magda looked up and nodded hardly noticeable. She was alive at least.

The others came at a run from the other parts of the castle. Broderick thought Elise had fallen on the stairs, as she lay at the base of one of the turnpike staircases that wove its way inside the eight-foot thick walls, but when she rolled her over, blood stained the dress around a jagged gash.

"Now go get us some bandages, Mrs. Buchanan. See if there is anything for the pain in the house too. Aspirin, if nothing else." Mrs. Buchanan left quickly.

Broderick carried her to his true bedroom with Dr. MacInnes and Magda behind him. An old suite of rooms, tucked in among the castle walls like a separate house. The ceiling was covered in highly carved plaster, the walls with panels of wood carving. A large diamond paned window kept it bright if covered in dust. There was a side room and shelves tucked in under the stairs. A set of stairs led up to a bedroom, the walls covered in very old Chinese silk while furniture from the orient filled the space.

"Get out of here." Broderick shouted at David.

"Do you forget I am a doctor?"

Broderick sat there trying to decide if he should trust the last of his guests. "Go get your bag, you're not helping her any just standing there," he finally ordered. As the door closed, Elise's eyes slid open.

"Christ, don't scare me like that," Magda hissed.

"Keep your voice down. I prefer Alexander not finish what he started," Elise forced out. There was no doubt she was in pain.

Elise pulled the dress top away from her side and he saw the wound. She had pressed her handkerchief into it to stem the flow of blood as she lay there faking a more serious injury. "Let him patch me up and then pretend I've died the next time David comes to check me."

Broderick narrowed his eyes. "Why exactly?"

"There's something wrong with all this and I don't know what it is. I just can't put my finger on it. All I know is that perhaps we can figure it out if I'm dead."

Elise closed her eyes before David could see her face at his return. He had a well-equipped bag and was able to dose her with something to kill the pain before he went to work on her side. Magda kept busy with getting a fire going to take off the chill, it hadn't been used in some time with him living in London.

"She would have bled to death if there wasn't someone here to sew her up correctly. They missed her kidney by a hair. You have to call the police," David finally announced as he finished up.

"My brother actually had the position before he left. Now the nearest police are several hours from here. That is the down side of a castle in the middle of the sea.

I suppose with Lorne away that duty has fallen to me too." Broderick kissed Elise's forehead as David walked to the door.

"I'll be back in an hour or so when what I gave her wears off. She'll need something more," the doctor murmured looking worried.

"Whatever happens protect her at all costs." Broderick muttered to Magda once the door closed.

"Why don't we just go shoot them all?" The woman snapped.

"Because there are 60 people here that could get shot, I've the children of the Earl's of Moerhab, the Marquess of Lisstone, and half a dozen other people here escaping London and the coast. The entire third floor is more like a boarding school. If we just lock them in their rooms they can shoot themselves out and be really mad and 60 people could get shot. She's right, at this moment her playing dead buys us some time. Tomorrow if we need to we'll go out hunting and have an accident."

~

Broderick worked up a mourning face when Emmon told him that the doctor was to return. With all of them just perched outside like vultures, he would have to act every time the door opened. The look on Broderick's face was enough to tell everyone it was too late when he opened the door.

The only problem was that the Doctor knew it couldn't be too late. He had seen the spot on the floor as Mrs. Buchanan attacked it with vigor. No one would be able to see it later when the question of murder came up, but he had seen it before when it was just an attack and it wasn't enough to kill her.

David closed the door to block out the others. "What are you playing at?" Broderick looked up from her side where he had returned to his vigil. The doctor pushed passed him up the stairs and made his own check.

She was alive even if weak. "Just what is going on that would make you try to sneak it passed me that she is playing dead. I will admit her wound is serious, but I got to her soon enough. Now I ask again what you are playing at."

"War business," Broderick snapped.

"I know I may not be serving, not all of us can, but you don't have to be so rude about it. Someone has to treat the men returning." David's thoughts were distracted when Elise's eyes slid open slowly.

"You trust MacGillivray and he still counts him as friend even after learning of the others," Elise grunted, her breathing heavy as she fought away the spasm of pain, finally silence returned. "He deserves to be able to protect his fiancée to the best of his ability until this is over."

Broderick wiped the hair from her face gently. "And what about me protecting my fiancée?"

She laughed until it hurt her and it turned to a gasp.

"Why is that funny to her?" David asked.

"Because a week ago when I left London I had never seen her in my life. It's all an act. She had been found washed up on the shore before I got here."

David smiled despite the situation. "Quite an effective act I must say. Gladys was telling me how happy you looked, what a perfect couple you make."

Elise reached for a glass of water by the bed. "Tell him the basics at least. If he was part of it, the bleeding wouldn't have slowed."

"All this death talk and I forgot why I was here. She needs more painkillers. Blast it all! Stabbings are not my usual patients." David dug in his bag until he found the vial. "So what is going on?"

Broderick pointed downstairs. Soon they settled by the fireplace as a light rain fell outside. David let Broderick be in silence with only the fire cracking to disturb the quiet.

"Alexander was in Norway dressed as an SS Major trying to catch Elise. It would make his wife in it as well. Oddly enough, we think they are here to snoop on me. My job puts me in contact with sensitive information, a lot of it." Broderick paused for a moment. Was someone in Turnbull's office in on this and had let it out that he would be home? He knew most of them too well. Someone in the government at any rate. It could be anyone. "That's why we're pretending," Broderick finally murmured.

"But what do they want her for?"

"Information she gathered in France."

David's eyes lit up. "You mean she's a spy?"

"She's with the resistance even if she is an American. She was in France when the Germans invaded," Broderick said quietly. The more he talked of her accomplishments the more he was determined to go free Lorne. The General sure as hell wasn't going to get him out.

"Why do you let them get away with it then? You've more than enough people around to overpower them."

Broderick went and poured himself a drink. "What am I supposed to do, rush Alexander with guns blazing and scare them so they take a hostage? What if it was your fiancée they grabbed? I have a house full of staff and children to worry about too. I may be a soldier, but no one else is. Shooting birds isn't like taking aim at a person."

"Oh. Still we can't let them go about killing anyone they think is involved."

Broderick finished off the finger of whisky. "That's why Elise wants to play dead. If she's not a threat anymore, perhaps, they'll not worry about anyone else. Mary, for instance, when she interrupted Cornelia helping with a headache, and who knows what they had really planned for that night. They may think Mary was helping her, when it was me that sent her. The rest of you are who worries me."

Magda suddenly appeared at the door.

"Is Elise all right?" Broderick asked.

"How did they get here?" She said with a grin. "I called about them when I was sick, the wives are always at home, committees, meetings, parties, the men go on trips, long ones. A month or more, but they always are around for events like this one."

Broderick's shoulders fell. "Of course they would pick Scotland, a U-boat could pick a deserted spot and let them out."

"Can we get it? That's the question."

David looked deep in thought before he started laughing. "Well now you have my help and I have an idea."

"I don't seem to remember you being too handy with a gun."

David's laugh settled into a wry grin. "True, but perhaps you have forgotten I am a doctor. I had to take all sorts of classes that can be used in interesting ways if you really want."

It was out of the corner of his eye that Broderick saw the Doctor's face. It was as if a bulb had gone off in his head and the light poured out. "And just what sort of interesting way do you have in mind?"

"Does the kitchen have some tinned meat?"

At that, Broderick laughed faintly. "We don't eat like this all the time. MacGillivray had hoarded his ration coupons just so you and Gladys could have a time like the old days would have been here."

"Then have the cooks go away or the power go out, some reason for us to eat tinned food for lunch tomorrow. I'll volunteer Gladys and I to fix sandwiches and I'll see those two don't carry through with their plans of leaving as we talked of earlier. Show them what I think of them ruining my Gladys' weekend. She's had little enough joy in her life."

A crash of thunder rattled the windows. Broderick looked out at the display of lightening. "It seems the weather is at least cooperating with us and will give a reason to have the power go out without comment and you can have your revenge." The doctor smiled at his words. "Elise is still going to remain dead though. I'll stay in here grieving. You can come to check on me as an excuse when she needs more injections or her bandaged changed. And let's hope they don't try anything more until your plan is pulled off."

"But the sub? If it's coming here somewhere and we take them out they can insert someone else without a clue who it is." Magda muttered.

Broderick only shook his head. "No idea at least not right now."

~

Elise's eyes fluttered open to find the light of a single candle valiantly trying to push back the gloom. The generator was off in preparation for the show tomorrow. "So just who is this ghost that saved my life?" She knew Broderick was awake somehow. She was too tired to move though.

"He actually was there, was he?" Broderick sat on the edge of the bed and pulled her hair aside. It was a simple gesture but he watched her eyes close at his touch. "My uncle four hundred years ago killed him."

She smiled weakly. It was all she could manage. "You would have thought he wouldn't go around protecting your guests."

"That uncle returned from war and found his daughter married to our ghost and father to the child she carried. The uncle killed her and the child. Our ghost was so distraught at seeing her laying there that he didn't see the uncle coming for him. He's had his revenge though.

They say the uncle was found literally scared to death on the wall. Our ghost has a habit of showing up when a woman in the house is in danger. He's forever making up for the fact that he didn't protect his wife that once."

"That's a sad story."

Broderick smiled. "Ghost stories usually are, but you have two of us to watch out for you now."

"Is he going to kiss me when I'm sleeping too?"

Broderick's smile widened. "If you were sleeping, you wouldn't know that I did. I think you were hallucinating on all that morphine David gave you." He didn't want to admit that to see her there on the floor had ripped his heart out. He was the one there to protect her.

Elise closed her eyes as sleep won. For a moment, he paused, but in the end, Broderick kissed her head as she slept.

~

Out of the thin dawn, a noise woke Elise. The drugs had worn off it seemed. Broderick lay across the room on the couch and if anyone had picked the lock, there was no way to pretend. Why should Broderick sleep in the same room as a corpse? Elise could see someone slink across the room as time went on and the only thing she could think of was to roll off the bed and under it even if it would hurt like hell. Elise tried to move to get ready for it when she felt the gun Broderick had given her under the pillow. Before she could do anything though, there was a loud thud from across the room. The sound had obviously woken Broderick as well. Suddenly the light snapped on, Broderick had another man pinned to the floor. Magda stood there with gun aimed at the man.

"Stay where you are," Magda called out. Both she and Broderick looked confused as they realized neither of them had seen the man on the floor before. He was not one of the houseguests. He was instead a wiry little man with angry gray eyes. He fought even though Broderick had a tight grip that didn't lessen no matter what he tried.

"Who in the hell are you and what are you doing in my house?" Broderick demanded.

Elise didn't give him a chance to answer. The confusion had lifted. "Mr. Davis I presume."

"Of course I'm Davis. Who else would you be expecting out in the middle of nowhere? Have this brute get off me." The young voice on the phone fit the face. He didn't look more than twenty.

Broderick started to move, but Elise stopped him. "Broderick don't let him up. Magda shoot him if he moves."

The pinned man got angry. "For Christ's sakes! Do you even know about what you're saying? You've been undercover with the General too long."

"Have I? I don't seem to remember ever having told you where I worked or how long, only that I had information." Elise paused for a moment. "Broderick, you remember me saying that there was something I couldn't put my finger on? Well, it was who told them I should be killed. I seriously think we had them fooled with our act, but that wasn't it at all was it, Davis? You, yourself, sold me out. Cornelia went down to make a call. I saw her do it and an hour later, I'm being attacked. What happened? Did she call to check in that they couldn't get anything out of Broderick. Magda there is why they were here, not me and you pounced when you found out where they were?"

Davis struggled as he tried to get free again. "I put out a notice to all concerned to look out for you along the coast. Anyone could have received that, Elise. If you want to start laying blame, look to your friend here."

"Yes, I suppose you called all your cronies and let them know I was missing along with regular channels. They would have gotten that message before they headed up here. They were overheard asking if they thought I was Lili." Broderick looked up at her as she thought on his words. He said nothing to confirm or deny the accusation. Playing dead had given her time to think and with his arrival, it made everything fall into its correct place. "Ah yes, and about Captain Sinclair. If he wanted me dead, I would have been killed a long ago. He even concocted a sham engagement and it would have worked. Magda here was the one that got sick and vanished for a few days, then reappeared. It would have made more sense that she was attacked than me. It was you that ordered them to kill me."

Elise watched Davis's face change. He wasn't so obvious as to let it fall, but she knew they had him. Still she didn't give him any pretext that would allow him to believe he had gotten away with anything.

"Until just over a week ago, no one in England knew anything of me. I never made reports to you. My work was all reported internally for the resistance. The British were contacted, not you specifically, but you were the one that responded. You received no other information other than that North Star was to leave Bergen on January twelfth and arrive in Aberdeen the next day. All you had to do was have someone meet me there. Did you panic? I can't imagine why you didn't just have Devon meet me and have him kill me then. It would have been far less risky than having me hunted down in Bergen. The resistance is quite active there, they helped me to no end getting me aboard the boat after we learned Alexander was looking for me. Oh yes, you made a mistake just now. I never told anyone my real name except those in this castle and even those that were tortured to give it up months ago never knew my real name. They just knew Lili Muller worked for General Meierhoff. Hell, they thought I was a turncoat German."

Davis sneered. "A fancy tale to dream up, but you still knew I was coming to get you."

Elise let out a snort that might have conceivably been laughter if not for the look on her face. "So why are you sneaking in here in the middle of the night? It would have been much more believable if this were breakfast or dinner last night. In addition, since you probably went and spoke to your confederates down the hall first, you would know I was supposed to be dead. With one hundred twenty rooms to hide my information, do you really think that I would have it on me still? I can't think of any other reason you came sneaking into a corpse's room."

"This was a secret operation. Should I have just knocked on the door and asked for you?" Davis defended.

For once Elise started smiling. "Why not? This is British soil, the house of a Duke of your Queen's realm, who sits in a prisoner of war camp fighting for his country. It is the house of the aide to General Turnbull. A man who should receive the report I'm to turn over first thing if you ever received it officially. It's not as if I was sitting in a traitor's house in France or even in Germany for that matter." Elise straightened her back in preparation for her words. "Does this castle have a dungeon?"

Broderick started smiling, but Davis didn't appreciate the look. "What would a Scottish castle be without a dungeon or a ghost? I like the way you think."

"Your brother's dead, you know," Davis spit out in a flash and when Broderick's grip loosened, Davis pushed him away. Magda fell as he slammed into her. Broderick scrambled to his knees and slugged him hard before he could get far, Davis sank to the floor in a heap.

Magda rushed over to her. "Are you all right? You shouldn't be up."

"Better than if you weren't here."

Broderick tied and gagged the traitor before summoning Emmon. They took him to a cell of the old dungeon where even if he yelled no one would hear him. It was little more than a hole into a cavern under one of the walls. No one had been in there since the 1820's when the castle had caught some smugglers off the coast.

Broderick came back in and sank on the edge of the bed as Magda returned with David to check on her.

"David, the plan goes, but for breakfast, we'll keep the power on. The eggs can be dosed as well as the tinned meat," Broderick hissed.

"Why? What's happened?"

"Someone was here. I think we're out of time. I'll come down late. They shouldn't do anything without me there. Feed them before then."

~

When Broderick came down for breakfast, everyone had almost finished eating. Gladys came over to him with giant tears on her face. David hadn't thought she would be able to act suitably if she knew the truth. Broderick himself looked broken up. They hoped that if everyone looked devastated, the others might actually worry that they had killed the wrong person. It only had to work after all until whatever David had concocted kicked in.

"I say, Broderick, now that you've grieved a bit shouldn't we do something about this murderer running about your castle? I'd think you'd want the killer of your fiancée brought to justice. You really should find the scoundrel that did this to such a lovely girl," MacGillivray announced.

Alexander noticeably paled at the comment, of course, perhaps the food was already working. Magda kept her head down as she stared into a cup of coffee. Her finger tapped a random beat against the cup, she looked up slowly. The corner of her mouth turned just enough to show a grin. She was a hard one to read. But the tap alone said it, a message had been sent. They had a U-boat in their sites.

"I've been looking into it since I got up. I should know by lunch. It's certain to have been one of the lesser staff, most have been here for years and are beyond reproach."

"It's a silly thought I have. It could even be one of us," MacGillivray elaborated even though he had no idea the death was a hoax.

Broderick wasn't going to say anything that might run them off early so he had to steer Bruce's mind somewhere else. "You're right. It could have been. It could even have been me, come to that."

Gladys sniffled. "What on earth could she have done to earn such disdain, Broderick, especially on the night you proposed?"

"Perhaps I found out she was stealing the family jewels or she was a fortune hunter." Broderick felt badly about deceiving the poor woman.

"Knowing you and your brother, there have been dozens after the family fortune and it never drove you to murder before," MacGillivray announced with some of his old kidding.

"True," Broderick started. "I suppose I have that in my favor, perhaps as all the books say the butler did it. Where is Hugh by the way?"

There was a bit of nervous laughter, no one wanting to laugh aloud when such an act had been committed the night before.

"We really should get back to Inverness, Broderick. I know it's a bad time for you, but we really must go as scheduled," Alexander announced.

"After what has happened, you must be crude to think of leaving Broderick to his grief all alone. I drove us here and I refuse to leave yet," Bruce announced with a booming voice. It put an end to the talk of leaving.

Broderick knew he would have to get the man a good old bottle of brandy for his unsolicited help. Talk turned to subjects less controversial. However, as they talked while Broderick ate, he and David noticed odd looks on the faces of the four they were after. Rebecca excused herself politely, but didn't hide it that she broke into a run as she turned the corner out of the room. It was only ten minutes later when Cornelia excused herself quickly from the table to leave Alexander and Aubrey there alone.

Mrs. Buchanan shuffled out after a moment. "Sir, I have to confess something to ye. It seems that when I left the under maid in charge of the eggs, she wasn't very careful. It seems that a bad egg got into the pan and ye know how Agnes is with her eggs. They are a little runny. When she saw Cornelia rushin' from the table she came to me cryin'. It was just the one pan not everyone got them."

Alexander looked up with a quizzical look on his face. "Bad eggs," he murmured before he leapt from the table. Iona winked dramatically at Broderick. No one could do anything to the food without her say so.

Aubrey looked around to find the others of his group gone. "I don't feel... Oh!" He jumped from the table and left in a hurry.

David started laughing jovially.

"David, how could you!" Gladys cried out. "A woman just died last night."

He kissed her gently. "While she may have been hurt, Elise is alive up in her bedroom."

Broderick held up his coffee in a toast. "Gladys, when the war is over and you've a child on your knee, tell them that your husband was instrumental in capturing German spies. He gave them all a strong purgative." Broderick couldn't help but laugh himself.

"There were no bad eggs?" MacGillivray asked.

"Not in the least," David announced drinking to Broderick's toast.

Broderick pushed his chair back. "Now if you'll excuse me, I have some Germans to see to the dungeon."

"Can I go to see how Elise is doing?" Gladys asked quietly.

"I think she is well enough, she probably would enjoy someone there besides me to look out for her." Gladys had to laugh finally. Broderick continued quietly. "She would have died if David hadn't been here." She sobered, but then smiled shyly as if the man she had agreed to marry wasn't such a wonderful man already.

~

The group headed to sit down to dinner that night when Hugh came and whispered into Broderick's ear.

"Very well, show them in."

"More guests, Broderick?" Bruce asked as General Turnbull entered and several of his men took position at the door. The old bull was just that, a short squat man with a paunch. His skull was bare and reflected the lights of the room. However, his was face dominated by bushy eyebrows and red veined cheeks and nose that drew attention.

"General! On time for dinner as always. The salmon is superb tonight. Per here is a wonderful fisherman."

Per, the captain from the boat, smiled happily at Broderick's praise. There had been no missing the plane flying low over Am Binnean and out to sea a giant explosion as the U-boat was blown to pieces. Magda was long gone though, taking their guest with her. She got him out for her own information, Whitehall wasn't part of it, at least she hadn't thought she was. By and far, her guest was the biggest information there was in the house though. Broderick was just helping an old friend with an out of the way place. They'd been there for several weeks before he had leave.

The General looked a little confused. "I thought I was here on business."

Broderick frowned. "Of course you are, but you're late. We found a way around not having any soldiers or police besides me. And got us a U-boat as icing on the cake. If you'll excuse me, I have to go get someone."

The General smiled as he sat down without an idea what had happened and speared a bite eagerly. Turnbull said nothing as he ate and then noticed he was alone in his indulgence, everyone else waited. Turnbull put his fork down and waited with the rest. Several minutes passed before Broderick returned with a very drawn Elise steadied on his arm. It was her first meal out of bed.

"Christ, Sinclair! Just what happened here?" Turnbull demanded.

"Rutherford Davis."

Turnbull picked up his fork again inpatient to get at his meal. "Yes I've heard of him. He was to be taking care of the report that this young lady was to deliver. Does some good work from what I hear."

Broderick straightened his back to delay what he had to say. "He ordered this done to her."

The reason they called him the old bull became evident as Turnbull's face screwed up and he saw red. "I'll have him drawn and quartered."

"Well the dungeon is the best place for him then," MacGillivray announced with a drink in hand.

Turnbull turned and looked at the other old soldier, but it wasn't with a look of charity. Turnbull was used to being in charge and definitely not having anyone talk down to him. "What about the Germans you mentioned the last time we talked," he finally said as he ignored Bruce's words.

"In the dungeon as well," Broderick answered as he seated Elise carefully in a chair.

"Well damn it! Why on earth did I drive all this way then? It doesn't sound as if you need me at all."

"If you hadn't been detained, you would have been here in time to stop this from happening to her in the first place," Broderick snapped annoyed. He'd worked for the General long enough to decipher the excuse he had given even if it sounded urgent. A woman was behind it all and not the General's wife, Broderick was sure of that. The General looked over at him, his eyes narrow. "Since you're late for all the excitement, she can just stay here until she's well enough to travel. They meant her dead. You can take them back to face charges. She can follow later and answer any questions you may have."

Turnbull was not happy. "A report came in a few days ago. It came to my attention just as I was to leave. I had to confirm it. MacGillivray, your son escaped from the POW camp and is safe with British forces." As Bruce hugged everyone within reach, Turnbull waved to a private and had him bring over a file. They handed it to Broderick without ceremony. They all watched as his face drained of color. Broderick said nothing still Elise could guess what it said. Davis had seen that report before he had come up, his attempt at escape was truth. Broderick's brother was indeed dead.

The General hardly seemed to care. "Now just where is the packet of information that started all this anyway?" Everyone turned to Elise taking the attention off Broderick.

"Emmon, can you have the center chandelier lowered? I'm not as strong as I was the day I put it there." Emmon went to the ropes that held them high above the dining hall and soon it rested in the center of the table itself. Elise removed a number of pieces of paper that circled the white candles and handed them over to the General.

"What code did you use?"

"I coded it double. I was worried I would get caught after I knew Alexander was looking for me in Norway."

The general frowned. "And if you had died?"

"There is a letter in Broderick's safe. I suppose Broderick I should apologize for not telling you earlier that I gained quite the skill at opening safes. I wasn't exactly writing letters to family. Broderick would have found it when he left here to go back to work, if not earlier. It told not only where to find them, but what codes to use as well. You may find out about the locations in France and other countries I passed through already attacked. I left the information on those with the resistance. They need supplies a bit sooner than you, I fear. However, there was a main reason they hounded me so relentlessly. You're looking at the defense plans for the northern coast of Germany."

"My girl, I could kiss you." The General slapped her on the back as if she was a man and she cried out in pain and for a time was unable to breath. "God, I'm sorry. I was so excited I forgot you had been wounded."

"Well I hadn't had the chance to forget about the pain and that was even before you slapped the damn wound," she gasped. David rushed for the morphine.

~

In the morning the prisoners, the General, and his men all left in a swirl of activity. David and Gladys stayed so he could see to her care. With Turnbull gone and unable to ask more questions, David ordered Elise to rest. It worked for a while, but since she was no longer on morphine, her sleep wasn't dreamless. A musty, dank, and inky blackness filled her mind. Disembodied boots overhead pounded with each beat of her heart. The door pulled open and light flooded into the darkness. Alexander's face peered down at her. Guns were aimed at her and the staccato when they fired brought her awake. She sat bolt upright. Elise could still feel the pain of the bullets from the dream far more real than the pain from her actual wound. As the dream faded, Elise could see full daylight between the heavy curtains and vaguely remembered Iona had asked if she wanted lunch. She hadn't even woken.

In the hall, Emmon stood up abruptly when she opened the door. "Where's Broderick?"

"I'll go get him for ye." Obviously, he was to make sure she wanted for nothing.

"Just tell me where he is. I could use the walk."

Emmon shook his head. "He said he was to be left alone, only I was to disturb him if it was important."

"Working I take it?" Elise guessed.

"Yes ma'am."

"All right, I'll leave him in peace, but I still need a walk. Will you allow me that?"

Emmon said nothing. He only held out his hand to lead the way, not lacking for anything meant an escort even to walk.

Walking the halls though was not getting the job done. It felt good to move, but it did nothing to rid Elise of the dreams of war. Especially not when Emmon stopped to show her the armory, hundreds of guns, knives, and swords hung in precise geometric designs. She blanched as she thought she could pick out the one that had ripped her flesh open. Making it more heart clenching was that more than twenty hung right next to it. Lately she'd been experiencing other dreams as well. Broderick's kiss came to her perhaps more often than the others, not the public ones for show, but the few times he'd kissed her forehead or cheek when he thought her asleep. Those had nothing to do with the parts they were playing or even the flirting that seemed nothing more than an extension of the show they were putting on, keeping in character. They weren't kisses that belonged to the reputation she heard of either.

Looking over her shoulder, Elise saw Emmon had fallen away from her side when Per had asked him about a boat to use. She slipped out of sight.

Broderick sat in the library alone when Elise entered the room. She closed the door to keep the heat from the fire in, the stone halls may not have been dank, but they still didn't have the same comfort as the individual rooms. Her eye caught a painting she hadn't noticed the first time she was there. A beautiful, ethereal woman in filmy white silk. Her picture made Elise feel like an ugly duckling instead of a model.

"My mother," Broderick murmured. "That picture is all that's left of her. Rather a mercenary I'm told. She died having me so I wouldn't know personally."

Elise turned to him realizing she had been caught. "I'm very sorry about your brother."

It was a moment before he acknowledged her words. "You guessed."

She nodded faintly and her eyes sought out the book she had looked at that first day. Indeed, she could see Broderick's precise handwriting had updated the entry yet again. "Davis never seemed clever enough to have thought of that himself."

"The report said he was shot in the back trying to protect a boyhood friend from being emasculated. He's been dead for close to a year and no one knew." Broderick looked up at her, his eyes full of sadness. "You show more concern over a man you've never met than that old bull. This morning before he left, Turnbull clapped me on the back and told me as a consolation I was a Duke now. The bastard doesn't care about anyone's feelings. At least the younger three aren't able to join up and I have to worry about them."

Elise, to Broderick's obvious amazement, slid the lock home. She may have still been pale from her wound but there was determination in her eyes as she lowered herself on his lap. "I forgot there was a war, forgot I was being hunted when you kissed me. Make me forget there's a war, forget the dreams until I have to leave and I'll keep you distracted from your brother's death."

"You've been a damned distraction ever since you washed up on the shore." The feelings from the middle of the night came back to him as he kissed her, but this time there wasn't the reluctance he had to let them come forward. When he picked her up, it was as gentle as a mother with its babe. He wouldn't hurt her wound even accidentally. He unlocked the door and carried her out of the library. "And if I'm going to be distracting you, it's going to be properly not some romp in the library. You've lived through enough already."

Emmon turned away when he caught sight of them disappear into the bedroom. He ordered their supper sent to the room.

~

Elise and Broderick stood in the chapel as the minister went through the marriage service. The chapel reflected a time six hundred years earlier. There in the midst of the dark, blocky castle built to withstand attack, weather, and sea, soared an airy gothic chapel filled with stained glass windows. The sun for once shone without and the floor danced with brilliant colors. David and Gladys turned and kissed. Gladys was a beautiful bride, in a beautiful setting that most could only dream of for their wedding. They had meant to wait, but until the war was over, none of their families would be in the same place so it seemed right that they just do it then in the chapel and not have to worry about two households anymore. Who was to complain about a honeymoon in a Scottish castle even if the war hadn't been on? The Duchess was there, not for the wedding, for the memorial they held for her husband's eldest son. She couldn't even be 50, and even at probably 45 she was a gorgeous woman, she was the one that should have been a model. It was hard to believe she had been a nurse for years, working two jobs at times. Even more that she was working with the worst of the facially wounded after trench warfare and in a mental hospital trying to let her aunt give her brothers to her again. Broderick said his father was long widowed, and she'd been widowed in the war when they met for a hedonist week on an island that was wiped off the face of the earth. Reports came in while she was there, the Germans had killed all that lived there. That small boat of survivors that made it ashore to tell the tale were all that was left, baring a battalion of 500 men that had joined the war.

As they headed down the hall to have the wedding feast Emmon blocked the way, his scarred face looked grim. "Can I talk to you, ma'am?"

Elise waved the others ahead. "Go on without me and get started."

Broderick went to walk past but Emmon took hold of his arm. "This involves you too."

"Now you're worrying me. What's happened?" Elise whispered.

"The runner brought a message for you," he handed over the paper to Elise and left them alone.

Elise couldn't open the note, her hand shook as she handed it over to Broderick. "Please."

Broderick stared at the paper what seemed forever before he finally read. "Received word this morning. Your parents died three years ago in an accident before America had even joined the war. Will have to wait to return. I have a job that needs your expertise. You speak Danish so I hear. Will give you briefing when you return. Car should be there in two days. General Turnbull."

Elise's eyes closed but Broderick caught hold of her before her legs gave way. When he put an arm on her waist, Elise rested her head on his shoulder. "Show me what freedom looks like again. Let me see why I'm doing this."

Broderick walked her out the front door of the castle without a word to anyone. There they found a blue sky that despite the season shone brilliantly.

~

"Miss Dutton, the car is ready to leave." The car had arrived the night before with some men to see her back to London. It seemed there were indeed questions and there was indeed another post to send her to that Turnbull wasn't going to wait for her to decide she had healed enough.

Broderick was asleep next to her. He had indeed been a distraction, a glorious distraction. But at the sake of the work he had to get done before his leave was up, work that was now truly his responsibility and so most nights after she had gone to sleep, he would slip off to get something done. Elise dressed quickly and then stared at Broderick for a long while before she kissed his cheek. Only then did she slip out. What else was there to say? Plans of after the war when there was little chance of surviving it.

~

After lunch, the castle was empty as the other guests disappeared. Broderick went back to work on the estate business. It would be another two weeks before he returned to London and by then Elise was back behind enemy lines on another assignment. Broderick tore into the General that he sent her off without any training still. Her talents were truly useful as a spy, too useful to waste in training her. All he was knew was that this time it was somewhere in Denmark, of course knowing Turnbull she could be in Italy for all he knew.

Elise was behind enemy lines before she remembered she still wore Broderick's ring.

~

Only days after V-E Day, Elise returned to London. The second job had indeed been in Denmark, with that at least, the General had been truthful. She was still only part of the local resistance though. She was the same as all the resistance fighters in Europe as they returned to their old lives or at least tried. As Elise had never been trained, she had no job with any organization. All she had been given was a letter for a ride on a transport back home. As she waited for the ship to load, she looked up and found General Turnbull standing there. The men all around saluted. Elise didn't even stand. "General?"

He was a bit red at her lack of respect. "You survived the war I see."

"No thanks to you."

His eyebrow raised a notch. "What did I do?"

"Do you know how many times I was almost caught because of your foul-ups and not the German's intelligence or the lack of equipment in the Denmark resistance?"

The General turned away at a crash in the distance. "Blame Broderick. He left me shortly after you were sent back in. He was the real brains behind my command. Never did find someone as competent to replace him."

Her heart stuck in her throat at his name. "Where did he go?" Elise tried to sound calm.

"I'm surprised you didn't know since he said he made the decision while you were there. When the push came to retake Malaya, he was resolved to go to see what was left of his brother's regiment liberated. The fighting is intense from all reports I've received."

Elise felt a little woozy. "Then he's dead too?"

"Last report he was still alive though the fighting is yet to end there. He made Major and it wouldn't surprise me if he was a Lieutenant Colonel by the time this is all over, with more medals than he'll know what to do with just like the rest of the family. He was nothing, if not a good man to have around, but I think you wouldn't need me to tell you that more than most. He's engaged so I hear, though I don't know when he found the time."

Her heart in her throat died. It had been over two years since they had seen each other, but still a little bit of her heart had stayed with him after all that time. A lot had happened to her and it sounded like a lot had happened to him as well.

A sailor interrupted. "Miss, the seaman here will show you to your private cabin that the Captain has given you." She picked up the suitcase next to her, it held all she had in the world.

"The Captain will take good care of you," the General said to her as she turned to follow.

"You've spoken to him about me? I find that odd since you've never paid me for any of the work I did for your side for the last two years. Soldiers are paid, spies paid, if I go by who paid me, I worked for the Germans all these years. All I have to show for this is a bag full of German marks not worth the paper they're printed on. Three years too late I had word that my parents are dead. I have nothing and you give me good treatment on a military carrier ship as thanks. Broderick was right. You don't care about anyone's feelings." She walked off and not one of the soldiers that stood around missed the show. General Turnbull held back the man that was to lead her and pressed an envelope into his hand.

"Give her that. She's earned it."

The sailor nodded and ran to catch up with Elise. When he handed her the envelope, she slowly slipped her finger through the seal. She drew out a check for twenty thousand dollars, she could only stare at pay for six years of work. Elise looked back to find the General had gone already. The letter with it thanked her for her sacrifice. Winston Churchill himself had signed it.

Still when she returned home, she found a bookstore that sat empty. No one knew where to get hold of her to inform her of her parent's death. Elise Dutton after all had ceased to exist. She felt like she had abandoned them even though they had received money from her Aunt as well and she had sent money when she could, at least before the war. There was no home to return to, no family to welcome her with open arms, and those in town, hardly even noticed she had returned at all. To them, she had never returned to help her family, nor had she worked in the effort to fight the war. They had no idea she had risked her life every day for the last six years. Her life was gone.

Elise sold the bookstore to a returned marine and his wife. To run a bookstore without a leg, would pose no problem after all.

~

Back in Europe there was more work than ever for a translator. Elise already had a job lined up, but she had one thing to do first. She looked down at her hand that still held Broderick's ring. She had to return it.

After inquiries, she found that Lt. Colonel Broderick Sinclair, Duke of Cairnmuir had returned from Asia and given up his position in the Army after V-J day. It had been months since she had stepped on that boat bound for America. The train dropped her at Inverness and the bus dropped her at the very end of its route in Thurso. Still she was many miles from even the village. She started to walk.

It was half an hour before a car stopped. "How far are you headed?" The driver asked only after she had gotten in and they were on their way.

"Am Binnean."

"You're late. The wedding started at noon, but don't worry, the party will be going on all night," the driver said with a great smile.

Elise couldn't say anything. She would have had to pick the worst day imaginable to arrive. She doubted Broderick's wife would appreciate a former lover coming on her wedding day to return an engagement ring, no matter the circumstances.

"I can get you to the reception in a flash," he added.

Out the window, she watched the land she had walked hunting with a party of spies. Her heart stopped when she saw the old ruined house where Broderick had taken her when she had asked him to show her freedom.

She had wanted to see the sky and he'd made love to her beneath it. Six months of hiding before she had crossed the channel, she still marveled at the open sky, able to stand out in it and be free. Denmark was just as oppressive. However, for five days she was free of war and responsibility. Six years as someone else hadn't been as hard as when she left his bed. When he had been there, she felt safe. That she had been alone in the hall was her only mistake.

~

In only an hour, she was within sight of the castle and the little village on the sea. Elise hardly noticed the driver until they stopped and he got out. Iona came at a run, threw her arms around the red haired man's neck, and wouldn't let go. "Me grand-baby. Alex, we thought we'd never see ye here."

"I wasn't sure I would make it for the wedding at all. I was bringing supplies in to Italy. A few months turned into more. I just got discharged a few days ago." He looked back at the car. "I picked up a hitchhiker on the road. She said she was coming here as well, at least I'm not the only one that's late."

Iona laughed. She had changed little. "I should have known ye'd find a date, even with only a few days' notice."

Elise figured there was no other way to get out of the situation now that she was there. She opened the door and slid out of the car.

Iona's mouth dropped for lack of anything constructive to do. "Go find the Duke right away," she was finally able to voice and Alex ran off.

Elise turned to leave as he did. "I should go. I just wanted to return this. I never meant to leave with it." She went to remove the ring and found that the two years with it on her finger, it was on too tight.

It wasn't Iona that grabbed her arm. She looked over her shoulder to find his mother, a duchess stopped her. She didn't look so unnaturally young anymore. The war was hard on her. Running one of the biggest hospitals in London it was little wonder. Losing a step son so soon after husband, Broderick running off to fight when he could have done his part safe in England. Alec had chattered on during the ride it sounded like even one of her own children had turned 18 and joined up. That was on top of seeing to an entire army's care. "You can't leave without seeing Broderick. He would never forgive me if I let you go. He's wondered what happened to you ever since you left here." Then as if in a flash, she let Elise's arm go and vanished.

"Since you left without even saying goodbye." Broderick's voice was quiet, but it felt like it would shatter her ears she had imagined it so long.

Elise couldn't say anything as she raised her eyes. She tried hard enough to hide what seeing him there again did to her, even if it was odd to see him in a dress kilt. She had dreamed of him on those cold lonely nights in Denmark. Those dreams didn't come anything close to the real man before her. "I came to return your ring." Six years as someone else and she knew she couldn't keep the hurt from her eyes.

"You don't have to rush off. The bride will be upset if that were to happen. She was most particular that everything be perfect. My brother and sisters have been anxious to meet the siren that washed up on the beach."

"Somehow I doubt she'd appreciate how you would introduce me to her, not with me returning what should have been her engagement ring." Finally, she had released it from her finger and started to place it in his hand. "I wish to cause you no embarrassment at your wedding. I didn't even know it was today."

Broderick's hand closed around hers when it came close. The ring was still solid inside her fingers. "Once upon a spy...I wonder if there is a happy ending to our story."

"What?"

Broderick grinned. "We were engaged when we last saw one another were we not? I'd like to know how the story ends."

She straightened. That was the end of the story. "It ends that you married another and I am on my way to Paris to pick up what I can of the pieces."

"Elise, tell me why you left without even saying goodbye. It means a great deal to me to know."

She looked at her hand in his in silence. She had no answer for that quickly anyway. "It doesn't matter now."

"Tell me anyway. It hurt that you left the way you did."

Defiantly she lifted her head and returned his gaze. "I was to return behind enemy lines. Any day I might have been killed. Four years I knew what to expect. There wasn't time for dreaming as much as I would have liked to."

Broderick reached over and tucked the hair blown by the brisk sea air behind her ear. "You would have found out that I never wanted you to take off that ring. It may have gone on as a ruse, but I meant it to stay there by the time you left. That was the only hope I had, that you never took it off."

He was running her heart through with each word. Elise turned to leave, but he didn't let go of her hand. "Well now you know why and now I know what might have been."

"Elise, look at me."

She looked back to him briefly, but the scene behind him kept her eyes riveted. A man with one arm missing was kissing Magda who was in a wedding gown as everyone cheered. It had to be her son that stood there laughing. An American Colonel started pulling them apart, he finally got hold of her and threw him over his shoulder. She watched as the man took Magda over to the tables for a feast where he very politely sat her down like the Princess she was.

"There has never been any fiancée besides you. It's been around for some time now that I had gotten engaged. You heard your own gossip from the General."

Slowly, very slowly, her eyes moved back to Broderick's face. She expected to see that damned grin of his, but there was no sign of it. He wouldn't gloat that she had believed that it was his wedding. "Everyone knew that it was a sham engagement," she whispered.

Broderick's smile was a little sarcastic. "You met the General. He was never one for subtlety. He heard some gossip, but I left without him ever asking if it was true. When you left, I knew I was miserable without you, that I missed talking to you before we went to sleep, looking at you across the table. It was the first time I felt that way and it's been the last time since you left me. From what I hear service men marry women they've known for a day."

"And that was before they shipped out. You'd be stuck with me for good without the chance of a bullet to end the union. Your reputation would suffer." Elise was finding it hard to remain objective as his hand trailed down her neck. It felt like he reluctantly pulled it away.

"It already has. I never corrected the gossip. I saw everything I wanted in life in our short time together." Finally, that grin of his returned. "I know you're not adverse to my touch, I seem to remember you enjoying it quite well in fact."

"Broderick...." She couldn't decide if she wanted him to stop or if she wanted to hear more.

"You didn't think of me at all, not one little bit?"

Elise willed her heart to calm down, but it was a vain attempt. "All the time, but it was all 'what if there wasn't a war'."

"There's no war now. No Lt. Colonel. No spy. No General to give either of us more work. There's time to find out what if. There's time to dream. Stay with me."

"You're crazy."

Broderick grinned triumphantly. He knew he had her when she could find no real objections. "Of course I am, about you. Why else would I have been looking for you ever since the General told me you were still alive? I even visited that bookstore of your parents' only to find out too late that you'd already sold it. Nice fellow that bought it, by the way."

Elise buried her head in his shoulder. "I've suffered enough thinking you were married. Can't we make it official? There's a minister right over there."

He could only laugh though. "Not on your life. The Duke of a castle more than eight hundred years old doesn't just get married on a whim. For one thing, MacGillivray would kill us if we did that. Second, that dress wouldn't do you justice for your wedding pictures. Third, the castle hasn't seen a really good party in a long time."

Elise bit her bottom lip as she tried not to smile. "Is that all?"

"The Queen rather expressed interest in coming to my wedding when I saw her last. You can't very well disappoint the dear woman after what she has lead this country through now can you?" Broderick's kiss took away the look of astonishment that filled Elise's face....

How could she stare at his mother standing there, watching him ready to throw her on the ground right there. "The Paris fashion houses are opening back up. I would imagine you wouldn't mind seeing all your old friends. If you wanted I know Christophe Martell from the old days, he would love to make a gown to reopen his store. That should take you time enough to plan a proper event." Phillippa Sinclair said with a laugh, somehow with the delight Elise saw in her eyes, even nude in the middle of the wedding wouldn't ruffle her feathers. Maybe there was hope after all.

"So who's the groom?"

"Oh well Magda went to America several times since we saw her and just a few months ago met a Yank to replace me. They're on their way to Czechoslovakia to try and help stem the Communists taking over there along with the rest of Eastern Europe."

~

And the spy lived happily ever after.

"Are you saying you weren't the only spy in the family?"

Elise smiled faintly. "Broderick wasn't a spy, he was in intelligence, the office part. He ran Magda until she gave up a couple years later when Communism couldn't be stopped. She settled on Kapheira to help rebuild it. He ran Henry Dunham until he died in the 60's. That's when he finally retired."

Ayda gasped. "The one they called a traitor? He was a spy."

Elise chuckled. "Perfect cover, a complete drunken lout of an Earl's son. He started in the early 30's and was running around Germany as Hitler came to power reporting everything they were doing. There are paintings on our walls he saved from being burned as degenerate, tracked down the owners after the war if he could. The few we have left belonged to people dead from the camps. It's his collection you'd love to see, he had over 100 of them. Those are just the ones he couldn't find owners for. He helped thousands get out of the region, had a stamp for Kapheiran visas he carried around when they just needed a country that wanted them to get out. He'd stamp passports and be in and out no one knowing it was him, while keeping up his cover of a degenerate lout. Later when it was harder he'd slip people passports for the island while drinking in a café or restaurant. And even later he'd have people pretend to be his servants until they were free of the borders. He was shot in the 60's, Broderick helped cover it up that he died of an illness while with his lover."

"Which paintings? I hadn't noticed any of that era."

"In my bedroom, there are only about 6 left. Broderick always wanted to keep them to himself I guess, a reminder of the old days. What we all fought for. Come by and see them."

There was a slight knock at the open door, and Ayda raised her head to find Hunter there. "Grandmother, the nurse is here with your medication."

Elise rose just as slowly as she had sat before patting Ayda's hand with the ring. "I've always suspected that Hunter takes after his grandfather. The distraction would be worth it."

Ayda kept a straight face until they were gone and then the laughter poured out.

CHAPTER 8

The possible Titian kept Ayda thinking on odd things. David said the story of the chalice needed details and more details kept showing up in the painting as she cleaned away five centuries of dirt. A painting of the Virgin Mary and yet it wasn't religious in nature, the painting was quite sensual in fact. She wasn't really thinking of embellishing her chalice princess story like Mary did with bawdy kitchen talk? When she finished for the day, she'd decided no. She couldn't do it, but she could get details. After dinner which Duncan kept Hunter from saying a word edgewise, Ayda headed to her laptop once more. She typed in two names. Alasdair Syncler and Eyja Eyverska, a simple search nothing complicated. Nothing connected the two, it was never a simple oversight that it was known she was his wife. But as separate people, details came to light as Ayda searched through the websites that came up. Alasdair looked to have served the king for some time even after the date of the wedding. He didn't leave service until 1183, it was then that the castle was started. His wife was only 15 when they wed, and she seemed to have not lived with her husband until then as well. There weren't many mentions of her, but there was one that hinted at something more. A wedding account, with Eyja listed, as well as Alasdair. It was before their own wedding date. Had they perhaps known each other then? Why on earth was she interested in making sure the cook had a good tale to hear? The chalice belonging to a princess was all she cared about, she had solved that mini mystery. Why did she still care? Sitting back the reason was simple enough, she was using it to ignore the fact she'd not come to a decision about Hunter, the job offer especially. She had gone to many of the festival events in the last few days. Another dodge and she knew it.

Did she truly wish to stay? If she took the offer, it would essentially be the end all be all. No job search, no grunt work, just paintings as far as the eye could see. A castle to explore, a townhouse with more to discover. Ayda was under no delusions that the list she had was even close to complete. The room with the chest had more she'd yet to get to, there was mention of another store room even. A collection that could truly take a lifetime to learn.

Ayda grabbed a sweater and walked out of the castle. A breeze off the water blew away the fog in her head. The distillery site was a hive of activity, machinery was digging foundations. Other than that though, there was the chapel and mausoleum holding the Dukes, set among the Sinclairs they ruled, a handful of tiny bed and breakfasts and the pub, the ever cheerful Cock in Hand. One lone gift shop filled with the standard highland gifts, Ayda almost laughed out loud, as she noticed for the first time front and center in the window were copies of the Once upon a Spy signed by the author. Beyond the post office and small grocery store, the school stood in a group of old whitewashed buildings on the edge of town by the water. Down at the dock, she found a small building busy with packaging seafood just off the ship. No other industry, no other culture, half a dozen shops sat empty along the main street. Hunter, the whole village, had their work cut out for them, keeping the place from dying altogether.

Hoping Ciaran wasn't around Ayda took a deep breath and pushed open the door to the pub. It was absolutely packed as a band played in one corner.

Finding a place at the bar, she looked around wondering who was descended from those in the stories she had heard. Which were the Vikings? She had heard mention that when the Dukedom was conferred, most all the men in Wrathe changed their name to Sinclair, a common practice to show their loyalty, but not usually entire groups at once. That was in 1328 and there were a lot of people since then. Were any of them Lindsay's, were they later? She almost laughed as she realized she was talking about 900 years of history. They were Scottish that was all anyone could claim. Though there probably were Lindsay's still running around. Forbes too, wait Jamison was a Forbes. So he was perhaps part of the men that came with the Countess of Ravensgard.

"What can I get you?" the bartender asked when he had a chance.

"A pint."

"You new to the rig? I don't think I've seen you before."

Ayda smiled. She certainly worked too much. "No, I'm working up at the castle on their art collection. Been a little busy I guess, not made it in much."

"So you're Ayda. Welcome."

And there was Hunter coming in the door. Everyone saying hi as if he was a long lost brother.

The music was good, she hated to have to leave because someone started calling her names. With Hunter there, if Ciaran showed up there would be problems for sure. People were dancing having a grand time. She'd hate for a fight to ruin it all. "Ciaran isn't expected tonight is he?"

The bartender looked over at her quickly. "That was you?" Ayda only nodded. "No, he left town a couple days ago. For good I guess, the house was emptied in the night, put up for sale even. Same sort of leaving his sister did, not a word to anyone. Phillippa would be rolling over in her grave."

"Phillippa? Elise's step mother in law why would she care?"

The bartender laughed faintly. "Maceachran's were her two brothers she worked her arse off to get back from her aunt. Only saw them again after some 9 years of fighting because Old Robert pulled strings when they met. They came here until university, Robert paid their way like they were his own children, they've paid for the whole family to go to school for 80 years, like they were family and they just screwed the family over. Lorne didn't deserve having his heart ripped out like that. Same way Hunter doesn't deserve being screamed at every time Ciaran sees him. Family doesn't do that to each other."

"He just took off?"

The bartender shrugged his shoulders as he pulled another ale. "The rumor of course is that his sister got a hold of him and he went to join her. He was the last one in town left of his family. Maybe he just got tired of it all." Hunter took the beer the bartender had just gotten ready. "We going to have a quiet evening Hunter?" The bartender asked.

Hunter grinned like proper delinquent. "Aye, you can start calling me names if you're getting bored already."

Ayda kept trying not to laugh. "You sound so tough until someone sees you're wearing a skirt."

The bartender started laughing as he was called away for another order.

"I didn't know you wore a kilt." Ayda added as Hunter was pushed closer to her as a crowd of people moved by. "Are all those jokes true? I've always wanted to ask."

"Give me your hand and you can find out for yourself." He whispered in her ear, not moving away after the crowd passed.

She should have expected that one. The men probably sat around waiting for a woman to ask just to pull out lines like those.

"Did you know I dance too? I'm here every time the band comes to play."

She ran out on him after damn good sex and he was still flirting with her. Ayda felt her heart beating faster even as she tried to slow it down. "And a little fighting too? Sounds like your usual schedule."

"Not tonight. Only when Ciaran defames the family honor. Care to join me?"

So he'd heard the gossip already. "What, fighting?" She said just to tease.

"Dancing."

Ayda turned around finding herself only inches away. Inches away from the only man that had ever distracted her from her goals. Damn if he didn't look good in a skirt too. "I've never danced like this before."

"Just hold onto me for dear life and you'll learn quick enough." He didn't sound like a future Duke just then turning on the Scottish accent as if he was nothing more than a highland fisherman.

Ayda took a deep breath and held out her hand. "Whisky first."

"You'll be Scottish before long with that request." The bartender called. "Just a minute."

"You're trying to embarrass me for a past indiscretion I take it." Ayda said only loud enough for Hunter to hear.

"What indiscretion might that be? Making me fall for you?"

She certainly didn't regret going to bed with him, but running out as she did ... Before she could say anything, the bartender pushed the shot of whisky in her hand. Not as smooth as the 50-year-old bottle she had tasted, this burned on the way down. He poured another before she had a chance to say anything. With the second down, the fact she'd yet to answer his job offer was a fading concern, the fact the man she had slept with was there ... eyes sad even if he smiled. Ayda put her hand out for him to lead her away to the dancing, not caring she would make a fool of herself.

~

Hunter was right. All she had to do was hang on to him. No mention of her leaving his bed, no mention of her job offer, she had too hard a time keeping from falling on her face. But making a fool of herself it was hard to do when the entire room was quite a bit more drunk than either of them. Hours later Ayda finally made it back to the bar.

"Now was that so hard?" Hunter asked when he rejoined her several minutes later. It was hard to hear though, the crowd had degenerated into a drunken mass of rig workers looking to let loose. "How about we get back before the police get here?"

"Sure." Ayda grabbed her sweater and the cool night air was a jolt to her system after the close confines of the pub. The moon rose in the dark sky over the hazy outline of the castle lost in a fine mist. There were no streetlights after leaving the main part of the street only foggy moonlight.

"This is what we do in the evenings when there's the option anyway." Hunter said quietly keeping in line with the hushed evening.

"Even after watching you I can't say I would have seen it, in a kilt even less."

Hunter's chuckle filled the quiet. "Mother forced us all to learn, she's the big dancer. I think I was five the first time. She holds a formal thing at the castle several times a year even. The Sinclair side is the military. This playacting at the pub though that's a favor for the owner, give the tourists something to see. She's worried if it's too boring all the rig workers will go to another town for their breaks. Ciaran is her usual actor, but since he's run off..."

"So you don't usually wear a kilt?"

"No." Hunter looked over at her out of the corner of his eye. "Too many tourists try to get their hands up it to find out what a Scotsman wears under one. Keep offering that I could be wearing lipstick under it if I was a good boy."

"What? Are you disappointed none tried tonight?" Ayda got out, but then she was backed up against a building. The warmth coming off Hunter seeped into her strong enough to take away the chill of the night. But he didn't touch her, and that was torture enough.

"I can understand you think it a mistake and I can keep my hands to myself, but don't make me sound like I'm moving on and in front of your very eyes at that. I've never been that man. I won't let you turn me into one to make you feel better that you ran out after your mistake."

Down the street Ayda watched as Roddy appeared in the police vehicle at the pub. "I meant me," she whispered sheepishly. "I haven't made up my mind about your offer, but I haven't been avoiding you, not on purpose. I get like this when I get a hold of a painting, that there's a mystery with it even more. Getting lost in it I admit gave me time to think."

Hunter's eyes closed slowly as her meaning sank in as well his words sounding very hurt. He'd opened himself up in those few words. His grandmother had been right there wasn't the sparkle to his eyes like before she left. She saw it every time she looked across the table as they ate in silence. Ayda leaned forward, not kissing him, resting her head against his chest.

"The last man I let get close, Brad, ran off as soon as he got what he wanted. He slept with me while he stole the job I had been promised out from under me. That's when I decided to get my doctorate, it started out to steal the job from him, but the more I got into it the more I fell in love with what I was doing. I could go be hired as his boss now and get his ass fired, but I don't want it. I have new dreams now that don't have to do with revenge for a broken heart. I guess that's why it's taking me so long to decide how to answer your offer. My last life changing decisions were made because of a man. It's been two months all I can think about is what happens to those dreams if it doesn't work out, never that I made a mistake. I never thought that night was a mistake, just when morning came I was scared if it didn't work out it would ruin everything." She hated to admit that an eighty-seven-year-old woman was right about how much the distraction was worth it. She pulled her head back and took his gaze full on. A look that bore right into her. "You're too much of a distraction if I'm in your bed. You're too much of a distraction if I'm not in your bed. What am I going to do?"

He kissed her forehead gently. "Guess you're screwed then aren't you?" He whispered in the heaviest accent that she'd heard since she came to Scotland.

"For crying out loud, I've got a pub full to deal with if you two aren't home with your parents by the time I come back out I'll have the both of you sitting in a cell for the night." Roddy's distinct voice called out of the darkness. Distinctly not happy to be called out at two in the morning.

Finally, Ayda saw a sparkle in his eyes that hadn't been there for days. "If I'm going to sit in a jail cell I'm going to be doing something worth it." Hunter lowered his head to kiss her. It was as if a part of her missing had come back when his lips met hers. Why on earth had she run away? Every inch of her cried out to take him to bed and never let him out. Every inch of her breathed in the smell of heather and wool from his clothes. She was in so much trouble.

"Break it up." Roddy pulled Hunter away. "Ah shite you could have said something. I thought old Maddy Sinclair was going to be biting my head off that her Jenny was out again." Without another word, he stalked back to the pub. It left Hunter smiling at her as Ayda tried to calm her breathing. Tried and failed.

"Best get you back, you've a long day tomorrow cleaning paintings, and it's late."

Did he know what he had just done to her? Oh yeah he knew, there was no doubting it as he walked off. He didn't even have to say a word and he was making her decision harder than ever.

~

Fully cleaned, the painting hung in the chapel. It was large, but somehow the painting alone made the room warmer, more earthy. Perhaps that was why it had been put away in the long history of troubles religion had often figured into it. Maybe it was too sensual for some to be seen in a chapel. With the light from the stain glass window pouring in, Ayda started taking photos, lots of them. Close ups of every face, even closer ones of the brush strokes. Something that might with great imagination be a signature. Then she just sank down in a pew and stared. She never heard Hunter's approach until a thumb caressed her neck.

"This is your excuse for avoiding me?" Hunter whispered.

She let the words slide. "If I can prove who I think it is, it's worth more than all the others, and it was just tucked in the storeroom behind everything else."

Hunter sank down next to her. "For a time, the chapel was hidden when Oliver Cromwell was massacring the country, during the reformation as well. The paintings were taken down and hidden, the doorway stoned up and covered with a tapestry and furniture. It was more than a decade until the king was restored, and the duke at the time had died. I guess what had and hadn't been in there at the time wasn't recorded, and some were missed being put back."

She kept from looking at him. She knew he was watching her, she could feel it even if she couldn't see him doing it. "Any idea how a Venetian painting got to Scotland in 1527 in the first place? French I can understand, with the long standing ties there, but not Venice."

"You want another story. A good family friend the Marquess of Lisstone does have a house there and we visited on more than one occasion, but that's 300 years later. I'm not sure how much it would help if I told you about a rather naughty party there for when I got my wings."

Ayda could only laugh. "No, I don't expect there are detailed stories floating around for every member of the family. Just, is there someone that traveled there for military reasons, marriage reasons, trading purposes? Putting someone there in the timeframe is crucial to verify the date the list has."

"You were the one going through all the papers. Nothing there?" Hunter asked.

Ayda only shook her head. "What's the official date of the chapel? Late Gothic I can tell but that's a wide range."

"No it's not from then. It was built after the English were run out of France. Joan of Arc, Hundred Years war, and all that. The men were all over fighting on the side of the French. The Duchess at the time was French, she brought the money to build it, but there were no men left. 1420's a good century before your painting."

"That's no help then."

"Come on." Hunter said after a moment.

"Last time you said that, we ended up in bed."

"Well, if you want to have sex in the armory, I'll certainly oblige you." He was already leaving when she caught up to him. The thought of both an answer and being in his arms again making her almost run.

"The armory?"

"Our little penchant of serving in the military it isn't just here in the castle. Had to keep track of who we could call on. Now it's more a tradition than necessity. It might just give you names of possibilities it's there for military reasons. That was the major reason why anyone in the family traveled anywhere. You said 1527?"

"Yes."

The armory still gave her shivers when they walked in. But why she couldn't figure, seeing as many of them were works of art in themselves. Maybe it was the fact that it was entirely possible that every weapon on those walls could have killed someone, an actual person's face was a lot different from an unused weapon there for decoration. These were no decoration, they all bore the wear of heavy use.

Hunter flipped open a large leather bound book and ran through it, his finger stopped suddenly among the ancient parchment pages. "I think purchased was glossing it over."

"Why, do you know how they got it?" Ayda quickly looked at the page where his finger pointed. "Lochlain Sinclair?"

"It didn't occur to me until I saw the name. That ghost story I told you. Lochlain was the father that killed them, and yes, it does explain how he got an Italian painting. The sack of Rome was in 1527, he was one of Charles, the Holy Roman Emperor's, supporters - well, a paid mercenary. I told you to be careful using that word. Took a force of men he scabbed together from wherever he could. A younger son, he had always wanted power and money in his own right. He was there, being thoroughly nasty to the citizens of Rome. Raping, pillaging, looting, I would say that painting you found was some of his plunder. He was never known to pay for anything."

"I should probably take it out of the chapel, then. The ghost might not like it. I can verify it and sell it. You could make whatever repairs you needed to the castle if I'm right, build an entire distillery, and still have money left over." Art had nothing to do with it anymore. What was she thinking? She'd need permanent equipment if she were staying. There was so much to do.

Hunter stepped closer to her. "I've been thinking that if you did want to stay," Was he reading her mind now? "There are several shops in town that are empty. If you wanted something a little more social than sitting cleaning paintings, an art school perhaps might be something you'd be interested in."

"Uncle Hunter!" they heard from the hall. "Uncle Hunter, my da is coming. He'll be here for supper with everyone. But he says it could be the last time before he has to go to the war."

Ayda forced her mind from the fact she was certain her thoughts had revealed what she truly wanted. If the family were coming there would little enough time to speak to him alone, let alone celebrate the fact. She couldn't think of anything else but celebrating after weeks without. Damn man was addicting. "Come on, let's go find Charlie, then."

~

With the family descending for supper, Ayda finally had a reason to put on the clothes that she had purchased in Edinburgh. The bathroom was covered in dark green art tiles, on the floor, walls, and ceiling, even the fireplace was filed with them. Verdant green plants took up every shelf, nook, and the mantle. Ayda finished dressing in front of the mirror with a sigh, she recognized it as the same bathroom that Elise had bathed in during her story. The dress was gorgeous, sage green that hugged every curve, with an unusual strap making it not quite strapless. This wasn't her family, though. Maybe if she was actually seeing Hunter, it might have been different. One night in bed wasn't usually the time to go meet the family. Now she was just intruding, despite what Elise had said. Ayda almost screamed when Hunter's face appeared in the mirror over her shoulder.

"I knocked. I guess you didn't hear me."

"Please, let me just go hide in my room. This is your family, and I'm not part of that."

His eyes closed slowly. "Duncan went to go wake grandmother to tell her everyone would be home and she didn't wake up. You don't have to finish dressing for the party."

"Oh, god." It was all she could bring herself to say. "The poor boy." She added when other thoughts came to mind.

~

Mary brought Ayda meals, and she worked in the old kitchen without interruption. That she wasn't family became even clearer as preparations for the funeral proceeded. All of the walls were filled again quickly, and women from the village came to clean and cook for the guests that would arrive. In daily life, it might not have been evident, but in death, everyone came to pay their respects. It was the large group greeted like family that intrigued her most, The Dunhams, she'd never expected them to show up en masse. Or for the Prince of the island to be among them. But there was no sight of Matt. Close to two hundred people stood in and out of the small chapel which was missing a pillaged painting, but as Ayda arrived, she was lead to the very front, next to the family. The three Sinclair boys standing there were a trio of family resemblance, Isobel was the only oddity with her red hair. The brothers tall, well-muscled, brownish blond hair a bit of red to it though. But they were certainly not identical. Hunter fell in the middle of height and bulk. Broderick was far lankier, more studious looking if that was possible. Lorne the largest of them all, not just in mass he was the tallest of the three.

Broderick and Elise were buried not in the mausoleum in the village, but under the floor of the chapel in the castle itself. Hunter's grandfather's slab already stood carved near the back, Elise's stood ready to go next to his. Head bowed as everyone prayed, Ayda slipped her hand into Hunter's. Somehow, even after the funeral was over and they entertained all of the guests, she never let go. It wasn't that he tried to stop her when she pulled away, she just never felt that she needed to. He needed her.

"I can't believe she's gone. The world surely has changed from when we met."

Ayda looked over to the voice, a small woman, hunched and ancient stood there. "Yes Mrs. Hartman it surely has. She always wanted to make it back to Kapheira one last time, the doctors didn't think she would do well." Hunter said.

"No one else is left, just me now."

"She'd be honored you were here. I know she never talked much of how you met, but you were always a great friend."

A tiny chuckle came from the woman. "Thank god she kept me out of that romance novel for sale in town."

Ayda looked at her quickly. "You're Princess Magda."

"Greg was a good man, I never regretted giving up some title for what I had with him. Elise was about the only one that called me that. The rules when I married Mr. Hartman said I couldn't use it anymore. She called though about you coming to stay."

"Where? Czechoslovakia?"

"No dear, the island. Kapheira. The Prince gave us a house there before the war, when I married my Prince. I still live there."

"Didn't it get decimated in the war?"

Her white hair bobbed up and down. "There was a boat that got away with my son, and others were away before they arrived. Half a battalion survived fighting. Some survived on the island itself, not many but enough. They all still have houses there, the kids and grandkids. They hid away the old treasures, and records. Oh, we rebuilt it. Slowly, but it's there. At least until the Prince started to muck things up. The current one, the former one was a complete god really. His son is the devil really, his grandson too."

"Matt?" He has seemed a sweetheart.

"Matt, oh no, Benedict is the bad seed. Matt's a doll. He rebuilt an entire town but when his father messes things up it never went anywhere. His friends have used it for years. Maybe you can come visit on your honeymoon."

"We aren't..." Magda walked off before Hunter could finish the words.

When people were heading to bed and back to hotel rooms, Hunter walked her back to her door.

"I'll see you tomorrow."

But when he tried to leave her, she was the one that kept a hold of his hand. She opened the door and he followed her in without a word. With gentle hands, she removed his clothes until he stood there in only his boxers. Hunter looked at her as if he couldn't believe she was doing this today of all days.

"Lay down."

"Ayda." He protested, but a finger over his mouth stopped him.

"Lay down." Finally he obeyed, watching her as she removed her clothes. Then she just put her head on his shoulder as she lay down next to him. A contented sigh was all she heard as he realized what she was doing.

~

"I don't want you to go." Hunter whispered the next morning as the sun came up. Did he know her eyes were open?

"How do you know?"

"Take the position, Ayda, finish your thesis. If I'm too much of a distraction, I'll keep my hands off. You belong here. I saw that even before we ended up in bed."

Finally, without even having to think about it, she nodded her head. Even a doctor of art would have to bide their time until a position opened and have to do the grunt work. There was none of that here. "Yes."

"I have to get out of here. We still have guests." When Hunter kissed her neck, it felt like a goodbye. "Thank you for last night," he whispered.

He got to the door as she dug the ring from a pocket in the clothes on the floor. "Hunter."

He looked back over his shoulder, but it wasn't until he saw the ring lying in her hand that he froze, hand on the doorknob. "Where did you get that? Father has been looking for it everywhere."

"Your grandmother gave it to me that day you found us talking. She seemed to think I needed it."

"Are you short on money? Why would you need it?"

Ayda couldn't help but smile. "Come here and I'll tell you." She waited patiently as he sat next to her. God, how did she ever resist being in his bed all day long? "She seemed to think that when the time was right, it would bring me back here. She also seemed to think that you figured into why I would want to come back."

"And she gave it to you?"

"I tried to tell her that her family would want it, but she seemed to think that it wouldn't be leaving the family. After Alice, I shouldn't have just left like that, I know it was thoughtless. If you can forgive me getting a little scared, would you consider giving me a second chance to see what might be? Your grandmother said life was too short. You have to take what time you have."

"What about your thesis?"

With all the funeral preparations being made, she'd had plenty of time to think on her life. Think without Hunter distracting her. "If I'm staying with your offer and I don't have to fit everything into three months, there would be time for distraction. Of course, if I have a job already lined up without it, then it wouldn't really matter if I take a month or two more. Writing it up is all I have left, and you are a rather large distraction."

"I seem to have no trouble getting my work done, why would you have more of a distraction?"

Ayda looked up to find a shit-eating grin and pushed him away. "I'm over here spilling my guts, telling you I'm willing to rearrange my entire life, and that's all I get? You're the one saying you wanted me to stay around."

"Now you know how I felt trying to keep my hands off while you came to that decision."

Ayda's protest stopped when Hunter ran his thumb along her cheek. "To seeing what could be," he whispered in her ear before he kissed her. Just when she ached for him to end the torment, he left to see to his guests. Damn the man!

CHAPTER 9

One Year Later

"Doctorate of Fine Arts restoration/conservation Ayda Rogers," the professor called over the loud speaker.

Ayda walked across the stage and shook hands before being handed her diploma. Yeah, Hunter had been a distraction, but the year wasn't because of that. It had just seemed that making it a definitive telling of the history of the art collection of Am Binnean castle was in order. The more she researched, the more she couldn't leave out. The paintings, the chalices, everything. A two-inch thick leather bound copy with gold lettering sat in the trunk to present to the castle library. She dedicated it to Elise. Never again would someone come in and be overwhelmed at an uncataloged household with paintings no one could even identify let alone find masterpieces hidden in the storerooms. More than 12 had been sold, and truth be told she had a list now of ones to work on finding new homes for on the walls of the castle. They'd been buying.

"Ayda, now that you have your doctorate, you must come and work for me. There's an opening what with Brad leaving. That thesis was magnificent."

Ayda turned to find a man that had turned her down for working with him as a possible thesis advisor. Brad had said she wasn't up to it. "Sorry, Mr. Hutchins I'm not one to take Brad's hand-me-downs. I've had the position of head curator with the Am Binnean collection for a year now. I'm afraid it's love. My thesis would have been done months ago if it wasn't."

His face fell. "If I can't get you," he looked over out of the corner of his eye, "can I get you to put in a good word with the owners? The museum simply has to have that Titian I saw in your paper."

Ayda tried to hide the smirk as she felt Hunter's hand rest on her waist.

"Now that the doctorate is out of the way, you can plan a wedding right?" he whispered in her ear.

Hiding her mouth near his ear, she whispered back. "Can I do something with a painting? The Titian?"

"Why ask me, you're the expert, and it's your future now."

Concentrating on Mr. Hutchins was hard with Hunter's hand reaching under her arm to find a breast. "It's yours for the right price."

"This is when turning you down for a job comes back to haunt me. Brad already screwed things up enough with taking off at the drop of a hat."

"I'll loan it to you for say 5 years, but the price will be made up in trade."

His eyes narrowed. "What kind of trade?"

"My area of expertise is painting restoration and collection management, and I'll be kept quite busy with working on eleven hundred paintings alone. However, the castle is one hundred twenty rooms with antiques of all sorts. The 857 A.D. watchtower is just about restored. Several swords need some work in the armory, I need a parchment from 1328 properly displayed, a fourteenth century chair needs to be seen to, three rugs have some issues. That's just a start. I won't break the museum's bottom line, but I want an agreement that I have use of your personnel for work as it comes up. I believe that security is one of your specialties, if you'd want to vacation at a Scottish castle."

His eyes started to sparkle. "Now, perchance? For a Titian, I can give you whatever you need."

"No, it will have to wait until after the wedding. I'm afraid the Duke is getting rather insistent his heir's son is born legitimately. There's a title to worry about, after all." Ayda ran a hand over her stomach. With the voluminous graduation gown pulled tight, it showed she was well on her way with that heir.

~

"So what is the story with the tower?" Mr. Hutchins asked as they sank down on a bench in the old tower itself. The drawings on the back of scratch pieces of papers just about had the last of the security system in rough idea at least.

Ayda smiled, he sounded so much like her not all that long ago. "It took more digging than most with it being so far back. I only pieced it all together recently."

"Tell me."

Ayda suppressed a smile. "Well there is a chest one of the oldest remnants I've seen here and inside was a quite elaborate chess set, ivory for material. There is a gold cup with Viking designs that dates to that period as well. I've dubbed it Auld Beginnings with the way things happened." She watched as Mr. Hutchins, Jerry, settled back in the shaft of sun that wouldn't last long, the slit of window that provided it was narrow and the sun set fast as they neared winter.

In the Year 1183

Alasdair Syncler rode his horse over the rise, an island, with little more than an old tower on it, greeted him. Hardly a tree broke up the expanse of sea, and sky. That tower was all that could be used as a beacon to find one's way. He might have received land for a castle, but it never meant accommodations or income. Nor did it mean people. When the opportunity came with a generous title and dowry of lands from the King of the Orkney's, he had married quickly enough. What better place for a third son that had no real inheritance. No village existed, no crofts. The title Lord of Wrathe was not expected. His father resented him being made all but a king of the land. It was in a good location for trade with the Orkney's though, that was entirely the reason to put the castle there instead of closer to Caithness despite the reason for his dramatic rise in station.

"I hear she is a fair woman, Alasdair." His cousin Lowrens murmured as he took in the sight.

"The little I saw her at the wedding, yes, I remember her as such. I've hardly said two words to her and it's been how many years? I can hardly remember anymore." They had both been little more than children when the vows were said.

Even though it was visible, it still took three hours to reach the tower and the shelter it would provide. As they finally neared, it wasn't as desolate as it seemed. There were people everywhere, at least thirty men. All fair skinned, Alasdair could only guess they had come with his wife. When you married a Princess of the Orkney's, that was the only guess to arrive at. The very people that the tower had built to protect against still gained the land, and now their boats were aground not far away. He, himself, had some twenty five men with him in addition to his party of friends and relatives. Many related, to some degree, but all barely filling their stomachs on the land they had on his father's estates.

"Princess Eyja?" Alasdair asked the nearest man he saw. No words, he only pointed to the largest concentration of people near the tower itself on the small island that looked like it had been flung off the mainland. No trees and yet there was timber enough to build a bridge and that was exactly what it looked like they were doing. The sun came out from behind the clouds and illuminated a woman's blond hair like gold.

She looked up quickly. "I hope you approve of the improvements I am making, husband."

Alasdair could only stare. There was no way this woman was his wife. He should have noticed that he had married a goddess. Had it truly been so dark? Golden hair hung to her knees in a large braid, her flowing mantle of dark red was thrown back leaving her tunic clinging to her curves, and what curves they were. Pulling herself from the midst of the crowd, she met him as he dismounted. His hound, a large black beast, ran up to his side and demanded attention after the long ride. When Alasdair finally turned he found himself eye to eye with her. "I don't mean to be rude but are you truly the one I am wed to?"

"I was only sixteen then and it has been four years since you went to serve your king. Trust me I was only hoping that the skinny boy that had left had become a man in his absence. We've been working on the tower since I received word you would be returning. I had hoped to have it finished, for the last 300 years it wasn't livable. You will have to sleep in tents along with the rest of us now."

"Eyja,"

Her back straightened. "Do not tell me you will hold me to my vows of being submissive and you are displeased."

"I think I should never have stayed away so long if I had known you grew so well. Show me what you have accomplished."

Her smile was like a ray of sun in the darkest night. "We just about have the staircase around the outside finished. It is useable but not safe as there is no barrier to falling yet. The four rooms in the tower have been made livable, but we've yet to move the furniture in. Mostly my people have been laying in food, we are a sea people, they brought their boats with them. I have agreed this year the rents will be in service to get things livable. We'll need to buy goods until next year when rent will be in food and other goods."

"Then I shall set my people doing the same. Farmers mostly, some herdsmen, a dozen knights and a musician, perhaps we should start plans for another tower, four rooms is hardly enough. We surely need a great hall most of all. You have been here longer and know what we will encounter." Alasdair tried to focus on what he was saying and not on his wife leaning far too close to him. God, they were wed, the marriage even consummated, and he hardly knew her. It felt most times that the marriage was solely an attempt to force the hand of the Lord of the Isles to throw off Norwegian rule. Alexander was trying to secure it for Scotland, but Haakon was having none of it. That was at the same time his marriage was announced, of all things, to the enemy. There wasn't any sort of enemy he saw when she started walking. If he thought he could get away with it, he would have taken her behind any sort of cover there was. Sure way to be killed with all her men there, but a handsome prospect all the same.

"There is a source of flagstones not far down the coast. A great hall is a fine idea. The timber will be harder to procure than stone though. A storeroom would probably be more practical in the near future once we purchase fish and crops. I'm trying to send word to see about purchasing supplies this fall still, but it is hard to find enough."

His wife shifted her stance and Alasdair was given a view of a breast straining against the cloth of her tunic. His trews were suddenly straining as well. "My King is sending supplies, and from my father, a ship should be arriving in a few weeks with enough supplies for our immediate needs. A late wedding gift from him. The bay just to the east of here would be a good place for the men to build houses for themselves. We'll put a village there for those that aren't farmers. Protected from the sea, good mooring for boats, and the stream goes right past there for fresh water. The land is there if they claim it officially so I can start a log. I have a priest with me as well."

"Excellent." Eyja exclaimed before a man called to her. Alasdair stood there unwilling to let his state be known.

~

Days passed as the men continued inching closer to making the tower safe. Up and down the coast in scattered groups, some fifty-five men started houses. As well as a small cluster at the river's mouth that quickly became a semblance of a village. Of the 100 perhaps that had come between them, the other fifty were women and children: wives, children, sisters, mothers. The mornings were for the tower and the afternoons for their personal work. Alasdair was almost certain there were already several couples forming between the two groups. Many were in family groups, so it was more like 30 farms all told. Though each might have several houses growing slowly. Rocks that littered the coast were gathered and quickly became ordered lines of walls. Several trips were made south procuring logs enough for roof timbers and doors and windows.

Days passed as he watched his wife working hard to make a new estate. He had been given a title after all, a kingdom. Alasdair Syncler Lord of Wrathe with a Princess as a wife. Looking over his realm, the tower only reminded him of his own state, tall and erect with nothing around. Desperate, there was only one thing to do when his wife hadn't shared a tent with him yet. He'd have to seduce the woman.

"Perhaps while we have the winches attached to move the stone, we might use them to move the furniture to the upper rooms. It would be safer than moving it up the stairs with limbs to be crushed easily," Alasdair finally announced.

"Fine idea." Lowrens commended and went to see it done.

Alasdair wouldn't admit to the man that it was so he could get Eyja out of a tent and away from all the others.

~

Alasdair walked to the hill that overlooked the tower, the hound coming to keep company. Beyond lay the blue grey sky and the matching sea. It wasn't much of a hill at all, while it gave a view of the tower, the tower itself was actually higher in height. The pinnacle of all he could see. Now there was a fine name for the house. Am Binnean rather rolled off the tongue, well he had a name if nothing else. Staying would take more work though. They had sheep in small numbers, a handful of fishing boats, and a half-livable tower. All that to keep 100 people alive with the fierce north winds blowing at them hard. The horses would need a place out of the weather before winter ...

A sound behind him made Alasdair turn and he found Lowrens riding closer. Only as he turned slightly to avoid a chasm did Alasdair notice another rider on the back of the horse. A woman, red haired as anyone had ever been.

"Who's that?" Alasdair called.

"My wife, Unuisticc."

Alasdair felt his mouth dropping. His cousin had never in his life talked of wanting a wife, and with Lowrens older, there had been longer for him to form that opinion. Lowrens slid off and left his bride still mounted. She leaned over and kissed him before she rode off though.

"Married? You?"

Lowrens looked to make sure she was out of earshot. "A tenant died two years ago leaving Unuisticc there alone with two children."

"And?" Alasdair prodded.

"What do you mean and?"

Alasdair only stared for a moment. His cousin had gone daft. "I mean you never mentioned her until this moment, you've never spoken of marriage until this moment. You have no house with a widow and two children and nothing to support you. Have you been without so long?"

Lowrens plopped down on the ground. "Thank me cousin. I've found out that the land is not as empty as it was claimed. Remnants of the old Picts dear cousin, a dozen families or so, scattered about."

"I thought the Picts were gone."

Lowrens shook his head. "Not by the name the Romans gave them, but the people surely still remain. They never left. My wife proves that. I'll sleep warmer than you this winter with a fuller belly. She owns the oat mill, her first husband was the miller. Only mill in some days journey, and she belongs to Wrathe dear cousin. Though she calls it Bad A'cheo, place of the mist."

Alasdair stood up straight at hearing that. "A mill. Then we can get some decent stores of food?"

"Aye we've a good deal in storage that we could let go, for you special price. That's in addition to what they all owe you in back rent. They were told of the change in lords and no one has shone his face for 4 years."

Several dozen tenants with established livelihoods, another thirty families that would hopefully be able to sustain life in such a climate, it still wasn't much of a life, but it was a start, a small one at any rate.

"She claims you all have no idea how to build a house. That one course of stone won't keep out the vaguest of winds. We're to invite all for a wedding feast tonight to show you all how it's done properly." With that, Lowrens walked off whistling a tune.

~

With the stairs usable if not finished and the rooms filled with furniture, between the two of them it took all the furniture they owned. The men scattered to finish their own homes before the cold weather set in with a design that would keep them far warmer. The house Unuisticc now shared with Lowrens had walls several feet apart filled with a layer of sand some four feet thick. The only wood in the entire structure supported the thatch roof and the place was warm as could be. The smaller projects would have to wait until life was secured. Only the natural cliffs of the island kept them safe from attack, that and Eyja's father almost within sight across the North Sea. The storeroom footing lay on the ground ready to be built but that could be done in the winter since there lay a surplus of stone about.

"Eyja, I thought we might walk?" Alasdair asked.

"There does seem to be a lack of occupation now that the men are all working elsewhere. Where should we walk?"

"I haven't explored much since I arrived. Show me wherever you wish."

She clasped her hands behind her back and made her way over the bridge in silence. Hips swaying as she walked, she was driving Alasdair mad.

He looked over at her not sure why the thought entered his head. "Where have you been living since I went to serve the King?"

"With my aunt. You had no house to offer me and my father had married me off so I was out of his hands."

"Why did you never tell me? You could have gone to stay at my father's estate. We could have at least seen each other. I was able to visit there even if I couldn't make it here."

"That far south and have everyone call me a Viking? No, I prefer to stay where I am welcome."

She surely didn't sound like the child he had left a week after they were wed, not that he was given the chance to get to know her at all. Maybe she never sounded like a child. In that, perhaps he did know why she had never come to his tent since he arrived. He had left her for four years without much of a thought. "You were never unwelcome," he admitted. She truly wasn't but once she was out of sight, he hadn't given her much thought.

"Perhaps not by you, but I did go to your father's once. Shortly after you left, I traveled there. I was not coming empty handed I had my dowry and household. I left after a week. I heard the women talking when they thought I didn't speak their language."

"My sister's I suppose. They always were backstabbers."

"Then we agree on something."

Her breath caught when his hand touched her cheek. "I have no commitments that call me away. Can we start over? I should like my wife to like me. I swear someone was watching through the keyhole. You can't claim we never ratified the union."

"Ratified the union?"

His smile couldn't stay away. "We never spoke before we said the vows. You claim it to be anything other than a contract?"

"Well, no, I suppose not."

Alasdair let his hand drift down along her neck, her eyes rose quickly when it grazed her breast. "Do you play chess?" She asked unexpectedly.

"Aye, though I am sure that I hardly rank with your skill."

Her smile grew. "If you win, I'll show you where your hand touches now."

"But if you win?"

Eyja hadn't thought it through it seemed. She caught her lip between her teeth in concentration. Was she willing to move faster than grass growing?

"If I win? You go swimming in the sea without a stitch."

"That's not a very fair trade."

"Then I suggest you win." She turned and walked back to the tower leaving Alasdair with a view of her hips swaying once more. Damn the woman!

~

Seaweed lay about everywhere to dry as Alasdair made his way up the stairs. Some of the Orkney Islands had so little else for food, they weren't going to let a food source escape notice. Already several pots of soup with the algae steamed in the cool day. He hadn't hardly stepped foot inside since all the work was completed. Opening the door he found four rooms, the ground level was the kitchen and temporary storage, the second level dining, the third held an office with a single book, the upper most level was the bedroom, and he'd never been invited to share the bed. An old watchtower, they had to add fireplaces on to the side so that they wouldn't freeze, a smoky peat fire burned there now. It took some doing but they had discovered a source for the fuel with Unuisticc's help. The mantle was covered with ancient gold vessels, each with intricate designs from people long since gone. His dowry was getting bigger each day. He had to keep wondering why with all the powerful men that were there for the taking, he had been chosen to wed a princess. A large bed covered completely in heavy wool hangings to keep out drafts stood near the fireplace. The table and chairs filled the other side. Away from the fire were chests holding clothes and valuables while the walls were covered in needlework. They definitely needed rugs.

"I changed my mind, husband."

"I am glad. I don't enjoy the idea of swimming in the sea in October."

Alone with no one to watch, her smile teased the corners of her mouth as she barred the door. "Now for every piece the other captures, we'll remove a piece of clothing. The winner gets to decide where we go from there."

Oh, thank god for unsubmissive women. Lowrens told of his brother's wife who, after baring her husband from bed, spent years without because she was too shy to say she wanted him back. "A much more pleasant suggestion." How mundane he sounded. She might have just suggested he watch her do needlepoint.

"But ..."

"Eyja, I have spent weeks waiting for you to get used to me being around again, no buts now."

Her finger over his mouth stopped him. "But for every piece we move regardless, we will tell one thing about ourselves. You say you would like to like your wife then you can do this for me. My father is a king. I had power in his household but I was never told anything. I was never told I would marry until it was already decided and then I was told you would be gone for who knew how long. Do not shut me away to do needlework. I've spent four years of it with my aunt."

"Gladly, Princess." He answered before he pulled her finger into his mouth.

She pulled it out of his mouth making a loud pop. "This isn't playing chess." Alasdair couldn't help notice her voice sounded a little husky though.

"Go set it up on the bed. The coverings will be far warmer than the chairs once you start taking all my pieces." She picked the ivory set up from the table and moved it to the bed. Watching her lean over was not helping Alasdair keep his mind on chess though, and she wanted him to tell her about himself, too. Lying on one side of the board, the smell of heather filled his nose, he'd smelled it on her, but looking to the floor noticed instead of rushes, heather was strewn everywhere. No wonder she smelled of it.

Eyja took the first move. "My cousin is the king of Norway."

Alasdair looked up at her. "Why would a younger penniless son be given a daughter of one king and a cousin to another?"

"The Norse prize warriors, which your family has always been." Her eyes lowered from his. "Besides I had seen you once and commented to my nurse that I liked the look of you. Next thing I know I'm being told we are to wed when we've never even exchanged a word."

Not having to swim in the sea any more, Alasdair moved a piece he was sure she would capture. If she had her way with him or him with her, either way it was the end he had dreamed of for the last weeks. "When did you see me?"

Her finger pointed to him, and he pulled off his shoes. Not very revealing but if he got what he wanted, he wasn't going to be doing it with his shoes on. "We were visiting to see my sister married, and you were a guest there. Watched you through the whole thing, mentioning it only once to anyone, but she must have told my father. Next thing I know we are wed. Now tell me something about you?"

"My father is a count, but I now outrank him."

She watched him as she moved her next piece directly where he was certain to capture it. He was starting to like his wife more and more. "I sing, dance, play the harp, do embroidery, and carry a knife in my tunic."

Alasdair took the piece she had just moved. "Show me."

"Tell me something while you undo the laces." Eyja turned her back to him.

"Chess is the last thing on my mind."

"Something I don't know."

"I've been dreaming of you ever since the day I arrived. I fall asleep with thoughts of you."

Eyja pulled the tunic over her head. Even with the fire, full breasts started to goose bump in the chilly air. Magnificent didn't start to describe the breasts he had caught glimpses of straining against her clothes. It was cool though, and she wore a pair of trews to keep out a draft beneath her hem. True to her word, there was also a knife in a scabbard on her calf. A small one, but deadly enough all the same.

"Move a piece," he offered. "It's your turn." Her eyes narrowed as she took off the knife. Maybe she hadn't thought it out as fully as he thought. She lay there half-naked and he only had his shoes off. If she kept up the same, it would end far too soon.

In the end, she moved one he couldn't take. "Will it hurt as much as it did on our wedding night?"

"No."

"Then move."

Watching her reaction, he moved one she could take. Without waiting for him to tell her anything or reminding him, she took his piece. She was both forward and a bit timid. Then again, their first time people were close enough to yell out encouragement, and her cry had brought a cheer from the next room. It never made for intimacy. Spending four years with soldiers, he knew far more now, in theory anyway, and he was certain this aunt would have never even spoke of the subject to her. He pulled his tunic off leaving them both in the same state. He left it to her this time, moving where she could take it if she wished. Staring at his crotch for a good long time, she finally took his piece. He pulled off his trews and he was naked. The wait left him standing erect, once free of their confines. He moved a piece again that she could capture and waited. She had said when someone won but frankly, they hadn't even gotten past their pawns.

Alasdair watched her eyes go from him nude to her still partially clothed.

All of a sudden, she moved her king out in the open where even a pawn could take it. Her eyes didn't leave his as he pulled the piece from the board.

"Well, Alasdair, you won the game. I believe I said the rules let the winner decide where it would go from here."

He reached out and pulled on the tie that held her last piece of clothing up. It fell down easily, and she stood there as he walked around her surveying his prize. Alasdair stopped at her back, his breath light on her ear. "If I have won, then I wish you to tell me what you want, Eyja. There is no one to hear, no one to call out if you scream in pleasure. That is what I have dreams of every night, me giving you what you have wanted in our separation. Tell me your wishes."

She turned her head. Her fierce blue eyes looked as if she was ready to cry. "You actually listened to what I said."

"I would truly hate for you to have those two kings in the family come hunt me down because I was acting like they did."

"There are three actually. The King of Denmark is a cousin as well..." Her argument halted when he ran his hands over her shoulders. Slowly following her arms, she sighed when he let his fingers brush the sides of her breasts.

Eyja tried to turn to face him, but he held her tight. "Tell me what you wish. You were the one admiring me at your sister's wedding after all."

"The cook at my aunt's liked to talk about men."

Ah, cooks. Have to love them. Alasdair thought an aunt surely wouldn't have. "And what did you hear that sounded interesting."

"She said a man could use his tongue."

"Did she now? So can a woman, but we'll save that for another time. It's what you wish right now." Pulling the chess board off the bed, he couldn't help but see her eyes watching his cock as he worked. She even licked her lips at the thought. "Lay down, Eyja."

"You're sure no one can hear? I still imagine whoever it was yelling on our wedding night."

He pushed her back until her legs hit the edge of the bed. Falling, dear god, the bed lined her up with him neatly. He could feel her heat, but he didn't enter. He just teased her folds with his cock enough for her to moan. "No one can hear, Eyja."

Scrambling back, she pulled out of range. Alasdair moved the covers and pulled them over both of them. Her squirming stopped as his tongue touched her ankle. Dragging it up the length of her leg, he smelled her scent long before he reached the junction of her thighs. Eyja yelped when he bit her thigh gently.

"Don't do that."

"Would you prefer here?" Applying the flat of his tongue to her folds, the only answer was a sigh of what he decided had to be pleasure.

"Marta said it was nice. She never said it was like that," she finally said after a moment. Her hips lifted every time he pulled back even a little, and she bit off a cry when he pushed his tongue inside her. He said he'd never torture anyone, but this was fun. He lost count of how many times he brought her to the edge only to pull back. His attack wasn't hard, but it was decisive and quick, her cry filled the stone walls.

Alasdair crawled up over her looking at such a peaceful face laying there, eyes closed. "Eyja, what else did your cook say?"

Eyes still closed her smile grew. "I don't think you'd believe me if I told you." Her eyes slid open as his mouth touched her nipple pulling it deep in his mouth.

"Alasdair, is this a new beginning for us? I truly don't wish to remember the first night we were wed."

He lifted his head up to look at her. "I hardly remember our wedding night, other than my father saying I needed an heir now. Perhaps you'll introduce me to your aunt's cook. I like her instructions far better."

Eyja pulled him up so they were meeting eye to eye again. "Then let's work on an heir. It is what I wish. Maybe we can go hire Marta away from my aunt. That heir of ours would not go to his wedding night as innocent as we were. She can tell him and save us the trouble. She would enjoy it far more."

"Yes, my princess."

~

Jerry looked around. They were sitting in the top floor of the tower. "This room," he muttered. "I think we should design a case for the chess set and gold cup."

Ayda could only laugh. "The chess set maybe, the cup is used to baptize all the Sinclair children. My mother-in-law isn't very technical, she might set the alarm off some Sunday, and we'd never get it shut off."

"Oh right, this isn't a museum."

Ayda smiled as he went to work on the back of a receipt designing a case. Maybe Marta was the sweetest woman known to man, but whenever Ayda thought of her, she was a large lustful woman with a bawdy laugh. She kept trying to not tell a story like Mary, she'd promised Hunter after all, but in the end she just couldn't deny the part the cooks of the castle had played. They fit there as much as the art did.

ABOUT THE AUTHOR

As a Peace Corps volunteer in Kenya a few years back I traveled quite a bit and now I just wish I was. A lot of the places I've written about I've been to, a lot of them I haven't. Rafting on the Nile in Uganda, living in a Montana ghost town, Puerto Rican beaches, African safaris, Mayan ruins, European youth hostels, the Black Hills of South Dakota all fill my scrapbooks. Now a daughter takes up most of those pages, but I still travel in my head every time I write. I currently live in the Pacific Northwest and look forward to filling many more pages. See more at www.jennifermuellerbooks.com.

31272591R00221

Made in the USA
Middletown, DE
24 April 2016